How Long Is Now

A Novel

Joshua Corey

SPUYTEN DUYVIL
New York City

© 2022 Joshua Corey
ISBN 978-1-956005-03-5

cover image: The Dog, Francisco Goya. c. 1820-1823

Library of Congress Cataloging-in-Publication Data

Names: Corey, Joshua, author.
Title: How long is now : a novel / Joshua Corey.
Description: New York City : Spuyten Duyvil, [2021] |
Identifiers: LCCN 2021030617 | ISBN 9781956005035 (trade paperback)
Subjects: LCSH: Corey, Joshua--Fiction. | Biographical fiction. | LCGFT:
  Biographical fiction.
Classification: LCC PS3603.O7343 H69 2021 | DDC 813/.6--dc23
LC record available at https://lccn.loc.gov/2021030617

For my parents.

The first step in re-creation is to cut the old lines that hold you right where you are sitting now.
—William S. Burroughs

FOUNTAIN

People ask me how I write so much. They don't ask *why* but that is what they mean. They can't quite conceal their fascinated disgust, so easily mistaken for envy. They peer sidelong at the freak that I am.

I'm sitting in my office on the campus of a small Midwestern college, not so many miles from the Chicago suburb in which my father grew up in a happy assimilated family in the slipstream of history, far from the northern New Jersey suburb in which he brought me up, the first child of this happy American father and his unhappy wife, an immigrant mother tormented by a past she had experienced without comprehending as the daughter of Holocaust survivors, Hungarian Jews sent to Auschwitz-Birkenau late enough in the war to survive it and come back to tell the tale. Or to not tell it, at least not in my hearing, save on the night of December 21, 1991, when Mom died of cancer. The men wearing latex gloves and professionally downturned mouths had already come and gone with the little that remained of her, scarcely eighty or ninety pounds of folded bones and skin, stunned and silent like a sparrow struck dead by its own reflection. The house was hollow with its own light, reflected from the black windows that surrounded us on every side: my father, my sister, my grandfather, and me. My grandfather, already translucent with the possibility of his own death, sat across from us at our kitchen table and told me, the only time he would tell me, of his work in the Auschwitz barber shop where—he imitated for me his precise gestures—he shaved the SS men as they joked and chatted with each other, yes, joked and chatted with him. Eyes almost closed, flipping his hand theatrically in the air to demonstrate the snap of the towel as he whipped it away from a freshly shaved and vulnerable neck. They tipped him with potatoes and the odd slice of sausage, just enough to survive until the liquidation of the camp, and then the death march into Germany during which he didn't die, followed by the haphazard journey back to a Budapest that would never again be home. There he was reunited with my grandmother whose own miraculous story of survival I'll never know—took my toddler mother out of the arms of the grandparents with whom she'd been hidden and back across Europe to Germany, to the displaced persons camp that the British ran at Belsen, and from there at last to New York, the Bronx, America, where she grew up into the sharp-tongued, chain-smoking, migraine-plagued mother I remember, whom I loved helplessly, whom my father loved from his helpless distance, who lives now only in her few poems, and in mine.

And Dad? He is gone too, more recently, still nearly in the now. He lingers in the bardo of this book, waiting for me to set him free.

This story is mine. It may seem a strange thing to say, since I wrote it, since so much of it is true, but I want anyway to make the claim. Mine. It's my life, a sliver of it. *My* story. I repeat this, desperately, because although it is mine I didn't make it. It was handed to me without my consent, readymade. Rimbaud: *If brass wakes up a trumpet it is not its fault.*

My mother who gave me language, my father who gave me a taste for living beyond the avenues of depression and despair.

In New York City they met, fifty years after Marcel Duchamp bought a urinal from a plumbing supply house on Fifth Avenue and submitted it to the First Annual Exhibition of the Society of Independent Artists, which refused to exhibit the piece. He signed it "R. Mutt, 1917." Some say that he collaborated in this work with the exquisitely titled Dada Baroness, Elsa von Freytag-Loringhoven, and the "R. Mutt" refers to the German *Armut*, meaning "poverty." Or maybe *Urmutter*, "Great mother." The impoverished great mother of art history, endlessly reproduced in galleries across the world, detached from all utility, a mischievous blank fired at culture itself. "My intention," Duchamp remarked, "was to get away from myself, though I knew perfectly well that I was using myself. Call it a little game between 'I' and 'me.'"

You can't flush Duchamp's *Fountain* but you can damn well piss on it. Can it make you cry?

Convulsively, almost automatically, do the words, the stories and places, they flow, they fill me, they find me out. My father's story and my mother's, tributarying out of a minor rift in history, trickling into my own.

I
THE JUDGMENT

THE END

Beside his bed, Dad's hospital bed, touching his gray swollen hand, that hand once strong and capable, so like his own father's hand, my Skokie grandfather, so unlike the hand of the small boy he once was, delicate, placed into the rough, wrinkled hand of my Yiddish-speaking great-grandmother, Bubbe Rosie, long gone now. Beyond that the pure gray horizon of conjecture: the old country, the *shtetl*, "Tradition!", Cossacks, a village in flames, the Pale. Outside the California sun pours its indiscriminate honey onto a bone-dry landscape; inside intensive care it's the fractured silence of life-saving machines. My American dad lies broken and mute, a loud object, tube down his throat, drains in his back, drains in his lungs that follow tubes down to catchment boxes on either side of the bed like cumbersome blood-soaked wings. Six days prior, while visiting my sister, he got up early to go get coffee and a newspaper. Careless with the stickshift, he drove her car off a cliff. Nine ribs shattered, also his back, also his neck. I flew out the day it happened, spent a week shuttling my grimly determined stepmother to and from the hospital, she and me and my sister in the court of Humpty Dumpty who will most likely never walk again. I touch his forehead, warm to the touch. His swollen hands. "Dad," I say. "Dad. I'm here."

He will not remember I was there. And even if he does,

I am there no longer. I'm leaving in a few days for a long-planned journey to Europe, to finish my book. This book.

A son walks over his father's body on the path to becoming himself.

I'm breaking with you, Dad.

NEW YORK, MID-1960S

Spring.

He drove the little two-door Chevy east, through snows of Indiana and freezing rains of northern Ohio, holding carefully to the wheel with hands at ten and two o'clock. Sometimes on the radio he found bluegrass or Hank Williams or a preacher's high sonorous hysterical voice, sometimes just the static between stations through which he caught snatches of speaking voices in the general hiss. Sometimes he snapped off the radio and just listened to the road for a while, until the steady rasp of the engine gave him a headache and the white stagger of the center line began to hammer his eyelids shut. He slept in the car to conserve cash and ate in little diners where he allowed himself, with his dark not overlong curls and sleepy eyes and sensuous mouth, to be mothered a little by the stocky dyed-blonde goyische waitresses. Pie and coffee, pie and coffee. In the hills of eastern Pennsylvania he glanced across black fields waking in the morning sun and saw a two-wheel buggy on a dirt road, the horse's breath clouding the air. Finally he began the climb, as he thought of it, though really it was more like a descent, northward through leafless but budding New Jersey, until he descended into the Meadowlands and saw the spires of Manhattan gleaming whitely in the afternoon sun. He was unprepared for city driving, so different from back home, unprepared for streets and avenues like scars cut deep into the earth, where a kind of metal bug life of trucks and cabs teemed. He drove precariously, one-handed, consulting often the scrap of yellow paper on which his directions were scrawled, a kind of squiggle out the mouth of the Lincoln Tunnel, having to turn right and right again to get back on track, straight up Tenth Avenue which turned into Amsterdam, nonplussed by unglamorous Upper West Side Broadway, counting streets— even goes east and odd goes west—finally hooking a left on West 91st and finding, miraculously, a parking space just a block from his destination, at 91st and Riverside. The car was crammed with his few possessions; he took only the duffel bag that had been sharing the drive with him sitting upright on the passenger seat, reasoning that he could get the rest later. He locked both doors and set out.

Brownstones hulked on either side of him and the sidewalk was punctuated every few yards by stark, spindly trees. There was no answer when he buzzed Hank's apartment, but this did not surprise him; his cousin had said on the phone that he didn't get home from work before six most days. He stood and then after a while sat on the stoop, buttoning up the thick cleanly woolen coat his mother had presented to him a week before he'd left. That and his wool cap made him look a little like a sailor, in spite of the hippie-ish curls of hair touching his collar. He thought for a moment of his draft status, how he'd slipped into 4F at the last moment because his doctor—his pediatrician since childhood—had found or claimed to find a heart murmur. Grinning, an unlit cigarette in his teeth—it made him look a little like FDR—Dr. Steinberg had scrawled his findings on a piece of paper and ordered him to take it to the draft board. A computer-typed letter informing him of his final status arrived six weeks later, enough time for Solly and Frank, guys he'd known in high school, to go from greasy jokesters to sober recruits, off to basic training at Fort Benning and Fort Dix. Guilt and relief mingled in the pit of his stomach when he thought of them, and then he put the whole thing out of his mind. Even from a young age, he was skilled at compartmentalizing. The present fits into its box, and it's on to the next thing, the next moment. He was young. All the moments in the world were his.

Raindrops were starting to spatter him. Not knowing what else to do, he returned to the car, humping the duffel on his shoulder that made him feel more than ever like a sailor on shore leave. He sat in the driver's seat for a while watching water streak the windshield, eddying in eldritch patterns around the squished bodies of bugs. Then the cold began to penetrate so he switched on the engine and then, out of habit almost, slipped it into gear. (He was a dab hand with a manual transmission back then. Automatics were rare.) Abandoning his perfect parking space he began to drive at random, following the park for a while back south, then hooking a left to follow 81st Street to where the Museum of Natural History squatted. Through Central Park, water glinting dully to his left, and then emerging on the East Side that struck him as somehow blanker and brighter than the West. He craned his neck to follow a Jackie O. lookalike striding along the sidewalk, slowing down to watch her until she stepped into a cab. He turned instinctively onto Park Avenue, but there was no glamor there, so he turned onto 60th and followed it to the FDR Drive. He got off the highway at 48th and snaked down to 42nd Street, pushing his way into Time Square, where the neon was coming into its full glory in the early dark. There was the Coca-Cola sign, just like in the movies; there was the giant Lucky Strike leaking real smoke into the sky. Broadway! Radio City! I'm really here, he said to himself. Home is the sailor home from the sea.

Back on 90th (this time he'd found, incredibly, an even better parking space right across the street from his cousin's place, so that he might be able to keep an eye on the vehicle from the front window) he hit the button and was immediately buzzed in. Incandescent lighting and the hygienic stink of wet white paint. With difficulty he lugged his duffel and himself up the narrow staircase and then went back for his most prized possession, the state-of-the art hi-fi that his father, who was a sales rep for a speaker company, had presented him with for his college graduation. It was topped with a forest of amplifier bulbs that glowed mysteriously when activated and caused the air above the set to ripple slightly in their heat. Cousin Hank stood in what looked like silk pajamas and an English dressing gown smiling in the doorway on the landing, and he could smell a strange trebly scent of cooking, matching what sounded like a sitar on the stereo. He braced himself for his cousin's kiss, which was hot and dry, Hank's luxurious mustache tickling his cheek. Hank was what his father—without rancor or dislike—called a fairy, and at this moment Hank was the only person in all of New York City that he could plausibly call a friend. Cousin Hank, a New Yorker. He was in awe of Hank's courage, when he thought of it. To walk away like that from his parents and his brothers and the smooth predictable Midwest. To step so trustingly into the arms of the city that had been waiting for him. He fought down a sudden slight sensation of panic.

"Come on in," Hank said. "Peter is finishing dinner. Do you like curry?"

He was confronted first by his own image in an oval mirror on the wall of the blind entryway, through which he had almost to contort himself in order to enter the apartment. Aladdin's cave, he thought automatically. Japanese prints hung on walls that had been painted a warm burgundy color, and an array of large, comically phallic candles glowed from the mantel over the fireplace, where somewhat to his astonishment a small fire was crackling. A strange low double bed took up the center of the room, with a sleek narrow hardwood armchair beside it that he couldn't imagine would be comfortable. How was it possible for two men to live in such a tiny space? How would it be possible for three? There was as far as he could see no other room in the apartment, save for a narrow door with a tapestry of an Indian elephant-god on it that presumably led to the bathroom. Two wicker chairs were tucked into a small round wooden table upon which a blue-veined china vase was sprouting daffodils. The miniature kitchen with its two-burner range was partially hidden behind a paper screen with what looked to be flamingos or herons soaring across it. He could just see the top of a man's head dipping and weaving above its edge. The air was hot and dry and smelled of dead violets and woodsmoke, masculine and yet somehow not. It was intimate yet foreign, like the city itself.

"Tea?" Hank was asking. "Or something stronger? You want a beer?" Peter dodged out from behind the screen to offer him a shy grin. Hank's roommate—no, he corrected himself, Hank's lover. He was taller than Hank by half a head, pale-haired, turtlenecked, with a blond mustache and goatee. In the 1980s both he and Hank would be diagnosed with HIV; Peter would eventually die of AIDS. Hank would not. Now Peter handed Hank a can of beer; Hank popped the tab and poured the contents into a heavy glass stein. "You like it? We got it in Hamburg. The glass, not the beer. The beer's from Milwaukee. Taste of close-to-home."

"Home!" warbled Peter. "He never shuts up about Chicago and his aunt's cooking. Your mother, right? And here I am slaving over a hot curry, and what thanks will I get?"

Hank sank into the armchair with a vaudevillian sigh.

"It's good," their guest said, meaning the beer, trying to mean everything: the subcontinental apartment, Peter and Hank's connubial bliss, New York.

"Sit down," Hank said easily. Seeing nowhere else he sat on the edge of the bed. *Their* bed. "How's the family? How's your dad?"

"Good. Everyone's good."

"And how's Auntie Lil of the miraculous kitchen?" Peter called. "Did she send any of that gilded fish with you?"

"Gefilte fish," he corrected. "Yes, she sends her love. To you both," he added after what he hoped hadn't been too long a pause.

"And what do they think of your little adventure?" asked Hank.

"They're not exactly thrilled. But it's okay. Mom, Aunt Lil, I mean"—his mother's name tastes strangely in his mouth—"is just happy I'm not overseas."

His parents and three sisters back home in festering Skokie, in the little bungalow his father had purchased weeks after mustering out of the Army, having done his bit as a quartermaster for the Manhattan Project, servicing the needs of Enrico Fermi and his unborn Bomb where they squatted underneath the campus of the University of Chicago. The quartermaster had grown up on Maxwell Street, a little pisher running errands for his own father, a Yiddish-speaking pants-presser and a tailor's son from what was now Ukraine. His mother's people hailed from Russia; all of them had crossed the ocean, as far as he knew, in plenty of time to avoid going up the chimneys of Dachau and Belsen. Unimaginable, his parents' past, and his own present as it might have been lived, or not lived, by a Jew born in the Forties. How far they'd come, from the smoke of Europe to brawling Chicago to small-minded Skokie, where they were three-day Jews at the Conservative shul and otherwise lived a life at once cloistered and assimilated. Cloistered, because everyone they knew, every neighbor and schoolmate, was also Jewish. Assimilated, because they all aspired to the American beyond, swam in its culture, rock n' roll and football and basketball and baseball and bobby sox climbing his sisters' knees and the Saturday afternoons spent in Solly's garage, fixing up cars for drag races and drinking beer and talking up the easy girls and talking down the prisses. There were a few frummers in the neighborhood, not too many, and from his seat on a milk crate through the garage's open door he would see them shuffling by in their flat black hats and beards trailed by women in wigs and long skirts and the children, sober miniatures of their parents, following behind them, eyes fixed on the sidewalk. They were entirely strange and somehow embarrassing, like the grade school baseball trophies his father had lined up like chessmen across the desk in his office. His father spoke disparagingly of the Orthodox at the breakfast table and his mother shook her pretty head. He himself had been a bar mitzvah boy, had stood in front of the darkly suited congregation and read a line or two of Torah—something from Leviticus, something about the right way to go about butchering a lamb. The beardless rabbi had lectured the congregation about Abraham and Isaac for half an hour after that, repeatedly laying his hand upon the boy's forearm as he did so, offering little disconcerting squeezes of emphasis. A father made malevolent by his faith; a son bound uncomprehending to his father's will. The rabbi's voice rose and fell with words impossibly distant from the bright shadowless postwar Middle West of which he was the scion; he soon forgot the strangeness of the letters marching right to left across a sheepskin scroll.

His Jewish destiny was professional, the shift from

wholesale to retail, from the son of peddlers to my-son-the-doctor. But he had failed to be admitted to even the most marginal of medical schools, dashing his parents' most cherished hopes. Here he was in New York with the ink just dry on his bachelor's degree, with a line on a position as biology teacher at a private high school not six blocks from where he was sitting. They would try him that fall; his parents had wanted him to stay at home until then but the idea made him almost cry out. He would get a job, any job; that and his savings from past summers spent caddying for the *machers* at the unrestricted golf club ought to be enough to get him by before September.

The curried fish with rice and vegetables puckered his tongue in a pleasing way. But his contributions to the conversation were monosyllabic, and finally Peter said something airily about meeting a friend downtown and slipped out. Hank did the dishes while he went through the contents of his duffel, as though looking for something. *Are we going to share the bed?* His panic dissipated once Hank produced a bed sheet and slipped it over the couch cushions, set him up cozy as could be with pillow and blanket, before slipping into his own bed with a much-marked copy of Carl Jung's *Memories, Dreams, Reflections*. Dad lay on his side for a while, feeling the tension running up and down in his body, listening to the pages turn, until finally Hank yawned, said goodnight, switched out the light, and went almost instantly to sleep. He went on lying there for a while, finally turning on his back, watching strange reflections from the street play across the ceiling, listening. He was waiting, he realized, for Peter to return, to slip out of his clothes and into the bed next to his cousin, where they would do… what? Faggot stuff? Would they kiss? Those mustaches! Won't they just sleep, since they know they're not alone? He fell asleep, wondering.

He awakened to long streaming light, his watch stopped. It could have been nine in the morning, or four in the afternoon. He was alone in the apartment. He went to the window to look down at his car, and saw that the passenger-side window had been smashed. Running across the wet street in bare feet to find everything but the amplifier and the contents of the duffle that he'd brought inside with him gone. The radio had been ripped out; a few colored tongues of wire taunted him from the excavated dash. Nothing to be done. He went back inside, stunned, and sat on the couch for a while. His cousin had left him a number and he dialed it.

"It happens, even in the best neighborhoods. That's New York," Hank clucked. "Look at it this way: you've broken your cherry. You're starting fresh."

Fresh. He rolled it, without saying the word, on his tongue.

For a moment he visualized himself getting back into the car and driving back to Skokie, smashed window and all, the whole trip out East but in reverse, the weary names of waitresses pinned to tags flashing before his eyes: Doris, Helena, Blanche. He could duct-tape a piece of cardboard to the window. He could get by without a radio. Or his father's stereo, for that matter. *I can't stay here.*

He got a room at the YMCA. Hank was sympathetic and Pete was surely relieved. He wore rubber shoes in grim concrete showers. He played chess in the rec room with strangers. He walked back and forth between the parks. He peered into shop windows. He read the classifieds. He sold the car.

Two weeks later he's in his new apartment on 89th Street a block and a half from Hank's. A year after that he meets Mom for the first time.

So who can say exactly, between that moment and the morning of October 2, 1970, in the earliest light, in Mt. Sinai Hospital, where it is that I come in?

SAILORS

This is the way of it. This is the anchor and the folly. This is the vision of a drowning man of a hearth glimpsed between frozen eyelashes, firelight sketching the path of a woman's back, something of her voice in the hull's shudder, the sheets' groan, the snap of the sails.

Following the traces of a sound, a throb, mechanical stuttering heart. The machine that breathes for my crippled father, in bruised halo, in state.

I give myself to experience because what other choice do I have? God?

God a kind of plasm or spasm that surrounds the heart of the sailor, who can feel his death between his teeth like the bit on a horse.

At the top of a letter to a friend the poet Federico Garcia Lorca sketched a jaunty little sailor, and wrote underneath, "We're all like the little sailor. From the harbors we hear the strains of accordions and the murky soapy noises of the docks, from the mountains we receive the dish of silence that the shepherds eat, but we don't hear more than our own distances. And what distances without end and without doors and without mountains."

Mishima: *The Sailor Who Fell from Grace with the Sea.* There's no more beautiful title, or beautiful truth.

Writing prior to meaning, following the skin of vision, rewriting nothing. The ship plunges into a valley of water, onset and hurtle, and the black wall comes rushing up to meet it. For a moment vision is obliterated. *Let me look into a human eye*, Ahab says to Starbuck. *It is better than to gaze into sea or sky; better than to gaze upon God.*

He doesn't remember the crash, doesn't remember failing to put on his seatbelt, turning the key in the ignition, releasing the clutch. He will never forgive himself that slipstream moment, that fatal confusion of first gear with reverse. California upside down in a smashed windshield. One life down. The rest is epilogue.

But what seemed like an endless plummet turns into an ascent, the spaceship's engines flinging it forward and upward on an arc to complete that of the Neanderthal's bloody bone in *2001: A Space Odyssey*. He saw it in the summer of '68 with the woman who would become my mother at his side, at their generation's hinge, levitating the room. What did they think of it? Merely trippy, something for the hippies? Or a true forecast of the future of imperial machines, black monoliths, entanglement with stars?

Which is more terrifying: the plummet into blackness or the ascent into blindness?

Wounded, adrift, Dad wriggles on the hook of time. I can spool the film forward, or backward, or freeze it in the hot light of the projector. Stronger than celluloid, it will not melt, but the image under scrutiny washes out more whitely, becoming ever more inscrutable. Cast back in motion, toward or away from the moment of newness, of natality. Then history becomes a matter for recall, a matter of stubborn fact. Haunted by the dangling strips of film taped to the old Steenbeck, each cut labeled IT MIGHT HAVE BEEN

OTHERWISE. What might have been spliced into that moment, or cut from it? The leap from New York to New Jersey that took place; the leap to Puerto Rico that didn't—if Dad had accepted a transfer instead of starting his own business, so that I, starring in someone else's movie, was named Sebastian, spoke Spanish, strolled behind brick walls lined with tops of broken bottles to bar my view of the sea. All the million dangling strips in which he's still alive, or Mom is, or the two of them together, still married, maybe even still in love. Maybe it's not a million chances, maybe it's only hundreds, or dozens, or one. There has to be one.

Our own distances. The lengths we travel, from birth to birth, like the tail of a strip of film slapping blind as it comes loose from the projector, its white cyclopean staring eye.

And all the films in which my parents never met, went their wayward ways, without begetting my sister, or me. How simple and easy it would have been for Dad to choose some other apartment, in the Village or in Brooklyn or Jersey City or not in New York at all. He might have gone back to Chicago after that first night of broken glass; he might have gone to Minneapolis, he might have gone to Los Angeles and tried his first-born's luck as an actor. He might have gone to sea, his old pediatrician Doc Steinberg might not have saved him from the draft, he might have volunteered to die in the Tet Offensive, he might have been Walter Sobchak at the end of *The Big Lebowski* weeping over Khe Sanh while The Dude brushes Donny's ashes off his Cowichan sweater, in his element at last. He might have wandered all over the world, a Candide with no Cunegonde, never meeting his destiny.

But why should I pretend to care about his destiny?

It's my turn to be the father, skinned to the animal loop of time.

Ten years since the January morning my daughter came leaping like a tongue of fire, long and red and screaming in the midwinter twilight. They placed the little thing in my arms and she smoldered there for a moment, until the nurses took her back and placed her onto her mother's belly, letting her crawl and climb, incredibly, the long inches between belly button and nipple. There she latched like she'd never let go. Swaddled in standard-issue terrycloth, heartbreaking underformed head concealed by a cotton cap, she gimbaled and rotored herself, uncontrolled, raw. As though the scrap of cloth in which she was wrapped was unspooling forever outward, taking in everything of the circumstances of her birth, her newmade ancestry, the early twenty-first century as fragile and fierce as herself. What did Virginia Woolf say of the moth whose last agitations she studied on a pleasant September morning, not too long before walking into the Ouse? *Watching him, it seemed as if a fibre, very thin but pure, of the enormous energy of the world had been thrust into his frail and diminutive body.* Yes. And in a flash she is older, my walking daughter, a free and independent person, speaking with fire that never left her. *I am the king.* Yes. Standing atop the foam rock at the playground, surveying her domain, the lone and level Midwest. *King.*

The child like an astronaut comes flying from the beyond toward the beyond. We, her parents, can offer her almost nothing by way of history, of origin. Yet she is helpless not to seek us. I touch my father's nerveless hand. Then, more gently, infinitely gently, as though it might break, the bruised and blackened egg of his unconscious head.

Dad sees Mom, standing there. He is still, somehow, standing there, seeing her, in the vestibule of a four-story walk-up on the Upper West Side, in a perpetual 1968, in the springtime of Prague, as buds stud the cherry trees in Central Park and de Gaulle resigns and the Soviets reach Venus and the Americans are orbiting the moon and the Family is seething in Canoga Park and a boy named Robert Rayford, eventually to be known as the first confirmed case of AIDS in North America, dies at the age of sixteen, and utopia is over before it's begun. *Because* it's begun.

Run the film in reverse, the first breath I sucked into my lungs, blowing out the greatest decade ever, that I'd never experience. The history I would inhale, and would spend the rest of my life releasing, redistributing. I wasn't there, I'm not there now. I travel from the beyond to the beyond.

SEPARATOR

Earbuds in, eyes tight shut, flashing forward out of ordinary time: airport lounge, night flight, taxis and trams, a parasitic particle surfing the melancholy waves of capital, filling the bitter bowl of Berlin that overflowed and ran dry and with painful slowness is trickling full once more. *Little by little by hook or by crook...* I picture an insect with Thom Yorke's face, squashed under a black bowler signifying the dead century (Magritte, Beckett, Robert Frank), pinned alive in a velvet box, twitching its limbs, wings stiffening; or more horribly, a creature extracted in its larval state, thoracic discs budding—and if one were removed by the tip of a knife the other three would grow grotesquely large in compensation: could such a creature, unpinned, fly?

Home three days from the disaster in California and my bags were repacked for the long journey. In spite of what was happening or because of it? I'd told anyone who'd listen that I was prepared to cancel my plans, and they'd all nodded and winced and not met my eye. *Of course you should go.* Or maybe it was *shouldn't.* I heard what I wanted to hear.

This morning in Chicago I packed my daughter's lunch, drove her to school, walked her in, knelt down outside her classroom door. "Back before you know it."

"I don't want you to leave."

Her frank, fierce gaze held mine. But there's a crack in

me through which something slips out. I kissed her on the forehead.

"Be a good girl."

"Goodbye," she said staunchly, and marched into her classroom without a second glance.

In the car driving me to the airport, Emily had life without me on her mind, driving one-handed as she does habitually, whirling us through light traffic toward O'Hare. Emily is an actor and her show was opening that same weekend; on the other side of the continent Dad was hovering more dead than alive. The timing of my trip couldn't be worse. But there we were.

"This weekend Joanna can put her to bed both nights. Then the second weekend my mom is coming to help."

"Do I hear quotation marks around 'help'?"

"You do not! Why would you?"

"No reason." The incomprehensibly bland commercial landscape of Chicagoland flashed by.

"Yes, okay, she drives me crazy sometimes." Tapping the wheel, not looking at me. "Are you excited?"

"Do I look excited?"

She risked the glance. "Not particularly."

"Well, I am."

"You look tired. Gray. Kind of lifeless."

"Don't sugarcoat it."

"I'm serious. You're all gray. Gray in the face and gray around the edges."

"It isn't every day," I said, "that my father drives off a cliff and paralyzes himself."

She felt for my hand and squeezed. "Babe, I know. I'm sorry." The highway hummed idiotically to itself. "But you've been out of it for months. Before it even happened. You know it."

"You think I should stay."

"I don't think that."

"You're glad I'm going?"

"I didn't say that." She reclaimed her hand.

"Maybe once I go you'll miss me."

"Of course I'll miss you." She worked a ragged thumbnail with her lower teeth, bringing her hand down to beep at an erratic taxi. "I miss you when you're gone."

We glided into the international terminal's departures lane. A woman in a yellow vest stepped importantly into our lane with her hand held high. We stopped and waited to be ushered to the curb.

"You're coming back."

"Of course I'm coming back."

"No, I mean *you*. The real you."

"Come back as the real me or don't come back at all?"

"On your shield, buddy." Her eyes, unsmiling. "Yeah."

Lingering with her dry kiss watching the car roll away surrounded by a churning crowd of tourists and immigrants. Slip the earbuds into my ears so I can walk with rhythm, can fly away with my everything band, the music that makes sense to me, twentieth-century tunes, mind flying to pieces, heart stuttering. Flying from marriage, from fatherhood, from my own father's ruins, from the equivocal employments of a poet on leave from poetry, from the panicky transience of a rapidly warming world, from life as it is lived toward the unlife of literature.

Dad survived his accident but that's just about all. He'll never walk again. He'll never carry his granddaughter on his shoulders again, or cook her an apple pancake for breakfast, or follow her on her school's annual 5K. The weeks and months ahead are a ferocious blank. They'll medevac him home to New Jersey, where he'll languish and linger, accumulating bedsores, lungs slowly filling from infections that the antibiotics are less and less able to keep at bay. He'll drift in the rigid canoe of his body. And I?

In my no-longer early forties, set in domestic ways, teaching indifferent undergraduates the ABCs of reading, I seize a chance at parabola if not escape. Bound for Berlin and then Morocco, the entire dubious enterprise subsidized by the prospect of the desiccated Interzone of a literary conference in Tangier to celebrate the centennial of William S. Burroughs, everyone's favorite homicidal junkie uncle, a weak magnetic field attracting and scattering assorted eccentrics, expatriates, musicians, professors, acid casualties, superannuated hippies, latter-day beatniks, evangelizing sodomites, the discarded relics of outmoded aristocracies, gatecrashers, and chasers after antique zeitgeists hoping against hope that transgression, counterculture, resistance to Control, and the supergaunt ghostly gunpowder visage of a dead man talking might still mean something in a desert kingdom on the margins of the trade routes of the twenty-first century, where the Mediterranean tips into the North Atlantic turbine, once and future empire on the transhistorical fade. November. The monarch remnants are winging their way to Mexico, the dead blooms have toppled off of trees in New York and New Orleans, in Chicago a young exterminator bends to his task with a prayer, perhaps, on his lips. A muezzin's call rattles the sky serrated by Tangerine hills. But Germany first for a long-planned residency, researching the heart of darkness, hipster heaven, *Berliner Luft.*

Emo on the plane, listening to Radiohead, time-image of self-sampling, bits of breath, a phoneme on the brink of subjectivity (the *huh*, the *ich*, the *je*), hands moving fast, cutting duration out of whole cloth, like this flight over the Atlantic traced on the airshow, pivoting off Iceland belching its lava, spitting its ash.

Even in California I was running. Days sitting tight in the Marin County hospital waiting for news, watching Dad's chest rise and fall and my stepmother's crumpled face and my sister standing stark by his bedside, her eyes impossibly large and liquid, proved to be more than I could take. One afternoon I escaped to San Francisco for lunch with Carlo in the same North Beach joint he always took me to, the kind of place where thin red wine ran more or less on tap and the linguini con vongole left a sensation of grit between your teeth. Carlo was a graying poet, an Israeli Jew turned equivocal unAmerican, me in twenty years in reverse. He saw something in me, probably not himself. He offered me his hand, eyes ironic as always, asking after Dad; I told him the news wasn't good, then quickly skipped on to my unchanged sabbatical plans over plates of pasta: three weeks writing in Berlin, followed by the Burroughs conference in Morocco. "I'm finishing my novel," I explained, as the waiter, a stooped old man with shoe-leather-black dyed hair, cleared our plates.

Carlo held up his glass of wine so that the rim nearly touched his right eye. "The novel is dead. I thought you were a poet."

"I'm writing fiction now."

"Is that what you call it?" Then he ordered me a cannoli I didn't want and sat sipping his espresso watching me choke down the dry parchment-like flakes clinging to their tube of unctuous cream.

"You haven't asked me what my novel is about," I said to Carlo, who really was a poet, and poor, but insisted on paying anyway. We stepped out together onto the blinding street. Not many miles away, across the Golden Gate Bridge, my father lay in his medically induced coma. They were operating that afternoon, bracing what was left of his spine with steel rods. My phone was silent in my pocket. *Call me if there's any change.*

"What is any novel about?" Carlo said, shrugging. "Shit happens, followed by other shit. Did the first shit have consequences that brought about the second shit, or is it all just same shit, different chapter? There's no such thing as causality. Who gives a shit?"

You can't expect a poet to be interested in novels. Walking, expostulating, Carlo moved on to a series of jokes, in extremely poor taste I thought, on my forthcoming travels to the Arab world. ISIS and Ebola were in the news.

Washington Square is the inevitable destination of any North Beach stroll that doesn't try to resist that city's formidable gravity. We wandered through the fug of body odor and marijuana until we found an empty bench from which to watch the Sunday painters work.

"Just remember," Carlo warbled, "when you're down on your knees in that orange jumpsuit that at least your skin isn't bursting to the touch like a grape. Jesus! You're a brave or foolish man."

"Morocco is very safe," I said weakly. "Tourism is a huge part of the economy."

"Don't get *ahead* of yourself!" For a moment I thought he was going to spray wine all over his antipasto, like a fourth-grader snorting chocolate milk through his nose.

"Oh my God."

"I'd feel safer in East Jerusalem with a KICK ME sign on my back," he said, waggling his eyebrows like Groucho.

I tried to get into the spirit. "Not DECAPITATE ME?"

"Jesus." Benjamin shook his head. "*Severance Songs* ain't the half of it." He clapped me on the back of the neck, hard, to make me feel it.

"Cut it out!" I writhed away.

"Exactly." He lolled on the bench and began to roll a cigarette. "It's never been more dangerous to be an American, you realize that? Whatever protection we once had, whatever innocence, it's gotten very thin. Even Americans don't like Americans anymore."

"Speak for yourself."

"Who else?" He lit his smoke. "Burroughs, Christ, that's

another one. Another slice of American madness served up for export. What's your interest in him?"

I explained as briefly as I could my thesis, my novel's premise: a writer on the trail of the most prophetic twentieth-century writers, William S. Burroughs and Samuel Beckett, a matched pair of lively cadavers, rough beasts, a pair of forceps by which I might grasp at the skull of the nihilism perpetually being born in our time of political hopelessness and climate dread.

"Sure, sure," Carlo said, nodding along. "Daddy issues."

"Excuse me?"

"Isn't it obvious? Burroughs, Beckett. Mama's boys, lousy dads, blind to anyone's misery but their own, which they universalize. Burroughs is an addict so everyone has to be an addict; Beckett's depressed so there's no reason for humanity to go on. Pretty flimsy if you ask me. A bid for the world-historical but from my perspective, Burroughs especially is looking pretty small nowadays."

"Beckett didn't have any kids."

Carlo waved his cigarette in front of his face. "Proves my point. Anyway, you should pay attention to what's in front of you. I say nothing about your own father, of course. But I'm serious about the danger you're in."

"Nobody's going to cut off my head."

"You're missing the point. I'm an immigrant. I see what's happening. I see your situation clearly. What you've never understood is that it's dangerous to be a poet. In this country the danger is mostly spiritual. But the Arabs, they've been humiliated continually by the West for hundreds of years. The ones who are lucky enough to have a country feel marginalized and for the ones who don't have a country it's much, much worse. What happens when you have no institutions you can call your own? No nation, no democracy? You turn to poetry."

"I thought they were Berbers in Morocco, not Arabs at all."

"You want to talk about Beckett? Think about Ireland, poor even in potatoes. The Irish had nothing to call their own but their history of humiliation and the fairies. So they went to the fairies. And when it turned to bombs and guns, it was because of those fairies. The poets. Why do you think Maud Gonne never gave Yeats the time of day? Because she wanted him to write her a weapon, and he couldn't or wouldn't. You get 'Easter, 1916' instead: *A terrible beauty is born.* She took the terror, he wanted the beauty. But you can't separate them. Beckett was still writing for that beauty, years after the fact, because after the war, after the Shoah, Ireland's homelessness became the world's."

"What exactly are you smoking there, Carlo? Can I get a hit?"

Carlo looked at the butt in his hand as if surprised to find it there. "Help yourself."

I took a drag, coughed, passed it back.

"The Arabs are the Irish of today. Don't laugh. Mahmoud Darwish was the Yeats of the Palestinians, but now the only poetry that matters is the poetry of death. The poetry of the deed. And wouldn't they love to get their hands on an innocent boy like yourself, to make a poem out of you. On camera, a live feed, for all the world to see."

"Shut up."

"All right, all right," Carlo waved his hands deprecatingly. "Don't get hot under the collar." He yanked his own while bugging out his eyes, Rodney Dangerfield style.

That was Carlo, bitter and brilliant, the breaker of bad news. I was a hostage-in-waiting. I was bait. Even if it wasn't true, it felt true. I was an American poet bound for the dark side of the moon.

"I'm a fiction writer now," I reminded him.

"So much the worse for you. The Arabs respect poetry. They know that *fiction* is just another word for lies."

The plane's engines throb time and space away. Radiohead ticks on. A flight attendant with the unlikely name—according to the tag on her uniform—of Loyola O'Rourke glides down the aisle carrying a smile and a tray of plastic cups of Champagne. As though there were something to celebrate about this crossing, from New World to Old, day for night, life for its opposite. Thoughts of the *Titanic*'s failed attempt to travel the other way; not especially morbid, since Emily is performing in a production of *Titanic: The Musical* while I'm gone, drowning nightly in the person of Ida Strauss, wife of Isidor the founder of Macy's, famous for refusing to board a lifeboat without her husband of forty years, impersonated in this case by a debonair gay man named Edward, a dear friend of hers whose path has crossed with hers on many a storefront stage. Now both of them will be singing to each other with passionate discretion every night in German accents: "Vere you go, I go." The show is a necessary fiction, a convenient explanation for why she isn't accompanying me on my mock-epic, aside from our daughter's need to stay in school. We follow the letter if not the spirit of our *ketubah*, the Jewish marriage contract, in which we pledged to let one another go as a condition of keeping together. But it's me who's coming apart: away from my family, mind's eye riveted to the picture of my father in his hospital bed, caught in the net of irretrievable accident.

Fingers curled around my pen, I close my eyes and concentrate on the music: music cleans up the affects, purifies them. Or maybe I've got it backward: maybe music, this music anyway, dirties up the scene, contaminates the fringes of consciousness where the waves of the outer world lap upon the shores of my mind. Burning the distinctions, smearing light over things like magnesium on bullets, making tracks, staining the objects with their origins. The plane itself is a tube of heavy light trailing tons of carbon through and into the sky, a black invisible arc, one of thousands at any given moment suturing the gap between there and here, Chicago and Berlin, for any reason at all. The immigration officer's question, Business or pleasure? But no answer suffices, a blank stare will not erase what's already been achieved. Riding the fragile and violent skin of civilization requires no effort: the enormous animal flicks a muscle like a horse registering the irritation of a fly, and I am catapulted to another continent. The Champagne dries out my mouth and I sit there wishing for water. In my ears Thom Yorke croons from his empty nightclub at the end of the world. The lights go down between beats. I'm a heart in the air.

NEW YORK, MID-1960S

One of his cousin's many friends—to him they all seem like versions of Peter, long and lean and twinkling through self-conscious facial hair, though one is a Black man with a Tidewater drawl and a bowtie and another is a heavyset balding Armenian who moves with a dancer's grace—had a lead on an apartment just a few blocks away. It was a studio on the fourth floor (but it climbed like the fifth) of a brownstone on West 89th, just half a block from Central Park where the reservoir bellied out reflecting the mingled blues and whites of the sky. People didn't jog in those days, in fact people hardly penetrated the park at all, a desert at all seasons, an island of wintry light populated by isolatoes walking alone with hands in pockets or walking alone with hands out, gesticulating, talking to themselves, in any case never on the level, never just looking out. There was no possibility of connection, there were no cell phones back then to explain the running voices and disconnected stares: these people were simply crazy, rogue thoughts of the city that had spat them out from somewhere deep within itself, or had been attracted from elsewhere only to be repelled by its mirrored metallic jagged surface, and had not bounced away but clung there, human detritus, negative images of the power and glory that had rejected them so decisively.

Facts embed themselves in fiction, like iron deposits

in otherwise non-ferrous minerals. Facts exert their own magnetic field which play over the fiction and shield it, perhaps inadequately, from the cosmic rays of the reader's regard. New York was cheap but the money he'd saved wasn't enough to pay the rent on his new apartment and feed him for the months until he started his teaching job. There was a Help Wanted sign in the window of the Florsheim's on 42nd Street, near Times Square; filling out the application he hesitated over whether to list his college degree where it said "Education" on the form. He went ahead and filled it in and was hired on the spot. All day long he breathed in the toxic, somehow hypnotic aroma of leather, talcum powder, ammonia, and feet. His shoulders learned to stoop from the constant kneeling, in a repeated movement vaguely reminiscent of the prince's gesture in *Cinderella*. No, not the prince: the awkward foolish monocled Grand Duke, henpecked by his feral King into first organizing a ball to marry off the Prince and then into discovering the identity of the elusive maiden who had succeeded above all others in capturing the Prince's heart. Again and again he knelt, displaying to his customers' indifferent eyes what was then a luxuriantly Brylcreemed head of lustrous hair, a compact helmet that he crafted each morning to conceal its real length from his boss. He saw no princesses in Florsheim, only men, men in suits and men in dungarees, men with hair jutting from their nostrils and men clicking their tongues noisily against their palates. Young Black men with conked hair or aerial Afros and young Puerto Ricans in sparkling white shirts and the occasional family of frummers, once six boys ranging in age from six to sixteen, all of them wearing dark suits, each of them needing to be fitted out with a new pair of heavy black brogans. He knelt before them one at a time, fitting their shy white-socked feet into the shoes while their mother stood by, a surprisingly young and attractive woman in spite of her ankle-length gray skirt and the unnatural mahogany shade of her wig, cut to give her bangs in a Louise Brooks-ish sort of way. Her eyes met his as he was struggling one of the older boy's feet—give the frummers this, their hygiene was good—into a pair of lace-ups and he thought he saw the corners of her mouth quirk into a proto-smile. Was she flirting with him? But at the register paying for her sons' shoes she was all business, producing a rubber-banded ball of one-dollar bills from the depths of a huge shapeless bag and flicking them out onto the counter with a practiced thumb. "Zank you," she said with dignity, not looking at him, as he handed her two heavy plastic bags full of shoes, which she in turn passed to her eldest, a heavy-browed thick-thighed boy who stared at him or past him with a kind of uncomprehending hostility. Her accent was identical to that of his Yiddish-speaking bubbe who'd emerged from the Pale of Settlement to sell apples on the Lower East Side. Was she his age as she seemed, or infinitely older? They departed, and he was disconcerted though not surprised to see the thuggish eldest son taking the lead, followed by the other five boys in a declining row, and the young mother, who didn't look back, taking up the rear.

By the end of each shift he was counting the minutes,

an ache like the tip of a boot driving between his shoulder blades; yet he was unwilling to return too quickly to his bare room at the top of all those dusty stairs; at the same time his meager salary permitted him few entertainments. Almost automatically his feet would carry him to the subway, but then while riding the noisy train something inside him would rebel and he would find himself getting off many stops short of 86th Street. He would emerge in the roaring dusk and wander, looking into shop windows or straying into Central Park if it wasn't too dark, trying not to stare too openly at the women he passed, the many beautiful women. His thoughts strayed back to the woman from the shoe store. How old had she been when she had her first son, now sixteen if he was a day? Surely not much older than sixteen herself. Did she love her husband? He pictured a short hairy man with a hunchback and an apron, then realized he was visualizing Fischbach, the deli man at Kaufmann's back in Skokie, hacking out slices of pastrami with his ingratiating leer. Did she *like* being so *Jewish*? Did she dream of making *aliyah* to Israel, still beating its collective chest a year after the Six-Day War? Her lips, he thought her lips had been colored the faintest shade of coral pink, as though she had applied a little lipstick, guiltily or defiantly, before starting her errand to Times Square—from where? Brooklyn, probably. It was a Friday: he pictured her with her children swaying on the subway, getting off in some dark shtetl he'd mentally transplanted to Flatbush, bustling around the house to prepare for Shabbos, standing before lit candles with her hands covering her eyes. Unconsciously his lips moved, words he hadn't said since his bar mitzvah ten years ago: *Sh'ma Yisrael Adonai aloheinu Adonai echad.*

He shook himself awake, ten blocks from home. Fat spattering drops of rain started falling and he jogged the rest of the way, getting thoroughly soaked as the clouds burst just as he was fumbling for his key to the outer door. Up the creaking stairs past domestic shouts and greasy smells, reaching his grotty top-floor apartment, panting and dripping in the little living room as the buildings opposite went gray and glassy in the storm. He put a can of soup on the stove, wrung out his wet socks and draped them over the shower curtain. He looked in drawers for candles and didn't find any. He sat in his kitchen and ate tomato soup, mopping it up with a slice of white bread from a plastic bag. *Never so alone, never so alone.* He was humming it, oddly happy, as if the words rhymed with the *sh'ma.* He put a record on the turntable and a percussive piano jazz started up. The rain was still falling. In untucked shirt and loose tie, barefoot, alone in New York, he swayed, clicked his wrists, lifted closed eyes, danced.

BERLIN

Fog of sleep deprivation coloring the otherwise perfectly blue autumn sky a cataract yellow in my mind. Bus ride, taking in the printed shirt, ice-cool glasses and goatee of a young man who would not be out of place in Bucktown or Brooklyn: a hipster is a hipster is a hipster. But this hipster appears to be traveling with his elderly parents, her with hair dyed purple-black, him gently balding, something stiff and grayed-out about the two of them as though they grew up in the defunct GDR; perhaps they did. The U-bahn's sinuous movement mesmerizes my jet-lagged brain, the way the unseparated cars wriggle together and apart and up and down as they pursue the tunnels. Remembering that that was the first thing they got back online, postwar: the U-bahn, when everything else was still smashed to shit.

The Berliners are out in force in the weak autumn sunlight, crowding sidewalk cafes, gesturing with cigarettes, flash in chic sunglasses. Two blocks from the Nollendorfplatz U-station to Winterfeldtplatz, where I am to meet the friend-of-a-friend who will give me the keys to his flat, where I can hunker down and write while he and his family head to Athens and then to some little island where *he* can hunker down and write. I'm tired, the kind of tired that creeps into you from the neck up. Sinus tired. Eyes aflame.

Winterfeldtplatz is an acre of stone at the foot of which stands a brick church, looking to my eyes at least weirdly out of place, brick being for the most part foreign to the architecture of bourgeois Charlottenberg. It is lined, today and every Sunday, with the tents and booths of a bustling market selling produce, fried meats, clothing, jewelry, and every sort of tchotchke. Well-heeled Berliners move up and down the aisles, baskets of flowers in their hands or else pushing complicated-looking strollers. There's a café by the square's edge where people sit outside in spite of the bite in the air. I spy Per in a blue coat and white scarf, hunched over an espresso, rubbing his hands against the chill of the fading morning and showing his ruined teeth. Smiling at me.

As soon as I sit down he springs up, offering to fetch me a coffee from the bar. I stand up to demur and he pushes me down again, lightly, the fingertips of his left hand splayed out across my chest. Traffic oozes around where I'm sitting, my red eyes fixed on the name of a bar across the way: SLUMBERLAND. Does Little Nemo drink there, all grown up?

Per returns with, I'm not sure why, a macchiato for me and a second espresso for himself. In conversation he offers up a peculiar mix of irony and earnestness, a saturnine world-weariness mixed with impish enthusiasm, made even stranger by his English, which combines his Scandinavian syntax with American idioms. His expression when he smiles, with all those misplaced and miscolored teeth, is entirely unlike the serious, vaguely patrician appearance he assumes when his lips are closed. He gives me that look now.

"I was extremely sorrowful to hear of your father's sufferings. Should you not be there with him?"

Taken aback, I sip my coffee for a moment. The jet lag presses down on my forehead like a hand.

"I *was* with him. His wife—my stepmother—is with him now, my sister too. There's nothing I can do to help. They practically ordered me to go."

Per jerks his chin sideways. "Family is important. Writing is more important?"

Is that a question? "I wouldn't say that. Not at all. But there's nothing to do out there. The doctors saved his life. He's recovering. All we can do is wait, so I'm waiting here."

"What do you wait for?"

I shrug uneasily. "I don't know."

"Berlin is a good place to wait," Per says after a pause. "Sometimes I feel I myself have been waiting here, for a long time. Since '89, in fact."

"What was it like then? When the Wall came down?"

"It was like a surprise party." Per shows me his terrible teeth. "The biggest surprise party you ever saw."

"I was in college," I say, remembering. "We watched it on TV."

Per makes a dismissive gesture, chopping the air with his hand. "What you saw is nothing. It is a feeling, impossible to describe. I've tried it many times. Imagine if that piece of paper"—nodding at the ten-euro bill I've placed on the table, insisting on paying for the coffees, I can do that much—"were just that. A piece of paper. You knew that all along, of course, but you also didn't know it. You never knew that *other people* could know it. Suddenly you are standing there with only this piece of paper between you, utterly valueless."

"It must have been amazing."

"Amazing is not the word." He shrugs. "But gradually things become normal again. You get used to everything. You pick up the piece of paper and offer it in exchange for a cup of coffee, and the waitress takes it. Keep the change." He laughs quietly to himself.

"I've wanted to come here for a long time. To see it for myself. It's the right place to finish my novel."

"If I were yourself," Per says, fiddling with his shirt's frayed cuff, "I would not be able to write any sort of fiction now. There is too much reality pressing in. It is your father in the hospital. It's a big deal." The colloquialism makes me smile; he misunderstands. He leans forward. "The mother is important, yes of course. Because she gives us language, yes? *Die Muttersprache*. But it is the father who teaches us the story. It is the father who shows us what we are to be."

"I'm not the least bit like my father."

Per shakes his head. "You must be like him. But you must."

"How can you say that? You've never even met him."

Maybe it's the exhaustion that makes Per so hard to understand. Or maybe it's his accent, an unfathomable blend of Swedish, German, and a kind of nasal bray that reminds me a little bit of Boston. "I have met *you*."

"I'm only here for a few weeks," I say irrelevantly. "Then the Burroughs conference. Then home."

Per spreads his hands. "Home is Chicago now?"

"Yes."

We really don't know each other all that well. Per was a friend of my wife's in a long-ago time, in New York. Their paths crossed only briefly, and I was a little too far from the intersection point. But we have met twice before in the States and are meeting for the third time now.

Per nods his head again, pleased, like a teacher who has finally gotten through to one of his dullest pupils. "Yes, Chicago, of course." He points an imaginary Tommy gun at me. "Al Capone. Bang-bang!"

"I really appreciate the place to stay."

"Berlin is a place to stay. I have stayed here for many, many years. I am not exactly fond of it; I would not say it is home. Yet I cannot seem to imagine living anywhere else. The Germans." Per bites off the word, shrugs. "They are *German*, yes? That is not what I mean to say. They lack imagination. Imagination of the other, I mean."

"It seems like a very international city. Multicultural even."

"That is not what I am saying. I am saying they do not *imagine* others. And it is strange to be other among them. To see yourself through eyes that do not see you at all."

Per's German, so far as I can tell, is accentless, flawless. He looks like he could be German, and after all, in this day and age, what precisely does German look like? I have already taken note of the many Turks and Arabs, the ubiquity of the doner kebab shops, the Africans and Vietnamese thronging the market at Winterfeldplatz across the street from where we sit, selling flowers and fragrances. Yet there is something blurry about Per, a roughed-out quality that is not German at all, almost *unheimlich*. Lines surround his eyes and mouth like so many parentheses and his graying hair clings in tight curls to the sides of his head. His ears are large and low, the nose a little on the small side. He does not look German, or Swedish, or anything other than, simply, European, European in the most generic and universal of ways. His nails, I notice, are bitten to the quick. Around the corner his wife and adult son are packing for their journey to Greece, where they will spend the winter while Per works on a new translation of the poems of Angelos Sikelianos. There is something furtive in his manner, in the way he slides the key across the table, the way that he nibbles more than sips at his second espresso. I feel myself an accomplice to a getaway.

Per stands and I stand with him; he grips my hand and forearm firmly for a moment, staring with intensity from dark blue eyes. "I am happy to be of service to you, my friend. Write well." He presses the key into my hand and I fold my fingers around it. I watch him walk away, still a little hunched, a sailor's gait.

What Per calls his "work flat"—the family lives in a larger apartment on the fifth floor—turns out to be a lair such as I have scarcely dared to dream of. I who write in stolen moments on the train to and from work, or when I ought to be grading papers, now find myself resplendent in the book-lined belly of a real writer's study. A large window swings open like a door to admit the mild morning air and view of a squared-in courtyard, typical of the city I'm told, cool and white, shaded with greenery, governed by the rectilinear forms that I can already tell will form my chief impression of Berlin. And a blue sky lids it.

The apartment is crammed with books, floor to ceiling, spilling in piles, covering the futon where I'm supposed to sleep, a surprising number of them in English. A sort of expressionist spoof on a Magritte painting stands high above the doorway, a mustached shabby-looking man in an overcoat and his basset hound in a landscape, looking sidewise out of the picture in a manner sure to unnerve me late at night. Books on the floor, books behind me on shelves, books in every room: I feel stalked by them, pursued. Everywhere I can feel the eye and hand of Per, author and translator, grinning buck toothed over my shoulder as I type or standing in the corner like a kid playing hide and seek, finger pressed roguishly to his lips.

Alone. I've longed for this moment. Over the work flat's little desk hangs a small painting of a blue river at night with a greenlit bridge and the sort of squat, hat-like houses I saw from the plane, a sailboat without sails in the foreground. It's not detailed at all, just color and brushstrokes, a signature in white that I can't make out. The Spree? The Seine? The path taken by Rimbaud's drunken boat? Clearly it's here as a point of departure, invitation to a voyage. How many of Per's own books have been launched from this dock? Fingers of green paint under the bridge mark the reflections of the lights in the water. You don't put your hand on a river and you can't clench it with your fist. You open your fingers and feel the flow.

In spite or because of the jet lag I lie between sleep and waking for hours of the night together, the images burning under my eyelids. Leaving the hospital after Dad's last surgery I made my way to the scene of the accident at a serpent's twist in the hilly narrow street below my sister's place in darkest Marin. The humpy hills carried redwoods on their backs, while a narrow creek wormed its way into the underbrush below, burbling inanely to itself. Shafts of light fell like spent arrows through the coniferous branches that shrugged around the spot, an unremarkable bit of roadway marked off by a pair of traffic cones, glimmering pinkly in the sun. The houses were ramshackle structures set back into the hillside, with outbuildings and platforms protruding pseudopodlike, some of them propped on stilts: decks, sheds, someone's hot tub suspended serenely on an insubstantial platform over a three-car garage. Scuff marks and torn brush mark the car's path down the hillside, an almost vertical drop of twenty or twenty-five feet, but if it weren't for the cones I'd never have spotted it. Someone spied me mooning there and came shuffling over. A man in his sixties I'd have said but infinitely worn and wizened, with a long gray beard wagging against a pouched midriff his Hawaiian shirt didn't try too hard to cover. I smelled him before I saw him: patchouli and pot, pot and patchouli. About Dad's age, I realized, but a man who'd traveled a different road.

"Can I help you?"

"No, sorry. I mean, yes. Can you tell me what happened?" The man stared at me owlishly. I gestured vaguely. "My sister lives here."

"Oh my, oh my," the old hippie said solemnly. For a moment I was afraid he was going to put his large, horny hand on my shoulder. "I was so sorry to hear about it. You've got to know what you're doing in these hills." He pointed at the cliff's edge. "My own wife's taken a tumble there. Me too, come to think of it."

"In a car?"

"Oh no, oh no. On foot." The old hippie chuckled to himself. "Once I was taking out the garbage and once, I don't know what I was doing. Taking a walk at night. My eyes aren't what they used to be. It's a ride, I can tell you! An unpleasant surprise." He gripped his left wrist with his right hand and met my eyes. "The second time I did a somersault and landed on my feet like a tumbler! Broke my wrist, though." He shook his head. "Your dad is lucky to be alive, you know."

Was he? "I know."

The old hippie fished around in his capacious parachute pants and came out with a top-of-the-line phone. "I took pictures."

"Excuse me?"

"Afterwards, I mean. We all heard it, you know. Tremendous crash. But somehow we didn't think anything of it until we heard the ambulance come."

I was calm. "You took pictures of my father's accident?"

"Oh no, oh no. Not while he was still in the car. After. Have a look."

Unwilling yet unable to resist, I took the phone from his hand and looked at the screen. There was my sister's car lying upside-down on the road below the cliff side. It looked like a toy car that a gigantic kid had arbitrarily picked up and squashed flat onto the asphalt, pressing down with his enormous hand until the windows popped out and the roof was half accordioned into itself. It didn't look like anything a person ought to be able to survive.

"Jesus."

"Lucky to be alive," the old hippie repeated. "See that? They had to cut him out." His hairy finger with its long yellow nail flashed over the screen, swiping left to show me the car from various angles. I thought for a moment I saw my dad's glasses lying in the middle of the road, perfectly intact. They were safe in their case now in my stepmother's purse. Who had thought to retrieve them?

And why had this old man taken the photos, and why was I looking at them?

"Thank you," I said. "I think I've seen enough."

The old hippie put his phone away. For a moment we both stood there solemnly, lost in thought, hands thrust into our pockets. A wind plucked at the trees, sending a few brown needles spiraling down into the dust.

"Terrible thing," the hippie said at last. But I could tell his mind was elsewhere. "You gonna stick around?"

"I'm going back to the hospital."

"You tell your sister we're all pulling for her," the old hippie said, and now the hand really did come down onto my shoulder and squeezed it for a moment. The watery blue eyes behind the round glasses met mine. "And for your father too, of course."

Nothing new here, reads the text from my sister that I send her at 3 AM Berlin time. *No news.* Then the dots of thought crossing so many thousands of miles. Then: *How's Germany?*

I put the phone away without answering and pull the thin covers over my head, breathing in for a while my own unwashed jet-lagged funk before exhaustion like so many ropes drags me down.

THREE WOMEN

But were there women before her? There were. Vera, the Russian immigrant, Elizabeth, the minister's daughter, and Cora. He met Vera in a bar on 42nd Street, having wandered in after a shift at Florsheim for a beer. She was tall, with dyed blonde hair and painted-on eyebrows and crimson lips, sitting in a scrum of coworkers, a Madison Avenue typing pool. "Buy you a drink?" Dad shouted in her ear, and she rose primly and came to sit beside him at the bar.

"A Manhattan," she said. "I've always wanted to drink a Manhattan in Manhattan."

"Me too." Their drinks arrived and he lifted his in a toast. "To Manhattans in Manhattan!" They drank. Where was this boldness coming from? The bar was crowded and her shoulder was rubbing against his. She smelled like baby powder.

"I am not from here," she said.

"Me neither!"

"I am from Georgia." He thought of Ray Charles singing in her accent and smiled. She smiled back.

She had emigrated to this country with her family, she said. Her father had been a Soviet consul to Cuba, and he had defected. They had moved to Miami but she had come to New York. "To live!"

"To living," Dad said, toasting her again.

Her apartment was a one-bedroom in a remodeled tenement on East 32nd Street. They walked or rather sloshed the dozen blocks together, stopping to kiss at every red light. But at the top of the stairs she searched her handbag and then announced, "I don't have keys."

"What about the super?"

"He is drunk," she said. She stared him down. "We go to your place?"

Back down the stairs, close to midnight on a Thursday, standing for almost half an hour on the corner trying to hail a cab, with no success. "I will wait inside," Vera told him. When he finally got the cab, he ran inside into the building vestibule, but she was nowhere to be seen. "Vera?" He ran up the three flights of stairs again. No one. He stared at her door for a moment, then knocked on it, hard. "Vera?"

No answer. He knocked again. "Vera!"

A door opened, not hers, and an older woman with a cigarette between her fingers and her hair in pink plastic curlers appeared. "Mister, you know what time it is?"

"Sorry. I was just…"

"Don't tell me what you were just. Go home."

"But I don't have her number." He fumbled. "Vera. Do you know her?"

The woman's face hardened. "Communist slut."

"She's not a Communist."

"Hah!" She slammed the door in his face. He stood there, bewildered and less drunk, in the dimly lit hallway. "Vera?"

When he got back downstairs the cab he had hailed was gone.

Dad met Elizabeth at Café au Go Go in the Village,

where there was a rumor that Bob Dylan had been playing semi-incognito gigs; already the decade was nostalgic
for itself. Dylan never showed up but Elizabeth did: another blonde, a natural one this time, the descendant of
Puritans—her father was a Unitarian minister in western
Massachusetts. She had liberal ideas and coral lips and pre-
ferred condoms to the Pill. They went to the movies and
took walks and had sex two or three times, and then one
rainy Saturday afternoon she called him to break it off.
He stood there turning slowly in place, winding the cord
around his legs, asking why.

"I'm not saying it hasn't been fun," she said to him, "but
I just feel it's time to move on. I need to actualize, and I
don't see you as being part of that."

"Actualize?"

"Don't get me wrong. You're a very sweet boy."

"Why are you calling me a boy? I'm five years older than
you."

"Don't be mad."

"It's because I'm Jewish, isn't it?"

"Don't be absurd. That's the most attractive thing about
you."

"It is?"

"Listen, that's why I'm calling, because I wanted to let
you down easy. I have a friend you should meet. Cora."

"Cora?"

Cora was a slightly rumpled woman in her late twenties
with John Lennon-style glasses and generous hips who had
been Elizabeth's roommate while they were both at Bar-

nard. She had long dark curly ringlets of hair and thick eyebrows and a dirty laugh that drew him in, though in his private mind he told himself that she wasn't his type. They met for drinks at Trader Vic's and went for a walk afterward and when they sat on a bench on the edge of the park she put her hand on his knee in an exploratory way. Not a bad kisser for a fat girl, he decided. A not-so-nice Jewish girl from the Bronx who nearly smothered him with her ardor, her massy flesh. She was in graduate school at CUNY for international relations and wanted to work at the U.N. She was also, somewhat to his surprise, a passionate supporter of Nixon: "Only a Republican," she said, "can end this war." It was one more perversity in a string of perversities: her appetite for bacon and shrimp cocktails, preferably in the same meal; her love of television game shows (her sister Lucy had once appeared, she said, on *The Generation Gap*, which had fanned her "huge crush" on the host, Dennis Wholey); her collection of traditional Dixieland jazz albums, for which he teased her mercilessly. They dated for seven weeks. Then one afternoon she came to pick him up at the shoe store. He looked up automatically when he heard the electric bell chime from where he was kneeling on the floor trying to slip a tasseled loafer onto the foot of a gray-haired man with a walrus mustache and white belly hair tufting between the snaps of his paisley Western shirt. Cora was wearing a close-fitting black dress that emphasized, he thought unflatteringly, the pear shape of her body, and she was panting slightly as if from exertion, with sweat on her forehead and red cheeks. When she waved at him he found himself unable to respond; he stared at her, then past her, his face frozen. He could feel her staring at him, looking into his thoughts. When he finally glanced up again her lips had thinned. She replaced the sunglasses she had just removed, spun out the door, and vanished into Times Square. A pang of guilt sent him lurching to his feet and out the door, but she was gone. Repeated phone calls only got him her answering service. Then the next day Elizabeth called.

"She doesn't want to see you."

"Why, for God's sake?"

"Because you don't want to see her."

"But I do!"

"But you don't want to be seen *with* her."

A small, fatal pause. "That's ridiculous," he said.

"You've got a lot of growing up to do."

"I—"

"Don't call us, okay?" The line went dead.

He felt bad about it, but not for long. He was alive in New York in the long zipless birth of free love. This was only the beginning, he believed. He was young, unattached, reasonably good-looking, a white man before he was a Jew, a man before all else. There was no reason it had to end.

But it did end, and wasn't there some small component of relief when it did? When the thunderbolt finally struck? When we finally choose love, is it not because we are in some small or large part tired of the chase, "the one," the *via negativa* that is, in fact, love?

New York in the Sixties, finite, the prize.

B-SIDE

On my screen Dad goes grayscaled, unable as yet to speak; he offers the camera a limp thumbs-up. His wife is contained, fierce and pointed across continents: *I believe he will walk again.* My sister's face a purple puffy mask. I sit at Per's desk and watch the rain where it spirals down into the courtyard; a tenant hurries through tenting his jacket over his head. The building at midday is dead, hollow, resounding with its own emptiness. Before me the notebook blank with pages, the capped pen. On the laptop screen the same shit I see in the States. The novel doesn't come. I thumb my worn and much-underlined copy of *Naked Lunch* instead.

Burroughs, deadskinned, in suit and tie, leaving moribund St. Louis and cold-water New York for sunnier climes where junk was cheap and the boys were cheaper, pining for Allen Ginsberg in his brief youth and beauty, spinning out his loneliness in what he called "routines," vaudevillian of the heated spoon, the talking asshole. In rainy Berlin I try to picture myself on his trail in sunny Morocco, the medinas, the quality of the sky, the cabs and colors and voices mingling French, Spanish, Arabic. Cities where white men like Burroughs and Beckett, the representative men of the twentieth century, came to feel their whiteness, to rub against something, to stand out against a multitudinous multicolored background. And let's not forget Paul Bowles, another B, rehearsing in his novels and stories the encounter of savagery with innocence, showing them to be one and the same. Three B's, then, under my pen in Berlin: exiles, seekers after experience or in flight from it, paths often crossing without, quite, touching one another: how thick and dull their senses must have been to need such quickening, thickened and dulled by gray America, gray Europe. Men without women. Men whose bodies mapped the flow of black bile from node to node, ringed, saturnine, men tapped into a seemingly universal flow that pulls others along, readers drawn like moths to the light of negative space.

I call my wife, willing her face to appear on the narrow screen I carry everywhere: no answer. She's asleep at home. Or she's awake but doesn't want to be reminded of my absence. Or she resents how I cast her as the rememberer of my sins. Her moods color the house, brightly or blackly, as thousands of miles away her absence colors the room. So I pull on my jacket and leave those colors behind.

Is it the first day? The last? The days pass quickly, the hours drag along. I stumble out the door into the light of others' lives, adrift, a man without qualities. Bread and coffee and *The New York Times* on my phone, crammed with distant irrelevancies. With my laptop slung in my messenger bag I wander the city, pulled up short by the intensity of its bustle, its resolute unprettiness. At noon I am adrift in a field of stelae, eerie with children and tourists wandering in a forest of stone, perplexed by the irreverence appropriate to another inexplicable tourist attraction: Memorial to the Murdered Jews of Europe. Not far away lines in the street mark the path of the Wall that once divided and ordered the universe, stiff and immutable until the coming of those days of 1989 in which I still thirty years after the fact can't make myself believe. What alternative could there be to the Cold War? Will we ever find out?

The incipient chill of autumn pursues me in and out of museums, galleries, restaurants, cafes. The global itinerant. I wish fiercely to be less alone, but there's no one I can see myself with. My life is here now, on the moon with moon people. Dodging sunbeams in the memorial, watching children play, Don't they understand what this place is for? The stones cast shadows on each other like so many sundials. Kids play hide and seek, not caring what time it is.

I meet an acquaintance for lunch, a fellow poet, an American who's lived here for years, working as a translator for an insurance firm. We sit across from each other in a farm-to-table place not far from the city center. Shane hasn't changed much—a few crow's feet, yes, and a gray skunk's streak in the otherwise lustrous black hair she wears in a severe bob. She regards me with entirely justified skepticism as I explain my reasons for being here. I don't mention Dad, there being too much and too little to explain.

"You're writing fiction now?" she asks, stabbing at her salad with an impossibly slender silver fork. "When did that happen?"

"Since poetry stopped making sense."

"Poetry or life?"

Shane sips white wine. I'm drinking beer, a sharp-toothed German lager, thrilled to have temporarily escaped the tyranny of the American microbrewed IPA.

"I just felt like nobody was listening."

Shane looks at me archly. "Nobody *is* listening. That's the whole point. If you had something to *say*, you wouldn't write a poem. Or a story either."

"I'm writing a novel."

"So much the worse." She drained her glass. "You know why I write? Because I'm alone. Nobody's wife and nobody's mother. I'm a woman of a certain age turning more invisible by the day."

"You're hardly invisible."

"I write for the experience of seeing what I can say when nobody gives a fuck," Shane says. "That's the only reason to write anything. Otherwise you should just shut up. Go home. Make love to your wife."

My father, I want to say. But what to say about him. What can this angry, angular woman tell me that I don't already know? *Make love to your father.* Isn't that what I'm doing, attempting, now?

The conversation ceases while the server swaps out our plates. An artful pile of pork tenderloin slices perched on a bed of infrathin swirls of red cabbage for me, six seared scallops arranged around a swirl of squid ink for her.

"You seem to have achieved a certain clarity," I say.

Shane spears a morsel of shellfish, chews, swallows, shrugs. "A.A. helps." She lifts her freshly refilled glass in a mock toast and takes a big swallow.

My eyes follow the wine's passage down her long elegant swallowing throat. "Does it?"

"Your face!" Shane laughs. "It's not really about drinking

for me. I mean, even drinking isn't about drinking, actually. It's about being seen. *Recognized.* You should try it sometime."

"I, uh. I'm not an alcoholic."

"Neither am I," she deadpans. She swirls the wine in her glass. "Not anymore."

"Aren't you supposed to say that you're in recovery, or something like that?"

"Am I?" She glances at her phone sitting quietly beside her plate on the table, a glass pet that purrs awake at the stroke of her fingertip. "There's a meeting at eight if you want to go."

I eat my pork. "It's a date."

We ride the gently swaying U-bahn east to Strausberger Platz and come out into a quiet leafy neighborhood rowed with the sort of modern six-story apartment buildings I've come to associate with those parts of the city not lodged in the nineteenth century (like my neighborhood, Charlottenberg) or the twentieth (the Stalinist wedding cake buildings lining Karl-Marx Allee). I expect a church or perhaps some sort of civic building, but we simply walk up to one of the apartment doorways and Shane presses the unmarked button for an apartment on the fifth floor. We are buzzed into a little antiseptic hallway and climb the many flights of stairs until I begin to distinguish the dry smells of electric heating and ancient coffee. Shane pauses before a surprisingly ornate door, with gold leafing curlicuing around its edges, and throws her shoulders back. "Ready?"

The apartment is book-lined, with worn wooden floors

and high ceilings; we stand in the large living room with the usual flatscreen on one wall facing a Biedermeier sofa and a loveseat and a leather wingback and an array of metal folding chairs. A bead curtain separates us from what I presume to be the kitchen; a big man wearing a denim jacket steps in from the corridor, rubbing his wet palms on his pants. Three middle-aged women in muted cardigans sit on the sofa with their heads bent together, whispering intensely. Shane plants herself in the armchair and crosses her legs in queenly fashion. But it's the big man who seems to be in charge. His bulk enfolding one of the folding chairs, he takes a comically small pair of reading glasses out of his jacket pocket and props them on his nose before he starts speaking, consulting occasionally a ragged spiral notebook in his massive hand. Of course I can't understand a word. Shane smiles brightly at me from the recesses of her chair. New people arrive—a well-coiffed old woman in a Burberry raincoat, a young Black man with gleaming shaved head, two men with blond hair gone to gray who could be brothers or lovers but who sit, as though by mutual agreement, on opposite ends of the room. The alcoholics gossip quietly while the big man drones on, some of them going out through the bead curtain and returning with paper cups of coffee in their hands. A sheet of paper goes round and I hold it on my lap for what I hope is a decent interval before passing it on to the next person, who scribbles something on it, probably their name, before they too pass it on. Shane, quite at home, has taken off her high black boots that now stand sentinel before her, and sits cross-legged in the armchair with her eyes closed, as though meditating. There's a hitch in the big man's basso, a pause; he wipes his brow. I realize that he has begun to recite the Twelve Steps, if only because I can recognize the numbers. I try to make out what he's saying:

"*Schritt eins: Wir ließen zu, dass wir über machtlos waren, Spiritus—dass unsere Leben unkontrollierbar geworden waren. Schritt zwei: Kam, zu glauben, dass eine Energie, die als selbst größer ist, uns zur Vernunft wieder herstellen könnte. Schritt drei: Traf eine Entscheidung, um unseren Willen und unsere Leben zur Sorgfalt des Gottes umzuwenden, wie wir ihn verstanden.*"

People sit quietly, listening, a few of them nodding. One of the middle-aged blond brothers has taken a small notebook out of his pocket and bends over his knee taking notes at a furious pace. We move on to a reading from *Das Blaue Buch*; someone hands me a worn copy and I open it at random, staring down at the page streaming with umlauts and untamed consonants as one of the women on the couch reads aloud. I am sweating under my collar and in the small of my back, though the room is underheated. I try to catch Shane's eye, to mouth *let's go* at her, but she's enjoying her joke too much, if it is a joke. She keeps her gaze fixed piously upon the page, understanding everything I don't.

The time has come for sharing. We sit quietly for a long moment and I think about standing up and walking out. But now the young Black man is speaking—in perfect German, of course, but with a lilting, vaguely Francophone accent—and everyone listens. "*Hallo, allerseits, ich bin Stephen und ich bin Alkoholiker.*"

"*Hallo, Stephen,*" we chorus. The woman on the end of the couch closest to me swings her head around and gives me the fish-eye for a moment.

Stephen tells his story, whatever it is, in animated tones, gesturing often with his large, beautifully shaped hands and smiling often in what seems a self-deprecating way. The others smile back at him, many of them nodding along. When he gets to the serious part he speaks more softly and the others look down at their feet or up over his head. One of the couch women—not the one suspicious of me—plucks a tissue from the box on the coffee table and dabs at her eyes with it. Stephen's gaze too is now set low, his eyes not meeting any of ours, as his voice drops into a monotone. Finally he stops talking and a silence balloons outward for a long painful moment, and then he says something else, just a few words, and cracks a smile. The room erupts in laughter. I laugh too, a beat behind. Shane is smiling at me with something like triumph in her eyes. We all clap for Stephen—Stephen who has been through hell and come back to tell the tale in a language not his own, in this anonymous apartment in Berlin, to a group of strangers who share his affliction, plus one who doesn't understand him at all.

By the end of the hour everyone has shared except for the old woman in the raincoat—she hasn't taken it off— and me. Shane's share is brief, only ninety seconds or so, but she too has the power to make everyone nod and smile and laugh with recognition. It's a peculiar feeling, to be inside and yet not part of a circuit that completes itself, a current that passes through these people who touch each other with the fundamentally similar morphology of their experience. Some, I have no doubt, lost everything before coming here. Some may have been or continue to be functional on the outside while taking every opportunity to fill the space inside them with alcohol. I can understand, at the very least, some of what the big man ("*Hallo, mein Name ist Klaus*") said at the beginning; *Leben unkontrollierbar* is *life unmanageable.* Shane's share ends and her face is flushed and I think of the wine swirling resinously in the glass in her cool white hand.

A silence falls. I look up from my woolgathering to see a dozen kindly faces all turned in my direction. "*Möchten Sie teilen?*" Klaus asks me kindly. "*Es ist okay, wenndu nicht willst. Es ist dein erstes Mal hier? Du bist sehr mutig.*"

What can I say? What could I say?

Hello. I'm not an alcoholic, at least I don't think that I am. I'm an American, and I'm here to write. I'm here because I don't want to be there. I'm here because I can't look my father in the face. I'm here because I'm halfway to being an orphan. I don't know why I'm here. I don't speak your language. Can you help me?

Shane nods to me, as though she can hear my thoughts. A flush climbs my scalp as I scramble for the only German word I can find: *Entschuldigung.* Excuse me. I'm sorry.

Klaus' eyebrows shoot up; the woman on the end of the couch stares at me with her lips parted.

"*Danke,*" I say to them, palms lifted. "*Nein danke. Entschuldigung.*"

Klaus stares at me through the tiny circles of his glasses, shrugs his sloped shoulders, and turns toward the woman in the Burberry coat. But she is curled up like a cat on the edge of her uncomfortable metal chair, sound asleep. *Das Ende.*

"Did you like it?" Shane asks me on the stairs. I stop to look up into her lit face.

"I didn't understand a fucking thing."

"Oh, I expect you got the gist." She watches me. "What do you want to do now?"

Her eyes challenge me. Is there something between us, beyond whatever I'm standing in for from Shane's perspective—for poets, for fiction writers, for married men, for men? She towers above me on the stairs, smelling strongly of cigarettes, sweat, perfume. The old woman in the Burberry coat comes lurching down from the landing and we step aside from her. She's affixed hot pink paint to her lips and offers us a hideously conspiratorial smile. We watch her round the corner and disappear. I am conscious of Shane's closeness, the faint white marks of powder on her cheeks, hot scent in the cold stairwell. I make my decision.

"Let's go to the movies."

Shane takes one step down so that we're on a level with each other and takes my arm. "Let's."

IN DREAMS BEGIN RESPONSIBILITIES

Alone in the dark, or with a woman at his side, paying as little as seventy-five cents per ticket, Dad went to the movies almost every week, sometimes twice. He saw:

True Grit alone.

Goodbye, Columbus alone.

Age of Consent with Elizabeth.

Midnight Cowboy with Cora, just before they broke up.

The Wild Bunch with Mom on their first real date. She was bored.

How to Commit Marriage with Mom on their second date. He laughed at the film. She laughed at him.

Easy Rider with Mom on their third date. She cried for the three of them, for Peter, for Dennis, for Jack. He held her close.

Take the Money and Run with Mom on their fourth date. They both laughed so hard they clutched each other shrieking, spilling their popcorn all over the cinema floor. People prepared to be annoyed twisted in their seats to look at the two of them and just smiled, they were so beautiful.

Midnight Cowboy with Mom and Hank and Peter, followed by a late-night double-date at a coffee shop on 43rd, Hank voluble and Peter silent in the conversation afterward until he burst out with: That film hates gay people. But it was a love story, Hank said gently, between two men. I don't care, Peter said. I'm sick of it. I'm sick of all of it! Dad stirred his coffee. Mom looked from one man's face to the next, each differently pained.

They Shoot Horses, Don't They? with Mom. He was bored.

Anne of the Thousand Days with Mom. Heavy bored.

One deadly hot summer afternoon they went down to the Village for a matinee of Warhol's *Blue Movie* at the Garrick on Bleecker Street. There was a line around the block, watched over by sweating blue-coated policemen. It's too hot, Mom complained. Dad agreed and they went instead to another theater to see *Winning*, with Paul Newman and Joanne Woodward. The next day the entire staff of the Garrick was arrested on obscenity charges that were eventually dismissed. I hear it was really boring anyway, Mom said.

On Her Majesty's Secret Service alone.

True Grit again, alone.

Women in Love with Mom and Hank and Peter. That's more like it, Peter said after. What are you talking about? It's exactly the same, exclaimed Hank. Mom was dreamy and afterward carried Lawrence's novel in her handbag for a few weeks, underlining passages with a ballpoint pen. *What was she short of now? It was marriage—it was the wonderful stability of marriage.* And: *This marriage with her was his resurrection and his life.* But: *Marriage was like a doom to him.* And: *It is awful to think what her life will be like unless she does find a means of expression, some way of fulfillment. You can see what leaving it to mere fate begins. You can see how much marriage is to be trusted to—look at your own mother.*

The Extraordinary Seaman with Mom. They left in the middle.

Butch Cassidy and the Sundance Kid once alone and again with Mom, and one more time in the winter of that year with a group of his salesman friends. Dad drove Mom crazy humming "Raindrops Are Falling on My Head" for weeks that felt like years. He never really stopped.

Alice's Restaurant with Mom. She found it unbearably sad. He was bored.

Bob & Carol & Ted & Alice with Mom. They were bored.

Breathless with Mom.

Army of Shadows with Mom.

A grim double feature he attended with Mom: *Night and Fog* and *The Sorrow and the Pity*. Nervous laughter before the lights go down, then silence, then a small steady stream of departures until the theater was two-thirds empty. She got mad at him for leaving in the middle of the second film and coming back with popcorn and a Coke. It's still a movie, isn't it? he said. You don't want any? Slurping noisily to make the point. They didn't speak for a week.

Castle Keep alone.

Marlowe alone.

Hello, Dolly! with Mom. Living together now.

While she was pregnant with me they saw: *Airport, The Angel Levine, The Ballad of Cable Hogue, Beneath the Planet of the Apes, Beyond the Valley of the Dolls, The Boys in the Band, Catch-22, Le Cercle Rouge, Le genou de Claire, The Conformist, Count Dracula, Diary of a Mad Housewife, The Dunwich Horror, Five Easy Pieces* (twice), *I Love My Wife, Julius Caesar* (a double-feature of the Brando version and the other one), *Little Big Man, The Molly Maguires, The Music Lovers* (alone), *Ned Kelly*, *The Owl and the Pussycat*, *The Private Life of Sherlock Holmes*, *Quackser Fortune Has a Cousin in the Bronx* (what is Gene Wilder doing playing an Irishman?), *Rabbit, Run* (Updike is his favorite author), *Ryan's Daughter*, *The Strawberry Statement*, *Suppose They Gave a War and Nobody Came*, *There's a Girl in My Soup*, *Tora! Tora! Tora!* (she left in the middle, Dad stayed till the end), *Which Way to the Front?*, *Woodstock* (the Garrick showed it all day and all night on continuous loop, people came and went, some took off their clothes, there was necking and more in the back row, the air was thick with pot smoke, some people camped out in the theater for a week, in that virtual sense I was there, they were there, New York City was there, at Woodstock), *Zabriskie Point*, *Zig Zag*.

I saw, or at least heard, or on some cellular level experienced, these films. And in this fashion, drinking Mom's Cokes and eating her popcorn, smoking her cigarettes and the occasional joint, registered in my nervous system every dilation of her pupils, every laugh, every tear of the world that made me, the world I can never know.

LODGER

One looks for it everywhere and finds it everywhere, evidence of the Wall, Caesarean scar of history on a city that seems everywhere suspended between the twenty-first century and the nineteenth. Pavement lines zigzag through the middle of the city, *Mitte*, indicating where it stood. Kitsch abounds: a gallery in a field upon which murals and graffiti are posed, the superannuated Ground Zero of Checkpoint Charlie where street performers pose in uniforms of the GDR and a stiltwalker dressed as Uncle Sam stalks about waving idiotically at the generally indifferent crowds. I make my way through them, reciting the small, melodramatic poem of myself: *Ich bin ein Jude.* In that morning's emails status updates on my father's condition (stable, and the breathing tube is out, but he is as yet unable to speak); an image of my daughter playing the piano, back straight, eyes almost shut; and from my mother's cousin Ava a report on the present absence I'm experiencing:

> *Did you know that your great-great grandmother Elenor and a couple of her daughters lived in Berlin in the early 1900's. my mother, visited her grandmother in 1927 and 28. One daughter died young, and the other one Ilona, was taken to Auschwitz in 1943 where she perished. GGma and Ilona lived in Steglitz Lepsiusstr 20. The other daughter, Hajnalka (English translation would be Dawn), was married to a gentile man [I misread this as "gentle"] Rheinhart*

*Rule (or the reverse, and not sure of the spelling) had a son,
but she died before 1927. My mother used to say that her
mother used to go to the cemetery almost on a daily basis. I
just wanted to let you know that besides Bergen Belsen, you
have another connection to Germany.*

Another connection. Rooted, Ava seems to insist, in
something other than the universal death that rippled
concentrically from this spot, that haunted the streets and
dreams of the grandparents and great-grandparents of the
people around me. *Ilona.* Who was she? She *perished.* It's a
good word, it suggests, doesn't it, something of the com-
pleteness of the annihilation that enfolded my mother's
family, from which by chance her parents escaped. Death
of personhood, death even of memory. The first generation
survives; the second generation is eager to forget; the third
generation obsesses about the past. Wasn't it Joseph Roth
who said that his generation was in the unhappy position
of having to put their grandfathers on their knees and tell
them stories?

Mom was two when the war ended; does that make her
first generation or second? Does that make me second generation or third?

What is my responsibility to remember what I never experienced, what she never knew?

All around me people speak in what Kurt Vonnegut
once called the mellow lower registers of the German language, speaking of anything and everything, but never do
I hear anyone say *Vergangenheitsbewältigung*, the German
word that means something like "coming to terms with the

past." Filled with sudden nausea, I start walking quickly, dodging the holiday-goers and passers-by, muttering from deep in my throat *Entschuldigung Entschuldigung*. But Berlin is everywhere I can go.

And when I do find my way to Lepsiustrasse 20 a few days later there's nothing there to see but a tawny stucco building of obviously postwar construction, deep in the leafy bourgeois neighborhood of Steglitz, distinguished mainly by its proximity to the *Bierpinsel*, a bizarre postmodern tree of a building whose name means something like "beer brush" and which unfolds in gray and colored petals like something out of a graphic novel by Moebius.

I meet yet another poet for drinks that night, a Canadian whose acquaintance I've made via Facebook, who unlike me is in a Berlin officially bought and paid for by the German government, a guest of their *Künstlerprogramm*. The bar is in Schöneberg, a macabre little hole in the wall decorated with the bodies of puppets and marionettes hanging from the walls and ceiling like so many lynched and deformed children. None of the other clientele are a day under seventy, while the bartender appears to be eighty at least; their dress and manner and rasping voices suggest an older, working-class Berlin long vanished from this quarter of the prosperous West. Ken is already there when I arrive: a slight, long-faced bespectacled man with close-fitting curling hair in a football jersey and jeans, with a notebook and pen, tobacco pouch and rolling papers, and a beer all arrayed before him like a workman's tools. We shake hands and sit down. The old men at the bar regard us for a moment with a sort of bemused tolerance, then turned back to their own conversation.

We fall into an easy rhythm, Ken and me. We discuss word spacing in poems and Canadian versus American approaches to the depiction of nature; whether or not I should take a side trip to Prague; the dismal state of the world economy; the dismal state of American politics (neither of us having any notion how much worse things could and would become); the generally deplorable state of Berlin restaurants and how little my experience reading Heidegger was helping me to decipher German menus. Ken is that rare man willing to think out loud and on his feet, doubling back on his own statements, so manifestly uncomfortable in his own skin that he sets me at ease if only by contrast. The pints, or liters, or whatever they are, go down gratefully as I scramble up the hill of the building buzz. Then a small comedy ensues when, having rolled a cigarette, Ken wonders out loud if he's allowed to smoke in the bar.

"They're smoking, those chaps right there."

"Yes, but they're standing by the open door. And it looks like they've been smoking since they were in short pants. No one's going to tell them to stop."

We split the difference by standing up at the bar, with the cool night breeze wafting in, and Ken brandishes his handmade cigarette to see if anyone will notice or object. The men at the bar grunt at us like quietly amused pigs, and one, a barrel-chested guy in shit-brown overalls and a flat cap squashed down on his bald bulb of a head, flicks out his lighter for us. But the ancient bartender shakes his head at us and wags his finger slowly in the air while the other two oldsters make a show of putting their own butts out. Ken sighs and I follow him through the acrid cloud out onto the sidewalk, where he lights his cigarette and inhales with profound relief. The overalled man follows us out, interested it seems by our Anglophone ways, and offers me one of his Marlboros. The three of us smoke in companionable silence for a while, broken only for station identification.

"You Americans?"

"Yes."

"No."

"Yes? No?" The man smiles at us, almost shyly, showing brown nubs of teeth.

"American," I say.

"Canadian," says Ken.

The old man strikes himself on the sternum with his closed fist. "*Deutsche!*" It isn't much of a joke, if it's a joke at all, but the three of us chuckle anyway. Ken and the barfly seem particularly amused.

The man was likely born in the 1940s. Same age as my father. If I recited to him my little poem, what would he say? Would he be embarrassed? Confused? Curious? Indifferent?

"Your father tried to kill my mother," I say in a conversational tone. "What do you think of that?" But of course he doesn't understand me. After a moment's blank pause, he smiles and bobs his head. "America very good!" he says. "I listen to your president when they make the *Mauer*, when they try to starve us. *Ich bin auch Berliner.* Very good!"

"I'm a jelly donut," Ken intones, sucking smoke.

"Very good," I repeat. The eager air nips at my ribs. The old fellow stubs out his smoke on the wall, claps me on the back with a meaty hand, and goes back inside. A moment later we follow and resume our stations under the doll heads, their blank painted eyes gone glazed in yellow light.

"You must find it weird, being here," Ken says. I've told him a little of my history.

"I just wish they'd stop being so *German*," I say. "Don't you think they're laying it on a little thick?"

Ken hoists his stein of Spaten, already half-empty. "Good lager, though." We clink glasses. Is this the fourth beer or the fifth?

"Does your wife like Berlin?" I ask. Ken is here for a year with his family.

Ken drains his glass, grimacing. "No. Which is odd if you ask me because she already speaks much better German than I do. We go to three classes a week—the *Deutsche Akademie* requires it—and she's already jabbering away. But I can't get the grammar through my stupid head. Worse than *amo amas amat*."

"My mother wouldn't buy a Ford, let alone a Volkswagen," I say distractedly. "But she spoke flawless German. Studied it in high school."

"Flawless German," Ken repeats. "Don't they wish it were so?" He nods as the barman brings us more beer. "Do you feel more Jewish here than you do ordinarily? More vulnerable?"

I press the cold glass between my palms. "It's like this,"

I say after a while. "The other day I was wandering around in the east part of town, in Kreuzburg. Lots of Turks there, right? The buildings there are different. Cheaper looking somehow, mass produced, like tenements, but with satellite dishes all over them. Lots of interesting graffiti. I was there because my map said there was a synagogue there, and I hadn't seen one yet, or anything at all Jewish except for the Jewish Museum. Morbid curiosity. I walked down to the canal there through this gritty little park and found a fenced-off building with plastic sheeting over the windows and cameras everywhere and a booth with a *Polizei* sign and one policewoman walking back and forth looking at her phone."

"Weird." Ken belched discreetly.

"It was deeply weird, and deeply depressing. Not a living place at all, you know? But the strangest part came when I was walking away and I met a man coming from the other direction. He was wearing track pants and a puffy coat and he looked like a Turk or an Arab, but he had the same guidebook in his hand that I was carrying, like he was a tourist."

"Like you," Ken points out.

"Like me. He looked at me and then he pointed at the building and he asked me something in German. I think he was asking me what the building was."

"What did you say?"

"I said *synagogue*, but he didn't seem to understand. So then I said *Jude*, Jew. He just looked at me. And finally I just said *Da*, because I know that means 'there,' and the policewoman was there, and he could ask her."

Picture it: two strangers facing each other beside the lifeless canal, one light-skinned, one-dark, each bearing a copy of *Lonely Planet* like a shield.

"Maybe I should have tried speaking French with him," I say. "I'm pretty sure German was his first language, and he didn't speak any English at all. Anyway, he said *danke* and I said *bitte* and we left it at that. Last I saw of him he was standing in front of the fence taking a selfie with a serious expression on his face. It doesn't mean anything, I suppose."

"If I were my brother Benji," Ken drawled, "I'd tell you that you ought to write a poem about that experience, which is what he says to me every fucking time I talk to him. But I'm not an asshole, so I won't."

"To Benji," I say, raising my nearly empty glass.

"To Benji!"

I haven't told Shane about Dad's accident and I don't tell Ken either, though something tells me he would understand. It's just that understanding that I don't want: the sympathetic grimace and nod, the stories of suffering unblocked. Ken too in his way is on the run. We have fled to the center of Europe to be away for a while from our questions.

I bum a last smoke and set out for home, detouring slightly to pay due homage to Haupstrasse 155, the perfectly ordinary building that a white plaque tells passersby was home to David Bowie and Iggy Pop from 1976 to 1978. Boys keep swinging. Here Bowie's still alive, the place standing in for the time he wore a skin of white fire, raking up as much coke as he could, keeping up with Iggy and Iggy keeping up with him, anonymous, almost unwanted, living entirely on raw eggs, his voice slipping through Brian Eno's mystical gates, the becoming of "Heroes," encapsulating what Bowie would later call "a sense of yearning for the future that we all knew would never come to pass." From the studio where he recorded those songs he could see the wall looming, his rapid heart slowing to beat in time with it, the scar at the center of the world. *"In dieser Zeit,"* the plaque informs me, *"enstanden die Alben >>Low<<, >>Heroes<<, und >>Lodger<<,"* Bowie's *Berliner Trilogie.* The street is empty but for the usual street things: streetlamps, cars, shadows, and the total absence of stars.

There's nothing to see here, any more than there was on Lepsiustrasse 20. Wherever I move in this city I'm at the epicenter of my own paranoia. That's my inheritance, the glamour of the dark side of the family, my mother's side. My woundable father saw it too and was drawn, overconfident, into its web, its map, its spell. *Nothing could fall.*

He's going home, the text from my sister reads, *to a rehab facility in New Jersey. It's going to cost the earth. Thank God for insurance!*

Thank God. I try calling my wife, drunk-dialing her in the small hours of Berlin, when it's still daylight back home. She doesn't answer and I don't leave a message. A moment later she texts me: *Busy. Anything wrong?*

Nothing in the world, I tell her, and I believe it.

II
THE STOKER

NEW YORK, 1967

They met by the mailboxes. Let it start like that: Dad in stocking feet, descending from his cramped fifth-floor eyrie through the stuffy blackness of the stairs, down to the vestibule where he hoped to find a letter from his mother, perhaps with a check from his father tucked inside, for the golf money was almost gone and the shoe store cut checks only once a month and it was the middle of an unseasonably chilly May. He ate canned food, hot dogs, pizza by the slice, and had overcome his initial embarrassment sufficiently to dine with Peter and Hank at least twice a week, each meal a mélange of flavors almost unbelievably exotic to a Skokie boy: turmeric, herbes de Provence, masala, fenugreek, tamarind spread with abundance on fish and lamb and chicken and sometimes no meat at all, only chick peas and cauliflower and leafy greens he couldn't name. Between that and the street food he didn't lose too much weight but still felt leaner and more haggard and bonier than before, with a semipermanent kink in his neck from looking up at customers from a kneeling position and a sore spot in his lower back from bending to retrieve and put away boxes of shoes from the humid filthy basement of the store. The check he expected from work would cover his rent and another cartload of Campbells but not a lot more. Already the knees of his only suit were shining and the other clerks, natty in knit ties and smelling richly of hair oil, had taken to laughing in low tones on smoke breaks and quieting up when he approaches. He wrote to his mother—never to his father—alluding to this and she in turn said something to her husband and he expected or hoped for at least enough for a new suit and a little spending money. He was tired all the time yet wakeful or fretful as spring advanced and the women's skirts got shorter, their necks and arms exposed to the light. He was tremendously conscious of them, all but spinning on the street when he encountered a beautiful woman sauntering or striding past him, something that happened more than a dozen times a day. Never had he seen women like this—Michigan Avenue back home was nothing to it—women in minidresses and miniskirts with long leg-hugging tights and stockings, women in Jackie O sunglasses and architectural patterned dresses, Black women with Afros and cherry-colored lipstick, Puerto Rican women with intricately braided hair, six-foot Scandinavians with feathery white eyebrows, all of them with bright open eyes and the same ironic twist to the mouth when those eyes glanced into his. He was a long way from the backseat fumblings of the Midwest, the bra straps and hairspray—stunning to think that each of these women had a place of her own, that he had a place of his own to which he might invite someone. Vera, Elizabeth, Cora, others. He kept his apartment—really, his room—spic and span, the way his mother would, spent too much of his dwindling stake on cheap reproductions of prints from the Met and a hand-tied throw rug and an Indian blanket to cover the holes in the couch and a plant, the first living thing he'd cared for since his dog Barney died, a Ficus that thrived ambiguously in the masked light of his single north-facing window. His only valuable possession was the hi-fi, now equipped with a turntable on which he spun the slightly scratched records he bought from a tall bent Black man on Amsterdam Avenue standing with injured dignity besides a baize cloth laid out on the sidewalk on which a pile of LPs were arranged in delicate semicircles, mostly jazz. Art Tatum, Bud Powell, Miles Davis: he had never been any sort of aficionado but the names were vaguely familiar, they spoke to him of the glamor of a New York that he felt he must labor to remain in touch with now that he lived in its grimy everyday. Late at night—it felt late, but he was too tired to stay up much past ten—he would play the same four or five records over and over, along with the solitary LP he'd brought from Skokie that the thieves had missed, tucked under his passenger seat—*Blonde on Blonde*, which is two records really. Long drawn-out sax solos and piano riffs alternated with the nasal whine of another Midwestern boy come to the big city to make good. Everybody must get stoned. Muttering small talk at the wall. Oh, mama. Beating on my trumpet. Break like a little girl.

But on this particular May afternoon he was padding almost silently to the ground floor, passing the other floors and doors. Fourth floor: Rosita Lopez, a retired dance teacher, whose kitchen stove vented it seemed directly into his own apartment so that he went to sleep dreaming of fried plantains and roasted olives. Her son Raul, a man in his forties, lived with her, a balding gray-faced cipher in a crisp white shirt and neatly creased black pants, trudging grimly down and grimly up the stairs once a day to and from whatever occupied him. Third floor: the family Rothstein, papa and mama and four children under ten years old, crammed into two bedrooms, sometimes sighted of a Saturday parading to shul, father in front followed by the three boys with their tallits showing, with the beshawled mother and toddler girl taking up the rear. Under his beard Shmuel Rothstein couldn't have been more than thirty years old and his wife was younger yet. Mr. Florio, the super, and his wife lived on the second floor—he was a garrulous black-browed Sicilian who once and once only invited him into the dark and cavernous apartment for a can of Schlitz that mustachioed Mrs. Florio brought to him, touchingly, on a plastic tray before beating a retreat to the kitchen. College boy, eh? You Jewish? You look Jewish. But I don't see you going to temple like the ones upstairs. Ah, Shmuel's all right, he'll even have a beer once in a while if you catch him in the right mood. A jeweler, richer than Midas, why they live here I'll never understand, all those kids and another on the way, ay yi yi. He sat on the rigid plastic-wrapped sofa and nodded and swallowed his beer and the visit hadn't been repeated, though there were evenings, as he made the cumbersome switch from Dylan disk one to Dylan disk two, that he almost hoped he might hear the super's hairy knuckles knocking on his door.

On the first floor there was another family, the Gardners, two tall limp blond astonished California transplants, and their teenage daughter. Professor Gardner, Mr. Florio had said, jerking his thumb over his shoulder to indicate the general vicinity of Columbia University. History, I think, or maybe economics. He had spied Mrs. Gardner one afternoon going inside the building with a younger man wearing a sharp narrow-lapeled suit, and the man had placed his hand familiarly on Mrs. Gardner's lower back as he ushered her in, as though it were his house, as though she were his wife. Mr. Gardner looked out at the world, he thought afterward, with haunted eyes. He saw little of the girl, Maisie, who looked to be about fourteen, though she must have gone to school somewhere. The Gardners were the only ones to have welcomed him to the building formally: on his third night there he'd answered a knock on the door and there they all were, crammed awkwardly on the narrow landing ducking their swannish necks, with Maisie in the middle holding a plate of cookies and a calculating expression on her face.

"I baked these for you," she said. "Mother didn't want me to but I said that wasn't nice."

"What Maisie means," her mother said with a pinched expression, "is that we didn't want to disturb you. But we're glad to meet you."

"We're the Gardners," said the professor. "I understand you're a teacher. Biology, right?"

He stood there holding the plate of cookies that Maisie had handed him. "I'm starting in the fall. Do you want to come in?"

"We can't stay," Mrs. Gardner said. Both of her hands were on Maisie's shoulders, physically restraining her from leaning farther in to suss out the mysteries of a bachelor's apartment. "But thank you."

"Enjoy the cookies," the professor said. His eyes were blue and tremulous. "Come downstairs sometime and we'll have a chat, one teacher to another."

"They've got a secret ingredient," Maisie breathed. "Do you like white chocolate?"

"I like every kind of chocolate," he said, smiling at her. The mother's knuckles on her daughter's shoulders whitened.

"Ow," she whined. "*Mother.*"

"Bye now," her parents said.

"Bye." The girl twisted her long head on her neck and dipped coquettishly as she relinquished the plate.

The cookies weren't bad. He washed the plate and left it on their welcome mat with a scribbled thank-you note on his way to work the next day. When he came home that night it was gone. And that was the Gardners.

That was everyone, save for the garden apartment, whose tenant had a separate entrance, and he had yet to encounter him or her. Mr. Florio hadn't mentioned a tenant there, only remarking that he and Mrs. Florio had lived there at one time but had to move upstairs last year because of Mrs. Florio's asthma. "We rented it right away," he'd said, but he hadn't said to whom.

The mailbox was empty; the postman hadn't yet come. He sat down on the hard steps, cautiously, having already torn a hole in one of his socks on a loose carpet tack. Might as well wait. There was nothing waiting for him upstairs but his Ficus plant and the same old records he was tired of spinning. It was a Tuesday, his one day off—he worked the other five days plus Sunday afternoons. He stared at the frosted glass of the inner door through which the spring light wavered gray and green. He knew he should be outside, exploring the city, meeting the day. There was something out there, he knew, some kind of adventure, a conversation he might have, a woman he might meet, if only he had the courage to meet it. But his back was sore and his neck was tired. The stale taste of milk from the raisin bran he'd had for breakfast seemed to coat his throat. What am I doing here, he said to himself. From upstairs somewhere he could hear a radio playing. What is everyone doing here.

He heard the outer door open and got to his feet. The mailman at last. A shadow appeared in the glass and he heard the mailboxes rattling. He opened the inner door.

A young woman stood there with bobbed dark hair accenting pale skin, wearing a black-and-yellow sleeveless dress with a large bag hanging from one elbow. He was struck by the largeness and darkness of her eyes. And she was barefoot, a pair of sandals dangling from their straps in her left hand. "Oh!"

He was tall, even taller on the steps. She had to look up. She smiled. He felt something tug loose inside his chest.

"A tall dark stranger," she said matter-of-factly. She stood up straight and stuck out her free hand. He took it. "No mail yet?"

"No." Oh.

"Shit." She grinned at his feet. "Looks like we had the same idea. You're not working today?"

"No."

"Then come outside and have a cigarette with me."

He didn't think of himself as a smoker, not really, but he accepted the proffered Kool and joined her on the stoop. Mild morning air, a morning feeling anyway, though it was really afternoon. The sun, as was its wont, haunted the other side of the street, leaving them in shade just two or three degrees below what he found comfortable. A guy on a motorbike zipped by, turning his head to take the two of them in. Two kids with no shoes sitting on a stoop, smoking.

She lived in the garden apartment—"which makes me the fourth Gardner, I suppose." It was her day off as well. She worked for the government. "Law enforcement."

"You're a cop?" he said with astonishment.

"Sort of. IRS."

"Oh my god."

Laughing. "Don't be scared!"

"I'm not!"

"No, really, don't be. If you're living in that tiny apartment they tried to rent me on the top floor then you've got nothing to fear from the taxman. Or are you a secret millionaire?"

"Hardly."

"Not yet, you mean. A boy from Illinois come to New York means one thing: a guy on the make. That you?"

"On the make," he repeated, entranced. There was a sharp edge and speed to her speech. New York, if not *Noo Yawk*. But also a refined quality, a delicacy, a little bit Hepburn, a little bit Rosalind Russell. She had taken the cigarettes out of a large terrycloth bag with a sunflower design like something you might see at the beach. It yawned at her feet and he couldn't help looking in. A library book wrapped in dirty cellophane, an almost comically large keyring like that carried by guards in prison movies, a compact, lipstick, smaller things. He realized he had been expecting to see a gun. "I guess I am."

"Thought so." She took a deep drag on the cigarette and let the smoke go into the sunshiny air. Something about her stance, weight on one hip, and the gleam in her eye reminded him briefly of Maisie Gardner.

"How did you end up working for the IRS?"

"It's a long story. I'd rather hear yours first."

"My parents wanted me to go to medical school," he explained. "But I didn't want to go. Maybe that's why I didn't get in. I didn't want it enough."

"Too bad. My folks would love for me to meet a nice Jewish doctor boy."

"How did you know I'm Jewish?"

"Don't kid a kidder."

"Are you Jewish?"

"Of course."

He was slow. "Living alone?"

"*Now* I am, thank God."

Hmm. "But you're from New York."

"The Bronx, originally. Then Queens."

"That's still New York."

"Oh, buddy. Queens is as far from New York as Manhattan is from Chicago. And the Bronx is on the moon. This place, where we are, this island, this street, right here. I've been dreaming of it my whole life."

Me too, he wanted to say. But was it true? His dreams, from this vantage point, were thin, sharded, absurd. She seemed to him beautiful, balanced, jagged and sharp. There was a ragged edge to her and an androgynous touch. Her eyes were ringed with kohl that couldn't quite conceal a purpler darkness underneath, the darkness of sleepless nights. She lit one cigarette off another. The sole of her left foot crossed over her knee was almost black.

"You're something," he said.

She laughed, brilliantly. "I've always wanted to be something for somebody. But finish your story."

"There isn't one really. I worked for my father for a little while—he sells stereo speakers for a Japanese company—and I couldn't stand it. I have three younger sisters and they're all at home. I didn't want to be a doctor, but I studied biology at Northwestern. Then my cousin who lives here told me about this teaching job, and I wrote a letter, and they gave it to me. I start in the fall. In the meantime, I sell shoes."

"Is that better than selling speakers?"

He laughed. "Not really!"

"So you're going to be a teacher, huh? I can see that."

"You think so?"

"Well for one thing," she craned her neck comically, "you're tall. And good-looking. I suspect you know that about yourself." She studied his non-reaction to this and nodded her approval. "It's not a boys' school?"

"No. Girls."

"Oh, they'll *love* you." She laughed again, as if at a private joke. He laughed with her.

"So what are you waiting for?" she asked him.

"Nothing. I mean, the mail. What are *you* waiting for?"

"Somebody," she said, looking into his eyes, grinning. "Someone like you."

They became conscious of someone, Horace the mailman, a lean dark-faced Black man with salt and pepper sideburns and a satchel on his shoulder, standing at the bottom of the stoop and looking up at them. He smiled unexpectedly at them with his head cocked slightly, like a bird. And my father felt, for perhaps the first time since he'd come to New York, *seen*.

"Pardon me," Horace said, and they stood apart, conscious of the distance between them, to let him pass. For some reason they both fell silent, overcome with barely repressed giggles. He had to look away. She put her hand over her mouth.

"Have a beautiful day now," said Horace, his duty done, walking away. She waved at him with her free hand and shouted after him:

"Have a beautiful day yourself!" Without turning around, the mailman lifted his hand in farewell.

My father stood up in his stocking feet and opened the door. With an exaggerated courtly gesture: "After you!"

She curtsied and stepped past him, and after a fractional hesitation he followed her into the intimate vestibule smelling of dust, of cigarettes, and something sharper and sweeter, as of an essential oil, musk, the fragrance of her, and the door closed and they were both together inside.

ANIMALS

The Natural History Museum on Invalidenstrasse, a massive nineteenth-century pile heaped with dinosaur bones, dioramas, the various fruits of taxidermy. I pause beside a model of a dodo, recalling the aisles of the Natural History Museum under white Bismarckian light, stopping in front of the dodo, its beak partially open as though Lewis Carroll had planted his sentence there: "*Everybody* has won, and all must have prizes."

In 1970, the year I was born, these animals were alive on the Earth: The Eastern Cougar, the Vietnamese Rhino, the Christmas Island Pipistrell, the Chinese Paddlefish, the Yangtze River Dolphin, the Po'o-uli bird, the Vine Raitea Tree Snail, the Pyrenean Ibex, the Nukupuu bird, the Western Black Rhino, the Aldabra Banded Snail, the Zanzibar Leopard, the Swollen Raiatea Tree Snail, the Golden Toad, the Dusky Seaside Sparrow, the Atitlan Grebe, the Alaotra Grebe, the Eungella Gastric-Brooding Frog, the Kaua'I 'O'o bird, the Christmas Island Shrew, the Amistad Gambusia fish, the San Marcos Gambusia fish, the Kama'o bird, the Guam Flycatcher, the Aldabra Warbler, the Galapagos Damselfish, the Marianas Mallard, the Southern Day Frog, the White-eyed River Martin, the Colombian Grebe, the Eiao Monarch bird, the Javan Tiger, the Madagascan Dwarf Hippopotamous, the Longjaw Cisco, the Round Island Burrowing Boa, the Phantom Shiner fish, the Guam Flying Fox, the Fijan Bar-Winged Rail, the Lake Peddler

Earthworm, the Bush Wren, the Santa Cruz Pupfish, the Madeiran Large White Moth, the Caspian Tiger, the Tecopa Pupfish, the Clear Lake Splittail, and the Blue Pike. They were all still swimming, flying, crawling, stalking, eating, breeding, and drinking on the day I was born. Gone now, preserved by photographs and the odd bit of taxidermy, some of them startling (the Guam Flying Fox is especially worth a Google). All of them unique, all of them sacrificed unthinkingly, which is to say simply obliterated, since the word *sacrifice* implies intention, a gesture at meaning or its making. No intention can be assigned to these extinctions: the animals are simply gone, lost passengers of the world I arrived in with no more clue than anyone else. One more helpless squalling bundle of fat and bone, here to claim more than my fair share of wealth and habitat like the good white American I was born to be.

Is it fair to say that no one planned any of it? If I take responsibility for my life, must I also take responsibility for the lives of the island creatures (Raitea, Christmas Island) that died for my sins? Nazim Hikmet: *You must grieve for this right now / You have to feel this sorrow now—*

In the colonial fantasia of the museum ancient bones mingle seamlessly with human artifacts as dry and dusty and extinct as the dodos and ibexes. Preserved objects of ritual: Athabascan totem poles, Siberian snowshoes, African masks. It would seem no less strange there to find an exhibition of Jewish foreskins alongside the shrunken heads. I was circumcised in the hospital; what became of that bit of flesh? Marked casually, almost meaninglessly, in the most delicate possible place. Genesis 17.12: "And he that is eight days old shall be circumcised among you, every male throughout your generations, he that is born in the house, or bought with money of any foreigner, that is not of thy seed." *This is My covenant, which ye shall keep.* Am I bound by a sacrifice not of my choosing, or even of my parents' choosing, since they enlisted a surgeon not a mohel, and he used anesthetic into the bargain.

In the old days the cinemas showed their movies in a continuous loop; you sat down in the middle of the feature and watched until the action circled round again so that you could leave, saying, "This is where I came in."

Dad and Mom, with no idea of the future, participating the perpetuation of the species, a hybrid of the easily assimilated and the immigrant: the Neurotic East Coast Secular Jewish Literary Male. A warbler, a grebe. I want to cry at their foolhardiness, but their faith is untouchable. It's me who's on exhibit in any museum I go to, prisoner to the gaze of so many plundered objects. They regard me pitilessly.

Pacific Islanders' shrunken heads. They sit in their cloudy vitrine, human remains, their sacredness violated and their aura enhanced by being transplanted so far from their context, from the New World back to the Old. Impossible, looking at them, not to feel conscious of my own throat and neck, not to stroke the undried apricot of my own ear. Panic of overidentification and imperial guilt. Carlo's cynical squint, pegging me as an American liberal bourgeois Jew, a poet no less, bound for a Muslim country, and the tabloid news for my kind is not good. Flashback to the parking lot of my daughter's school where I passed the time of day with another dad, a former Navy SEAL turned commodities trader, dapper and regal in gray checked pants, who gently upon learning of my travel plans informed me that his former colleagues considered all of North Africa to be "in a field state." Smiling, shaking his head: *brave man.* Now, in the museum my own hands at my throat, the vision: voices shouting in a language I can't understand, clad in an orange sardonic Gitmo jumpsuit, soaked in the terror stink of my own sweat, blindfold ripped away to reveal the bright blinding disk of desert, featureless except for the film crew setting up in front of me, bored, paying out cables, taking its time; the masked man behind me, someone I've probably gotten to know over the weeks and months of my captivity, perhaps even traded jokes with, perhaps even pleaded with for instruction in Islam, a word that means *submission*; on my knees, saying the words of the script that's been written for me, perhaps provided on a teleprompter newscaster-style, or more likely written in chalk on a slate held by a boy jihadist wearing a scraggly and unconvincing beard whose eyes refuse to meet mine or else, even more jarringly, smile at me pleasantly.

Firm pressure on my shoulders forcing me to my knees, brutal star of the sun, the moment of disbelief, the long knife that has been brandished at me so many times now at my actual throat, a rough palm pressed to my forehead. Pain. And after that? The moment of consciousness: for how many seconds would I still be seeing, perhaps feeling the wind tickling my cropped hair, crazed tumble of cloudless sky as my severed head is set down, not ungently, on what used to be my back, trophy of spite, repaying the wages of humiliation, grief, rage, and fundamental powerlessness? What can the brain know, the eyes and ears and lips and tongue and teeth and scalp, detached from the inverted tree of the body, its nerve endings, its second self curling under the sternum (seat of feeling attacked in cruel self-knowledge by the samurai committing seppuku), its acreage of skin forming the porous boundary between micro and macro, world and world? Perhaps as long as a minute would remain to me before consciousness lapsed and fled down the drain to wherever consciousness goes at the last, tunneling inward to the last synaptic flashes or, just possibly, outward to...

Stop. Stop. I am no journalist. I am not Daniel Pearl. I am not a name made sacred by what it restores, in memory, to men that were lost, men as beloved by their loved ones as the shrunken heads' original owners must once have been. Names are magical, of ritual, fragments of reality at its least endurable and most vivid. The names of victims are printed and listed and seemingly without end. Names bring specific griefs with their own specific gravity. Horror has no content, just a turning in what's inside, coming out. Massacres of innocents and near-innocents, horrors that implicate us all. If the shrunken heads seem merely remote, grotesque, even comic, it may be because of the overlapping ripples of atrocity.

What these tribal people did to each other, what some agent of empire did, probably with supreme casualness, to claim or trade for these heads, to pack them for storage or display them in a ship's cabin, so that they ended up here, without brain and without skull, stuffed with sand, orifices sealed and faces blackened so as to retain the vengeful souls of the slain like a genie in its bottle, to challenge and absorb their power, as standing reserve, first for the good of the tribe, then for the good of the empire, for the education of the souls of tourists and middle school students come to gawk or take sober notes.

It was precisely at the moment that the soul's power was absorbed by the tribe that the head became a mere souvenir, of value only for the money or trinkets that a warrior might receive in exchange from a white man. Now, behind glass, what energies do they still radiate, or absorb—these pouches of mute flesh, these signifiers of barbarism and of the barbarism of signification—the will to *render* the things of this world, to bring them into meaningful patterns, turn them into language, wasted as words?

I stand outside myself looking back at them, penetrated by a blind gaze. A loose and uneven redistribution of subjectivity, matter. William James compared the universe to "one of those dried human heads with which the Dyaks of Borneo deck their lodges. The skull forms a solid nucleus; but innumerable feathers, leaves, strings, beads, and loose appendices of every description float and dangle from it, and, save that they terminate in it, seem to have nothing to do with one another." The heads of the town way up to the aether—what James calls "This imperfect intimacy, this bare relation of *withness*." I am *with* those heads in space if not in time; with the bodies of the murdered, if not their souls. Out of one museum into another, surrounded by extinct animals; out of the street and into the present's whited sepulcher, Berlin, I tear out of your museums to hurtle back into you, your broad unmazy streets that lead everywhere in history for a Jew, toward Rome.

NEW YORK
—CHICAGO—
NEW YORK

The city, the city, the city at the end of everything. Three thousand miles away, three months before my birth, the Family would go on trial and just like that the Sixties that he had dreamed through, dreamed outside of—the decade's psychedelic surfaces, its braless girls, its dream of total revolution that would leave everything but the American soul unchanged—would end. The JFK Sixties, the Beach Boy Sixties, the space-race Sixties had colored the first years of Dad's young manhood. When the revolution came or tried to come—in Dallas, in Selma, in Los Angeles—he was still in college, commuting from home, head down, nose to the grindstone, in thrall to his parents' dreams for him and his own inchoate unspoken resistance to those dreams. The immigrant thing that he would never have guessed was integral to his experience had its hooks in him, mainlined from parents molded by the dual catastrophes of immigration and the Depression: the drive to succeed, to push beyond the beachhead of buying and selling into the land of milk and honey, doctors and lawyers. Like many another patriarch his father had come to rest on the mountaintop, making a good living and yet unable to cross into the Promised Land of country clubs and European vacations. That was on my father's shoulders. All around him temptations crowded, sweet stink of grass, miniskirts, the taunting voices of Grace Slick and Janis Joplin, the sit-ins and the be-ins, dark convulsive violence before the hangover dawn. The girls, the drugs, the politics, he looked at them all, sampled here and there, but none of it entered his heart, he was shielded as though by bulletproof glass.

The long hot summer of '68 sent him home for his first visit since he'd moved to New York: he quit the store gratefully, only a month now between the salesman and his new identity as a teacher of biology to uninformed uniformed girls. He put on his only suit to fly home on his father's dime. If New York had been intolerable with its sticky shoe-sole heat adhering to every surface, Skokie was differently so in its silence, its postage-stamp lawns, the late-model cars drifting and shimmering in light the texture of ozone and oil. His mother fussed over him as if he'd come back from the war; his sisters stood blinking at a distance; his father was on the road selling speakers. The war: Vietnam like a pebble in his shoe, a wince of mingled fear and shame every time he caught the news on TV or heard from his mother ventriloquize the grief of other mothers. His yiddishe mama always in motion to and from the kitchen, fluttering around her daughters, his high-school-age sisters in pastel miniskirts and exaggerated eyeshadow who were parking in cars with men his age, pursuing off-the-shelf dreams of love. They sought a man they could care for the way their mother had cared for him, the number-one son, clothes always beautifully pressed like the crisp new five-dollar bill she pressed into his hand every time he left the house, whether it was for the week or for an evening. Sometimes he caught his sisters looking at him with eyes shining not with envy but wonder: how could anyone be so cared for, so loved. He took it for granted of course but it oppressed him too, those unverbalized dreams of the once and future Jewish mothers. They colonized his heart and twisted in his gut as he sat again for the MCATS in a drafty high-ceilinged room with long windows pulsing summer light off the lake, unable to recall the distinction between mitosis and meiosis. One more try, his mother had said, but what he heard was *one last chance.* When he got home the TV was on with pictures from downtown, showing waves of long-haired young people breaking their skulls on the shoals of the police. It was happening almost exactly twenty miles away. His mother brought him his dinner, touched his shoulder, reassuringly or warningly, as though restraining him from diving into the chaos on the flickering kitchen TV. The touch was unnecessary. He chewed, staring. The scene might as well have been in China for all that he could recognize of himself in it. Who were these people and why were they so angry? He couldn't possibly be so naive, he even chastised himself with the accusation, and yet when was the last time he'd picked up a newspaper? There was no need for news in New York: New York *was* the news if you lived there, a jittery handheld camera turned upon the city's narcissistic surround. In Skokie there were papers fastidiously bundled for the trash man every week; there was CBS and Walter Cronkite, good old kindly Uncle Walter, whom his entire family watched religiously, shaking their heads as they knew Walter would like to do, but didn't, as the solid old postwar dispensation shivered itself to pieces a little bit more every evening. His father, a New Deal man since before he could vote, was speaking openly now in praise of Nixon, and his youngest sister had a poster of Nixon on her bedroom wall and records of Nixon's speeches that she played on a small white turntable that had once been his when she was going to sleep. "He makes me feel safe," she explained. On the little screen the paunchy pale face of Mayor Daley was moving its liverish lips. He had somehow sidestepped the life in which he'd have been halfway through medical school, or starting his residency, engaged to a beautiful nurse. Where could teaching high school biology on the Upper West Side lead or leave him? He tried to imagine the future. On the screen they were reporting from Saigon. His mother stopped behind him, he could feel and smell her (lavender, juniper, Johnson's baby powder) and heard her breathing. They were both looking at the TV. "Oy," she murmured. "Those poor boys."

Those poor boys beat their heads against the brick wall of the times, marching to war or marching against it. Dad did not. Martin and Bobby were already dead and Nixon was already unstoppable. Soon they'd be protesting the Miss America Pageant and *Hawaii Five-O* would debut on CBS. In Mexico City two years prior to the day of my birth hundreds of students will be massacred in Tlateleco. Two weeks later Tommie Smith and John Carlos stand in eternity in the same bloody, fists raised. Dad went back to teaching the apolitical divisions of cells. All is consigned to the past.

The New York to which he returned was the capital of everything yet somehow faraway, secure, provincial, remote from what they were calling "the Sixties," isolated from "Chicago" and "the Family" and "People's Park" and "Bobby Kennedy at the Ambassador Hotel." New York wasn't square exactly, and that suited him; he'd never thought of himself as square. But it was not a city that he could ever imagine losing its head. There was too much action for that, too many non-sequiturs walking the streets. Now that he for sure won't be a doctor (the MCATs for the second time a bust). Now that he was teaching biology, he felt closer than ever to science, and Dad's New York was not a bad place for science. He took his ninth-graders on field trips to the Museum of Natural History and the Bronx Zoo and a lab at Columbia where they conducted clinical trials with rhesus monkeys with pink indignant buttocks pressed against the edges of their cages, scandalizing and delighting his girls. On an eleven-inch black and white television rolled into the classroom for the purpose they watched Apollo 7 take flight, as the girls speculated ingenuously about the likelihood of the astronauts discovering little green men and bringing one home as a pet. The prestige of science, particularly American science, was at its apex. He told his girls about Watson and Crick, about the first human heart transplant, about the power of the pocket calculator and the advent of the dawn of computers. It was, he told them, an exciting time to be alive, the most exciting time in human history. Barriers were falling everywhere: in space exploration, in undersea exploration, in discovering the secrets of the human body. His girls spent an afternoon making models of DNA helixes out of pipe cleaners. They dissected salamanders and frogs and mice, giggling nervously when he puts a slide of a female mouse's reproductive system on the projector. They watched filmstrips with the shades pulled down while he stood in the back by a cracked window glancing out at the asphalt play yard, fiddling with an unlit cigarette, daydreaming. Usually his thoughts found themselves winding their way back to Judy. What was she doing just then—what was she doing *exactly*? She'd accepted his departure for Chicago with disconcerting nonchalance, fallen back into conversation with him upon his return as if he'd never left. Was this good or bad? Was she really a fed? She'd described her job's daily round: how she dropped in on businesses in arrears, sometimes accompanied by grim-faced men in white shirts, black ties, and black windbreakers with MARSHAL printed on the back. There was never any trouble: the defendants, when they saw her, she said, just went limp. One man had stood up behind his desk when she came into his office with the marshal, tall and dignified with white hair and a white handkerchief poking out of the pocket of his silk jacket, then sat down again abruptly in his chair and began silently to cry. A lot of the people she busted were immigrants—South Asians, Serbs, Puerto Ricans—which made her feel a little funny, she said, as the daughter of immigrants, of refugees even, as a refugee herself. Her father had been born in Hungary, was now a hairdresser and cab driver in Astoria, and she doubted his books would stand up to more than casual inspection. A bit of a shady character, her father, a charmer, a goniff. Dad met him that October, this father, he'd come into the city and insisted on meeting them at Rockefeller Center, of all places, and bought them hot dogs and smiled broadly, as if the entire place belonged to him and he was showing it off. He was a small, dapper man in a fedora with a green feather in the band, wearing a wide-waled corduroy suit, displaying pointed yellow teeth under a luxuriant black mustache, smelling thickly of Sen-Sen and cologne. Judy seemed a little embarrassed in her father's presence, almost squirming as he bragged about how he'd been able to get a cabdriver's medallion in just six weeks because of the big boys he knew from the courthouse, just across from the little shop on Queens Boulevard where he cut hair. Lawyers, judges, upstanding businessmen, in and out of the shop all day, busting balls, dropping tips for the races, settling disputes and parking tickets with a wink and a smile. He walked up and down in front of where the two of them sat on a bench by the fountain, waving his arms like a man giving a speech, or an orchestra conductor. His accent was thick, almost impenetrable at first. Mom caught Dad's eye when her father wasn't looking and waggled her eyebrows up and down, Groucho Marx style, but he could tell she found her father's performance painful. "He wanted to impress you," she told him later on the subway back uptown. "Did he?" He hedged, smiled, shrugged. "He's funny, isn't he. Isn't he funny?" She repeated this word as if trying to discover its meaning. He put his arm around her and, he didn't know why, kissed her on the forehead. She relaxed into his body and the subway car's sway. "My mother would have loved you."

"When did she die?"

"A while back," she said, her voice closing.

She unfolded it to him in hints and echoes, lying with her legs thrown over his as they sprawled on her bed—a big brass bed, like the one Dylan sang about all that summer long. They floated together in the golden shadows of her basement apartment, the air perfumed by a stick of sandalwood and colored by the rasp of a needle gliding in the center vinyl of an untended record (not Dylan: Judy Collins, *Wildflowers*). The dapper little man in the cloud of cologne was wearing a secret under his tailored sleeve, a series of numbers, like all the parents of friends and cousins she'd grown up with in the Bronx, slapping down their mahjong tiles and jabbering away in Yiddish and Hungarian about anything but how they'd gotten there. "He was in the camp," Judy said softly. He did not ask which camp but the name hovered between them, its strange soft soughing *ow* with the whisper of static at the end, a bubble of ash. Her father's barbering and scavenging skills had saved his life, or so he'd led his daughter to believe.

Her mother had also survived, but could not survive the cancer that had claimed her when Judy was ten years old. Now her dad had married another survivor, a hard-faced woman named Magda—"a real cunt," she muttered into his chest. She went home to her father's new house in Queens as infrequently as possible, and her father had taken to visiting her out here once a season or so, always in Midtown or the Village. Neutral ground.

She was a survivor. Born in Budapest, sheltered by her father's parents, whom she barely remembered—Bubbe and Zayde—from whose arms she'd been taken after the war, brought to live with her parents in a displaced persons camp. "Belsen! Can you imagine? The Brits took it over from the Germans—it never stopped being a camp. It was a little Israel when I was there, almost its own country. We had schools, theaters, concerts. Everyone was making everything from scratch." Finally, when she was almost six, the necessary visa was approved—distant cousins, here—and she'd come to this country, to the Bronx wilderness, without so much as a doll or a shawl to call her own. There she'd pieced together an American girlhood, shedding almost instantly the Hungarian accent that her father dragged behind him like an anchor.

As for her mother, she'd never learned English at all. But her brother had been born here, was still in high school, a poor student, a *luftmensch*, always on the brink of dropping out. Dad met him, found him a loose-limbed greasy-haired galoot of a boy, red-eyed mumbling "Groovy" and "Far out," destined to flunk out of City College and after that the Air Force, destined for a life of flunking out of things until the day he found, of all things, Jesus, and remade himself as a Christian, a pastor, the father of blonds.

Throughout her childhood their mother had been a ghostly presence, shaking herself out of dark depressions to oppress her daughter with obsessive dictates on how she wore her hair, whose houses she could visit after school, piano lessons, French lessons, elocution lessons, working as many levers of the baroque anachronistic bourgeois education of prewar Hungary as she could find in her immigrant borough. Dad wondered at Mom's precise and sharply edged mid-Atlantic speech, thrown into sharper relief by her father's accent and her brother's affable Outer Borough honk.

It was all strange to him, strange and improbable. He knew about the camps, of course, and in Skokie he'd seen survivors clumping and drifting by the doors of kosher markets, the marked men and women clothed entirely in funereal black and white. The images of emaciated figures in their Buster Keaton striped pajamas were to him distant and unreal, less real indeed than the strange, disquieting images of naked African tribeswomen he'd studied surreptitiously in the pages of *National Geographic*. He couldn't bring it close to him. *Never again, the six million*—they were just phrases. He was a happy American boy, child of a postwar era so heady and prosperous it scarcely knew what it was post of, barely aware of anti-Semitism as a living and malevolent force.

Looking at her in repose, sitting in a kitchen chair with her knees drawn up, a cigarette burning between her fingers, her eyes seemed to him Oriental and elsewhere. He had taken her dark aura, her air of tragedy, to be affectations, remnants of the Beat poetry she read to him from tattered paperbacks after they made love, her face a chanting mask: *I saw the best minds of my generation….* He could not discern, behind her flashes of depression, a darkness deeper than his own rare dips in mood. The world was before them, after all. They would be young forever.

"Turn the record over," she said, eyes closed. Smoke climbed the ladder of the air.

The days and weeks turned into months. He couldn't figure her out, and that kept him flushed, imagining, on edge. With her bobbed hair and short dresses and green felt cloche hat, she was the spit of a 1920s flapper, in spite of her far from flat chest, which she deplored. Her favorite film was *Thoroughly Modern Millie* (1967); she'd seen it four times. But she was also the closest thing to a hippie chick that he'd ever dated, what with her books on crystals and astrology and the sticks of Indian incense that she bought from the same head shop his cousin Hank frequented. Her politics were pinko, yet she worked for Uncle Sam and the taxes she helped to collect were paying for the bombers running sorties over Vietnam and Cambodia. Her reading was eclectic and convulsive: one week it was all Dostoyevsky and Mailer, the next week Dorothy Sayers and Agatha Christie, the week after that nothing but P.G. Wodehouse. She called Dad "Gussie" when she was pleased and "Jeeves" when she was annoyed, until finally he asked her to stop. She was an Anglophile and a Francophile. She had a good singing voice and went on Sundays to Black and Baptist churches in Harlem where she could clap and sing. She said she was an atheist. She dragged him to Ethical Culture meetings and Unitarian Universalist services but they never darkened the door of an actual shul. His eyes were open, wide, but it was as if he saw things more slowly than she did, or not at all. She was quicksilver, a mind alight and restless. He basked in her flame.

This is getting serious, he said to himself. He wrote a letter to his mother, telling her about this remarkable woman he'd met. Walking toward the avenue with the envelope in his hand, knowing that the action he contemplated was irrevocable. He watched it slide like a tongue into the stolid blue box. Soon they would know. The family would know. And what would be the next, inevitable step?

His heart began to imitate her movements, restless in his chest like a robin on the hunt, bobbing and dropping, the even keel quite gone. He caught her turning away and pulled her to him. He kissed her hard, hard, his mouth driving like a beak, and she opened.

On what part of her body were the numerals printed, the expiration date she bore? No one knows the anniversary of their own death. But I know. I can read them now, the terminal digits on her wrist: 12/21/91. Dad has his number too, for the moment obscure, though the accident shines ghostly through my picture of him, the line of before and after. It glows greenly over the scene I imagine, two young people living at the top and bottom of the same West 87th brownstone, a nice Jewish boy and a girl not quite as nice, a minor accident of history, in love.

She crooned to him, returned his ardor, handed over what softness she possessed, holding back, for now, the edge of her tongue. She smelled to him like soap and smoke, and he crushed her close. He would never again feel so alive.

NEW YORK, NOW

"You've got it wrong, you know," Hank says, putting the pages aside and glancing at me over the tops of his glasses. Nearly eighty, kindly, transparently bald, reclined in a striped djellaba from his own journeys to Morocco in the Seventies. Summer. Phlox and yarrow bob in the breeze in the little garden attached to Hank and John's Upper West Side living room, just blocks from where my parents met. John, Hank's husband, a painter, chops greens in the galley-like kitchen; my wife naps on the couch with a splayed paperback copy of *The Tempest* rising and falling on her stomach. Our daughter is home in Chicago being looked after by my mother-in-law. Everything else is in the past.

"Your father got here *before* I did. Sixty-four, sixty-five at the latest. He was the one who welcomed me here, not vice-versa. I knew nobody when I first came to New York. He had had a life here for years."

I brush this inconvenience away. "Was my mom already in the picture?"

"Not yet. He met her in, oh, '67 I think it was. She moved into his building and not the other way around. And they took their time getting married. Before, that was their happiest time."

"Before I came along?"

"Before they left the city," Hank says. "Yeah."

The room warms with the smell of simmering olives.

John is cooking us a chicken tagine, keeping up the Moroccan theme.

"I can't use that," I say. "I lose the whole theme, the Sixties, the *late* Sixties. I need him younger than that. More naive. Anyway, it doesn't matter. I'm giving up on the memoir. This is fiction now."

"Why?" Hank asks. He's been retired for a good while, but habitually resorts to the psychotherapist's trick of the open question. The pause that pries you open.

"It just is," I say stubbornly. "This is the story I have to tell."

"But why not just say what happened?" Hank asks, consciously or unconsciously quoting Robert Lowell.

"Because I don't *know* what happened. That's part of the point. I'm writing about things I can't possibly know."

"You could ask," Hank says, looking at me over his glasses. "*I* know."

We are poor passing facts, whispers Lowell.

"Leave him alone, Hank," John says, chopping.

"As if *you* didn't care about accuracy? This man," Hank says to me, "only paints his own family members, always from photographs. He wants to get it *right*." John smiles absently and addresses himself to his root vegetables.

John's paintings have the quality of dreams—stark present-tense faces unhooked from linear history, shading shades of brown and yellow skin, with John's great-grandmother the enslaved matriarch hovering visibly or invisibly over every triptych or panel he paints. In every painting of every ancestor, the creation of the world. Countless refractions of a lost original. Color extracted from black and white.

"It's fiction," I say again. "Something imagined, not recalled."

Hank raises his hands in surrender. "If that's how you want it. But it's not what actually happened."

It happens here. It happens now.

"Wake your wife up," John says, grinning at me happily now, sideways like a terrier. "I need her to taste this."

"It's not really about them anyway," I tell Hank, "or you either, with all due love and respect. It's about the greatest decade in human history, and how I missed it, and how missing it shaped who I became."

Hank raises his eyebrows and John shakes his head, smiling to himself as he lays dishes onto the table. My wife opens her eyes once, unseeing like a cat, and closes them again.

"You're sure about that?" John asks.

"Sure about what?"

"Sure that you know what your book is about."

"It's my book, isn't it? Aren't you sure about your paintings?"

The painter's vision is not a lens, / it trembles to caress the light.

"Far from it."

"Photos or not photos," I say, "you have to imagine it. Ancestry, right? Where you came from. Where you're going."

John shrugs. "It's a wise child that knows his own father."

"I would have written it this way anyway," I say, "no matter what had happened to Dad."

"You're sure about that." Not a question.

My wife sits up, reciting the side she's been studying for an upcoming audition:

Had I the plantation of this isle, my lord—

I' the commonwealth I would by contraries

Execute all things.

"Another country heard from," I say.

"You should listen to your cousin," she says.

"Which one?"

"Both of them."

Lie there, my art. But how to escape the cycle of quotations, questions, repetitions?

"Dinner's ready."

He flashes upon my inward eye, my father in his sickbed, looking for all the world like a falling man whose parachute didn't quite open in time.

DAS KUNSTHAUS

Shane and I see a fair bit of each other. The days drift by without my managing to write much of anything, anything at all, while the Burroughs conference, the one in Tangier that's my official excuse for this existential lark, creeps closer. Shane says she's having the same problem getting any writing done. She makes a living as a corporate translator but does the job only late at night, leaving her days empty and open, a blank book waiting for poems that mostly fail to arrive. She takes me to more movies, not the arthouse flicks I might have expected but dumb American comedies with German subtitles: *Bad Teacher*; *Horrible Bosses*, *The Hangover Part II*. We sit in the theaters with plastic cups of lager and Shane laughs so hard that the beer comes out of her nose. I wonder when she'll try to kiss me, or I her, but it keeps not happening. Then comes one particularly vacant afternoon that I've spent lying on the floor of the work flat staring at the ceiling while rain titters at the window. My time in Berlin is coming to its inconclusive close; the novel I came here to write lies in fragments around my body, like the wreckage of a crashed airliner painstakingly reconstructed by investigators but lacking key components, the explanatory black box above them all. I lift my buzzing phone: the text, from Shane, reads simply, *U Ornanienburger Tor*. I stare at it a while before punching the station into Google Maps.

About half an hour away on the S-bahn, on the north

side of the Spree, not too terribly far from the Hackescher Markt where we've been meeting for our lowbrow film festival in the evenings. I scroll back through my other texts, the ones I haven't answered. Two from my wife, one from my sister, a whole slew from my stepmother with details about Dad's upcoming surgery, his fourth, this one to screw together the pieces of his cervical spine the surgeons were unable to reach in the last round. *They have to go in through the front,* she writes, *on the other side of his larynx. It may damage his swallow reflex, and the doctor says there's a chance he'll never be able to speak again.* And from my sister, in all caps: *PLEASE CALL.*

I text Shane: *I'll see you soon.*

Rocking on the S-bahn flying over the city with the Berliners, many of them young, tattooed, and bearded in the best Williamsburg style. Pretending to text I snap a photo or two, capturing the red-eyed man slumped into the shoulder of his lank-haired blonde girlfriend on the row of seats across from me, their aura redolent of another age's heroin chic. The guy opens his eyes and meets mine. He leans forward—he's bigger than I'd realized—and says something that sounds even more aggressive than he might intend, because he's saying it in German. I shake my head.

"You photographing us?" he says in English. "Huh? You take our picture?"

I deaden my face. "No. No, of course not."

He extends his grimy hand across the aisle. The other passengers watch attentively, as though seated at the play. "Show me."

"No. No way."

His fingers spasm together like a spider flailing its legs. His girlfriend, whose eyes had also been shut, now opens them, revealing startling Liz Taylor amethysts that pop like an android's eyes against the smudged kohl that surrounds them.

"And what did she say then?" Shane asks, brushing shoulders in the wind as we stride up Ornanienburger Strasse.

"She said 'Fuck you, Yankee.' In a Russian accent."

"I love it!" Shane shrieks.

"I'm glad you're amused about me almost getting my ass kicked in an international incident."

"So what happened then?"

"Nothing. They got off at the next stop." I decide not to tell Shane about how the guy loomed over me before they did it, leaned hanging from the straps to dangle his head over me and let some saliva slip down from his mouth to drop with a splat between my feet. How the two of them staggered off the platform then, laughing. How the other passengers then, and only then, looked primly away from my blazing face.

"People have had it up to here with tourists. You can't really blame them."

"I *don't* really blame them."

She stops and points. "We're here."

Here is a massive concrete gothic industrial-looking building more or less squatting in a large, overgrown lot, with ornately colored plastic tubing strung between the bars of the chain-link fence that separated it off from its sedate and prosperous surroundings. But what really catches my attention is the high white wall at one end of the building looming over the street, covered with a black and white mural. Above a grimly stylized image of a man's face reminiscent of the mask worn by Klaus Maria Brandauer in *Mephisto* (1981) are printed the words HOW LONG IS NOW. Since I am a poet in the company of another poet, however, we must not neglect the line breaks:

HOW

LONG

IS NOW

Words unbidden in my mind, young Morrissey's hair falling into his eyes: *I am the son and heir / Of nothing in particular.*

"What is it?"

"It's called the *Kunsthaus*," Shane tells me. "It was a department store at the turn of the century—this was the Jewish quarter, you know."

"Are department stores automatically Jewish?"

She shrugs. "Anyways, later on an electric company bought the building, and they say that the first German television transmission was from here. After that the Nazis took it over, like they took over everything else. They used to keep prisoners of war in the attic. After the war it was a technical school, and then after the Wall fell they were going to demolish it, when a group of artists moved in and started squatting. It had a kind of unofficial status for a long time—there was a restaurant, a movie theater, and of course many artist studios. But it's all over. In six months the new owners are going to evict absolutely everyone and then who knows what will happen. Maybe they'll knock it down after all. They'll probably turn it into condos."

"So what's inside now?"

She takes me by the hand. "Let's find out!"

Shane leads me in through the sculpture garden—a tatty piece of ground marked by a disheveled array of sculptures of almost inconceivable ugliness—a graceless faux-Giacometti here and a boxy imploded pseudo-Calder there. Creatures of barbed wire and hacked wood, a Koonsian inverted mermaid with a fishy torso and pornographically spread legs sitting on a wicker chair, with a Sally Bowles-style bowler pinched between the fish's gaping lips. There's a grand piano that looks like it was raped by a bandsaw and a boxy upside-down Trabant covered in peace symbols, wheels slowly revolving in different directions. Queasy, I turn away.

"What's wrong?" Shane asks.

"Nothing. How do we get in?"

The entrance off of the garden is more like a tunnel than a corridor—we pass between layers of paint-spattered cinderblock underneath exposed bulbs to reach a massive orthogonal stairwell spiraling vertiginously up toward a faint reincarnation of the natural light we've left behind. I can hear tinny music, a dull industrial scraping sound, distant laughter; I smell mud and dust and marijuana and ancient shit.

Shane's eyes sparkle. "Come upstairs," she says. "There's someone I want you to meet."

We are climbing the stairs but it feels more like a descent as the music gets louder and someone in some indeterminate location makes a hideous rasping noise, as though they were blowing a raspberry into a bullhorn. The sound cuts off abruptly as we poke our heads above the level of the highest floor, where the stairs simply terminate in mid-spiral so that I have to use my hands to pull myself up on the same level with the floor—hands and trousers now practically soaked with dust. Shane, more agile, is already standing to one side waiting for me. The room is vast and stretches away from us. Toward one end an enormous curtain of red and amber beads ranges from one exterior wall to the other, while the opposite side terminates in a mirrored wall with a wooden bar running along its length, like in a dance studio. A few fluorescent bulbs burn on the ceiling, but most of the light rubs its face against the long filthy windows ranging either side of the enormous room, a thin gray garlic-skin-colored light that I will forever associate with the skies of Berlin. Then a vibration thuds through the soles of my feet a split-second before the loud enormous gush of water through pipes. A metal door groans open and a young woman steps out, slinging one arm through a strap of her overalls. She walks over to us and accepts a cigarette from Shane while the two of them exchange a few low, muttered words in German. She's got closely cropped bleached blonde hair and what appear to be Sanskrit tattoos on both forearms. Shane gestures between us, her hand trailing smoke.

"This is Olga," she says. "The one I was telling you about."

She hasn't told me squat. "Of course," I say. "Nice to meet you."

Olga takes a slow drag on her cigarette and squints at me. She says something in German and Shane laughs. "*Nein, nein,*" she says, smiling at me. I laugh to show I'm in on the joke. Then Olga says something else.

"*Englisch, bitte,*" I say.

Olga shrugs. "You want to see it?" Her accent is Slavic.

"See what?"

Shane raises an eyebrow at me before turning back to Olga. "Yes, of course."

"This way.'"

We proceed in a line toward the bead curtain, shimmering dull gold and rust in the washed-out light. Just as we are about to reach it the strands part and something pokes through that I don't recognize or understand—a gigantic red-eyed hairy head that waggles back and forth at waist height, gibbering maniacally. I stop dead, glancing at Shane and Olga's faces, trying to read their reactions and so judge my own. Olga looks bored, Shane amused. I try to slow my breathing. The head stops its waggle and the eyes fix on mine: two hands in black rubber gloves thrust through the curtain and press themselves against its cheeks, tilting to one side in a grotesque parody of innocent curiosity and wonder. I am on my heels. Then Olga turns and says something else in German to Shane before turning back to the hairy head and hands. "Cut it out, Viktor," she says in English. "We have visitors."

The head withdraws, leaving behind, for a moment,

the hands, which also then withdraw, as the beads waver and scrape themselves across the floor. A moment later the whole figure pushes through the curtain, turning the beads on either side of him like waves, stirring up little cyclones of dust. A man, six feet tall, burly, in overalls identical to Olga's, wearing a gorilla mask and sleek black rubber gloves that go all the way back to the elbows. He steps up to me and extends one of the gloved hands. I shake it gingerly.

"Stop clowning, Viktor," Olga says in a bored voice.

Viktor doesn't remove the mask but says something either too muffled or too remote from English for me to understand. Shane comes to my side, if not to my rescue.

"He really is a clown," she says, as if that explains everything. "And an artist. He and Olga live here. They're siblings."

"I see."

"For what I do I have to wear a mask," the gorilla says in unctuous and nearly accentless English. "I prefer it."

"And what do you do?"

"I was just about to show you," says Olga. "Come on."

The four of us push through the curtain more or less simultaneously, sending the little plastic ovoids swinging and spinning in unpredictable moiré patterns behind us; I think of the urine that astronauts eject into space, each droplet instantaneously crystallizing into a fragment of gold that will swing in orbital clouds around the Earth for forever and a day. The curtain's fingers have waved us into a makeshift theater: haphazard rows of rusted metal profoundly uncomfortable-looking metal chairs before a low platform with a rippling black velvet curtain hanging over it. The windows are blacked out and the light that filters in to the space through the curtain is striated and yellow and casts our long shadows over the walls. A sixteen-millimeter film projector is propped up on a wooden stool among the chairs, cyclopean and unstable. The gorilla lopes over to the projector while Olga pulls back the velvet curtain to reveal the pitted gray cinderblock wall that will function as a screen.

"Sit," Shane orders, and I sit in the least warped of the chairs on the far left edge of things, while Olga ties the curtain and her brother the gorilla curses and fusses with his machine. Shane sits in front of me and I study the back of her neck for a while; then I realize she is speaking in a low voice and bend forward in my seat so I can hear.

"...so I told them about you and Burroughs and they both were just so excited to show it to someone who knew him!"

I glance at the gorilla's back, then at Olga who stands with her hands thrust in her coverall pockets, exposing long canines in what I take to be a friendly smile. "But I didn't know him!" I hiss into Shane's ear. "He died in Kansas in 1997! I've never even *been* to Kansas!"

Shane turns her head to show her severe, somehow Egyptian profile, and puts a finger to her lips. "Ssh. Don't ruin this for them!"

The gorilla has stopped fiddling with switches and celluloid and now turns to face us, making what sounds like an elaborate speech which is, however, muffled by his mask, and is in any case in German. Shane translates: "He says it's a great honor to meet you and he's familiar with your work." (*What work?*) "He says the footage he's about to show us is rare." Viktor pauses. "*Very* rare." A rush of new words. "He says the Burroughs estate doesn't know about it and if they find out they'll try to steal it and that that wouldn't be fair to…" Here Shane frowns and says something in German to Olga, who says something German back. Shane shrugs and looks back at me. "Fair to them, I guess. Anyway, it's only ninety seconds long and they've never digitized it, he says. This is the only copy."

"Why?" I ask, not sure what I'm asking. Why do they think I knew Burroughs? Why do they want to show me this film? Why is Shane making me into a liar? Why am I in this building in Berlin? What am I doing here?

Olga has pulled a separate, second curtain, made of what looks like soiled bedsheets sewn together, across the bead curtain behind us, to make the space darker. The sheets billow gently against the beads, which drag themselves across the concrete floor in short, patternless skritches. I feel endarkened. Enwombed. Shane, startlingly, takes my hand and gives it a squeeze.

The gorilla turns on the projector.

The film is black and white and begins with the usual numeric countdown: 7, 6, 5, 4, 3—there is no 2, no 1. Then a handwritten title card appears but it's too brief and in any case too German for me to understand anything except the date: 1976. Images flash in upon me: the American Bicentennial, the sands of Coney Island where I dig industriously with a plastic shovel while my little sister splashes in the surf in her polka-dotted swimsuit. I know without looking that Mom is behind me on a folding lounge chair, shrouded in a floppy cotton hat and wrapped in a towel in spite of the heat, a murder mystery in her lap and a cigarette burning between her fingers. And standing up to his knees in the water in front of me the lanky form of Dad in his trunks, his hair long enough to hang in wet ringlets around his ears, his back to me shading his eyes as he looks out at the distant shape of the Statue of Liberty rippling in the heat. Masses of people surround us, a confusion of colors and noise amid the stink of Coppertone and sauerkraut. Then like a slide shifting abruptly it's night and I'm propped up in Dad's lap out of my mind with sunburn and exhaustion but with eyes wide as the fireworks leap over Liberty's shoulder to explode in red, white, and blue succession impossibly high in the sky. My sister and mother are somewhere behind us, lost in the crowd; I don't look for them. I shrug more deeply into my father's arms, who points in the sky, showing it to me, showing the world as he'd found it to his only son. "Look! Look there!" The blank overheated night sky exploding again and again into particularity, marked by this moment, the nation's birthday, an unrepeatable sliver of time.

The flash suspended, the colors drained. An overexposed shot of bright white light that then adjusts as the camera takes a shaky step backward to reveal a window, long and narrow, through which dark masses of foliage can be seen, a view it might be from a castle window above a forbidden forest, a view of legend. The camera takes another step back—there's no sound—and wheeling captures what appears to be somebody's living room, sparsely furnished with a white leather sofa and a Bauhaus-looking chair. All tubes and waves, and a coffee table crowded with bottles, an enormous overfull ashtray, what looks like a Pollock painting covering one wall, and a high glass table serves as a bar. But it's the people that the camera is interested in, a small klatsch of them standing and gesturing behind the couch, on which sits a slender figure wearing what appears to be an English tweed suit, with a snap-brim fedora concealing his face. Something about the movement of the narrow hands and the point of the chin instantly convinces me that I'm looking at William S. Burroughs, folded to resemble nothing so much as a praying mantis with his big Midwestern ears sticking out from under the hat in imitation of the elbows thrust out from his side. He looks perched on the edge of the sofa, ready to escape. Behind him in a black suit with no tie, big belly thrusting out of his button-down white shirt, gesticulating with hands, fingertips, and his great wagging beard, lips in constant motion, is Allen Ginsberg in conversation with a woman, much smaller, who stands listening ironically with one hand holding her elbow and her other hand holding a cigarette, her stillness in stark contrast to Allen's excited bob and weave.

The pose is so characteristic that I have to suppress an exclamation, though it isn't and doesn't even really look like and in any case cannot possibly be my mother. No. Long black hair hides her face but then she tosses it aside, glancing irritably in the direction of the camera and then offering it a sharp sudden smile. Now I cannot suppress a gasp at that haughty, glamorous face.

Shane giggles. "I know, right? Susan Sontag."

"Have you seen this before?"

She squeezes my fingers. "Keep watching."

My eyes follow Burroughs, though the camera, jittery barely keeps him in frame, drawn like a bird to the light and movement of Ginsberg and Sontag's cross-purposed conversation. She glances at the camera; he's oblivious, talking freely, shoving his glasses up higher on his face and then unselfconsciously picking his nose. Then there's a jump cut and the position of the camera has reversed so that it's facing the windows, which flood the screen with white light. Shadowy figures move in front of it, merge with it, emerge. Something flashes out at the viewer—a hand. Then the gray begins to reassert itself but for a moment it's like watching sheet lightning, light bearing the scars of ancient celluloid. The frozen metal of the chair I'm sitting on numbs my ass. I squint into the light.

"Plato's cave," murmurs Shane.

Now I can see clearly two figures, one facing the window with his head in profile, one turned more earnestly in the first figure's direction. Burroughs has shed his hat, he's talking with his chin tucked low into his chest but his eyes are alive and searching the face of his interlocutor, who stands with hands in pockets, a man as tall and narrow as Burroughs, shockingly narrow in the hips, fleshless, beaked. The profile is unmistakable. The lips move, saying something very brief, and Burroughs, astonishingly, laughs. The gorilla slaps his knee and laughs with him, and Olga—who is still standing next to the screen, watching not the images but us—again shows her disturbingly long and pointed teeth. In a room in 1976, William S. Burroughs is laughing at a witticism made by Samuel Beckett.

Beckett and Burroughs, bookends, paring down existence to an arbitrary minimum in the black-and-white century. For Burroughs it was junk, for Beckett, words. But words were also a kind of drug for Burroughs, a desperate man, his only weapon against the Ugly Spirit, himself: "We are the language the letters disintegrate, fade to gray shadows." Beckett was addicted to nothing but nothingness, grinding down and down, grimly, ecstatically, into the dark: "In other words, they like other words, no doubt about it, silence once broken will never again be whole." Permanently old, permanently past the contemporary and therefore always ahead of it: so many black and white photos of these beautiful ascetic old men, Burroughs stooped and ironic in his English suits, Beckett all craggy nobility and steely hair and eyes. Improbable survivors of privileged boyhoods and inexplicable torments, most of them self-inflicted. Both defined by the darkness of their humor, a perverse taste for misery that Burroughs infected with glamor and that Beckett stained with truth.

Burroughs, the laughing man, whom I have never heard laugh in any of the many recordings I've heard of his voice; Burroughs was disturbed by the purity of Beckett's unbelief. Burroughs the public agent, the rebel against "Control," who never met a conspiracy theory or a system for self-improvement that wasn't worth investigating, sometimes for decades. "Beckett is quite literally inhuman," he once wrote. "Beckett closes off whole areas of experience…. You could imagine his turning in disinterest from an extra-terrestrial." He clung to the distant, distasteful praise that Beckett had offered him through a third party: "Burroughs…. Well, he's a writer." On the screen I see it happen, Beckett turning away from Burroughs's brief bark of a laugh, looking out now through the window over the forest or park below.

The horizon of Beckett's work offers no escape, even or especially in imagination, from life on earth. Like Burroughs, Beckett had passed through a personal crucible, though at a less terrible cost to others. Where Burroughs has been quoted again and again claiming that he would not have become a writer if he had not shot and killed his wife Joan Vollmer, Beckett transformed himself by abandoning the English language that had for him become too supple a medium. He broke his addiction to what the "Anglo-Irish exuberance and automatisms" of James Joyce, at whose feet he once sat, transforming himself from crapulent scion of the Protestant Ascendancy into the austere sly ethereal existential effigy of poetry after Auschwitz, witness to the emptying out of values in the wake of the inane slaughterhouse of the twentieth century, by choosing to write in French.

The scene moves on—the camera, for reasons of its own, is studying an uppermost corner of the ceiling—but the two men so briefly glimpsed linger in my mind's eye.

Is it too much to say that by turning to French, Beckett killed the Joyce in himself; whereas, Burroughs, in his more literal fashion, killed the heterosexual scion of privilege in himself by killing his wife? "The death of Joan," Burroughs wrote, "brought me into contact with the invader, the Ugly Spirit, and maneuvered me into a lifelong struggle, from which I have had no choice except to write my way out."

Every writer works with two intertwining materials, his language and his life. Beckett estranged himself from both in a fashion that Burroughs could not understand. And yet what is the "cut-up" if not a technique for killing off the author and putting words at liberty?

A lone man or a pair of men, in shabby clothes, discolored and disheveled, with the air of refugees or clowns. Comedy of the missed connection, the lost opportunity, the incommensurability of the will. Heads thrusting out of urns, out of sand. Trembling at the limits of masked eyes. Country roads and sandy wastes give way to inhuman cylinders, blank spaces, decomposed pronouns.

The camera prowls the room, searching for its famous quarry: four writers of the late century, among the last whose images we can recall, images that persist above and beyond and in spite of what they wrote, the last wisps of glamor that being a writer could possess. Its movements chop the air.

Beckett had little patience for Burroughs's cut-ups: "That's not writing, that's plumbing." But Beckett essentially cut himself into another language, trying to kill the author in himself: "I seem to speak, it is not I, about me, it is not about me." To free the creatures from their creator, into their abandonment: "It's a lot to expect of one creature, it's a lot to ask, that he should first behave as if he were not, then as if he were, before being admitted to that peace where he neither is, nor is not, and where the language dies that permits of such expressions." It is a fundamentally theological, Protestant impulse, almost Miltonic, unbinding the creatures of language so as to show them the error of their ways, all ways, any way, no way. We are a long way from Burroughs' insect overlords, and terrifyingly near to the virus of life itself. Then again, maybe Burroughs saw it too, writing blurred lines into *The Soft Machine*: "I-you-me in the pissoir of present time."

Burroughs had no sense of God, only of puppets and puppet masters, only a proliferating network of agents whose agency—their actions on behalf of evil—matters more than whatever forces or entities they may claim to serve. Sinister doubles of themselves, Mr Bradley Mr Martin, watching the Penny Arcade Peep Show they themselves star in, his characters are as notional as Beckett's, though admittedly more full of literal spunk: sex is comic for both writers but Burroughs is living out his fantasies, as gleeful and methodical as Sade, whereas the nominally heterosexual Beckett is shamed by the remotest possibility of his participation in the perpetuation of the species. For Burroughs conspiracies are sufficient to the evil of the day, forming a functional metaphysics: Burroughs, the libertarian gun nut, forever imagining enemies to shoot at. Beckett, though armed briefly by the Resistance, rifle trembling before his bad eyes, never fired a shot in anger. The enemy was always within: "There I am back at my old aporetics." A poetics. Beckett was by far the better writer. But so what? Both men were out there on the edge of the literary possible. Both of them were free in a way I can scarcely imagine being. They confronted themselves.

Ginsberg and Sontag steal glances at the grand old men, half in love with them both.

"Nothing is more real than nothing."

The film is over and the three Berliners are looking at me expectantly, and I am stumbling my way through these thoughts. My mouth moves but nothing comes out but English, cut-up English.

Rapid chatter from the gorilla. Shane looks at me, flushed with triumph.

"He says to ask you how much."

"How much? How much what?"

"How much will you pay?"

"Pay for what? For this? Nothing."

"Nothing?" Shane exclaims.

"*Nicht?*" say Olga and the gorilla together.

"I mean, I don't have any money," I try to explain. "He should try the Burroughs estate. Or Beckett's for that matter, or maybe a museum. I don't know."

"No money?" the gorilla demands. I shrug. He advances, stabbing with the fingers of both hands toward my chest. "American?" he says accusingly. "And no money?"

"Sorry."

The air has gone out of the room. Viktor's mask seems set in an expression of rigid disappointment. Then Olga shrugs and says something that makes both Shane and the gorilla laugh.

"What? What did she say?"

Shane wipes her eyes. "Never mind."

"Are you laughing at me?" Stupid question: of course they are.

"Let's get a drink," Shane says, standing. "You have money for a drink, right?"

"Of course," I say, huffily. I stand too and sway there for a moment, all the blood having gone out of my legs. The gorilla snaps the roll of film off of the projector and tosses it to Olga with alarming casualness; it flies through the air, trailing a tongue of celluloid derisively behind it. Olga catches it neatly and thrusts it into the nylon shopping bag that serves her as a purse.

The artist, says Burroughs, creates an object capable of doing him harm. That's the test of its otherness, its separate life. Needle, and thread.

And Beckett: "Another devising it all for company. In the same dark as his creature or another." *Company*, his most autobiographical text. "The dark cope of sky. The dazzling land."

Dad never remote enough from my thoughts, hovering six inches above my left shoulder, crippled insect. Dad. Stay there.

In the low-ceilinged bar on Linienstrasse we hoist foaming glasses and each of us toast our chosen avatar:

"To Allen!" shouts Viktor, whose pale sweaty face still bears the marks of his mask.

"To Susan," Shane says, grinning fiercely. "What a cunt!"

"To Sam," says Olga, smiling at me with venomous sweetness.

And what shall I say? Shall I offer a toast to the unknown and barely competent cameraman? To my father between life and death? To the twentieth century within which my life forever threatens to shut itself up, tight as a nutshell drum? But it appears I have no choice.

"To *el hombre invisible,*" I say, lifting my glass up high. "To Bill."

NEW YORK

The first time they slept together, or rather just a little before, they sat naked on her mattress with their legs crossed, smoking the pot she'd been gifted by her brother, a great brown twist of weed that exactly resembled her brother's goatee. "You just sit with me and breathe," she'd ordered him. "No touching, not yet."

He was happy to go along with it, happy in his lean nakedness and happy to be in the presence of hers. "What are we doing?"

"It's tantric meditation. You're going to love it."

Her brick-and-board bookshelf was weighted down with cheap editions of the Vedas and *The Portable Emerson* and everything by Carlos Castaneda and a fly-eaten copy of the *Whole Earth Catalog*. He felt relaxed and unhurried, high without anxiety, taking in the pungency of marijuana and underneath that the sharper, almost metallic taste of sweat. There was a charge between them, in the little space between them, the inch or so that separated the knees of their crossed legs, the rise and fall of her breasts, the skunky tang of their pot-infused bodies. Then she said it, high and casual. "I was married, you know."

"I didn't know!"

"You didn't ask."

Studying her until she rotated her bare left hand at him in a mocking gesture. *Go on, ask.* He asked. "You're not married anymore?"

"Divorced. I'm a divorcée, like in the paperbacks. Sexy, right?"

Suddenly she seemed much older to him, though they were almost exactly the same age.

She punched him, playfully. "Ow!" He rubbed his arm. "I thought you said no touching."

"*Say* something, genius!"

"What do you want me to say?"

"Okay, if you have nothing to say, ask me something." She rolled her shoulders and he watched her breasts appreciatively. "Ask me anything. Men never *ask*."

"Who was he? Or is he?"

"A guy I met at City College. From the Bronx originally. He was my TA in my Intro to Philosophy class. He was going to law school."

"On the make, huh?"

"Exactly. But first he wanted to make it with *me*."

Was she trying to make him jealous? He preoccupied himself for a moment with the lighter, trying not to burn his thumb as he applied the flame to the bowl, mostly making a hash of it. "So why did you get divorced?"

"First ask me why I got married."

"Okay. Why did you get married?"

"To get out of that *house*. To get away from that bitch who was always in my business and my idiot brother and his asshole buddies and my gangster father who's never known *what* to do with me. To get out of the *Bronx*. To get away. David helped me do that. It was a marriage of convenience."

"Was it convenient for, ah, David too?"

"Maybe. I don't know what was in it for him, actually. Maybe it was the way I looked at him from the back row. Or maybe he needed a cover story. He was probably gay."

"What makes you say that?"

"I don't know. Just a feeling."

Three weeks, five weeks maybe after his return from Chicago he had said to her, very seriously, "What is this?" "What's what?" "*This.* Us." "This is this." "So are you my girlfriend?" "Ugh." "So you're *not* my girlfriend." "Ugh!" She pushed him in the chest and he pushed her back, more gently. He thought that Cousin Hank might help, so that night he brought her over. They took to each other immediately; inside of ten minutes they were passing a joint back and forth, laughing like maniacs on Hank's couch while Dad sat on the edge of the wicker chair and grinned uncomfortably. What is this? He knew that a report from Hank would eventually filter back to his parents, and a favorable report from Hank, beloved degenerate that he was, was likely to be perceived unfavorably. He couldn't decide if he was glad or happy about that. Anyway, she was hardly hung up on gays, and neither was he, he decided. This is the new life. No—correction—this is life, full stop. Life at last.

Was she his girlfriend or not? Was this sex or not? She had been married for all of six months to David R., a possibly gay lawyer in training, and they had gotten divorced ("the most fun we ever had—we went to Reno, better than our honeymoon"), and she had moved out of his place and taken this apartment and her job with the feds and that plus alimony ("It's not much, he's glad to pay it," she insisted, "he feels guilty, that's David, your classic schlimazel, feels guilty about everything except what he's really guilty of") made her independent, free. Free enough to drop pretenses: they were kissing now in the undersea grotto of her apartment, in the jingling seashell of her bed, curling her shorter body into his longer one, taking him in hand ("It's okay, I'm on the Pill") and inside her, kissing him over her shoulder, and he let himself go, as completely as he ever had, feeling himself embraced as he never had been before. (Hot piss-yellow halo surrounds this scene, conceals it from my view, basic creepiness of picturing your parents fucking. "Sir, I cannot conceive you." "Sir, this young fellow's mother could." But this is not the moment. On the page, they are avatars, not my parents, of anyone's sex, of my own. Look into the light.) When it was over, she rolled to her feet and put the record back on, starting from the beginning, and got back into bed with him, pressing her breasts against his back, arms wrapped around him, cool flesh and hot flesh, in the autumn of the Sixties, underground. He was asleep before the end of the first song.

It's life's illusions I recall
I really don't know life at all

HOW LONG IS NOW

Her face flickers in and out of view: it's midday back home and she's got a show tonight. A tonight that comes after my tonight, which is concludiing my time in Berlin, inconclusive, the novel still unfinished, if anything more unfinished than when I arrived. We are arrested by the unspoken, by ordinary weirdness, kidding back and forth, pretending not to pretend. Dad is useful, I can blame my strangeness on him. He's in a rehab facility in New Jersey where they sit him up on the side of the bed, trying to learn to do with his arms what he used to do with his legs, buttocks, back: to sit up. Sister and stepmother stand in abbreviated constellation around him, dark star crushed beneath the sheer weariness of the ordinary thoughtless things like using the toilet that now require foresight and planning. A shower can take half the day. How am I helping, you ask? By staying the hell out of the way.

She looks tired, tired of single-mothering it. How must I look in my midnight euphoria, propped against the background of someone else's books, wincing from the crick in my neck? An hour ago Shane was here, glancing at spines, taking down a few titles in German, glancing at me over her shoulder with an unreadable, challenging expression on her face. *What are you going to do about it?* What am I going to do about anything? Unfamiliar angles of her cheekbones, quirk of her lips, The Pixies racketing like tin ghosts from the phone in the back pocket of her jeans. *You think I'm dead, but I sail away….*

It's the angle I'm sitting at, probably, on this futon with the consistency of wet concrete and a single lumpy pillow like a sack of flour. Blue Prussian night pressing down on the work flat's windows and somewhere in the building's depths a sound like a baby's howl. My wife is in the kitchen, sunlit, stretching.

"What are you doing now?"

"Cleaning. I never stop cleaning. And getting ready for my voice lesson." She sings me a scale. Even over the miles on a shaky connection with one shitty speaker the church-bell ring of her soprano comes through.

"Beautiful," I say, meaning it. She flicks this aside.

"My voice teacher says I have to unlearn everything, but not right now, not in the middle of the show. I have too many bad habits. So right now we're just doing damage control, and when it's all over she's going to go to work on me. Like a gut-rehab."

"Your voice has great bones," I say. "How's our girl?"

"She asks about you sometimes."

"That's good, I suppose. Right? Tell her I miss her."

She sings another scale: "I will I will I will I will I *will*."

"What you're doing does sound scary," I tell her. "Like you have to give up your voice to get it back."

"That's exactly how it feels." Her eyes, if we were together, would now be searching mine, that tiny back and forth flicker of the pupil assessing my actuality, and hers. Now they slide away from her phone's little lens. "Are you going to miss your friend?"

Don't guess which friend. Keep it light. "Not as much I miss *you*." Trying to make up with emphasis what we're missing everywhere else. Distance. Skin.

My wife dismisses friendship with an elegant dismissive roll of the fingers of her left hand. I control with an effort the impulse to look away, to drop the screen. "Are you excited about Morocco?"

Our fears sleep in separate bedrooms. She's worried about Ebola and dark-eyed maidens. I'm worried about hashish and sharp knives.

"Can't wait." Burroughs to Kerouac, April 1954: *Whenever I encounter the impasse of unrequited affection my only recourse is in routines.*

"And your father? Have you talked to him?"

I shrug. "The same."

"I called him yesterday," she says. "Or at least I tried. It costs him so much energy to talk. Your sister put the phone up to his ear and I told him we were thinking of him all the time. That we love him."

"Thanks for doing that."

"When was the last time you talked to him?"

"As you just pointed out," I say after a pause, "he can't really talk yet."

"He can listen."

"Really?" I say, playing bitter. "I wonder what's changed."

"Everything." Her eyes scan the screen in search of mine. "I'm only going to say this once. He's your father. The only one you've got. It's a miracle he's still with us."

"Some miracle."

"I know it's hard, but you're thousands of miles away. Isn't that a safe enough distance?"

"I'll call him, okay? I'll call him right now."

Emily sighs. "Please don't turn me into your mother."

"She's dead and my dad's a cripple. What else am I supposed to do?"

"Nothing." Her face is closed. "Nobody's asking anything of you. And you can't say 'cripple' anymore."

Oy. "So we're done here?"

"Finished." Rueful, rigid. "Safe travels. Have fun."

"You bet. Love you." The screen goes dark.

Three weeks in the bubble of solitude that a few minutes of screen time aren't enough to pierce. Shut my eyes to the blankness of the room. Dream of travel, insertion and extraction into contexts I leave virtually unmarked. On a beach as if thrown there. In the distance walking the margin between dunes and water a woman in a black and yellow dress walking away from me, hands trailing by her sides, dark hair comma'd by the wind. Is it Shane? Is it my wife? Following after, shaking off a voice insinuating my ear: *on a wave of mutilation.* Without looking at it I feel myself slipping inside the trough of the sea sliding away, presaging the tsunami of my recurring dreams. The sand sucks at my feet. The woman isn't getting any closer but I see her glancing out to sea and her profile catches at my heart. That sharp black brow. The wave is coming for us, the sky is blank. I pass one of the inverted horseshoe crabs I used to encounter as a child on the beaches of Maine, terrifying me with its shattered primordial clockwork insides.

This one's still alive, somehow dragging itself up the beach in spite of being on its back, too many legs waving in the air, pointed tail drawing a long straying S in the sand. The woman has stopped as though waiting for me, I can almost touch her with my outstretched hand. Then the wave is on us. We are tossed stiffly like dolls; we are dolls, short of joints, like the action figures I used to toss in the deep end of our swimming pool when I was ten. This tiny shredded segment of something. Fifty-two pickup. I'm in the pool with Bernice, the department store mannequin my mother used to dress as a flapper and kept in an alcove of the house as a kind of joke. Blank face, coquettish crook of the elbow. I'm tangled with her in the black water, without breath. The crab's going home.

They say in dreams every person you meet is a projection of yourself. But surely some selves are more porous, commodious, unlordly than others. If there's an afterlife it must consist entirely of scenes from one's own life—the filmlife flashing before your eyes, protracted by the dying consciousness into a subjective eternity. Hell is other people? No. Hell is other people deprived of their otherness, reduced to shades and shadows of your own blinkered inescapable self. Wherever you go, there you are. And heaven? Heaven must be forgetting, a fall into imagery without origin, a permanent slideshow of beloved faces that do what only the not-self can do : recognize and claim us for their own. Heaven cuts the silver cord of memory and turns it into dreams.

Daylight grays the room. I want to resist it, to turn my

head aside from the wild dark of psychology. Surely we are not so trapped and solitary in our skulls. Surely there is more to my mind than my body. If my father comes through this, will he know that? Believe it? Is it only the perishable that offers hope, in the network of sheathed cells branching and radiating from the spinal cord, fist opening in the gut, quivering from fingertips, not limited by the skin, partaking of the smoothness or roughness of the air, its temperature, smells, the last image imprinted on the retina linked by imperceptible means to the first light of the first moment of life, red light of the womb, blue light of the hospital, white light of the nursery, green light of the sea, yellow light bathing the faces of long-forgotten schoolmates who have already met or will meet their separate ends but for this convulsive moment are parts of a living world with its pets, its insects, its grilled-cheese sandwiches, its textbooks, its allusions to the Spanish Armada, its first kisses, capillary expansions in the cheeks to register the heat of being seen, reflected in others' eyes, who circling now elliptically the fallen consciousness offer the best hope I can imagine of glimpsing the eyes of…? To be finally fully seen with the body of history behind you? What happens when that cord is cut?

Burroughs from the trap of his personal rot-hole: "the purpose of writing is to make it happen." To make something happen in the mind of the reader, his reader. A stroke in defiance of the seemingly impermeable barrier between mind and Mind, mind and other minds, mind and history, life and matter. Magic, most simply, changes the mind. Ritual magic brings others into the circle. But if the magic only happens when we are alone?

Cut-up voices. Burroughs writes to Ginsberg in 1960 from London: "Nothing is true. Everything is permitted." And: "COME OUT OF THE SHIT WORD THE FOREVER. ALL OUT OF TIME AND INTO SPACE. FOREVER."

Texting back and forth with Shane, whom I'm leaving behind, probably forever. *Didn't you like me?*

I liked you fine, I type. *I still like you.* And when she says nothing: *What happened to the film?*

A kind of digital shrug. *Viktor has left Germany, and Olga went to Munich. I don't know where it is.*

If they still want to sell it they should come to Tangier, I write. *There'll be lots of folks there who'd be interested. They could auction it off, I'm sure.*

I knew you didn't really like me.

The glass brick weighs down my hand as I sway and swing on the S-bahn for the last time, airport bound. I flinch to my sister's text: *Dad asked for you yesterday.*

And underneath that, what I wrote an hour later boarding the flight to Tangier: *How does he seem? What else does he say?*

Three dots like the tail of a thought. Rain slashes against windows and I try to picture her, my sister in the California night sitting upright and correct in a hospital chair, listening to the ticking and beeping machines, tapping silently at the glass with her thumbtips. His body recumbent, broken, imperfectly concealed by sheets, tubing, metal, breathing.

He can't talk very well yet. But I gave him my phone to write on.

Shane writes *Fuck you.*

A pause.

Don't be scared, says my sister.

My thumb hovers as the engines whine. And then in all caps the screenshot. Dad's words:

I WANT TO DIE.

I WISH IT
WAS THE SIXTIES

In delirious love, on the subway, in the classroom, coming everywhere into contact with her eyes, her body, her voice. The last days and nights of the Sixties pass them by, contact them glancingly: the Living Theater, Central Park be-ins, the imperceptibly increasing pressure of the Silent Majority, the countdown to Apollo 11. For the only time in his life he is living without a television. The city is enough, with her in it: waking in winter light at her place, padding yawning out the door and up the stoop and into the building up to his apartment to shower and dress, down again offering a friendly hello to the startled mask of Professor Gardner, he's off to work, in sportcoat and tie, eating an apple, taking the six blocks to the school at a trot, at that hour in that age the Upper West Side almost somnolent, last of the meat and flower trucks lined up at the bodegas, street people that he knows by sight to greets with a nod or a wave or—*gimme some skin*—a low five. Into the high door of the Boyleston School where he'll have maybe fifteen minutes in the faculty lounge going over his prep for the day before the students swirl in, identical tartan skirts, the eternal schoolgirl, giggles mostly ceasing when he steps in front of the board, calling the roll by memory—Clara, Lucinda, Charlene, Estrella, Jennifer B. and Jennifer C. He's on automatic, as though he'd been teaching for years, wondering where she is right now. Still in bed—her

work schedule to him is a mystery, she lies there all morning some days—or taking the subway, head high, with the
red neckerchief she sometimes wears that makes her look
a little like an air hostess, or typing a report in her grim
acoustic-tiled cell of an office (in spare moments composing a poem, a song, a little paragraph of wondering about
her life), or with one of her marshals down on the Lower
East Side preparing to bust some hapless evader. He gets off
work at three and comes to meet her in Midtown, where
standing on a planter he looks out for her in the streaming crowd, eyes ready to be caught by the flash of red at
her throat, her sly smile, mouth meeting his. Home hand
in hand like schoolkids, up to his place or down to hers
to cook an inexpensive ethnic dinner—hotdogs and potatoes lavished with paprika and steamed on the stove—or
else out on a double date with one of her girlfriends, most
of them outer borough girls like her, their newly acquired
chicness in hairstyle and nail polish matched by the cuf-
flinks and heavy watches of the sleek sharklike Manhattan boyfriends they had conjured for themselves, every
last one of them destined for a partnership and a house
in Westchester; or else complemented by the scruffy attire
and long hair of another kind of boyfriend, shaggy draft-
card burning would-be Dylans perfecting their sneers. At
these dinners he is conscious of himself as a Midwesterner,
a hick, and rushes to fill the space in himself this creates
with questions about the others. He's good with people;
he can talk to anybody. When he walked out of Florsheim
he was one of their most successful salesmen and Salman,

his short sweaty boss, had physically blocked the exit as part of an attempt to convince him to stay. More than once they've gone out with Hank and Peter—fast friends by now, they talk to each other for hours about their upbringings and foibles, a sort of mutual lay analysis, begun at dinner and continued until late at night at one or another apartment, she had a water pipe and the four of them would sit around smoking it, the hash making Hank and Judy more and more voluble even as it inclined Peter and himself toward dreamy silence. Only later it would occur to him that Hank had presented her with a misleading impression of his family, what they were really like—Hank the bohemian outlier to a staunchly conventional tribe of Jewish American materialists. Nor did he realize that her lifestyle, her habits—the late hours, the cigarette butts everywhere, the dishes stacked in the sink, the general atmosphere of funk and languor—were not fungible, temporary phenomena but integral to the structure of the woman he now found so mysterious and alluring but would someday find inscrutable and infuriating. After all they lived apart as much as together, and if he couldn't dispel with a joke or smile the black mood that sometimes radiated from her he could always retreat upstairs to his own place, bearing with the equanimity of his momentary virtue the stony glare of Mrs. Gardner or the implicit opprobrium of his letters from home demanding more information about this peculiar girl from God knows where. Moods: they came over her swiftly and without apparent provocation. He'd find her sitting on the floor of her tiny bathroom crying and when he knelt

down to hold her she started hitting him hard on the shoulders and chest until he got up and walked into the bedroom
and stood in front of the mirror, pulses pounding feeling
absurd. Finally he stalked out again, out of the apartment
and out of her life, to find his phone ringing when he got
upstairs and her voice on the other end, so gentle: "Come
back down." Down he went, bewildered and angry, only to
find her standing there in the center of the apartment, feet
together, arms at her sides, eyes downcast, like a dancer at
the start of a performance. Before he realized it, she was in
his arms, her cheek on his shoulder, and the heat leaping in
his chest drove the cold edge of his anger away.

Whenever her period started she'd call in sick, having somehow persuaded her supervisor that she was the
sufferer of something chronic, and spent the day in bed,
leafing through magazines or a trashy novel, smoking her
cigarettes, listening to the radio, or just lying on her side
and looking out the window. Which, since her apartment
was in the basement, merely looked out on another wall.
Growing up with a houseful of sisters he thought that he'd
learned a thing or two about women's bodies and women's
moods, but there was something strange and impenetrable about hers—the crying jags, the downward twist of the
mouth—that seemed of a piece with her aura of European
exoticism. Sometimes the strange word *Jewess* flitted unbidden through his mind. Though he'd spent his first dozen
years on the South Side, he was a suburban kid at heart;
she was a creature of the city, its changeability, its smoke
and steel, confident even in its griefs, in a way that held her

outside himself, though intimate, a part of the city through which he glides. What she saw in him he could not guess, or did not try. It was enough to be near her or, having been spurned, to be recalled to her side. She was a force to be negotiated with, elemental, and he bent himself to the task, while on some level deeper than imagination a future took shape.

When did the proposal happen? In late December, or at the end of November, or a week or so after New Year's Day. Walking past a jeweler's on Broadway, his eye was drawn to a woven white gold ring that he purchased the next day for the entire contents of his savings and thrust into his pocket, ready for the right moment. I don't get to see this moment, or even to imagine it, this moment without living witnesses. But in my mind it is one of the shards of the last year of the last heroic decade: the spring, summer, fall, or winter of 1969. These are the sharp edges of a personal history, so close to mine but not mine: the meadows of New York, before conception, before New Jersey, outside of history. Dad spiraling into his marriage, his life, as I spiral farther out of mine.

III
THE METAMORPHOSIS

THE MUTTERING
SICKNESS

From the plane, the outskirts of Tangier sprawl below me. Hundreds of boxlike buildings, white walls, a few red roofs, not a lot of green. Clouds cast calm shadows on seemingly random acts of development. I look around at my fellow passengers, a mix of Mediterranean tans, blacks, and browns. I see a man I had noticed in the airport waiting area clad in a spotless white djellaba and tarboosh, wearing what look like huaraches from which his long toes protrude. He's traveling with a woman in a black hijab and veil that reveals only her eyes and eyebrows and elegant hands and a pair of what looks like expensive low-heeled Italian pumps. In spite of the cloth that conceals all but a few inches of her skin, I can see that she's at least a decade younger than her husband. They have two children with them, a boy and a girl in Western dress—the girl about eight in jeans and a jumper, the boy about five wearing Osh Kosh overalls, and the girl bosses the boy around. They sit with their mother in one row, the father sits in the row ahead of them, eyes forward, ignoring his family. Is this a religious seating arrangement, or just the vagaries of travel? The girl, who has beautiful dark eyes and braided hair, could be my own daughter. The boy squirms in the seat beside her and the mother leans across their bodies to do something, adjust a seatbelt maybe. She is disappeared though in public; I imagine her uncovered, not with her husband but with other women, in a festively decorated but windowless room somewhere, laughing, gossiping, sharing a pot of mint tea. Most of the other passengers, like her children, wear Western clothing. I too wear Western clothing. I am hurtling, low, like a stone skimmed across the surface of the ordinary toward the putative exotic: one jump, two jumps, three. Terror that may fade when my feet touch ground. For what feels like the first time in my life, I am going somewhere I can't imagine, marked as white, a human American man, a Jew, foreign with a foreign language lodged in my throat.

In the pass the muttering sickness leaped into our throats, coughing and spitting in the silver morning.

As we taxi to the terminal, I spy a trio of single-engine planes parked at the edge of the tarmac; one is upside-down, wheels in the air. I try to take this as a metaphor for my disorientation and not an ominous portent; I try not to see my sister's overturned car. It's a small airport with no jetway; we have to descend metal stairs onto the tarmac, which makes me feel like Kennedy deplaning at Love Field: *Dallas loves you, Mister President.* The air is mild and tastes of ozone. Two men in French-looking uniforms loiter by the main door; the older one exactly resembles Claude Rains as Captain Renault in *Casablanca*, down to the white gloves and mustache. Only his skin is dark brown—Rains/ Renault as native, the colonizer absorbed by the colonized. Inside the airport feels small, precarious, empty. I pass through customs without earning a glance and note that of the four immigration officers checking passports, one is a woman in the same uniform as the others, hair face and neck exposed. A modern country. I try to line up for her but get shunted to a bored pudgy-cheeked young guy who looks through, or past, me as I hand him my passport. "Bonjour," I say helpfully. He doesn't respond, just stamps the passport and hands it back to me, his eyes traveling over my shoulder. One of the other officers has stepped into the booth of the female officer and is speaking to her over her shoulder as she considers another passenger's passport; I am struck by the intimacy of his pose, his low voice and hers. He puts his hand on the back of his chair as he all but whispers to her. The family from the plane is waiting patiently for them to conclude their discussion; I can't see the veiled eyes of the young mother. What does she think looking at this woman in the uniform of the modern state? Does she feel envy, pity, indifference? The scene passes; I pass. Her husband has noticed me glancing at his wife and I feel his eyes burning the back of my neck. But when I look back one last time he's staring straight ahead, stroking the ends of his mustache with two fingers, standing in a circle of privacy orbited by his children and wife.

My phone bangs around in the cargo pocket of my trousers, beating time against my left knee, a heavy glass conscience. There have been no new texts from home. I picture Dad groaning his way through physical therapy, clinging desperately to a metal bar against which he's supposed to brace himself with the muscles that still function, and struggling to fully inflate his lungs against the metal webwork reinforcing his shattered ribcage. Or maybe he's sleeping now, eyes darting back and forth beneath thin lids, floating on an opiate cloud. Or maybe he's just sitting up in bed, staring straight ahead, confronted by the new distance between head and toes, a distance he will never again cross. His body is a ravaged landscape, despoiled but not deserted by consciousness. It's not that I can't imagine his suffering. I don't want to.

Beyond passport control there's a murky high linoleum hall with a kind of café or kiosk crammed into the far corner of it, and there, sitting in a close gawking knot with their luggage heaped about them, my colleagues from the college are waiting for me. The four of us form a sort of troupe or band, two of us writers, two of us musicians, united for the purpose of performing pieces inspired by the life and work of William S. Burroughs. Four white men on the sliding scale of middle age, half out of our minds already with the otherness of Morocco, and the giddiness of re-enactment. Eager to touch ourselves the city that touched Burroughs, city of legend, the Interzone. I name us for the Beatles-like dynamic that sets in the moment I'm in hailing distance. John, the mastermind and inventor of our little band is the Burroughs scholar in rimless glasses, restless, always physically and mentally in motion. George is the tallest and the most talented musician, on his own dreamy wavelength, his head haloed by graying blond hair, always a few steps ahead of or behind the rest of us as we drift through Morocco. Ringo the clown, theatrical, laughing at himself and us. The oldest of us, as it happens, and the only one with previous experience of Morocco dating back to his mid-Seventies youth (when he might well have crossed paths with cousin Hank). He is gifted with an unexpected lightness of touch, keeping the beat. I'll be Paul if you like: the cute one, the sentimentalist, the face.

We exchange handshakes and hugs. "You must be exhausted," I say, for they've flown straight from Chicago, without having had my weeks to acclimate to Euro-African time.

"Yeah, but I don't feel it," Ringo says. "*So* stoked to be here."

"Amazing!" says George.

John takes me aside. "How's your dad?"

I don't know how to answer him. John's own father died recently after years of physical and mental ill-health. At roughly the same time, his wife lost first one parent to a car accident and the other to cancer. He of all people can understand what it means to care for a once-vital parent, to bear witness to their rage and humiliation in the face of irreversible decline. Is that why I can't meet his eyes?

"He's okay," I say to him. "I mean, as well as can be expected. He's receiving excellent care."

John searches my face, files whatever he finds away, and turns while nodding to face what surrounds us: North Africa, the fist of Tangier thrust simultaneously into the most ancient and the newest of seas. He lifts his arms to it, in benediction and astonishment: we're all feeling it. Africa.

"This is crazy," John says as we walk outside the airport, waving his hands to take in the electric blue sky, the surging crowds of people, the motorbikes and battered cars hurtling within inches of each other. We are immediately swarmed by taxi drivers, and pick or get picked, by a large smiling mustachioed man in an army jacket. He piles us into one of the ubiquitous, dilapidated Mercedes that make up the bulk of the grand taxi fleet in this country (the petit taxis are ancient Toyotas and Datsuns). We bounce around the stripped interior of the car, hurtling onto the ring road, though we have yet to give the driver a destination. John is looking at his phone.

"Are we going to the hotel?" The conference doesn't begin for three days. We had talked back in the States, vaguely, excitedly, of taking some sort of tour or side trip beforehand. To Marrakech. To Casablanca. The thought fills me with sudden weariness: I long for the anonymity of a hotel, for air conditioning, for a well-made bed.

"I've got a surprise for you," John tells me. The others grin and nod. "Tell him to take us to the train station."

I'm the only one who speaks a little French; in my more paranoid moments, I think this is the only reason I've been invited into the group. "*Nous allons à la gare, s'il vous plaît.*"

"*Oui, monsieur.*"

"We're going to Joujouka," John says. "It's all arranged."

"Holy shit!" High fives all around.

Joujouka is a village in the Rif Mountains where Burroughs and Paul Bowles both spent some time, as did Brian Jones and his own little band, the Rolling Stones. It's the home of the Master Musicians of Joujouka, a legendary group of traditional musicians and healers. Ornette Coleman recorded with them; Brion Gysin hired them to be the house band in a Tangier restaurant that he owned. Burroughs called them "the four-thousand year-old rock band." John had spoken of the possibility of our being able to see them while we were planning the trip, but I had dismissed it as another one of his wild speculations.

"It's all arranged. There's this Irish guy who's their manager, and the conference organizers got in touch with him and arranged for some of us to come to the village for a special performance. We'll stay all night as guests of Joujouka. They'll play for us. It's going to be amazing."

"Wow."

The outskirts of the city are crammed with what looks like new construction, dozens and hundreds of concrete pillarlike buildings—most of them half-finished, construction sites indistinguishable from demolition sites. Cranes and rebar and cinderblocks thrusting everywhere out of the earth like teeth. The city proper, *la ville nouvelle*, seems modern enough, contoured and sloped by hills; the edge-of-land light reminiscent of San Francisco, though the architecture we pass strikes me as colonial, Mediterranean, a hodgepodge of the styles of the powers that once were: Spanish, French, British. There are minarets, of course, utilitarian in appearance, made of concrete like everything else that postdates the International Zone, with perfunctory arabaesques of green and black snaking the walls, and loudspeakers protruding from the top. The days of the muezzin climbing to the top of the tower and calling unassisted to the faithful must be long gone.

We wait for the train in the high-ceilinged largely empty station populated by pigeons and a pair of soldiers that flank a single policeman, stalking the few waiting passengers on their endless languid looping patrol, submachine guns only one flick from readiness, left hand resting on top of the barrel, right hand around the grip, finger on or near the trigger. Guns frighten me in any context, on the hips of American cops as much as in people's bedrooms and glove compartments, so it's particularly unnerving to actually be in the sights of these weapons as they pass by, to pick out the round black eye of a gun aimed directly at my midsection. The government of Morocco is an official ally of the U.S. in the so-called War on Terror. King Mohammed VI, whose portrait (saturnine in a dark suit, perched with studied casualness on the edge of his throne) is everywhere. He is a secular leader with a strong vested interest in suppressing radical Islamist and jihadist elements, particularly those that might come from traditional enemy Algeria, Morocco's neighbor to the east. These men with their guns supposedly stand between us and the fanatical young men who would blow people like us up, hold us for ransom, decapitate us on YouTube. But it's hard to suppress an impulse to put one of the station's marble columns between me and the soldier's weapons every time they pass by.

We sit on our small pile of bags in a dusty corner of *la gare*, sipping strong coffees from the station café. Already each of us has fallen into a portable screen of some kind: John is reviewing our travel plans, George is emailing home, Ringo plays Candy Crush. Me, I'm making up for lost time, after weeks in Berlin spent writing nothing.

When the time comes, we board the train—clean, modern, comfortable, first class. There are other conferees aboard who have signed on with the mysterious Irishman's Joujouka tour; we share our compartment with an Australian trance-music specialist and an American rock-n-roller turned academic (a more familiar type than you might expect), both fervent Burroughsians. Passing and mixing among the other compartments, I am introduced to some other travelers and hangers-on; it's a male-dominated crowd but there are a couple of female academics: a young Taiwanese-American media theorist and a zaftig middle-aged filmmaker, sitting with the rock 'n roller's dewy blonde girlfriend. Also present is Gabriel, a dapper Englishman in a snap-brim fedora and scarf, generally acknowledged to be the world's leading scholar of Burroughs's work and one of the organizers of the conference in Tangier. It's a giddy combination: the strangeness of the landscape sliding by outside (trash-strewn scrubland dotted with half-finished houses, hills, farms, herds of goats, vineyards, drainage ditches, men in djellabas and women in hijabs walking slowly in fields or across ridgelines) and the familiarity of the atmosphere inside, which is like that of the hotel bar at any academic conference I've ever been to, minus the alcohol.

A conversation takes shape about Burroughs's relationship to celebrity: "Why did he do that thing with David Bowie?" "It was an advertisement for himself." Topics include Burroughs's loneliness, his desperate need for a "routine receiver," the reader whom he conflated with the loved one in his letters to Allen Ginsberg. His sharply conservative slightly antiquated ways of dressing—Gabriel's is a good imitation, though he foregoes a tie. "Like Harry Dean Stanton in *Repo Man*," I offer; "Great film!" the others chorus. *Cops dress kinda square... It helps to be mistaken for a cop.* Burroughs, Beckett, Harry Dean: thin men wizened before their time, borrowing Death's authority with which to penetrate the underworld. Orpheus's tailor.

"I'm fascinated by someone so perfectly inhuman," says the media theorist.

"Don't believe the hype," says the trance-music specialist with gauges in his earlobes.

"I mean someone with such a powerful yearning toward inhumanity. Someone with such an advanced death drive."

The trance-music specialist sits up a bit straighter. "You've got it ass-backwards if you'll pardon the pun."

"What pun?"

The trance-music specialist sighs. "You're mistaking the social death of queer people for half-baked Freud. Burroughs spent his whole life trying to feel alive in ways that a straight society denied to him."

"I still don't see why it's a pun," says the media theorist. "Anyway, I'm not interested in the real Burroughs, as if there ever were such a thing. I'm interested in the image he projected, and the afterlife of that image in modern culture. I don't want to spoil my paper for you..."

"Go ahead," the trance-music specialist says drily.

The rocker interrupts. "The real question is how the culture manages to assimilate such a foreign body. How does the rebellion of someone like Burroughs and the other Beats—"

"Burroughs wasn't a Beat," harrumphs the documentary filmmaker. "That's just *branding*."

"How does rebellion against society end up by becoming a prop to that society?" the rocker persists. "'Jack Kerouac wore khakis,' remember that?"

"Burroughs wasn't selling anything."

"The hell he wasn't!"

The pot simmers without boiling. For all our investment in the life and work of an infamous drug addict, pederast, and wife-murderer we show ourselves to be a disciplined, decorous, almost Puritanical bunch. Gradually, the regular rhythm of the train overtakes the disconnected hyperbole of the argument: one by one my fellow travelers open books or laptops, or close their eyes. The train lurches to its pauses at little platforms like islands in the green debris of this country. New passengers board, some in traditional clothing and some looking like they just stepped off the Champs Elysée. A little girl with a white bow in her hair looks in at us, yanked along by a mother in a conservative but stylish claret-colored dress. Clink of the tea cart passing by. John, George, and Ringo have all yawned themselves to sleep.

Hills high to the south—valleys and plains to the north—we're following the edge of the Atlantic, hazy sun sweeping the waves, passing villages of dust. The ancient name for Morocco, *al-maghrib*, meaning "west," derived from the verb *gharaba*, "to depart, withdraw." Onetime edge of the world, facing the wall of sea. The shells of houses straddle red earth hills, black trashed gullies, grasses, blue plastic bags sprouting from spindly branches of stunted trees. People and children fly by, following paths in the hills. An old man in a brown djellaba stands wizardly in his peaked hood atop a ridge following the train with his body, a figure out of time, raising his arms in silent benediction or commendation like the silent Auditor in Beckett's play *Not I*. Hills on either side crowd in the train, creating a sense of enforced intimacy. *Africa*. Hushed English accents, Americans, Australians.

Birds take flight—the first birds I've noticed. Black and white plumage, maybe herons. The farmland that appears is well tended and clear of the profuse trash that lines the tracks in thick almost orderly lines. Flocks and herds, vineyards—wine no doubt produced for export. We could be in Italy—the chilly impoverished Etruscan Italy that D.H. Lawrence loved, before the coming of Futurism and the Fascists. Buzz of the life force rooted in the soil and air. Flickers of pre-modernity. But every shepherd has his cell phone; I see one djellabaed man leaning on a fence post with his glass rectangle pressed to his ear, eyes disinterestedly tracking the train.

Cows, stark black and white, browsing by a train platform. A row of pointed trees in the distance. A boy in a bright pink windbreaker, a disconsolate herder of sheep. More signs of construction. Is it poverty or something more complex, some process of transformation arrested by our passing glances? The King, the rocker tells us, is investing heavily in infrastructure, people-pleasing, trying to stay ahead of the Arab Spring. The vegetation is lush and ragged by turns. Passing or piercing a low lake. Palm trees, mounds of rubble. Lushness of Assilah. Red poppy-like flowers. Surf.

Two young women, heavily made-up, hair and faces fully exposed, wearing knee-length skirts, lug suitcases past the compartment window. No one pays them any mind. Modernity embeds itself in the torn-up landscape, which stoically ignores it.

Sun starts to set, bright orange haze kindling eastern hills. Trees now, ranging up and along the hills, not quite a forest. An orange grove. Tuscan light.

People walking on the earth, without roads or paths, walking steadily and purposefully in the landscape that is theirs. I leaf through a paperback of *The Spider's House*, Paul Bowles's sequel of sorts to his far more famous novel, *The Sheltering Sky*. It describes Fez in the run-up to Moroccan independence, the arrogant lazy detached narrator Stenham deprecating the life of the committed. "They are there, of it," he muses, "and I am here, of nothing, free."

Staring at the blinking cursor on my laptop, wincing at the hash I've made of my novel, typing up a few notes on Burroughs, staring at nothing. I open a new document, the blank whiteness of the screen a void I try to spoil. Vacuum abhorred by words.

The light winds down in the western sky, glimpses of the Atlantic gone goldenrod, the discarded-looking wind-swept beach towns, a few donkeys, a boy untangling a goat from a wire fence. The train slows; my disheveled and mop-topped companions are waking up, rubbing their eyes, replacing their glasses on their noses. I type, furiously, one last sentence before shutting my laptop with a snap. The next stage is here.

THE SIXTIES END

She was a woman with a job that could have become a career, a life in government service. With her talent for languages (she spoke French, German, Hungarian, and a bit of Spanish) and inquisitive mind she might have become a professor, or a translator at the U.N., or a journalist, a teacher, a writer. Second-wave feminism was in full swing and there were fewer obstacles than ever before in the path of imaginable lives. On a commune in the Pacific Northwest, in a women's collective on Martha's Vineyard, on a farm in Ecuador, or simply New York, always New York, city of her dreams, where she already had established for herself a foothold, an anchor, a point of view. With her critical eye and indiscriminate appetite for books she might have become a second Susan Sontag; with a little more distortion, a Patti Smith. She could have been anyone. So why did she become my mother? Why did she, having married once for the purposes of escape, marry again? And why did she marry *him*?

Fear, implanted by her parents, implanted by their experience, her experience, the fundamental instability of the world, the possibility that had been disclosed to her of everything and everyone she knew simply going away. The atavistic fear that leads a woman to attach herself to a man, as Ishmael grasps the coffin of Queequeg after the Pequod goes down: a form of security, a clinging to existence. Let life happen later but for now, simply float. She floated for twenty years, their whole marriage, for the rest of her abbreviated life.

If not fear, what then? Love? Love for this goofy, gawky, not unhandsome galoot from the Midwest, striding at right angles away from his parents' dreams? He had attractive qualities: he could at least once in a while draw out and realign the iron filings of her moods and depressions, was always moving or making plans to move, a slightly awkward but never inhibited dancer. If she proposed to him a new movie or gallery or restaurant, even in a neighborhood then unfathomable, practically off the map—a Puerto Rican place in Washington Heights, a then-exotic sushi restaurant just off the West Side Highway—his answer was always, Yes. Maybe she was the one trapped inside the coffin, afraid of life, and he was the one knocking at the door inviting her to come out. Maybe they invented each other, from a distance that closed rapidly, two volatile elements that might find or make in one another a kind of stability, a picture that could last. Maybe. The voice of conjecture, the voice of the Unnamable, coming between them, me, us: *I'll ask no more questions, there are no more questions, I know none any more.* Did she think it would last forever, their brownstone idyll, her in her garden apartment and him in his miniature penthouse, meeting and parting and meeting again always centered on her bed? *It issues from me, it fills me, it clamors against my walls, it is not mine, I can't stop it, I can't prevent it, from tearing me, racking me, assailing me.* Did she look back with nostalgia on their salad days from the house in New Jersey, the houses, the suburban meetings and greetings, the travels to France and Italy and England always home again, or did she look back with something resembling horror, disgust, astonishment: the role I've played in what I've become? *It is not mine, I have none, I have no voice and must speak, that is all I know, its round that I must revolve, of that I must speak, with this voice that is not mine, but can only be mine, since there is no one but me....*

No sailor can remain at sea forever and a day.

She said yes. By the time of the wedding, I was on the scene as proof of concept, in utero, as blastocyst or embryo, tail coiled under me, biological crossroads of two sets of Ashkenazi dreams selected nearly at random in the city of New York a year and a half before Nixon put an end to Bretton Woods and three years before the birth of my sister and four years before Nixon's resignation and five years before the fall of Saigon and six years before Son of Sam and President Ford in their different ways told the city to drop dead. But it's all over for us long before that, because my sister will be born in the suburbs after we've left the city behind to make its fate without us, city without which there could be no us, city in which, apparently, a happier us could not be. Wasn't. There's no wishing to have gone straight, no one to watch out for a simple twist of fate.

The photos radiate happiness, giddiness, a new start. I can't help wishing that for them, looking at it. For them and me and for us.

JAJOUKA, JOUJOUKA

El-Ksar el-Kebir has the ramshackle feel of a frontier town, sour tang of exhaust fumes mingling with the dust that somehow sharpen the colors, the many colors of the clothes of the men and women circulating in the streets, on foot and in horse-drawn wagons and leaning precariously on the running-boards of ancient cars and trucks. The Burroughsians pile out onto the platform and stare blearily about, looking for our contact, the Irish historian, bassist, and fixer who acts the Master Musicians' exploiter and protector; he's our ticket to Joujouka. Gabriel is on his cell phone; the others mill up and down in front of the station deflecting the attention of cabbies and touts. No sign of Nick or any other Westerner other than ourselves. The train pulls out, bound for points south—Rabat, Casablanca, Marrakech, who knows?

"Let's get a coffee," John decides. He and George and Ringo wear exhausted skins over febrile bones, the jet lag warring with the prickling unfamiliar. We cross the perilous street, pausing to pat the nose of an inquisitive horse, to a café where chairs and tables are arranged haphazardly on a sort of platform above the street. A widescreen TV shows soccer. Men in Western suits without ties sit with other men wearing djellabas, sipping tiny cups of coffee and tea. They show no interest in us, or in the small mob that has surrounded the knot of bewildered Burroughs scholars waiting across the way.

"*Café pour tout le monde*," I say to the waiter, a very old man in an untucked white shirt that appears to be a few sizes too big for him. He nods and withdraws.

"Where's your guy?" Ringo wonders.

"He'll be here," John says. "I just got a text from him. He says, and this is an exact quote, 'Delayed by sheep.' What do you think that means?"

"Exactly what it says," George offers. "That's what makes for traffic jams around here."

The coffee arrives, black and strong. John knocks his back and asks for another. The rest of us sip delicately.

"So explain to us again this Jajouka situation," I say.

"*Jou*jouka," John says. "You see, apparently there's been a kind of schism in the Master Musicians. They've been led by the same family, the Attar family, for generations. Back when Burroughs knew them, and Gysin and the Rolling Stones and all that, they were led by a guy named Hadj Attar. His son Bachir took over, but it seems that some of the Master Musicians didn't like his style and they wanted to elect a new leader. Bachir wasn't having any of it, so there was a split. He's the leader of 'The Master Musicians of *Ja*jouka.' The others, the ones that our guy helps to manage, are 'The Master Musicians of *Jou*jouka.' They spell it differently, but it sounds the same."

"In Arabic or in English?" George asks.

John shrugs: who knows?

"So which ones are the real Master Musicians?" Ringo asks.

John shrugs again. "Some of the folks from the conference didn't want to come here because they didn't want to offend Bachir. They see him as the authentic link."

"To what?" I ask.

John points with his chin. "He's here."

Four battered Mercedes have lined up in front of the station and members of our group are getting into them. A lanky, grinning man in a faded army jacket with a mop of black hair is moving back and forth and talking a mile a minute, sometimes to the conferees and sometimes to his drivers. He looks a little like Nick Cave. We pay our bill and recross the dangerous street to join them.

"Glad to meet you!" Nick says, shaking each of our hands and looking each of us in the eye. He speaks with a light brogue. "Fantastic that you could join us. Listen, you need anything, *anything*, while you're here, I'm your man." He waggles his eyebrows at us mock-conspiratorially. "I've done a count and you're the last, so let's get going!"

Nick packs us into the last of his fleet of half-ruined sedans: our driver, Jamal, speaks neither English nor French but talks to us anyway in a rapid smatter of Arabic and Spanish. He is, we later discover, one of the Master Musicians in person; there seem to be dozens of them and they are all brothers and cousins and nephews of each other. Riding shotgun, I try to put on my seatbelt but can't make it work; Jamal admonishes me with a finger-wag and a smile; perhaps I have insulted him by demonstrating such tactless concern for my own safety. Reluctantly, I let the seatbelt dangle, holding on to the buckle with one hand as a sort of talisman. The gearshift has no handle and Jamal risks impaling himself on the sharp point every time he changes gears; the dashboard is covered with what looks like dirty sheepskin. Nick folds himself into the lead car and the little fleet spins off, somewhat disconcertingly all in different directions. The four of us goggle about like mad at the diesel-scented streets. We roar past horse-drawn carts with people sitting on them crammed back to back, facing outward in a ring, legs dangling, some of them women in vivid purple and pink and orange hijabs and headscarves, like petals of some strange hothouse flower. People wander into the paths of oncoming vehicles without concern, sometimes with small children in tow. There are women in the streets and riding in the backs of wagons but the visible clientele of the many shabby cafes we pass are entirely male: men in djellabas and shirtsleeves and suits sitting in rows, staring out at the traffic. The town is a seemingly chaotic collection of nondescript off-white buildings, colored by the women's clothing and by the many market stands we pass displaying huge heaps of oranges, avocados, grapefruit. Jamal lurches cheerfully between first and third gears. A toothless man squats by a cage filled with squawking hopeless chickens; another stand presents as an open-air butcher shop with goat haunches pinned to a wooden rail. We dodge other cars, make abrupt turns, pass a row of market stalls where the universal smog is cut by scented heaps of bananas and tangerines, before barreling through the familiar horseshoe-shaped gate or *bab* of a low white wall. Suddenly, we are in the countryside: the town is gone, the traffic has evaporated, the others are far ahead of us, our car is alone on the earth.

The engine has no muffler and conversation is impossible; anyway, we are too busy snapping pictures of everything, including our own astonished faces. The sun is gone by now and the sky over the foothills of the Rif Mountains is a pearlescent purple. Wide-open rolling spaces, few trees, yet another herd of goats silhouetted against the sky. The car slows frequently and sometimes suddenly to avoid the numerous potholes and the brakes emit a high piercing squeal every time. Climbing higher, headlights on, turning off the main road onto washboard concrete, struggling up the grade past a few squat shadowy buildings. Low bushes, a few more rooflines: we have arrived in the Little Hills, in Joujouka.

We park or rather stop in the middle of the road beside a crumbling concrete wall with a blue corrugated-steel door fitted into it. Watched by a few young boys who have materialized from the shadows we pass through the door and down a winding path to a low house with a large open tent erected next to it, where we are met by a group of vigorous old men in traditional dress with beautiful angular planed faces that they present to us to be kissed in greeting: these are our hosts, the Master Musicians. *Salaam alaikum, alaikum salaam, shukran, shukran.* In the yard of the house wood has been laid for a bonfire; through the open door bright electric light illuminating a room that is somehow bare and elaborate at the same time with its whitewashed walls, colorfully cushioned benches, and rugs. A small, somewhat younger-seeming group of musicians is inside, singing and playing on a violin (held upright like a tiny cello) and on traditional drums, the tebel and the tarija. This is not the trance music we will hear later, the rhythms of which communicate a powerful *baraka* or blessing with healing powers. This is just for fun.

An intermission is arranged in which to get settled. John, me and a heavyset Englishman in a Nehru jacket whose arms seem too short for his body are led to the house of Tiktik, a Master with a striking resemblance to mid-period Marlon Brando. He will be our host for the night. George and Ringo are barracked elsewhere. Tiktik's house is a windowless white island in a sea of mud; stepping through the metal door we find ourselves in an open courtyard with three small trees growing in it, the minimum number needed for Tiktik's place to be called a *riad* rather than a *dar*, or house. There is a sheltered corner with benches, cushions, and a low table to which we are conducted and served mint tea, followed by coffee and a dry sort of cake. Tiktik serves us himself. There's no sign of his wife or of any other woman, though a couple of small boys scamper by. Tiktik sits between us as we talk, smiling and patting me or John on the knee paternally when he recognizes a word, but it's hard not to escape a feeling of awkwardness: we speak no mutual language yet he feels obligated to remain with us, part of a conversation in which he cannot fully participate. The history of colonialism interposes its long, awkward body between us—or maybe we simply don't make a sufficient effort to include him. Ignorance takes up space. Tiktik lights his pipe and takes a few puffs and the unmistakable odor of *kif* floats out into the courtyard. A giant beetle ambles by on its way from the moony shade of one tree to another.

The Englishman, a self-described "literary journalist," stuffs his own pipe with shag tobacco; his quiff of whitish hair and sly, sensuous eyes make him resemble a more heavyset version of the French literary critic Roland Barthes—another B, another frequent visitor to Morocco in pursuit of a sensual freedom denied him in the West. He surveys the scene and declares, "Burroughs wasn't an experimental writer, not really." Tiktik nods as if in agreement. "You can't be an experimentalist if you have no notion of what you are actually *doing*. He borrowed the prestige of scientific method but there was no science, you know, no science whatsoever. Yet he was *steeped*, positively steeped in the literary tradition. That's the only reason his work has any value."

The mingled aromas of different smokes perfume the air. "I've always cared about the work, not the persona or the legend," John says.

"How can you separate them?" I ask.

"I'm completely opposed to the romanticism of Burroughs the junkie sage or whatever," John says.

"Oh, I quite agree," puts in the Englishman.

"But the root of experiment is experience. How can you separate Burroughs's experience from the experiment of his writing? Don't you have to print the legend?"

"Experiment is a form of skepticism," John says. "I express my own skepticism by not working with received forms."

"I mean, if we don't care about Burroughs's life, his experiences, then why are we here in Joujouka?"

Tiktik, hearing a familiar word, looks up and nods and smiles at us encouragingly.

John leans back to take in the stars becoming visible above Tiktik's courtyards. "Because it's awesome, that's why."

Excusing myself to visit the bathroom which is no bathroom. Certainly no one could ever bathe there. You crawl through a tiny door into a tiled room with a hole cut in the floor and two grimy pedestals to stand or squat on. *I-you-me in the pissoir of present time.*

"To experiment means controlling the conditions," the British Roland Barthes is saying when I come back. "But Burroughs's conditions controlled him. He was an addict with a good education, that's all."

"Control is what it was all about for Burroughs," says John. "*Breaking* control. That's why he liked doing cut-ups."

"Yes, yes," the Englishman says impatiently, "but that wasn't even really Burroughs. That was Gysin."

"Burroughs was the channel, it all passed through him. The whole twentieth century."

"So he's become a museum piece."

"Well, there's Gysin's line, 'writing is fifty years behind painting.' Don't you think that's still true?"

"Yes," the British Barthes says thoughtfully, "only in place of 'painting' I suppose you'd have to put 'video' or 'performance' or 'conceptual art.' Maybe it's still true of painting as well."

"A permanent fifty-year lag," I say as if to myself. "What does that mean?"

"Burroughs expected writing to evolve beyond words," John says. "He wasn't sentimental about words and neither am I. What both of us wanted to destroy is *literature*. Literature is just dead and buried speech, a whited sepulcher. That's why most people prefer dead authors. The ones who've been dead long enough not to stink." He nods at me. "This is where we disagree. He's a romantic."

This is an old routine and I smile so that the British Barthes will see that. "Yes, I still want something from language, from literature, because literature is always pointing at something we can't quite have. John's answer is to burn it all down but I just keep chasing the horizon. Tomorrow never knows."

"One of you is very cynical," the Englishman says enigmatically. Tiktik arranges his face thoughtfully as he looks out into the courtyard. The *kif* smoke is thick and dizzying.

"All I know," I say, "is that the older I get, the more respect I have for what I don't understand."

The British Barthes points his pipe-stem at me. "Does that include yourself?"

Tiktik stands up and says something in Mahgrebi that we understand without understanding: Time to go.

On our way down to the village from Tiktik's *riad* the overweight Englishman, who has a swinging, almost drunken gait in spite of having taken no *kif,* slips and falls on the muddy path and sits there on his ass for a minute, cursing elaborately. We help him up and through the gate and down to the main house where six Master Musicians are playing and singing to a rapt audience of Westerners. George and Ringo wave to us sleepily. Nodding and winking to each other the Master Musicians, the youngest of which appears to be in his late sixties, pass the rhythm from hand to hand, drum to drum, flute to flute. The music is hypnotic, tidal, not so much unmelodic as melodically woven over spans of time that extend impossibly, almost geologically, building in slow intensities toward distant yet approaching peaks. The room is long and bare, with benches along the plain whitewashed walls and an open carpeted space in the middle; the Master Musicians play at one end and their guests, the Westerners, fill the other three sides. We have yet to see any women in the village, other than the white women attending the conference. The Master Musicians delight in inviting these women to dance, particularly the younger ones. What must they think of these shameless women with their uncovered necks and faces? Yet the vibe is far from lascivious, the smiles on the Master Musicians' faces open and delighted. A boy maybe eight years old with marvelously fluid hips stands up to dance, and a mustachioed old man who's only a few inches taller than the boy, wearing a pink button-down shirt and gray sweater vest, wriggles bonelessly alongside him. The Master Musicians sing loopingly, raspingly. We are all grinning like idiots. After a pause for dinner—great heaping tajines of chicken and lamb, round loaves of bread called *kesra*, and liters of Coca-Cola—no alcohol of course—we head outside to the now-illuminated tent where fourteen more Musicians, wearing dark red robes, gold turbans, and gold slippers are lined up ready to play. Eight of them wield reedy high-pitched penetrating wind instruments called *ghaita* and the other six have drums: a *tebel* (played with sticks), four *tari-ja,* and a *def,* played with the hands.

Now the music begins in earnest. For hours they will wail away without pause, wordlessly, in rising and falling reedy rhythmic waves at an ever-increasing volume. We sit in a semicircle in front of them—off to one side in another corner of the tent are younger men, villagers, there to see the show or to see us or simply with nowhere else to go. The air is fragrant with *kif* and hashish, of which a number of the conference-goers partake. As the hours go by, some can't tolerate the rhythmic unbuilding intensity and have to wander off to catch their breath or to look up at the stars, which are numerous. Some of the jet-lagged stagger off for naps and come back with the music still going. People get up to dance, then sit down again, then get up again. I rest by a tentpole where Nick Cave is chatting up the media theorist.

"This music is sacred to Pan!" he shouts at her. He gestures broadly at the night wrapped shawl-like around the core of light radiating from the tent. "A few hundred meters from here is the cave of Bou Jeloud, the pre-Islamic goat god who bestowed the power of the *baraka* onto an ancestor of the Attar family and grants fertility to the village every spring."

"Where are the women?" the media theorist shouts back at him.

"Here and there," Nick says mysteriously. "Look!"

Three slender figures with scarves around their heads are dancing sinuously in front of the band. The men from the village are laughing. The media theorist gives them a hard look.

"Those aren't women!"

"You're right! You see, every year Bou Jeloud comes to the village to give fertility to its women. But he wants a wife in return! The villagers didn't want to give up any of their women, so they dressed up a boy as a woman instead, to fool him. Naturally, he's disappointed, but it works every year!"

The boys dance on, grinning shyly at each other.

"But will *we* see Bou Jeloud?" the media theorist asks.

"There!"

Someone has splashed the woodpile with kerosene and lit it and huge flames are forking the air. As the music surges to another crescendo a shadowy figure comes tumbling out of the darkness and capers around the bonfire with his knees flying high. It is a man in goat skins, with a peasant's straw hat hiding his face, wielding an olive branch in his right hand. He comes somersaulting across the grass, then runs up into the tent and whips the evil spirits out of us: children, young men, visitors. He whips the media theorist across her back and she leaps back shrieking, but with a delighted expression on her face. Joyous panic. Grinning, silhouetted, he does a high-stepping dance suggestive of hooves in front of all the Master Musicians before flying back to the bonfire. He is Bou Jeloud, the little god. Everyone is on their feet to dance with him. I think of Viktor in his gorilla mask, twist my head from side to side. Could he be here?

On the outskirts of the bonfire, barely visible in the shade of an outbuilding, I catch my only glimpse of the village's women, hunched in a little row with their wrists resting on their knees, their teeth gleaming in the dark. It's a show, we are the show. We are dancing, I am dancing. Lean shadowy forms. Eyes of Burroughs in the shadow of his hat. Smoke, drifting. Glint of the olive leaves as they shake, striking me blind.

Black beetles of Joujouka. Firelit on a hillside in the bowl of the Rif, Moroccan night. The dancing boys who are girls who are boys. What is ordinary, blank, bitter, in the divided village, Masters versus Masters, the young men bored and restless, the animals dumb as animals, stars in the sky, canted Orion, the music blasting us out of the tent, into the tent, shoeless on carpets, alive and everywhere, trespassing, at the end of the century of Burroughs, the century of Duras, the century of Dylan Thomas, the century of John Berryman? Predictions are hard. Three hundred years ago, one thousand years ago, "the four-thousand-year-old rock band." Bou Jeloud springs from the bonfire, somersaulting, blood and salt and skins. Streaks of light, museum spirit, one of the dozen consorts of Aisha-Astarte, great god Pan (who gives his name to PANIC, to the unspeakable realization that EVERYTHING IS ALIVE), first-person-shoot-er light rendering the North African night wavery, leaking stars, blind corners of bushes, horns and drums blasting *baraka*, unless the placebo effect works its wonders. Pre-Islamic Sufi dance out of time, standing Master Musicians like stolid minarets. Every sheep hangs by his own legs. Rumored ritual *sahar*, the casting of spells, *sukeel*, herbs combined to create a trance and open the subject to suggestion. With the other gobsmacked Westerners I am yanked out of my defensive crouch to caper with the goat-man, to feel his branch strike my shoulder, driving out the Ugly Spirit, out and onward, spirit driving writing out of restlessness. Oh goat god hear my prayer and give me the gift of rest in music, the silence that makes possible a sound. Sparks ascend, bodies sink. Because it's not "nature" whipping me with an olive branch in the night to drive out my demons. Bou Jeloud drives demons into me too.

Drunk on singing, we shake and swivel as the drums syncopate. A language I can't understand stitches us together. What do we want? POSSESSION. When do we want it? NOW.

Optimism, says the theorist Lauren Berlant, is cruel, another form of trauma. Optimism interrupts habit, because the spliff in my hand isn't part of a narcotizing routine but something other and unexpected. Because optimism promises that bad history will not, for once, repeat itself. Smoke rips me open with the possibility of something new. Wild eyes of the god in mine. I patch myself with stars.

Cliff edges all around us: the stage, the village, perched precariously on the lips of the mountains. One false step and I'm over the side, joining my father in the stark pain that resists oblivion.

Lying on the ground with the music behind me and beneath me, I hold my phone to the sky. There is, unbelievably, a signal. How far into the desert must I go?

Your father is a fighter, my stepmother has texted me, I don't know how many hours ago. But that's the last thing that he is.

On a rigid bed in Tiktik's house, I lie exhausted and sleepless in a tinnitus tunnel, getting it down. Flames pass through the back of Bou Jeloud's skull out his eyes into my eyes into my mind: *this black witch-shape against an orange background of fire,* Gysin wrote. Black overwhelming wave, mountain blocking out stars, cutting contact, the word-lines' consummation, the cruel perfection of dreams.

NEW YORK

"I'm pregnant."

Didn't it start like that? An ordinary morning in New York City, restless at her desk, jumping each time the phone rang while around her the grimy, colorless business of tax collection went on? What did they used to say, in the bad old days before you could pee on a stick, when the condom was forgotten and the Pill failed?

"The rabbit died."

He stood in her tiny kitchen with all its lights burning against the January dark, wearing the flowered apron he'd given her that she only wore for a joke, a succulent hash sizzling on the stove. He did that sometimes, cooked for her—snuck downstairs to her place to which he had the key with an armload of groceries, fixing up for her the simple dishes he knew how to make: a roast chicken in the inadequate oven, a pot of spaghetti and steam, burgers smashed flat on cast iron and served on toasted English muffins with sautéed onions and mushrooms on top. Later in life he became a gourmet chef. He learned how to cook all the Indian dishes Hank and Peter had introduced him to, threw fancy dinner parties with his second wife, and whipped up canapés and hors d'oeurves with feverish aplomb. But for now it was enough to make something, anything, to serve her, to feed her, to bind her more tightly to him. She came in through the door in her winter coat with her nose wrinkling at the smoke funneling up from the stove, to encounter across the countertop his eager kiss, stepping back squinting (she didn't wear glasses around him, not then, not yet) at the wreckage of plates, pots, pans, cans, gasping a little at the greasy heat, stripping off the coat and throwing it down (why not) onto the floor, putting her hands on her hips, looking up into his bewildering shaggy face. Said it.

Said it and studied him, no myopia now, on the balls of her feet. Everything his face did now, every shift in his weight, every realignment in his posture, mattered. She was braced. She did not, could not, know how this man—only a year younger than she but in that moment he seemed a child—would react.

He looked down. His pupils contracted. He took half a step back and lifted his face with his nostrils flared, lips writhing. It was the most fascinating, the most horrible spectacle she'd ever seen.

"But this is *wonderful*," he said. Still clutching a wooden spatula in his hand, he maneuvered around the little step-ladder she used to reach the higher shelves (she was a full head shorter) and swallowed her in his embrace.

She fought the panic down, forced her upper body to relax, though her legs were trembling. "You're sure?" she demanded. "You're sure?"

"I'm sure."

He knew about the abortion. She'd told him and he hadn't been shocked. He knew, he had to know, that they had options. She felt her chest pound against his sternum as his long arms enfolded her. Was he really such a fool?

"I love you."

She was in, all the way in. And he said, or she heard: *I'll take care of you.*

"The hash is burning," she said.

He cursed, whirled away from her, grabbed forgetfully at the pan, cried out, seized a towel, and used it to shove the cast iron pan off of the glowing coil. Turned on her sucking on his fingers where they'd been scorched, with the smiling eyes of a madman.

"Are you hurt?" She had a cigarette in her mouth and a lit Bic in her hand.

"Let's open some wine," he said, shaking his head at her question. "Let's celebrate! Let's get married!"

"Let's start with the wine," she said, laughing. Some part of her was giving way. He was so big in her tiny kitchen. He was a fool. His right hand was glaring red where the hot iron had touched. She loved him, all right.

She lit the cigarette and sucked smoke deep into her lungs.

"Let's," she repeated. Half-smiling. "Let's do."

MORNING
IN MOROCCO

The morning after Bou Jeloud is grainy, washed out, white. John and I meet wordlessly in the shadowy recesses of Tiktik's *riad* for a breakfast of coffee, honey, bread, and hardboiled eggs, served to us by a middle-aged woman, the first Moroccan woman we've seen up close, wearing a pink headscarf and a housecoat, little smile cracking what looks to be a habitually stern and reserved expression when we bashfully repeat our *shukrans*. One of the smaller boys we'd seen the previous evening comes yawning and scratching out of a doorway, and the woman hisses a stream of syllables at him; he stands there listening, without changing his expression, then retreats back through the door by which he entered. She flashes us the smile again, as though in apology, and leaves us be. John and I look at each other in wonder.

"Never anything like this," he says as if in response to a question.

"Never," I agree. We drink coffee out of clay bowls, warming our hands.

After breakfast we take our first look at the village in daylight: low houses stud the rocky, grass-strewn hillside. There is a walled-off area with "JAJOUKA" handwritten on a small sign above the gate. Louche, smiling, garrulous Nick Cave comes strolling out from under the shadow of one of the rare trees to tell us that this is the compound of Bachir

Attar. "Friendly, isn't it?" He points out the broken glass embedded on the edges of the walls. "Notice anything?" The glass comes from assorted vodka and whiskey bottles; you can still make out the Absolut logo on a few shards. "This is a *halal* village," Nick says in a serious tone. "But where did he get those, eh? And he calls *us* the infidels." More in sorrow than in anger, Nick shakes his head.

A boy drives a line of goats along the wall as we circle the compound out toward Bou Jeloud's cave; the animals step gingerly on the gravel and bleat at us, rolling their uncanny eyes. Nick points out the cave's location, down a slope of the hill across what I presume to be a creek or river. "He's probably sleeping it off."

But when we return, inevitably, to the low white house with the performance tent outside it and the black smear of ashes where the bonfire was, there's the old man in the same pink shirt and gray vest that I remember seeing on the previous day, and his face is unquestionably the same one I'd glimpsed under the brim of Bou Jeloud's hat. He presses his palms together and grins at us from where he and some of the other Master Musicians are sitting on the swept concrete porch of the house. In their white djellabas, sipping their cups of mint tea, they remind me of nothing so much as Southern planters gathered in some gauzy pre-Civil War tableau. Among them is a man I'd noticed the previous evening who with his darkly tanned skin I'd taken for Moroccan, in spite of the SLR camera he was wielding with considerable dexterity. It wasn't until I heard him cry a valedictory *Rock and roll!* at the height of the performance in a broad New Zealand accent that I realized that he was, in spite of his appearance, a Westerner, one of us. He is to accompany us on the next leg of our journey, across the center of the country to Fez, where he lives.

"The cars will be here in a bit," Nick informs us—George and Ringo, looking considerably more fresh than they had on the day of their arrival, have rejoined the group. "Why don't I show you the temple?" It resembles a *riad* with a courtyard open to the sky, walls crumbling, a pair of crooked trees at the center, one bent toward the other like a deaf man trying to hear. "People who need healing, who were possessed, the mentally ill," Nick explains, "were tied to these trees. The Master Musicians would play over there and flood them with *baraka* to chase the madness out."

"Does that still go on?" George asks.

Nick grins. "Of course."

The courtyard stands in a column of air, a column of white light. The trees, beseeching, tortured, bend their arms toward me. I shut my eyes. The Master Musicians are playing, bent to their instruments, spiraling breath into notes, beats, a regular human rhythm. Sprawled under the trees, in chains, the mad and the sick, beating their heads in helpless time. Out of the sky he falls, a dad of glass, shattering into a body from which he will never again take flight. He lies on the ground in pieces, in chains. The music assaults and assuages his incommunicative flesh. The face remote from the skull. The skull and shoulders and upper arms, the chest above the nipples, infinitely removed from belly and genitals, hips and thighs, knees and feet. All the king's horses and all the king's men. All the magic of the music, filling me with the clarity of my own emptiness. The logic is remorseless: I can still walk and my father cannot. Thousands of miles away, across the sea. My phone, glass ingot, weighs me down with the possibility of reconnection. I am not free.

Nick leads us into a cavelike interior chamber with a few prayer rugs and water-stained walls to which a chill damply clings. He indicates a donation box into which we dutifully stuff a few dirhams. I stand there alone for a moment after the others filter out, trying to feel the vibrations of the place, the way I've tried to feel other sacred places: cathedrals, national parks, cemeteries, the memorial tree in the Budapest ghetto where my mother was sheltered as a girl, the names of the murdered tied to its branches like so many silver leaves. But I feel hollow. Instinctively, I pull my phone from my pocket to check the time and notice, with something like relief, that last night's signal has gone. No one sees me. I am alone on the earth for what feels like the first time in years.

I snap a selfie in front of the madness trees.

On the train to Fez, Sandy the expatriate from New Zealand reveals himself as a leading candidate for Most Interesting Man in the World: broadcaster, actor, writer of political thrillers, playwright, stand-up comic, investigative reporter, NGO factotum in Africa and Asia, founder of a Buddhist monastery, a traveler who's been everywhere on the planet except the United States, now living in Morocco with his third wife in a Fassi *riad* that they restored themselves. He shares our compartment from Joujouka and tells us everything we need to know. Bargaining: let the merchant name a price, starting with an object you don't actually want, then shift to the one that you do, ask its price, offer one-third of what he's asking and work your way up to half. Demographics: count the satellite dishes to learn how many families live under a given roof. Cultural sensitivity: a story of how he replaced "Hallelujah" with "Un di li la" in a Leonard Cohen concert he once promoted in Fez so that the Islamists wouldn't freak out. Details about his life slip out—discovering at the age of fifty that he had been adopted at the age of three, and that his adoptive family had gaslit him about his former life, the memories he had of his birth parents, who had given him up when they divorced. "Are you Jewish?" he asks me unexpectedly, and I freeze up for a moment in the rain compartment, in the silver tube slipping its way southbound into the heart of the Maghreb. What makes him say that? I do not have, I don't think, particularly Semitic features—I lack the stereotypical schnozz. Dark hair, pale skin. Something about my mouth, maybe? My cheeks? My eyes?

"I grew up thinking I was Jewish," Sandy says with a disconcerting giggle. "I even wrote a play once that won an award for the Jewish Play of the Year. Can you imagine?"

"But you're not?" I say stupidly.

He laughs again, louder, so that it seems to ring through the entire train car, laughing at the universe and the joke it had played on him. "I knew from a young age there was something between me and my parents, something they would never tell me. I thought that maybe I was the son of Holocaust victims. You know, someone from the *Kindertransport*, and somehow I'd wound up in New Zealand instead of England. Turns out I'm just another bloody low church Anglican. And nowadays I'm a Buddhist, if anything. But a part of me will always feel Jewish."

And he isn't scared to be here, I thought enviously. He's scared of nothing and no one in this life.

"Did you ever find them?" I ask. "Your birth parents?"

He shows his yellow teeth. "You'll have to read my memoir to find out."

For the whole four-hour train ride Sandy doesn't stop telling us stories about his astonishing life, as the landscape rolls past at a stately pace and the Moroccan woman in a muted turquoise pantsuit sharing our compartment sleeps or pretends to sleep through it all. Sandy dismisses our choice of hotel—"you're not in America now, lads"—and from the Fez station packs us into a grand taxi with instructions to the driver to take us to the guesthouse or *dar* run by a friend or protege of his, from what we can gather a former houseservant. He stands on the curb waving to us as the taxi lurches away, grinning wildly, a weatherbeaten man utterly at home, alive to the outside of things where he happily clings.

"The Moroccan chamber of commerce ought to put one of him in every train compartment," John says as the cab bumps us along through modern Fez to the medina.

"Worth every penny," Ringo agrees.

Voices in the darkness in the night of Fez an hour before

dawn, standing on the rooftop, where men should not go by day: for the roofs above the city evoke an imaginary interior reserved for the secret life of women otherwise concealed behind blank crazed walls. They say that not so long ago any man found on a rooftop was immediately apprehended as a thief or an adulterer and punished either way with death. There are no windows in these houses, they are all turned inward toward courtyards or atriums, toward a silent invisible domesticity the direct inverse of the life and cries on the street. The silence makes itself felt as I listen, begins to hollow itself out with echoes, the sun working its way up to the crest of the eastern hills humming faintly as it rises: murmurings in the street, a pigeon's coo, somewhere a long way off the whine of a motorbike stuttering in the purple dark where overhead the stars are going out. Cold in my fleece, hunched, glad for the hot cup of coffee that John, climbing out onto the roof deck like a submarine captain climbs into his conning tower, puts wordlessly into my hands. Now light defines its objects, picking them out one by one, the laundry lines, the satellite dishes, the cats—I have never seen such a city for cats, living as these do free of cars: they lurk everywhere, in streets and on rooftops, in the few trees, a white cat pinks by with a kitten in her mouth. Scruff of the neck, skin of our teeth: what can be seized gets seized from outside, by the skin, even ourselves—*get a hold of yourself!*—as a forced smile promotes happiness, as certain postures induce thoughts—*Kneel,* commands Pascal, *and you will believe.* As if on cue the muezzin starts his cry, like a lookout spotting a whale, a subtle buzzing layer atop the noises of dawn. George and Ringo appear, blinking in the new sunlight, surveying the golden bowl of the city.

"Goddamn," I say.

Shyly smiling Fatima appears with breakfast for the gentlemen, we take it on the patio, coffee and fresh-squeezed orange juice and thin crepe-like pancakes and the darkest richest honey I've ever tasted—the product, she tells us, of cactus flowers. Smiling, discreet, young, with no head covering but somehow cloaked in modesty, or is that only the distance I perceive between us, as Nazarenes and faithful? But I am no Nazarene. George generates a low, appreciative whistle as Fatima withdraws.

"I could get used to this," he says.

"Being waited on?" Ringo needles.

"All of it." George's gesture takes in the rooftop, the dome of sky, the mountains, and the sounds of the city, the cries and conversational murmurs that float up to us from the narrow streets.

Ringo tells us a story about his ex-wife, how she went down to Mexico and saw a house there—"a villa, really"— and bought it more or less on a whim.

"Just like that?" I ask.

"Just like that. Apparently you can do that sort of thing in Mexico because it's so cheap."

"Probably not as cheap as here," John remarks.

We sit there for a moment in a colonialist daydream. There's a book downstairs by the owner's wife detailing how they acquired and remodeled their house here. Lavish photographs show its transformation from a weather-beaten ruin into a modest palace with fig trees and fountains and intricately tiled floors. Can you really simply buy this feeling of *being there*, a feeling of solitude enriched by the senses, and keep it forever? Is that what Beckett's Murphy was rocking toward, tied up in his chair? What Burroughs pursued—ecstasy, ex-stasis, standing in the stream of a life without obligations—while someone like Paul Bowles stood even further aside, contented as a cat in his malice? Giving up on the idea of home and thriving in a place foreign enough to pierce the skin of irony I wear at all times like a mask? What would that be like? To step into the sincerity of being nowhere. An image seizes me with momentary terror: dabbing the air with my feet as I lift off and float away.

"We should get going," John says.

The medina of Fez is an imploded villa, a village on steroids, no city at all, vast and unconquerable. It is entirely walled and nearly ceilinged by awnings and arcades—you play a game of peekaboo with the sky when walking its narrow, carless passageways and streets. We enter through Bab Bou Jeloud—uncanny, really, how the goat god follows us on our travels—the blue gate with the familiar keyhole arch like the ancient portal between East and West. But the gate is only a hundred years old and a product of the French protectorate, which sought to preserve the medina as a kind of living museum in which the Moroccans themselves were the chief exhibit.

Nevertheless that electrical sensation, the otherness

of the present tense, is alive in us as we pass through the gate into the mazy alley-like streets. There is an open plaza crammed with cafes and fruit stands to be negotiated before beginning the long descent down the main drag, the Rue Talaa Sghira, an endless souk winding into the heart of the old city, or I should say old cities, since Fez has really two medinas: Fez el Bali, which dates back to the 8th Century, and the "new" medina, Fez Jdid, which has only been around since 1276. Heart of the city or the cities, if that's the phrase, since no place I have ever stood so vividly conveys the experience of the Infinite Sphere, whose center is everywhere and circumference nowhere—an attribute of God as formulated by the twelfth-century French theologian Alain de Lille. Though in the original phrase, as reported by Borges in his essay "Pascal's Sphere," it is at least an *intelligible* sphere. As outsiders and tourists we cannot hope for such intelligence; I can only try and contain the overwhelming feeling of endless sphericity by resorting to my smartphone, which even without wifi can present a nearly navigable sketch of the veins and capillaries through which we pulse. So we ward off the phrase's descent, as Borges tells us, into Pascal's formulation not of god but of the universe as "a *frightful* sphere." I picture Rover, the sinister weather balloon that traps No. 6 in the Village in *The Prisoner*. I picture, spinning spherical in the air, my sister's falling car.

Dad loved an adventure. My phone fills with photos to show him at his bedside. What will his exhausted eyes see? The awful monotonous might-have-been of his own life?

What his retirement should have been? Put that away, I tell myself. Stay here.

Fear and exhilaration are close cousins. Reds and purples and golds, wools and furs, donkeys heavy-laden with propane cannisters, wheelbarrow-like wagons crammed with oranges, tinny Arabic pop from radios, scents of honey and sweat and leather, all clothe our descent into the old city or cities. And everywhere men men men, no women. Bright-eyed, standing or squatting men in djellabas and modern dress, calling out to us in a fractured blend of Mahgrebi, Spanish, French, and English. Trained by our suburban upbringings to avoid the eyes of strangers (*stranger danger!*), hopped up on suspicion, I and my companions deflect, look aside, murmur repeatedly the phrase taught us by our Kiwi guide: *La shukran*—No, thank you. Try to look like you know where you're going.

The Medersa Bou Inania is one of the only Islamic sites in the country open to infidels, a fourteenth-century school erected by Abu Inan Faris—a sultan, my guidebook informs me, less known for his piety than for his murderousness, as well as for the feat of siring 325 sons over the span of ten years. It was perhaps a rival to the Karaouine Mosque also known as al-Karaouine University, the oldest continuously operating university in the world, which non-Muslims are not allowed to enter. They say that Abu Inan was strangled by his own vizier—but the building remains in use, and is said to be one of the most beautiful examples of the period's architecture in the country. Its green minaret pops into view from time to time as we wander back and forth, but the building itself eludes us until we resort to asking a young bearded man in a white tarboosh outside a carpet shop: "Medersa?" He speaks no English but nods enthusiastically and leaves his shop long enough to lead us to the massive gate set in an otherwise undistinguished stretch of wall, bows and smiles and leaves without asking for any payment. "*Shukran!*" we shout after him, and grin at each other. The charmed feeling of the morning has persisted.

As it happens, the Medersa is about to close for lunch but we are able to slip inside and stand in the middle of the sunlit courtyard blinking at the strange combination of spareness and intricacy. There are few architectural flourishes or structural details to look at, but everywhere startling carvings in stone and wood. As is typical of Islamic art there are no representations or figures of any kind, only patterns suggestive of fractals and the beautiful looping curves of Kufic Arabic script, not in this case quotations from the Qu-ran but instead words of praise for Abu Inan, who is even vaingloriously referred to as Caliph. Perhaps that is why the Fassi suffer foreigners to enter the medersa, though there is an off-limits space for prayer that we can look into but not enter. The tension, if you can read the Arabic or know what it says, between the beauty of the design and the bloated banality of a tyrannical ruler's pathetic quest to be misremembered as a good guy, is dizzying. We feel ourselves inside a patterned language, without images—we are ourselves the images caught in this language. But it has nothing to say to anyone alive.

No one is here except a few other tourists—Germans, or

Austrians, or maybe Swiss—and the bored-looking big-bellied man in a white djellaba and black vest who charged us five dirhams each when we came in. He's looking at his watch and looking at the door and thinking about his lunch. We snap a few photos and run our hands over the smooth carved knots of cedar, remote from the hysteria and fanaticism with which the artifacts of Islam are usually presented to Westerners on television and in the movies. It's just another monument, albeit a living one—the Medersa still serves as a school, though no students are in evidence. History breaks and flows here as a stream does on a rock—shaping and marking the site, but too gradually for us to notice. It is the stream of time and events that we dip our fingertips in, as it passes us by, that eventually seizes and drowns us. But for now we are only passing through.

Walking the medina. The workshops are wide open as the windowless dwellings are not, and we are repeatedly invited to enter low cavernous rooms where men and boys sit on the floor weaving baskets or stitching leather or stringing beads. Faces, by turns inquisitive and indifferent, appear and disappear, blank stares, gentle smiles, eyes sparkling ironically. Sometimes one of us makes the mistake of touching something—a leather satchel, a musical instrument, a hassock, a bit of jewelry—and immediately the bargaining begins, and the other man is not easily persuaded that our apologetic shrinking from the encounter is not simply a somewhat unsociable haggling strategy. I have found no better account of the mystery of shopping in Morocco than that of Elias Canetti in his little book *The*

Voices of Marrakesh:

> *In the souks, however, the price that is named first is an
> unfathomable riddle. No one knows in advance what it will
> be, not even the merchant, because in any case there are
> many prices. Each one relates to a different situation, a
> different customer, a different time of day, a different day
> of the week. There are prices for single objects and prices
> for two or more together. There are prices for foreigners
> visit the city for a day and prices for foreigners who have
> been here for three weeks. There are prices for the poor and
> prices for the rich, those for the poor of course being the
> highest. One is tempted to think that there are more kinds of
> prices than there are kinds of people in the world.*

John is the most avid bargainer and his pursuit of a
leather satchel for less than the price I paid for mine diverts
us for the better part of an hour. "We must remain friends!"
cries the middle-aged shopkeeper with the salt-and-pepper
mustache, and it seems entirely earnest, as if he and these
Americans he's just met were friends before and shall be
friends hereafter, provided the transaction comes to a sat-
isfactory conclusion. Each party ratchets up and down by
degrees until something changes, the temperature of the
transaction warm but not heated, and the bargain has been
struck. It is tempting simply to pay the first price offered,
but it is equally tempting to bargain hard, to assert one's de-
termination not to be taken advantage of, even though pric-
es are low—the 500 Moroccan dirhams John is originally
asked for the bag is only about $50, much less than you'd
pay for an article of similar quality back home. We revel in

inconsistency, in our contact with a pre-modern economy still stained by the personal, by feeling, by whim.

Meanwhile, all that life is swirling and crying and cooking around us, around a million corners, and the parade of goods is never ending: silver necklaces, grilled meats, stacks of round loaves of bread, stacks of mangos, fresh fish, ceilings hung with ouds and other stringed instruments, dazzling rich arrays of red and orange and yellow spices, T-shirts, pewter hands, flatscreen TVs, soccer jerseys, carpets. We eat meat from sticks, we take photos of each other wearing fezzes. George, an expert guitarist, teaches himself how to play a *gimbri* right in front of our eyes, bending its three strings into a fair approximation of "Smoke on the Water." The pair of shopkeepers—one old, one young, one tall, one short, with identical mustaches and green djellabas—applaud and I half expect one of them to request "Stairway to Heaven" or "Free Bird." Before we know it we are the proud new owners of a *gimbri*, a pair of drums, a *ghaita*, and a set of heavy metal castanets or *karkaba*, which we lug along through the afternoon streets, idiot grins plastered to each of our faces.

Toward nightfall we have turned and turned around again and could be as lost in time as we are lost in space, in the electric thrum of the medieval. We must *smell* lost, because a group of young men materialize and begin speaking to us all at once in a confused babble of French, Mahgrebi, Spanish, and English. One of them, a young man with thick black hair wearing an Adidas-logo tracksuit, asks us where we want to go in reasonably clear English.

"The blue gate."

"No, the movie theater near where we're staying, what was it called?"

"This way," Adidas says, and strides off without looking back at us. We look at each other, and at the other touts, who shrug and stand aside. Adidas doesn't wait. We hurry after, duck around corners and through passageways narrow enough that I have to turn sideways to navigate them. Unexpected corners, wall fountains, a group of boys kicking a soccer ball. Ringo points at a sign that reads *Bou Jelud*.

"Doesn't that tell us where to go? Wait a second."

Adidas keeps walking, so we keep following. Electric cables with an improvised look string back and forth between buildings, netting the darkening sky above our heads. Few lights, yellow, with insects surrounding them. "Does this feel right?" someone asks. "Are we going the right way?" Shrugs. We're deep now in unsuspected canyons of the city, climbing after what felt like a long descent. Walking a long time. Suddenly we round a corner and our guesthouse appears. We look at each other. Adidas stands there expectantly. We file inside. Adidas starts speaking to us rapidly in French, in Spanish, in Arabic, but he seems to have forgotten his English. No one is in charge. We rush past his waving indignant arms, hurry inside and shut the door. For a moment, silence. We look at each other. Then he starts knocking.

We're exhausted, sprawled on the narrow cushioned benches in the atrium, hungry for wifi. The bell keeps ringing. "Should I give him some money?" "How much?" "How much is a hundred dirhams?" "Too much?"

Hands slap the heavy wooden door, echoing through the corridor into the high handsome room. We can hear what sounds like shouting now in the street, like a crowd of people is gathering. We don't look at each other. I have a working cellphone and I call our host and explain the situation. "You did the right thing," he assures me, so quickly and smoothly and reassuringly that I'm certain he means the opposite. "I'll be right there." I relay the information. We sit there, staring at our laptops, while the shouting and the doorbell ringing goes on, trying not to visualize what's happening outside, what we imagine might happen.

The shouting increases in intensity, then suddenly dies down. We hear a key in the lock and our host comes in, spreading his arms apologetically: "I'm so sorry about this." John and I go outside where Adidas is waiting calmly with his arms folded. The crowd that we heard has vanished, or maybe it was never really there. I shove a hundred dirhams into his hand, far too much: if we'd paid him going in ten would have been sufficient. But I am no longer paying for the man in the tracksuit's services; I am paying for him to go away. My cheeks burn with shame. He accepts the money without comment, his eyes looking into mine: dark brown, thickly lashed, a little bloodshot, unsurprised. He bows to me—I could vomit—nods to our host, and walks briskly away. The host gestures firmly with his arm across his body.

"Inside. Back inside, please." And then, more loudly and distinctly: "You are safe, my friends, you are safe!" We file back inside.

For the rest of the evening we avoid each other's eyes.

NEW YORK

"What are you writing?" *What are you, writing?*
"None of your business."

They were married in the spring. She was already pregnant with me, as the year was pregnant with everything the child won't know—my parents as people, the city they'd take me out of before I turned two, the summers we'd spend on the coast of Maine where the clang of bells in buoys marked my childhood with its own genre of longing. They were living together in the three-bedroom apartment on the first floor and he was forever urging her to be careful going up or down the steep steps. She was still smoking, though not as often. He looked at her sitting at the little kitchen table in sunlight the color it was a year ago when they first met, her hand covering the notebook and what she's written there.

He was angry. "I was only asking."

"I need something that's mine," she told him. "Not yours. Not the baby's. Mine. Don't you understand?"

He didn't. He didn't understand why she'd quit her job the day after she'd told him she was pregnant, leaving him to shoulder the burden of rent and groceries unassisted— he'd dropped the teaching gig and was working for Merck full time while pursuing an MBA in the evenings. He didn't understand why she left dishes in the sink from breakfast all day long, adding a plate and glass at lunchtime, and dumped in everything else at supper, leaving him to wash the lot when he got home at ten, fuming silently while she read in bed or sprawled on the sofa with her hand on her belly watching Johnny Carson do his shtick. He couldn't understand why she turned her face from his when he kissed her goodbye in the mornings, still warm and tousled in their too-small bed, burrowing more deeply under the pillows. Did she get up after he left? What time? Sometimes he came home from work and she was still there, though the dirty dishes and full ashtrays told him she'd spent at least part of the day upright. Sometimes she watched him washing the dishes or sweeping the floors with a red face and his mouth twisted downward, her own expression unreadable. She sighed and looked down at her belly. "I hope it's a boy."

He tried to imagine his own mother behaving in this fashion, doing anything other than *doing*: stripping beds, cooking breakfast, heading out to the dress shop where she's "helped out" for the past fifteen years, coming back to fix lunch for her children and husband, heading out again to get her hair done, home again to clean, to cook, to clean some more. It was impossible. This impossible woman whom he loved, who said she loved him, who was carrying his child—and, he thought with irritation, nothing else.

The wedding reception. Her father had insisted on playing the role of the big shot, though she knew he couldn't afford it: she'd let him, saying she enjoyed the image of her stepmother's apoplectic face as her husband wrote one check after another. But in fact he did it on the cheap, in the backyard of the house in Richmond Hill with its yellow-brick patio and a small but artful garden planted with hydrangeas and tulips. The bride wore a white flapper-style dress cut just about her knees and a broad lacy garden-party hat; the groom wore a dinner jacket with a yellow rose in the buttonhole, though she hated roses. His family, of course, had been appalled: they had not been invited to the ceremony itself, a brief hour at the courthouse, but had to cool their heels in the little back garden while the clouds threatened rain and Dad's dad tried to make small-talk with the bouncing vulgar little father of the bride and the bride's stepmother sulked in the kitchen sucking down one Bloody Mary after another. His sisters clung together, whispering, teetering around on their heels, bewildered by the crammed-together roofs of the neighborhood, the smell of cooking fat that clung to every surface, the little Black boys pedaling down the middle of the street shouting in what sounded to them like another dreadful language. The towers of Manhattan seemed impossibly distant from low-slung vulgar Queens: "If this is the Big Apple," shrugged the oldest, "I don't think much of it." Worst of all had been his mother, who hadn't seemed to understand that his wife's stepmother *was* a stepmother, and so kept popping into the kitchen to take the other woman by the hand and plead with her in a quavering voice to look after her only son as if he were her own. The stepmother, drunk, had stared at her as she stared at her stepdaughter, with blank-faced brittle disdain. Nevertheless, when bride and groom stepped out of the taxi and swept along the short little path through the trellis into the garden, all had stood and applauded, and for a moment they were stupid with smiles, swaying pleasantly with the vertigo delivered by any irrevocable act. They had told no one about the baby, not yet visible at two months. They drank Champagne—her father hadn't stinted there—and danced to the three-man bluegrass band hired from somewhere while the guests crowded against the wall of the little house to make room for them. It started to rain and they all had to cram inside the steaming little kitchen and living room, limbs adhering to the plastic covering the furniture, and his youngest sister found a seat on the knee of one of his business school buddies and the temperature rose as quickly as the noise level. In front of everyone she slipped out of her stockings, complaining of the heat, and stuffed them into his inside jacket pocket. Everyone was drunk. Her eyes, shining, held his. And they closed their mouths to the question blurring one other's suddenly small-seeming and childlike faces: *What have we done?*

One afternoon in late summer, he came home early with a stomach bug and found the apartment empty. He took off all his clothes and sat on the toilet for a while, groaning. Then he went to the front window and watched the street for a while through grimy blinds that were doing a pretty poor job of keeping out the heat. Where was she? He thought of his mother and his sick days home from school, how she'd sit by his bedside with her brisk, worried, kindly face, feeding him little tidbits, searching under his bed for dropped comics and toys. He'd sleep in his fever and wake and always, it seems, find her there watching him, sitting at his bedside or leaning in his bedroom door, her face a mirror that reflected only love. The apartment was dirty—he realized how rarely he saw it in this condition, in the daytime, with the sun streaking in, showing off the layer of dust that clung to every horizontal surface, the fingerprints on the doorway molding, cobwebs glistening in the corners. His gut knotted and relaxed. He drank glass after glass of tap water. He lay on the sofa. He sweated. Then he remembered the notebook. It was on top of the refrigerator—not exactly hidden, he told himself. Not exactly private. He fetched it and brought it back to the sofa and lay there with the notebook propped up against his knees, covers closed, for a long time. He'd put the chain on the door so he couldn't be surprised—if she asked him why he would answer—what? That he'd felt too weak to be alone? That didn't make any sense. He got up and took the chain off the door again. He sat down and opened the notebook, confronted by the numerous swirls of ballpoint script, began leafing rapidly through pages, looking for his name or his initial. When he didn't find either he began at least to look for references to the pregnancy, to his son (he was sure I'd be a son). What did it feel like? What was this thing, this creature, that had come between them, quite literally into their bed, an obstacle constant and growing? This moon in her belly, reflecting what sun's gravid light? But there was nothing written there that he could recognize as relevant to his need. Summaries of books she'd read, observations about the weather, snippets of conversation with friends about nothing in particular, descriptions of places she'd visited and lists of places (Venice, Budapest, Berlin) she wished someday to visit. Toward the end of the book, the most recent entry, he read the simple sentence *R seems tired.* Tired? He looked at himself, his body. Was he tired? What exactly was it that he felt, was feeling, when he saw her now: in the mornings when she was still asleep, in the evenings when she seemed withdrawn into dreams, on the weekends when they forced themselves to act as if nothing had changed, went to movies and Central Park and galleries and cheap restaurants, and *he* was the one asking her, a protective hand on her arm, if she was tired, if she was feeling well, if she needed to rest. It seemed incredible that she could not see him, did not think of him, remember where he was on the outside. He willed her to come home right then, to find him naked on the couch with her diary, to confront him. But nothing happened. A car honked down in the street and someone shouted something in Spanish. The electric fan whirred, pushing the heavy air like a bell-boy hauling a suitcase from one end of the apartment to the other. He felt empty. He got up and put the diary back where he'd found it, turned on the little black-and-white television and lay down and went to sleep.

There had been another summer afternoon years previously, at the end of her first marriage. David did not come with her. She found herself in a repurposed kitchen in an anonymous brick bungalow in darkest Brooklyn, in air streaked with the stink of jet fuel and the roar of heavy planes rumbling down into Idlewild, fewer than fifteen blocks away. Lying down on the cushioned table waiting

for the muscle relaxants to kick in. The doctor's antiseptic grip, glint of his glasses, his hiccups ("Excuse me" he said each time in a light German accent). The icy forceps he warmed for her by pressing them against his suit-panted leg. On the ceiling the doctor or the doctor's wife has pinned a travel agency poster of a Greek island, a blue dome and white walls ringed by the wine-dark sea. As he worked she concentrated on the photo. There was a balcony there, and she was a woman in white, wind catching her skirts, walking her widow's walk, looking out to sea, wondering what would come, what man, maybe, would sail over the horizon, coming back to reclaim her and his kingdom. Something shifted and relaxed inside her body. A sentence from Lawrence's *Women in Love* unfurled in her: *Why not a bath of pure oblivion, a new birth, without any recollections or blemish of a past life?* My life is the prize, she repeated to herself. My life is the prize.

When she came home and found him there naked and asleep in front of Walter Cronkite she stood there for a while in the doorway, considering. Whatever hormones and electrical impulses passed through her body at that moment were also passing through me. We stood there, neither in nor out, considering my father's prone body. Finally she came in and shut the door, and marched into the kitchen, and stared into the almost empty refrigerator.

Vietnam flickered soundlessly on the little television. Dad opened his eyes. "That you?"

"Yes."

"You cooking?"

"Yes."

He closed his eyes again.

The white hum. A Chinese take-out carton; she took it out and sniffed plum sauce gone bad, making her gag. Pregnancy had temporarily returned to her sense of smell, cutting through the cigarettes she'd cut down on without quite stopping. "There's nothing in here."

"I'm not hungry anyway," he said. "I'm sick." When she didn't respond he pulled himself up somewhat nearer to a sitting position and shouted it, a little shocked by his own hoarse vehemence. "I'M SICK!"

He heard the door to the apartment open again, then close. He closed his eyes. He was counting to himself. He was waiting for the arrival of something that he would never name.

TRAINS

From Kebir to Fez, from Fez to Tangier. Imploded anonymous villages on steroids, the medinas. Shantytown pulling away Fez falling behind the old cities la ville nouvelle white buildings gridding chaos of landscape in motion bound for Tangier. Sunlight, rebar, turned earth. Half-finished houses straddling raw hills, black dirt, grasses. An old man in a brown djellaba sits on a milk crate on a ridgeline watching train and world slide past. Intimate hillsides. Blunder of voices speaking English in the air-conditioned car. Stepping onto each platform to feel the stillness of the train.

Cut word lines. The French I sort of speak is the frayed rope to which we cling. *Je voudrais. Nous nous voulons. Nous sommes hommes americains. J'aime votre pays.* Late in a legacy of well-meaning white folk seeking friction, heat and light. The Master Musicians' cheeks touch ours—we brush against them shyly. Laughing incredulous on the train. Who are we when we're alone? *Feeding the stranger.* Metabolic junkies addicted to whatever can catch us on the run. *I coped in a bucket of tar.*

Buzz taking root in soil and air. Flickering modernity. A Fez graffito en anglais: *Not zombies we are ULTRAS.* Political situation. Divine right of kings. Men in djellabas with mobiles pressed to their ears. It is written in strangers' eyes: *Je suis un juif.* Don't look away.

Cows, goats, sheep, chickens, dogs. No cats from the

train, nothing undomesticated, nothing that self-beautifies. Cats love rooftops and a god's-eye view. A woman traveling alone in our compartment plays with her phone or dozes through our excited chatter. Does she understand us? Does she understand us. Like a yo-yo that sleeps for a while alive before snapping to. *Earthbound ghost need.* Nail me to a train.

People walking on the earth—not roads, tracks or paths but the earth. Figures scaling the unscalable. In the medina there's no outside. Walls climb to nowhere. We tread through someone else's living room in muddy shoes, too excited to apologize. *The fact of addiction imposes contact.*

Passing or piercing a low lake. Now Atlantic breakers. Palm trees. Mounds of rubble. Lush Assilah. Red flowers that could be poppies. The War to End All Wars. *Les gares* are guarded by two soldiers and an officer, the soldiers in kelly green berets, grease guns leveled at the populace which includes us. They walk and walk, never boarding the trains that come and go.

Tuscan light. An orange grove. *A Man Within.* Took the Kiwi for a native, didn't I? Yet Dad is in the landscape, comes out of hiding from everywhere I look. Treetops sprout like fingers. Hilltops of his knees. Ridgeline of his crushed chest. Hot whistled wind of his breath.

The one-eyed gimpy cat at the Tangier train station we spotted begging like a dog. Now we're passing a ragged black and white dog at a small white depot stuck in the middle of nowhere. Now we pass a burro ambling on a field streaked with silver water. A white heron with curved neck standing still in a pool, eyes akimbo, a bent question mark in the mirroring water. *Where do they go when they walk out and leave the body behind?* Out between towns a woman in bright pink with shopping bags in both hands walking steadily. To where?

Sandy's poker face, looking each of us in the eye: "If you eat dead-hand couscous you'll never feel happy again."

Sand of sleeplessness weighting the back of my head. Hazy Moroccan light filtering into our eyes, finding the rods and cones. Slow oil tanks slipping past. Retrospective. A woman on the platform in ankle-length lemon-colored coat with a leopard-print headscarf walks by. Poured concrete mouths flapping tongues everywhere. Industrial minarets: *Towers open fire.* Powerlines. Steel.

A waltz to the music of emerging infrastructures. Count the satellite dishes. Towns end definitively. A river. Cliffs. Scrub and burnt orange earth.

Unwashed tender skins. Stubble field. Sulphur cliffs catching fire in the sun. Then night in our moving workshop. Traveling blank through time. Internal night. Interzone yet to be imagined. Animal figures silhouetted by fire. We look at them. "I thought I had more going on in this sequence." Following tracks laid down by conquerors. Substance from standstill given to flow. Bouquet of folded dirhams blossoming between the tea seller's fingers. Virtue has gone out of me. The eye is captured.

I am never here.

Calling all agents to reactivate. On the train from Fez in the settling night. John props his iPad up against the window and sets it to film our journey in stop-motion: the first stations, bright yellow lights of Meknes, scattered lights of the countryside, the dark, the dark. Filling in gradually our reflections in the window—writing staring fiddling with musical instruments chatting dozing. One woman with us in the compartment, alternately speaking soft rapid Arabic into her cellphone or feigning sleep, doing her best to conceal her irritation with the noisy Americans. We are coming together out of the shards of our separate experience as foreigners into the dubious light of William S. Burroughs's colorless eyes. Tangier when we arrive is just another city. Bowles: "The place was a counterfeit, a waiting room between connections, a transition from one way of being to another, which for the moment was neither way, no way." The days of the city as international zone are long gone, but a faded cosmopolitan luster still reflects from the whitewashed colonial architecture, the names of streets and cafes, and the nearly imaginary view of the coast of Spain from high vantage points: the crumbling walls of the Kasbah, the Place des Nations. Burroughs called this city home for about four years, during which time he transformed himself from a mere wife-murdering drug-addicted trustafarian pederast into the visionary author of *Naked Lunch*. The artist, says Burroughs, creates an object capable of doing him harm: "a frozen moment when everyone sees what is on the end of every fork."

We arrive by night, flashing in a petit taxi from the station through the Ville Nouvelle which in Tangier is almost all of the Ville, wide open European streets a shock after the intricacies of Fez. The hotel is a long dark tunnel of a lobby: only the fez perched jauntily on the concierge's head signifies that we are not in Brussels or Des Moines. But this lobby is filling with excitable Burroughsians, direct from the airport, mixing with a few of the people we'd gone to Joujouka with. There's our rocker friend, grinning around his cigarette, coming up behind John and George and putting his arms around them both. *Music on the beach*, that's the word going round, irresistibly. George and Ringo sensibly beg off to go to bed but John and I follow the little crowd out into the night, up a hill past sealed shops to the Avenue Pasteur, which becomes the Avenue Mohammed V, where coming down toward the black spinning plate of the sea we reach the Avenue Mohammed VI, edging the beach, passing glass towers and neon nightclubs spaced a little too far from each other like an elastic Miami Beach. It turns out the music is inside one of these clubs and not the beachside bacchanal we'd imagined: a smoky nightmare crammed with Europeans and incongruous tikis and a white guy with long curly hair doing his best Jackson Browne impersonation while everyone crowds around the bar shouting and drinking. John and I stand on the edge of things, appalled, glancing at each other: our travels in Joujouka and Fez have infected us with an ascetic lust for purity, a mistrust of graven images, a fresh disdain for alcohol and those who cling to it. Wordlessly we walk out and catch a cab driven by a sullen man who speaks neither French nor any other language that we can discern but who gets us back, eventually, to our hotel. We part in the lobby and head to our rooms. Mine is bare and sad and shuttered, the carpet slightly sticky underfoot and a tint of sewage coloring the air. I open the shutters and the window and lean out into the Tangerine night and catch up its density and smell in great snuffling breaths. I'm in a black-and-white movie, a pure simulacrum. In Casablanca, we were told, a replica of Rick's Cafe from *Casablanca* does bang-up business, laid out to exactly resemble a cafe that never existed except on a Warner Brothers soundstage. *Hide me, Rick! Save me!* On the iPad my wife's face is weary and distracted, bright kitchen daylight haloing her hair.

"I don't know," I tell her. "I'm kind of an outsider here. I'm no Burroughs scholar. The people who love the Beats mostly peaked at fifteen years old. They're all so damned pleased with themselves to be here. Otherwise it's horse laughs and name tags like every other literary conference I've ever been to. They're not even eccentric. I feel so far away from it all." I pause. "I miss you."

"I miss you, too."

Do I believe her? Does she believe me? A temporarily single mother watches her husband stray through foreign lands, tempted on every side by drink, by hashish, by lithe young graduate students with eyebrow piercings and *Nothing is true—everything is permitted* tattooed somewhere on their bodies. Space isn't elastic: it stretches and breaks, like time. Chicago isn't just thousands of miles away, it's literally behind me in time, and to her I'm part of some entirely notional and elastic future, untouchable, remote.

"How's your other husband?" I ask. She looks at me

blankly. "Edward," I say. "Herr Strauss. 'Vere you go, I go also.'" I don't know why I ask this; I never ask after her friends. Silence in reply. "I sink ve haff a bad connection."

Lying in bed in mental pursuit of Alamut, the castle of assassins, singular vision of paradise that I will not discover here any more than I've discovered it in Chicago or Ithaca or San Francisco or Missoula or New Orleans or any other place I've been. Did I glimpse it in Joujouka, in the goat god's mad, savvy dance? If I were anything more than a tourist, anything more than a mayfly clinging to the surface of the river, might I not discover at last my proximity to life? O paradise of the word! It exists in the mind inviolate, sweeter than honey, passing unscathed between the whirling blades of intellect. No abode of *houris*, no *marabout*, no castle in the air. It is the dream pressing against the actual, the actual giving it shape, dream of undeformity. Dream of an escape from every constraint, from every lived moment of complicity with the Ugly Spirit. No blood orchid need flower for me to inhabit this land. In black ink rather my shining love.

Images of Dad skim across my screen: shots of him lying in bed, still intubated but with eyes open, his wife standing next to him with her hand resting on his forehead in a priestly gesture, his daughter standing on the other side clutching his hand, wearing a tense tight smile. In his gaze I read my father's terror, the roaring in his ears that had been forestalled for a while by unconsciousness and denial. These images carry no news, no shock, only sadness. What does he see when he closes his eyes, as the machine breathes for him? "A voice comes to one in the dark," Beckett wrote. "Imagine."

The pixels that bring me pictures of life at home show only overexposed windows, halos crowning the dark unstinting heads of father, sister, stepmother, wife, each in their own way entangled, stranded at the crossroads of my father's bed. Alone and overtired in the uncomfortable shit-smelling Tangerine hotel, in the dark, penetrated by wifi radio dreams, pierced by the eyes of strangers, called to pray in an incomprehensible tongue. Running breathlessly ahead to the woman on the shore, under the black wave, perpetually turning to show her face in profile, trying to get ahead of it. *Mektoub.* It is written. What is my present tense? What is the future of a fate sealed yet unobserved by anyone, the day I was born? Or back of that, behind that: my parents. My parents growing up, one in Skokie, one in the Bronx, the recombined strands of Ashkenazi DNA meeting in Manhattan. And back of that the DP camp in Belsen. And back of that Budapest, the war. And back of that the void, history's intense inane, the awful absence of pity, continuity, legibility. Beckett: *From time to time with unexpected grace you lie.*

Out of nothing we must make something....

A life in dreams severed from my life....

For the period of time in which you are required to face death, you are immortal...

Journeying toward sleep in the specious present.

A COOK'S TOUR

The sun smacks the surface of the sea with its silver ladle, splashing its shards of light into shaded eyes, under the loom of the Spanish shore that seems to hover above our heads. Many sordid histories meet at this old crossroads of the Cold War: spies in the Cafe de Paris, listening beggars in the Petit Socco; "that steep, shadowy-white seaport," Truman Capote once called it. Out the window of my sewage-smelling room in the Chellah Hotel I see palm trees, white buildings, and a basketball court where uniformed boys are playing soccer. How would Matisse paint it? The proportions of Fez are reversed: the sprawling Ville Nouvelle surrounds and bears down on the tiny kernel of medina like an octopus forcing open an oyster. But there's still enough old city to get lost in. Dapper Gabriel gives us the medina tour, debating out loud with absent biographers over where Burroughs lived, how literally to take his claim that he was in spitting distance of Bowles, miming for us the theoretical loogey hawked from a rooftop into the hidden garden where Paul and Jane reclined in their respective cocoons of hashish and spite. We climb up to the Casbah where a break in the wall gives out to the Bay of Tangier. By night the dim lights of the Spanish coast seem to hover too high in the air: Europe as UFO. Cats come to greet us. And it's up there, improbably, inevitably, that my phone rings.

"I have to take this," I tell my Burroughsian confreres. "I'll see you at the restaurant."

Gabriel looks from one face to the other, confused. "His father," John tells him. "He's in the hospital."

"Ah?" He nods, shrugs, seems to bow a little. "I'm sorry to hear that. We'll leave you to it." He turns to the rest of the party and raises a finger in the air. "Come along, children!"

I stand in a gap in the wall in chalky light, the vista of the Mediterranean blackening in front of me. The signal is utterly clear. My sister is in New Jersey, visiting Dad at the rehab center in harsh daylight. I'm on North Africa's floating edge, entering the dark.

"He looks better," she said. "A lot better, you wouldn't believe it. His color's come back and he's got a chair and he can go outside. I spent the morning with him. But he's depressed. *So* depressed. It's like he's not even in there, you know? When I talk to him? He can only whisper but even so, it sounds like he's very far away."

I search for words. "How long are you staying?"

"A few days." Her eyes say: *As long as it takes.*

"Can I talk to him?"

"He's resting now. Try us later." A long, indecipherable pause. Her voice is clear of tears when she asks, "How about you? Where are you, anyway?"

"Morocco."

"Wow," she says absently. And for form's sake: "What's it like?"

"It's amazing. The most amazing place I've ever been. So beautiful. I can't quite put it into words."

She says, "Huh."

"You're pretty brave," she adds. "Traveling by yourself."

Am I?

I walk slowly down the steep cragged passageway from the Casbah down to the main drag we'd passed on our way up, rejoining my companions outside a fish restaurant I recognize from an Anthony Bourdain travel show. There we dine lavishly on seafood tagine and cumin-roasted grouper, drinking a thick nonalcoholic blend of sweet plum and fig and grape juices that seems nevertheless to be getting us drunk, given how loudly everyone is laughing at one another's Burroughs stories. One of my tablemates, a scholar in her sixties, who interviewed him in the notorious "Bunker" in New York City when she was an undergraduate, pronounces him "a gentleman." Fork in the air, lips pursed, shoulders back, by alchemy she conjures an invisible cigarette, the spindly legs crossed at the knee, the diffidence, the parchment voice and cigarette-paper face. "People talk about his misogyny—and it's true!—but he was always a sweetheart with me." *Sweetheart.* For a moment we can all see him, the magisterium of transgression, sitting primly with our young scholar in the cavernous warehouse room. I want to ask her about Beckett and Sontag and Ginsberg and the film that shouldn't exist and that no one else at this table, I'd wager, has seen. For a moment, I could make myself the center of attention; I could present, if only to their imaginations, an irreplaceable document of an otherwise unrecoverable moment in American literary life. But I say nothing. I've kept my eyes open, in and out of the hotel,

looking for anyone who so much as resembles Olga or Viktor, or Shane for that matter, or anyone in a gorilla suit. Gabriel would give a great deal to be in touch with them, I'm
sure. He presides over the table with his long fingers, in his
elegant linen suit, thinning hair swept back from a widow's
peak, listening and looking and laughing with a certain reserve. What does it mean to love another writer so much
that you devote your own life and writing to them, to the
arduous task of preservation and resemblance? He doesn't
look much like Burroughs, it's true, but when he puts his
gray fedora on and stands erect he transforms into a figure
of dark midcentury glamor. His shrewd eyes, passing from
face to face, pause for a moment on mine. I force myself to
meet his gaze and after a moment, with an ironic twinkle,
the drawn handsome face passes on.

The waiter, who is also the owner, presents us with trays
of berries for our dessert. Around us, in the little dining
room, artifacts of fishing kitsch: nets, stuffed swordfish,
a wooden effigy of Popeye the sailor. How could Spain,
my final destination, be anything more than anticlimax?
Burroughs to Ginsberg, 1958: "Unless I can reach a point
where my writing has the danger and immediate urgency
of bull-fighting it is nowhere, and I must look for another
way." It seems incredible that bullfighting still goes on, but
it does; and young men still go to Pamplona for the chance
of being gored and trampled every year.

Academics, men and women, rich by local standards,
vulnerable to the same charges of tourism, Orientalism,
and exploitation that enfold Burroughs, that enfold Bowles,

that enfold this whole conference taking place in one of what Rimbaud called "the wet and peppered countries." *Je est un autre.* He was only sixteen when he wrote that, with just three years in front of him during which he'd burn through all the absinthe and transgressive sex and poetry that the nineteenth century could handle. By nineteen Rimbaud was no longer a poet; he looked to Africa for what he could not find in verse, becoming a tubercular merchant of coffee and a runner of guns in Yemen and Ethiopia, dying one-legged and notorious at the age of thirty-seven. He haunts, or ought to haunt, any Western writer who seeks to awaken their genius in the so-called Third World. To discover and riot in a world of fantasy constructed piecemeal from the half-comprehended glimpses of a poorer people's reality. "If brass wakes up a trumpet," he remarked, "it's not its fault." The dead white writers I pursue, sub-Proustian mama's boys to a man—if they have anything in common it's their flight from one sort of privilege into another, capable or so they hoped of converting the dead brass of their lives into vivid trumpets of experience—burning with the white-hot flame of desires they dared not fully express at home. What am I, what are we, academics and fellow travelers and nostalgists, doing here if not re-enacting that exploitation, without at least in my case even the excuse of seeking to derange, systematically or un-, the oppressive rules of the game?

But it's not sex flaring in the loins of this particular literary tourist; I am pushed more than I am pulled. Death drives me forward toward its livid unknown; I hang back just enough to jot a few notes on my way down. What is unspeakable about my desire is simply and entirely that it is, in fact, unspeakable. I paraphrase, I swerve, I double. *Verde que te quiero verde.* The ship on the sea. The horse on the mountain.

Walking with the others in the salted evening air, following the pure stink of Gabriel's Cuban cigar, foam scribbling the beaches, I try to feel what they felt, what Gabriel and the others are pretending to feel: contact with the reality of the unairconditioned world. There are troops of boys pursuing each other in the shadows of the dunes; there are shrouded figures in djellabas hunched in the dark with their heads on their knees, resting or unconscious. A circle of light seems to follow us, to shield us, a suite of scribblers, each composing a novel in his or her own head of which they shall be the star. In New Jersey, in the rehab facility, the day drags on. Dad lies half-upright in his bed with my sister at his side, her eyes red, the ward crawling with warring septic and antiseptic smells, while a small flatscreen television plays. Maybe they're watching Bourdain—another of my B's and at the time of which I'm writing, not yet dead. Maybe, somehow, they're watching me. Reading this. Surviving my story.

Our performance takes place on the penultimate day of the conference in the late afternoon, in a dark room ringed by elaborately carved wooden walls, viewpoints strategically blocked by wooden pillars here and there, floor hidden by thick dust- and sound-absorbing carpets, the ensemble presided over by the obligatory portrait of the tensely smiling king. We are preceded by an aging folk singer whose interminable talk-song about New York in the Seventies has everything to do with his own fleeting encounters with fame and sordid glamor and little, so far as I can tell, to do with the conference or with Burroughs or his work. Only after all the air and life has gone out of the room and the audience is yawning and wishing for coffee does it become our turn. One by one we step out from the room's corners, each of us playing one of the instruments we purchased in the Fez medina with more enthusiasm than proficiency. Ringo has the *ginbri*, George has the *qaraqib*, John has the *taghanimt*, I have the *def*. Videos taken on the fly assembled over feverish hotel room evenings flicker on the screen: stuttering shots of our car ride to Joujouka, Boujelud dancing before the bonfire, orange-sellers and water-sellers in Fez, the darkening view out the window of the night train to Tangier. We stand in a line and chant the Burroughsian sentence that gives our group its name: *In the pass the muttering sickness leaped into our throats, coughing and spitting in the silver morning.* Repeat it, repeating it: language is a virus, human beings are its carriers, everything else is a void to be fucked or that fucks you, gigantically, in the ass. With the old B-movie actors like Randolph Scott, growling *cut 'em off at the pass!* Playing pass ord. John and I do our best Abbott and Costello at the center of the stage while Ringo and George pluck gamely along beside us.

"So we fucked each other…"

"Couldn't reach flesh!"

"In the pass the muttering sickness..."

"Animaled the hairy men..."

It's falling flat, or else the audience has already been flattened by a long day of listening to interminable papers on the North African adventures of Burroughs and Bowles, or by the terrible folk music (faux music), while all the time the sun has been tracking invisibly westward across the sealed shutters leaking mingled light and dust into the room. One of the organizers leaves mid-performance and is followed by a trickle of others; cooler air and smoke wisps and voices from the lobby wafting through the now-open door. But the pass... what passes? The nagging notion that there's something within us unexpressed by words—or worse, that something is deformed by them, as a childhood photograph comes to obliterate and replace the event it memorializes, or how the stories your parents repeat about you render you helpless to resist them, to be defined by them. Life and language, warring siblings, the pretty one and the smart one, or is it the other way around? Language for Burroughs was one more block, one more inhibition implanted by the not-me that he tried to destroy. Thus cutups, thus shotgun paintings, thus the post-Burroughsian Burroughs of Lawrence, Kansas and the house of a thousand cats from which he emerged only to cut the occasional Nike ad. What in his wake can we do but try and make his rejection of language's deformities somehow audible, legible? To re-appropriate what he appropriated from junk and rent boys and marginalized cultures and thus by alchemy set ourselves free?

The lights go up and we take our bows to tepid applause. As in Fez, when shamed into silence by the insistent pounding at the door of our guesthouse by the indignant tout, I find that we can none of us bear to meet each other's eyes.

We could get a drink—there's wine and beer in the hotel—but somehow it still feels wrong to drink alcohol in Morocco; as though it were possible to be only half an infidel. So as John goes off in search of one of his old-time Burroughsian compadres, and George and Ringo retreat to their rooms and the screens connecting them umbilically to their actual lives, I wander outside, past the knot of smokers, tasting the salted air, in search of something to take the edge off the anticlimax. Any excuse not to return to New Jersey and the image of crashed Dad immobile in his chair, flanked by wife and daughter in grim *pietà*. So I drift north toward the medina under a pinhole moon, exhausted, floating leglessly over the city like Emerson's transparent eyeball: *I am nothing, I see all...*

The Sour Meêgazine is perched on the lip of a bluff overlooking the harbor, along the northern edge of the Avenue Pasteur. Tourists wander among the brass cannon pointed out to sea, defending the city from the notional enemies to the north. I hear my name called, and see Gabriel leaning against one of the cannons, tipped-back fedora lending his lean face a disarmingly frank and open expression. He's rolling a cigarette on the cannon's butt, inches from the touchhole. "Good thing it isn't loaded, yeah?" He offers it to me and I shake my head. We stand together for a minute while he smokes, looking out at the evening water coated with its haze of history and dust.

"I looked you up, you know," he says after this endless pause. "But there's nothing there."

The idea of being a ghost appeals to me. But this can't be true and I tell him so.

"Oh," Gabriel says, waving his smoke in the air dismissively, "you're *there*. Your Twitter handle and your poetry, and so on. But you've done nothing on Burroughs that I could find, peer-reviewed or otherwise." He eyes me curiously. "When did you start working on him?"

"Honestly? Just for this trip. It was all John's idea. I know the two of you go back a ways."

"Friends and rivals." He chuckles at the thought—his form of chuckling being to actually say the syllables *Hee-hee*. "For a while it looked like he was going to be the leading Burroughs scholar in the world. But now I suppose it's me."

Being used to the self-aggrandizement of academics, I only nod noncommittally.

"That's why I was surprised to see your name mentioned in the email I got this morning."

"What email?"

Gabriel glances to the left and the right, as though expecting to catch someone spying on our conversation, then draws a folded piece of paper from the inside of his cream-colored jacket and hands it to me. "Take a look."

A print of an email sent from what is obviously a dummy address. It reads:

Dear Professor,

We have the materials for which you have been search-
*ing and for which we understand you will pay **top dollar**.*
You can confirm this with our agent: he has seen the mate-
rial and can attest to its quality and ingenuity. Show him
this message and he will affirm. We will be in touch tonight
with next steps.

Very truly yours,

Viktor Himmelfarb

My name is printed, by hand, across the top of the page.

Gabriel has been studying my face. "Himmelfarb. An assumed name, I assume." He chuckles again: *hee-hee.* "But you are the genuine article, are you not?"

"How do you know it's me?" I say, my cheeks hot.

He retrieves the paper from my grasp, refolds it, and points down the Avenue Pasteur. "Why don't we continue this discussion over a glass of mint tea?"

One of Burroughs and Gysin's cut-up collaborations flits through my mind as we stroll down the Avenue Pasteur toward the Place de France, traffic roaring to our left and the dark platter of the Mediterranean hovering to our right:

Calling all reactive agents
Recalling all agents active
Calling agents all reactive
Recalling agents active all
All agents calling reactive
Calling all active agents re

We settle at one of the outdoor tables, watching the roundabout churn. A tall beggar with a stringy beard encircling a nearly toothless mouth hobbles up to us and Gabriel says something sharply to him in Arabic; the man bows, pressing his fingertips together, and withdraws. The waiter arrives with a tray of mint tea already on his arm and deposits the glasses in front of us. Each glass is tubular like an egg, nested in an arabesque of wire—a zarf—that curls upward to be pinched precariously between thumb and forefinger. The tea is so hot, so sweet, that it curdles on my palate like cognac. Gabriel watches my face, folding his elegantly tapered fingers together on his knee.

"Well?"

"I'm nobody's agent," I say, and Gabriel tightens the lines of his mouth and nods slightly, like a chess player acknowledging his opponent's thoroughly conventional but nonetheless effective move. "But I think I know what your correspondent is talking about."

"You've seen it?" It's my turn for a tight nod. Gabriel sits up straighter. "Would you describe the film to me please? As best as you can recall?"

I do so, haltingly. The view of the wooded area, which must be somewhere in the vicinity of the Tiergarten. The sofa and Ginsberg's moving lips and hands—the man never seemed to shut up. Burroughs' long face, and Beckett's, and Sontag flitting between them like an especially glamorous moth. The film's abrupt end.

Gabriel waits to see if I have anything more to say, then nods. "The episode described has been well documented," he says. "It was their second meeting, you know. Barry wrote about the first one." He's referring, I infer, to Barry Miles' biography, *Call Me Burroughs*, which includes this description of the two literary giants' inability to understand each other:

In February 1963 Burroughs paid one last visit to the Beat Hotel [in Paris].... It was on this visit that Burroughs met Samuel Beckett, one of his literary heroes. Beckett had two objections to his fold-in method. He called it "plumbing" over and over again in the conversation and complained, "You're using other writers' work." He thought Bill believed that the writers he used for fold-ins—Shakespeare, Blake, Rimbaud, Beckett himself—had answers. "You should see what I've done with your work, Mr. Beckett," Burroughs said. But Beckett objected, "There are no answers! Our despair is total! Total! We can't even talk to each other. That's what I felt in *Naked Lunch* and why I liked it."

"Pretty much all the principals wrote or are otherwise on record about the second meeting, the one that happened in Berlin," Gabriel tells me. "Burroughs wrote about it in *The Adding Machine*. Sontag spoke of it in an interview. Ginsberg sent a postcard about it to Peter Orlovsky. There were a couple of professors present as well." He dismisses the professors with a twitch of his lips, leans forward. "But nobody ever said anything about the encounter having been filmed. There weren't even rumors of such a thing until quite recently. Then again, from what you describe, they might have been filmed covertly. The technology for such a thing was unusual in 1976. But very far from out of reach."

I keep my face neutral, aware of Gabriel watching it all the time.

"My understanding is that there have been no digital copies made," he says at last. "We are talking about film, celluloid. A single print with no negative. Am I getting warm?"

"I only know what I saw," I say after a moment's hesitation. "It was screened for me in Berlin. Film, yes, on a projector and everything. Why is it so important to you?"

"Burroughs," Gabriel says, ignoring me, pulling back one finger at a time as if counting. "Beckett. Ginsberg. And Susan Sontag. That's all you saw? There was no one else?"

"No one else I recognized. The professors, I guess."

Gabriel drums his fingers on the table. "Have you seen *Film*?"

"The film? I've just told you—"

"Not *this* film. *Film*. Beckett's film. The only one he had a hand in making himself."

"Oh yes," I say, remembering. "Buster Keaton."

Film was made in New York in 1965, starring the great silent film star who would die just a year later. It's not impossible that one or both of my parents saw it in one of the arthouse cinemas of the time. A curiosity in black and white, with no plot to speak of: a man, played by Keaton, referred to in Beckett's script only as O, does what he can to evade the camera's gaze as he walks down a street, hugging the wall; climbs a stairway; enters a room; and sits down in a rocking chair (shades of Beckett's uproarious *Murphy*), where he considers and eventually destroys seven photographs of himself at different ages, from infancy to cyclopean manhood (he has an eyepatch). Confronted by the camera, E, O covers his eyes and shrinks into himself until he seems to have shriveled into nothingness. The credits roll over an eye, evocative of *Un Chien Andalou*; when the eye closes, the film ends. "It's a movie about the perceiving eye," Beckett said, "about the perceived and the perceiver—two aspects of the same man. The perceiver desires like mad to perceive and the perceived tries desperately to hide. Then, in the end, one wins."

"There are no comparative studies of Burroughs and Beckett, of much merit, anyway. That I know of." Gabriel sips his tea. "And yet it seems unquestionable to me that not only are they the two greatest and most characteristic writers of the twentieth century but that they are almost mirror images of each other. Not in personal habits so much, though nowadays I suppose one older white man is supposed to be as good as another." He coughs out another *hee-here*. "But I submit to you that while it was Burroughs who did the most to evade the demands of Control, up to and including his own ego, it was Beckett who did the most to dramatize the tragicomic failure of such operations. In spite of everything, the eye"—or maybe he's saying *the I*—"persists."

"Your point being?"

"My point," says Gabriel, setting down his tea glass with a clink, "is that your film represents nothing less than the pivot-point of the twentieth century. The encounter between two avatars of the unspeakable, of the obscene reality of Cold War regimes of total control, the grandfathers, knowingly or not, of our present debased era of total self-imposed self-surveillance, which extinguishes the I"—this time he lifted a forefinger of clarification—"for the sake of the eye." He touches the orbit of his own and stares at me for a long moment, in a pose like a secret salute.

"So you're saying I should put the film on Instagram?"

Gabriel laughs, a hard bark, emphasis on the second syllable: *ha-HA!* "No. On the contrary. I want you to give it, or rather sell it, to me. I will study it closely. And if it is what I think it is, I'll see to it that it disappears."

"Disappears? Why?"

Gabriel sighs, slumps back in his chair, becomes preoccupied for a moment by a speck of some sort of fluff that has attached itself to his suit lapel. After a moment he disengages it and releases it into the waning sunlight, a breeze from the ocean luffing it into the traffic's continual combine. He looks at me with his lips pressed together in disapproval. "Playing dumb? Or just hard to get?"

"I—"

Gabriel raises his hand. "I see you require me to play the game through to the end. Very well: if I must, I must." He puts the hand down. "I have seen the film you described. I know exactly what goes on in it."

"Then why did you act as if you hadn't seen it?" I say irritably. "Why make me describe the thing?"

"It was a test," Gabriel says drolly, biting off the tip of each T.

In a moment, I tell myself, I'll rise from the table and

walk away from this lunatic and his obsessions and his poisonously sweet mint tea. "Did I pass?"

Gabriel's face becomes serious. "Have you asked yourself the simplest, the most basic question yet? Who was the filmmaker? Who was the man behind the camera?" He raises the admonitory hand again. "The *secret* filmmaker. The *covert* camera."

"No idea."

Gabriel folds his arms and tilts his head on one side, looking extremely pleased with himself and what he's about to say. "The CIA."

This is the part where you walk away, I tell myself. Aloud, I say, "You've got to be kidding me."

"Think about it. When did this meeting take place? 1976. In what city?"

"Berlin, of course."

"*Not* Berlin," Gabriel says, wagging his finger. "*West* Berlin. Remember? The Cold War was on. The Wall was still up. The Soviet Union still existed. And the Stasi, the East German secret police, was still very much a going concern. Its agents were all over the city—both cities. Nothing went on there that they didn't know about."

"So what are you saying? The CIA and the Stasi were spying on a couple of writers? Why?"

"Try not to be quite so intolerably naive. The intelligence services were much concerned with writers like Beckett and our man. Burroughs had been under FBI surveillance since at least the period in which his wife was killed. And Beckett, remember, was in the French Resistance. On the right side against the Nazis, yes? But a lot of people on the right side were on the wrong side as far as the CIA was concerned. Communist sympathizers. Fifth Columnists. And Beckett by this time was as famous as any writer alive. A Nobel laureate. A considerable asset to whichever side might plausibly claim him."

Gabriel's eyes are alight. I can no longer tell just how far he might be trying to pull my leg.

"You've got to be kidding about this."

"Is it so farfetched?" He leans forward, counting off the fingers of one hand. "Number one, the CIA infiltrated and provided funding for the *Paris Review* and a number of other prestigious literary magazines. The propagation of post-modernism, if you will, in service as a propaganda weapon against stick-in-the-mud socialist realists. Number two, the covert funding, and some would say, the restructuring, of American literature via the academy, to place it under institutional influence and control. I suppose you know all about how they subverted Paul Engle in the sixties."

"Preposterous."

"You'd have to say that, wouldn't you?" Gabriel sneers. "Aren't you supposed to be some sort of 'creative writer' yourself?" He says the words as if he were describing something slimy.

"I have a lit PhD," I say shamefacedly. "And I didn't go to Iowa."

Gabriel dismisses this with an elegant twist of his fingers.

"The conclusions we must draw from the existence of

this film are quite grave," he goes on. "If the CIA is in the room, with a camera no less, of which the other persons in the room appear to be unaware, then one or both of the writers in question is likely an agent. Theirs or ours, it doesn't much matter. The damage to Burroughs' reputation would be serious enough—Burroughs the CIA asset! But the damage to Beckett's would be catastrophic."

"Bullshit," I say. "If anything, their reputations would be enhanced." A thought strikes me. "You don't like Beckett very much, do you?"

Gabriel darts his eyes. "What makes you say that?"

"You said that Beckett and Burroughs were the two greatest writers of the twentieth century," I tell him. "But Beckett stands head and shoulders above Burroughs, and you know it. It was Burroughs who sought Beckett's approval, not the other way around."

"Now you're being absurd."

"Am I?" I lean forward. "I think you want to squash this film because it shows Burroughs the fanboy. Burroughs the starstruck. Burroughs in love with handsome Sam Beckett, who wanted nothing to do with him."

Gabriel licks his lips, shrugs, laughs, spreads his hands. "Believe what you want," he says. "Here's the real point: I want that film. And I'm willing to pay for it. Communicate that to your principals."

"They, ah, didn't exactly authorize me to make you an offer."

Gabriel makes a move. "Name your price." He takes a Mont Blanc pen and a chic leather-covered notebook out of his coat pocket and slides them across the table. I open the notebook to the first blank page and write the most outrageous number I can think of. I slide the notebook back to him.

"Can I keep this pen?"

Gabriel's eyebrows lift and drop as he studies the notebook. "Yes," he says, as if to himself. "All right." He puts his hand out for the pen and I reluctantly return it to him. "You want cash, I suppose? Or can I Venmo you?"

I clear my throat. "I don't exactly have it on me."

"I wouldn't want it if you did." Gabriel puts the notebook away. "The authorities here aren't my biggest fan. They tolerate the Burroughs microindustry—they have no choice, it brings in dollars—but they don't like it. I get hassled at ports of entry all the time." He glances at his watch. "I can't stay any longer, but I'll be in touch. Arrangements will be made."

It's long past being a joke. We stand up together and shake hands.

"Be seeing you," I say, cupping one hand over my eye in salute. He hustles out onto the sidewalk, an elegant sidelong figure in his cream suit and fedora. He whips around into the steady pedestrian traffic and is gone.

"Being," Beckett once said, "is constantly putting form in danger."

I sit down again, laughing quietly to myself. Who or what is Gabriel, and why does he want me to believe these things? Why is he willing to pay so much for a forty-year-old strip of eight-millimeter film on which a group of writers—half-forgotten, like all writers today—commune with one another so awkwardly?

It can be as impossible to encounter someone in real life as it is on the page: isn't that why I became a poet? Because I fell into language and couldn't climb out again, because characters are never real to me, only organized patterns of simulated speech colliding and separating, the same whether on the pages of *Northanger Abbey* or in *The Sheltering Sky*. Bowles captured it best, maybe, the gulf between people that's the gulf between words, expressed in the world of his novel by the immense Sahara and the three young women who wanted to drink tea there, one dune following the next until height and remoteness became indistinguishable from death. "The desert—its very silence was like a tacit admission of the half-conscious presence it harbored." One thinks of the protagonist of one of Bowles's earliest short stories, "A Distant Episode," an arrogant and hapless professor of linguistics whose desert journey ends with his tongue being torn from his mouth. Bowles was a composer before he was a writer and *The Sheltering Sky* moves like a symphony or maybe an opera toward the whiteness of anticlimax, Kit's survival as a kind of holy fool or *majdoub* who seems to take the entire white man's burden of colonial exploitation into her own body, willingly sacrificing herself to the sexual whims of tribesmen who probably never existed outside the perfervid Western imagination inscribed in the music of Bowles's writing.

I'll be coming home soon, I text my father. It's the first time I've written to him directly since the accident, though

I don't know whether he's using his phone or not. And where, wherever, is home? Home for Dad is a house in New Jersey with stairs to climb almost everywhere you went: stairs to enter or leave, stairs to cook or watch TV, stairs to work or to bed. He has been evicted from that home as surely as he's been evicted from walking, from eating solid food, from wiping his own ass. He has become a body that functions now only to contain whatever remains of his spirit, like a broad and shallow bowl. A stubborn fact, a life clinging to the bare exterior of existence. *Don't die*, I write. But I do not touch Send.

Night is falling over Tangier, settling its dusk and dust over the growl of cars, as I go on sitting irresolutely at this table outside the Cafe de Paris. The wifi comes and goes. I open up my notebook and take out my pen and press the tip against the page. Nothing comes. Nothing flows.

"You are a writer?" asks the man at the next table in lightly accented English. For a moment I freeze like a child found under a bed; I suppress an impulse to bolt from the table, the city, the Arab world. But when I finally turn I see an elderly man in a three-piece suit, balding at the temples, white mustache, gold spectacles. A newspaper is folded in front of him commuter-style. The suit conveys a frayed respectability and the eyes behind his glasses are gentle.

"Yes," I say, trying to conceal my embarrassment. Was he here the entire time? Did he see me with Gabriel? Did he overhear?

"And American?" he asks, his voice rising almost girlishly with what must be feigned surprise.

"Yes."

The man purses his lips. "And this is your first time in Morocco?"

"Yes. How did you know?"

"A guess." He offers me his hand in a short gesture made from the elbow. "I am Mr. Ahmed."

"Monsieur Ahmed?"

"*Ah, vous parlez francais?*"

"*Pas exactement.*"

I say my name and he repeats it once or twice, as if memorizing it. He makes another gesture with his other hand, a stiff encompassing wave. "What do you think of my country?"

"Wonderful," I say. "It's a wonderful country. I've never seen anything like it."

"You have seen only Tangier?"

"I've been to Fez. And I went to a village near Ksar el-Kebir. Joujouka. You know it?"

"Marrakech?" he asks me. "Fez is the most Moroccan Moroccan city, I believe. But Marrakech is the most beautiful."

"Not Marrakech. Not this trip."

He nods again. "You have come to Morocco to write?"

"Yes. Well, no. I'm here for a conference. An academic conference. On the American writer William S. Burroughs. He lived here for a time."

"Burroughs," he says, in the same sage neutral tone that could have indicated profound knowledge or no knowledge. I think of what Gabriel said about the Moroccan government's distaste for the writer. "Yes."

He is silent for so long that the conversation seems to be over; I am searching for a question to ask, or an excuse, when he bursts out with, "I am also a teacher!"

"Really?" I say, trying to convert it at the end into an acknowledgment rather than a question.

"I teach English," he says gravely, "in the American school. For many years. I am now retired. I lived in England for many years. But not America. I visited America for the first time last year."

I nod, trying not to appear confused by the chronology.

"It is a cold country, but civilized. Morocco is also civilized."

"America?"

"England." He shakes his head in a way that makes it clear to me that, whatever America's merits, being civilized isn't one of them.

"Oh, yes. Um. What are your students like?"

"We have Moroccan and international students. It is a very famous school. Do you know the poet Ezra Pound?"

"Yes!" For the first time I feel myself on solid ground. "Yes, actually, I wrote a chapter of my dissertation on…"

He rolls right over me. "It is a famous association. The son of the poet Ezra Pound, Mr. Omar Pound, founded our school in 1950, when Tangier was still an international zone."

"Fascinating."

"Yes." He lifts a finger in a schoolteacherly way, anticipating questions. "He did not know his father well. He did not believe in politics."

"You mean his politics were different from his father's?"

"That is not what I said."

A waiter appears, and I ask Mr. Ahmed if he would permit me to buy him a tea or coffee, but he declines with an elaborate two-handed gesture. "You are the guest here," he reminds me.

"Same again," I tell the waiter, who bobs his head and withdraws. "You were saying?" It seems best to let Mr. Ahmed have his head, conversationally speaking.

"Mr. Omar Pound was an international man for an international time," Mr. Ahmed says, touching his newspaper where it lay folded as though it offered evidence of his statement. "Born in Paris. A student in England and Iran. Then he lived here for a time with his family and then New Jersey. You know New Jersey?"

"I'm from New Jersey, actually."

"Yes, New Jersey. He lived and died there. He died not so long ago. I have visited his grave."

"You have?"

"Yes. He died in Princeton and is buried there. Albert Einstein also died there but he was not buried. I was disappointed when they told me that there is no grave to visit."

"I see."

"The poet Ezra Pound and the physicist Albert Einstein," he says, steepling his fingers. "Two geniuses. They would not have liked one another."

"Because Einstein was Jewish?"

"Of course." Then, significantly: "I have great respect for the Jews."

I assume a friendly blankness.

"There used to be many Jews in Morocco," he says. "Every city had its *mellah*. Now there are very few. You have seen the Jewish cemetery?"

"I have." It's outside, at least. I passed it several times on my favored path from the *ville nouvelle* into the medina. Whitewashed walls and a high rusty gate. There was no way inside that I could see.

"There is a synagogue as well. Not far from here." He gestures with his thumb.

"I'll, um, have a look."

"Would you like for me to write down the address?"

The hairs on the back of my neck rise. I try not to be obvious as I search the street for sinister men in a cluster crossing the street to accost me, or heaped together watching from a nearby car. Mr. Ahmed is a CIA plant if he's not a terrorist; maybe he's somehow both. In a moment he will invite me to another cafe, or to his home, and I all unwary will follow him, only to find myself followed, bundled into the back of car or van, whisked away to a boat or the Algerian border, in a matter of weeks or hours to find myself waterboarded in a cinderblock room, or else clad in the orange jumpsuit of my nightmares, in a desert backdrop, lamb to the slaughter listening hard for the sound of scraping knives like Carlo's laughter...

Mr. Ahmed mercifully interrupts the paranoid train of my thoughts. "You are staying long in Morocco?"

"No, not long. The conference ends tomorrow. Tonight, in fact."

"Pity. I have not read your Burroughs but I have heard some things about him. What would you say I should read if I wanted to be introduced?"

"Um…"

"He is a novelist, yes? Like you?"

"Uh, no. Not like me. I'm a—I write poetry." I say this wincingly. Never admit you're a poet to the person you sit next to on an airplane or bump into at a cocktail party. But it turns out that Carlo was right: Mr. Ahmed's eyebrows shoot up toward his hairline and he regards me with a look of what I can only describe as deep respect.

"A poet," he repeats. "Wonderful."

I dip my head to hide my shame.

Mr. Ahmed bows his own head. "I would be very pleased to hear some of it, if that isn't too much to ask."

"No, of course, I mean, that's kind of you, but I couldn't."

Mr. Ahmed's look of disappointment is so apparently sincere that I feel even more deeply ashamed.

"I literally couldn't," I explain. "I don't have anything on me." I'm not holding, I don't say. "I don't memorize it, or anything."

Mr. Ahmed nods, but the look of disappointment continues to crease his face for a moment. Then he lifts his eyes to the canopy of the cafe, clears his expression, and chants:

> *I have no name:*
> *I am but two days old.*
> *What shall I call thee?*
> *I happy am.*
> *Joy is my name.*
> *Sweet joy befall thee!*

Mr. Ahmed opens his eyes and smiles and nods to me, like a prompter, as though expecting me to finish the poem. But I can only return to him an idiot version of his smile. He shrugs slightly and closes his eyes again.

> *Pretty joy!*
> *Sweet joy, but two days old.*
> *Sweet joy I call thee.*
> *Thou dost smile,*
> *I sing the while.*
> *Sweet joy befall thee!*

The waiter, who has returned mid-verse with more mint tea, stands listening attentively. When the poem is over, he bows to me and to Mr. Ahmed and walks away again. No one else has paid the least attention. Mr. Ahmed beams at me.

"Very nice," I say at last. "Is that...?"

"Mr. William Blake," Mr. Ahmed says. "He is my favorite English poet. Do you not find that fine? 'Sweet joy befall thee!' It could be a verse from the Koran."

Now I feel certain that masked men are about to descend upon us both and haul me away to a bloody desert death. But there are only cars, men with newspapers, hurrying oblivious passers-by.

"Your Mr. Burroughs, is he anything like Mr. Blake?"

"I don't know," I say, warming my suddenly cold hands with the tea glass. "Maybe."

He plucks a pen from his coat pocket and poises the tip

over the margin of his newspaper. "Where must I start with him?"

"Um. Well, the most famous book is probably *Naked Lunch*."

He writes it down on the edge of his newspaper, frowning slightly. "*Naked... Lunch.*"

"The Brits always call it *The Naked Lunch*," I say irrelevantly. "I don't know why. Anyway it's not an easy read. Actually, none of it is easy, except for the really early books. One's called *Junky*." I do not want to say out loud, even to this sophisticated Muslim man who has lived in Great Britain and taught in an American school, the title *Queer*.

"*Junky*." He writes it down, then looks me in the face with his amiable grin. "Stories of low life, eh? A song of experience! Like your Henry Miller, with his *nostalgie de boue*."

"You could say that."

"Do you know Allen Ginsberg?" he asks, surprising me again. The image flashes before me once again: Ginsberg on the couch with Sontag, talking and talking, unapologetically picking his nose and flicking the boogers to the ground.

"Yes! I mean, not personally. He's been dead for a while." Mr. Ahmed waits. "Actually, he and Burroughs were quite close." Burroughs was in love with him actually, but I don't say that. "Ginsberg, Burroughs, and Jack Kerouac are considered the three primary members of the Beat Generation." I glance up at the setting sun blaring in the windows across the avenue, half expecting to see projected there Viktor and Olga's film.

"Of course. I have taught Mr. Ginsberg's poems to my students. We read *Howl*, and also 'A Supermarket in California' and 'America.'"

I nod vigorously to show my enthusiasm. He closes his eyes and for a moment I think he will recite more poetry—bracing myself for the uncanniness of *I saw the best minds of my generation* from the lips of this elderly Moroccan. But he only swallows and shakes his head and, owl-like, opens his eyes again.

"What do your students think of them? Those poems."

He shrugs. "They are students, like students anywhere. They are bored, I think. They do what they are told."

Moloch in whom I sit lonely!

"It has been a pleasure to meet you," Mr. Ahmed says abruptly. He stands up and tucks the newspaper under his arm where I can read the words NAKED LUNCH carefully inscribed atop a looping Arabic headline: a cut-up in waiting. "Now I must go."

We shake hands formally, bowing ever so slightly at twenty-degree angles. He picks up what looks to be a trilby hat from the seat opposite him and put it on, completing his transformation into a thoroughly British figure—an Oxford don or maybe a retired colonel. He adjusts his hat and, not knowing what else to do, I shake his hand once again.

"Thank you for the recommendations," he says. "And enjoy your conference. It ends tomorrow?"

"Yes. Then I'll be leaving."

"For America?"

"Uh, no. Not yet." I suppress the urge to look left and right, like Gabriel. "To Spain."

"Ah, Spain! I have been there many times. You go to Granada?"

"Sure. I mean, maybe. I don't know."

"You must go to Granada," Mr. Ahmed says significantly. "It is the most beautiful place I know. The Alhambra. Go."

"I will go," I tell him. "I will."

He offers me his hand for a third time—two fingers of it—and I hold them gently in goodbye.

As he walks away, a white-bearded man in a black djellaba and tightly laced Nikes who was peering at us from the edge of the sidewalk steps over to the table, picks up Mr. Ahmed's coffee cup between thumb and forefinger, and drinks the dregs. His eyes are red and tremble in their sockets. I turn away.

The synagogue turns out to be a stately white building with absolutely nothing liturgical or religious in its appearance. It could be an embassy or a hotel. As with the cemetery it is fenced off from the sidewalk, though this fence is all iron and does not obscure the entrance. It reminds me of the synagogue I saw in Berlin, walled and guarded, with no sign of life, Jewish or otherwise, going in or coming out. But this shul is, I learn later, miraculously still in operation; Chaar Raphael, you can look it up. I imagine they have more than the usual trouble putting together a *minyan* there on Friday nights. But then again who knows?

Morocco, shadows and light. Photo of Bowles lying at full length on a rug wearing a light brown djellaba, surrounded by white-clad Master Musicians in their gold turbans, themselves surrounded by the blackness of night. I can feel the chill surrounding the fragile circle of light and music; I can almost meet Bowles' steady unsmiling gaze. White-haired white men that populate this ghostly journey. I think of Dad's hair, not too plentiful before the accident, surely less plentiful since. Will he go completely bald, completely white? Will he get the chance to become old?

I wander down the hill from the Boulevard Pasteur, following little tributary streets, and come to the black border of the beach by night. Beyond it, the small waves. Beyond them, Spain. Beyond the night, the next day, the end of the conference, and what cannot, in any shape, be known. The earbuds are in and I am listening to a halting, thorny performance for solo piano of Hungarian composer Zoltán Jeney's "Arthur Rimbaud in the Desert." A series of halting half-note progressions with long spaces between steps that seems to stop just when it might be getting somewhere, and then begins climbing again. Dune after dune after dune after dune.

Surely it's time to come home.

NEW YORK THEN

A few weeks before Dad's accident, before the flight to Berlin, I spent a weekend in New York to give a few poetry readings and to see a few friends. I stay at an Airbnb in Prospect Heights in a gorgeous brownstone owned by a Black guy named Mitty and his shy beautiful daughter Saniya. You do better on Airbnb if you reveal a few personal details, and Mitty told Saniya that I was a poet. At their kitchen table she showed me a poem of her own:

Sun on the playground
Can't catch me
I'm home
Asleep!

"I like that a lot," I told her. "What does it mean?"

She looked at me like I was an idiot. "It means there's no sun when I'm sleeping."

"Right. 'Course."

The apartment was walled in by high bookshelves, murky paintings on the walls, a narrow back deck and narrower back yard. I trained to Manhattan to give a reading and to see my cousin Hank and his husband John, and afterward they bought me a late dinner in a hipster imitation of a Fifties diner; meatloaf and milkshakes for me and John, while Hank ordered an egg-white omelet with all the vegetables the kitchen might possess. John asked me about my plans for Morocco. Hank reminisced about how back in the

Seventies he'd rented a car and driven all around the country with his boyfriend of the time.

"It's a magical place," he said. "I fell in love with it."

I asked after John's work. The last time my wife and I were in New York together we had gone to visit John's studio in Washington Heights where he showed us some of his paintings: sculptural, iconic portraits and tableaux of generations of his African American family, going back to slavery time and beyond to a fantastic Africa out of Douanier Rousseau, a pastoral blaze of electric pinks and greens. Nude men danced together in scenes reminiscent of Matisse, while in another painting a figure resembling John himself sat hugging his knees at the planet's edge, looking up at the stars. The more recent paintings were political—stark figures of Black men shot down by demonic red-eyed police. But what drew me in most was a large painting in which the members of his immediate family crowded together on a train station bench, no one figure meeting any other figure's gaze. The small boy perched on the right edge in a red sweater looking out at the viewer was recognizably John. The room they waited in was abstract except for lines indicating a wooden floor, an angled suitcase at the bottom right, and at the upper left, a white and black accordion shape—a radiator—somehow reminiscent to me of the fatty streaks that unsettle the faces in Francis Bacon's portraits. The radiator squatted like a scream in its corner, kitty-corner to the watchful boy.

In the diner, John shrugged at my question.

"It proceeds," he said. "I'm happy." The simple truth.

John rarely shows his work. When he sells it, he sells it to friends. He took up painting after a long career as a professor of art history, with all the weight of the Italian Renaissance in his head. Somehow, late in life, he'd found it in himself to become an artist, to paint only what he sees. He's the bravest man I know.

"There's fulfillment, and there's success," he reminded me. "Don't confuse them."

"Your father," Hank said, returning to an old theme, "never should have married your mother. She was so *alive*."

"Don't you mean," I said, "that *she* should never have married *him*?"

"Either way," John pointed out, "if they hadn't gotten married, you wouldn't be here."

"Maybe I'd have managed somehow."

The next day I woke up alone in Brooklyn. I strapped on my trainers, whittled down my possessions to the front door key and a twenty-dollar bill, and went for a run along Flatbush, through Grand Army Plaza, past the facade of the Brooklyn Public Library, a glorious monument to the faded age of great public works, waving as I passed at the golden image of Walt Whitman embossed in the doorway between what looks to be Melville's White Whale and Poe's Raven. Into Prospect Park, blowing hard, slowing to a wander through strangely bucolic meadows and fields, looking over arched bridges into algae-blooms, avoiding ornery swans, surprised by space, surprised by un-city.

Mother space, father time. New York: ground zero of my life, crossing paths obliquely with Lorca and the Spain I'd yet to see: "first landscape / of shocks, fluids, and murmurs / that seeps into a newborn child." But I never got to be a New Yorker myself—a strangely painful fact. I was only born there, though there are certain smells—the scorched stink of pushcart pretzels, the fermented vapor of urine rising from hot asphalt—to which my memory stakes a claim. But fathers are ambiguous, DNA tests aside, and the city's role in my development entirely phantasmatic. His face emerges in mine, I thought as I jogged along raggedly, more so every day. My father, and his father, and a step back, and a step back. What descends to my daughter? My face in hers.

A step forward, out of Brooklyn, out of the past. No one understood that, in a few weeks' time, he would wake up early in my sister's place, decide he wanted a cup of the coffee she doesn't drink, and without waking her, pad into her kitchen and pick up her car keys, head down the wooden steps whistling to where her VW stands waiting on the edge of its cliff…

Out of the back-and-forth of generations an urgent wish to stop time. I proposed a bargain, with God or the devil, it scarcely matters which, the moment my daughter was born: Let nothing more happen now, ever. Let me disappear in boredom as if into the most placid and silent of lakes. For the sake of what we call love, let all happening end.

But there was no one to bargain with, and happening… *happens*. As the dead beloved goes on moving behind your shut and sleeping eyes. As my father turned the key in the ignition and the engine rumbled one last time to life.

The sweet Brooklyn day passed in the bliss of unforeknowledge. I talked to my wife on the phone; I drew circles and X's in the pages of my notebook and filled the spaces with words, gleefully heading each page NOT FOR THE NOVEL NOT FOR THE NOVEL. And that night I went to see the Irish actor Lisa Dwan perform Beckett's *Not I* at BAM, running late from daydreams, pausing just long enough to fold a New York slice into my mouth before I arrived at the theater. I was ushered into a space of utter blackness; even the exit signs had been masked with black cloths, though the word EXIT still gleamed dimly, redly, like light pressing through eyelids in the dark. Finding my seat with my fingers, apologizing in the hush, nearly trampling an indignant older woman whose silver-spangled purse provided the closest thing to a source of light. Without preamble a spotlight singled out—Mouth. Past performers of the role—Billie Whitelaw, Julianne Moore, Juliet Stevenson—typically took twelve to fifteen minutes to run the catastrophic cataract of Beckett's lines. Dwan did it in nine minutes and fifty seconds. *Out, into this, into this world...* I don't know how it's possible for Mouth to move— in the other productions I'm aware of the performer has to be fixed in a chair, or thrusts her head through a board— but this Mouth did, indeed, seem to move, floating like a half-paralyzed dragonfly from one end of the invisible stage to the other, teeth sparking in the darkness. *Imagine,* it cried, *not suffering!* An exuberant performance of misery, mystery. The voice pursued itself, relentlessly, impossibly, reaching higher and higher pitches of intensity. A woman's soul, lacerated by words cut out by Beckett like a boy cutting paper dolls, in order to feel *something.* It turns out a body's not necessary for voices. A tube of air and anguish hovered there, capped by white and red.

The applause tumbled around my ears. In the men's washroom during the intermission I was pretty sure I saw Philip Glass in front of me drying his hands on a paper towel, talking animatedly with a bearded man. I couldn't make out what they're saying and tried standing a little closer, but they were borne away by the general scrum. They passed out of the room, Philip flicking water off his fingers in a repetitive drumstick motion. He passed me by.

Two more short plays followed. A woman paced a strip of carpet while her unseen mother refused to die. And a woman rocking in a chair took her time dying in tight light. Women and mothers and dying. I didn't see Philip Glass anywhere standing on the street afterward, wishing I still smoked. I walked home in light rain.

While walking, I called Dad to tell him about it, though I was out of the habit of telling him much of anything beyond the doings of his granddaughter. We followed the mandatory minimum of speech out of shyness, habit, fear. Fear of what? Past a certain age your father's not your father anymore. True? He was in New Jersey, as yet uninjured, only an hour and change from Brooklyn. I could have met him in that now-then. I could have seen him one more time, whole. But I didn't, saying only to him repeatedly, as a fellow lover of theater, *You should see it, Dad. You oughta see this one.*

A father is a weathervane. The cock crows, thinking it rules the roost. But it is only a whirligig spun by every passing breeze.

CAFÉ CENTRAL

I wake late on the last day of the conference and wander down through the sounds of vacuum cleaners and the street ricochet of motorbikes, and drifts of smoke to the hotel dining room: the Americans are half-crazed with happiness over their freedom to light cigarettes indoors. Round bread dipped in honey, yogurt, dates. My colleagues sit on the terrace by the swimming pool, from which a tall morose man is scooping fallen leaves with what looks like an ordinary garden rake. We exchange greetings and complain about the cigarettes and reassure each other that yesterday's performance did not in fact fall flat. How strange to sit with them, these men I work with, familiar faces made more familiar by the foreign feeling that surrounds us, an intensity of connection that will fade once we return to the States and our separate lives. We represent a broad waddling band of middle age, from John on the cusp of forty to Ringo who's nearly sixty. Morocco is like a fragrance on our skins, activated by November heat, soon to dissipate—meanwhile it's snowing in Chicago. I smell smoke, the sea, dry leaves, car exhaust, honey on my fingers. The conference can't hold us. We go for a last stroll up the hill through the streets of the Ville Nouvelle until we reach the medina, slowing our pace to take in the density of colors and people walking, shuffling, standing, squatting, and smiling in its narrow carless passageways. We find the Petit Socco or Zoco Chico, a kind of narrow hypotenuse of a square at the center of the old city lined with cafes, the regular haunts of Bowles and Burroughs and all the rest: Café Tingis, Café Central, Café Al Manara. We climb up to a second floor terrace, and take seats with a view of the square.

Café Central, wrote Bowles in 1958, was the favored destination of American visitors and residents: at any time you might spot there Barbara Hutton, Truman Capote, Somerset Maugham, or Errol Flynn "trying to hide his face behind the pages of a newspaper." Bowles was sentimental about his adopted city and deplored the rapid changes after Moroccan independence that threatened to destroy "this lively oasis of the past in the midst of today's dreariness." At the same time he was a pragmatist, and unlike most of the other expatriate writers who came to Morocco had a deep understanding of and interest in Mahgrebi culture: he translated the work of Moroccan writers and storytellers and made it possible for a number of writers and artists to publish or sell their work in the West. Strangely, or maybe just pragmatically, he never learned Arabic, relying on his fluency in the postcolonial lingua franca of the country: French and Spanish. You could call him a colonialist with a conscience—maybe no writer since Henry James is as closely associated with the disasters that can occur when Americans, high-minded and otherwise, intrude upon a culture and history that they do not understand in search of their own personal enrichment, spiritual or otherwise. Bowles was no rider of the Marrakech Express, which many nevertheless followed to his door in Tangier, where he received them patiently, in later years most often from his bed, suffering the hippies, fools, and "tourists" his louche protagonist Port Moresby criticizes in *The Sheltering Sky*. The tourist, Port says, "accepts his own civilization without question; not so the traveler, who compares it with the others, and rejects those elements he finds not to its liking." It seems to me that this distinction is a little simple: time was I would have embraced Bowles' definition of "the traveler," but now it seems the height of arrogance to assume that I might simply "reject" the "elements" of my upbringing, my language, and everything else that's shaped me. Sitting with my colleagues around a table on the narrow balcony of the Al Manara overlooking the square, sipping from our glasses of sweet mint tea, I know that we are much closer to tourists than travelers. We have come to Morocco, we've heard the Master Musicians, we've been lost in Fez, but not once, even for a moment, have we stepped outside the literary bubble that the likes of Bowles and Burroughs helped inflate for us. In the sun, watching both drab and colorful djellabas stream by, spying what looks to be another American in the cafe below bent over her notebook scribbling away, I know myself to be living inside their texts, if not inside textuality itself. *Mektoub.*

"How long have you known Gabriel, John?"

"Gabriel?" John creases his forehead. "Forever. Since I was a graduate student and went to my first Burroughs conference. I think that was in Binghamton. I presented a paper on heroin and postmodernism, and Gabriel liked it enough to publish it in the journal he was editing at that time. In a way he launched my career."

"Heroin and postmodernism?"

"Don't get him started," George interjects, but it's too late. Ringo rolls his eyes.

"Different drugs belong to different literary genres," John explains. "You ever noticed that? Heroin is postmodern because it's absolutely negative—it zeroes out the personality. Death of the author so that the text can live. Alcohol is the opposite—that's literary realism—lethal, ordinary, all that John Cheever kind of crap. Who do you think was more trouble at a party, Burroughs or Cheever? I rest my case."

"What about other drugs?"

"Uppers are science fiction," John says suavely, ticking off the list on his fingers. "Without amphetamines no Philip K. Dick, who is a genre unto himself. Cannabis is poetry, eh?" He digs me in the ribs. "Poetry and the personal essay."

"I hardly touch the stuff," I say stiffly.

"And psychedelics?" Ringo asks, smirking.

John slaps the table. "Nonfiction!"

"So would you say he's a trustworthy person?"

"Who, Gabriel?" John giggles. "I mean, I never loaned money to the guy, but I'd say so. Why do you ask? Did he ask you to write something for him?"

"Something like that."

"Great! We'll make a Burroughs scholar out of you yet."

After tea and a browse through shops buying trinkets we wind our way down to the seaport and enter a mazy indoor market crammed with butcher's stalls and buckets of red, brown, and yellow spices. A severed and skinned cow's head eyes us dolefully. I narrowly avoid stepping into a milk crate out of which a dozen severed goats' legs thrust their hooves. Men and boys move around and through our little group at a rapid pace, shouting instructions at one another and ignoring us completely. "This way," I say, thinking a wider doorway means the way out. And it does, but only through a massive fish hall, where table after table stands groaning with the catch of the day: a million gleaming sardines, sharp-finned bonito, mullet, marlin, a pair of surprised-looking swordfish, and on the floor near where the daylight comes in is stretched out a tuna the size of a canoe. It is staggering, and in an odd way heartening, to be confronted by this evidence of the sea's continued abundance, though something tells me this display would have been dwarfed by the catch even a dozen years ago. Our fish dinner at Popeye's comes to mind: it is easy to imagine the genial owner who served us portion after portion roaming the aisles of the market, pointing at the freshest and most savory prospects for his restaurant while one of his employees followed behind with cash on the barrelhead and a cart full of ice. Did Brion Gysin do the same for the restaurant he called 1,001 Nights, the palace showcase he created for the Master Musicians, another fantasy of Morocco from within Morocco?

"There is an end of the world feeling in Tangier," Burroughs wrote to Ginsberg. "Something sinister in complete laissez-faire." Those days are long gone and the fantasy of Interzone was never anything other than that: a colonialist fantasy imposed on the unwilling, backgrounded and exploited "natives." We who return to Morocco in the twenty-first century re-enact a fantasy of isolation and autonomy: "imagination," wrote Paul Bowles, "is essential for the enjoyment of a place like Tangier." Is it not the nature of the imaginative life to try and realize itself, to erase the boundary between itself and life, in the face of every consequence? We risk little: there is no madness for us here, no descent into drug addiction or alcoholism, only the fantasy from a distance of destructive Others—named *Ebola*, named *Islamic State*—that up close dissolves into any cityscape's gumbo of smiles, frowns, and blank indifference.

A banquet bids goodbye to the conference, to the fantasy of dropped names. It takes place in a heretofore hidden room of the hotel, palatial, ornately carved, with a dance floor on which male and female dancers gyrate. The first woman modestly covered, the second a belly dancer, exposing a quantity of flesh that would be unremarkable back home but here seems almost criminally provocative. A spectacle that by beholding it marks us all as outsiders, as surely as do the glasses of wine poured for us by the smiling waitstaff, who seem to enjoy watching us watching. We eat fistfuls of olives and dates, lamb, slices of an enormous *pastilla*, huge heaping salads, and between courses we clap our hands awkwardly; some of us even dance. As I watch my fellow conferees I swell with unexpected affection for my tribe, my people: literary geeks and nerds, male and female alike, shaking our awkward butts, chasing after whatever stale whiffs of glory that continue to be emitted by the legends of those names: Kerouac, Ginsberg, Bowles, Burroughs, Gysin. Somehow we've carved out a subcultural niche for ourselves that survives, against the grain of a society whose principal addictions, caffeine and media, are designed to foster ever-higher rates of productivity and ever-decreasing quantities of pleasure. The music—played by younger men than the Master Musicians, with a more Saharan and Berber quality—whirls us in circles and ellipses; at one point an incongruous conga line forms. I am not a graceful dancer but I've had a little wine: I put my hands lightly over another man's hips and a woman behind me grips my waist and we sway around the room together. We are celebrating ourselves. We are celebrating, in spite of everything, the work of the imagination.

It's around nine o' clock when I return to the Café de Paris, and I sip mint tea with my notebook spread open before me watching the djellabas and jeans skirting by. There's a moon in my mind, moon over Morocco and my last night. The notebook remains blank. Mr. Ahmed does not appear. As I'm getting up to go the waiter—an extremely tall, extremely thin man with sallow skin and a disconcertingly Hitlerian mustache, touches me on the elbow. "Monsieur was with us yesterday?"

"Who's asking?"

He bows, skips backward, extends his fist and opens it. A slip of paper is rolled up in his palm like a cigarette. "For you, please."

I take the paper, give the man some dirhams, and step into the lavatory to have a closer look. The paper is thin and flimsy, like a cash register receipt. In fact it *is* a receipt, for three mint teas at this very cafe. But on the other side a few words have been scrawled. *Granada. Sunday. Casa de Lorca. 15:00.* That's all.

So it's not only Mr. Ahmed who wants me to go to Granada, I think. Unless he wrote this note. But why?

I raise my wife on Skype. It's daytime there. She's sitting in the bay window with a cup of coffee, eerily composed, shadowed by gray winter light. She smiles tightly at me, then looks away.

"I kissed Edward."

My stomach drops. "So?" I say lightly. "Isn't that your job?"

"Yes. I mean, no. I mean, I kissed him. I *really* kissed him." She studies her hands. "Offstage."

"Oh."

Someone outside goes clattering by noisily on a motorbike and I can't hear what she says after that.

"What did you say?"

"It was a party for the last show, the afterparty, just me and a couple of the others. We stayed out late, later than anyone. The sidewalks were icy and he walked me to my car. And he kissed me."

"I thought you said that *you* kissed *him*."

She shrugs. Why won't she look at me? Because she can't, because video chat, no matter how smooth the wifi connection, offers everything but connection.

"I thought that Edward was gay."

"He is."

"So it didn't mean anything."

Her cheeks turn red. "That's not up to you."

"What are you saying?"

"I'm saying that I'm confused. And that you should know."

"I should know that you're confused?"

"Yeah."

She looks into a space I can't occupy. "Did you find what you were looking for yet? Are you coming home?"

"Dad's going to die," I say. The words are torn from me and I'm breathless.

Her face. "Honey, no. You don't know that."

I don't know what else to say. So I say something stupid, or rather I do something stupid: I move my mouth as though saying words. Her face was flowing, rippling with remorse. Now she only stares at me, puzzled.

"What? What are you saying?"

I am moving my lips, gesticulating. In the little window where I see myself I look insane. Not angry exactly but intent, energized. My lips forming the words that Emily's taught me all actors use when they're on stage but have no dialogue, when they're pretending to speak: *peas and carrots peas and carrots.*

"I think we have a bad connection." Off camera there comes a long slow yowl. "And your daughter is calling me. I'll call you back."

Her expression has precipitated into pity.

I'm no longer "talking." I stare at her. Not at her, but at the tiny camera lens on my iPad, so that it will look to her as though I'm looking into her eyes, even though I'm not, I'm not, I'm not.

"I'll call you back," she repeats, and the screen goes black.

My father is my go-to-jail free card; I can still play that. *You won't see me tomorrow,* I can say. *I want to see him one more time before he goes home from the rehab place. Before he begins in earnest his career as a cripple. I want to tell him it's okay if he's done with all this, if he's ready to go. If I were in his shoes I'd want to die. Wouldn't you?*

I'd want to remember him the way he was when he was alive.

Riding the ferry, propped on the precipice of my own existence—marked from where? From when? The moment of conception, in that brownstone on West 89th. The photos I still have of Mom's pregnant belly, Dad's smiling mustached face floating in front—he looks like Groucho posing with the Man in the Moon. Pointing his finger at what will be me. The labor before the birth, at Mt. Sinai Hospital, in the pre-dawn hours of October 2, 1970. The light that blinds the blind infant, the smack of cold air followed by the doctor's hand, the nurse's arms, warm wet cloth and then warm dry cloth, the bassinet, discovering sleep. More photos: at home in the shared apartment being bathed in a metal washtub, my mother's lips fixed in a shushing O, holding—I can't remember this—me by the feet long and hysterical. Even in black and white I am all squall, tiny and red. Bottles, booties, cries in the night, she sacrifices her sleep for his, and his. Well-wrapped in the park in a secondhand stroller, snow on the ground, Simon and Garfunkel somewhere singing about a home *where the New*

York City winters aren't bleeding me… Blank months while sights, smells, sounds of the city touch my skin and mark me for exile, as the apartment seems to shrink and Dad is finishing his MBA, and Mom is too tired to do anything but shake her head in an ambivalent sort of way. New York is going down the tubes; street crime is rampant. *For the baby,* he insists, and how can Mom refuse? Signing documents: the lease on the shop where he'll start his company, then the lease on the rental house. The city is a memory; the photo record is no help here. We are in Old Bridge, where Dad is running for the school board, where Mom has to buy groceries with food stamps. Dad is gone all the time building the business that will ensure our middle-class comforts; Mom is home watching her belly swell. We move to Plainfield, where my sister will be born; there my un-photographed memories start. Hot sidewalk, cool grass, Big Wheel, frost heaves, gravel driveway, trees trees trees, hills, glass and ceramic tchotchkes shelved in the orange-painted den, Dad shaving in the little Victorian bathroom over the pedestal sink, Mom slumped with a cup of coffee in the kitchen the color of a ripe banana, riding my rocking horse, all the chess pieces, fireworks at the Bicentennial, maple leaves, deep snow, striped shirts, standing in line for *Star Wars.* The precipice is behind me and ordinary life sets in. Decades flash by until it happens again, is still happening. What was my father thinking, expecting, as he wondered whether he'd make payroll for his employees this week, as he wondered if the checks his wife writes at the super-market would bounce, coming home every day to find us there, waiting for him? What was my little sister thinking, flashing teeth and hair, tumbling and squealing in a perfect unquestionable world? What was my mother thinking, brooding with her Salems, standing out on the back porch watching us and then turning away, letting the screen door slam, going back inside to her Agatha Christies and her sewing machine and her solitude? What happened to the books she was going to write? What happened to the poems? What became of the life she might have led, with my father or without him or after him, the subsequent life, the second act? On weekends we shuttled back to the city in its incomprehensible Seventies squalor, all four of us, to visit Hank or my Vitalis-smelling grandfather in Queens or to see the requisite sights: the Statue of Liberty, Radio City, the Empire State Building, the World Trade Center—vividly I remember standing with my whole body pressed to the smooth metal southeast corner of the north tower looking straight up at the impossible possible, the sky at a greater distance than I have ever seen it since. We rode the ferry to Staten Island and back again, passing the time, the overripe dirty yellow the color of the taxicabs, wind ballooning my windbreaker, following the line of my father's arm as he pointed up to the Statue and then down to the Atlantic and then across the Garden State he reminded me was home. My sister pulling me by the hand this way and that, the water rolling, I don't remember Mom on these trips though she must have been there, frowning enigmatically behind Jackie O sunglasses, smoking, smoking, looking out over her children's heads over the railing at the elongated fist of Manhattan, knowing in her bones it was a paradise to which she would never return, and the person responsible was crouched beside her son, his arm extended over the water, turning back to grin at her. She stubbed her cigarette against the bulkhead, sending sparks flying, lips rigid, studying impassively her husband's smile until it faded away.

IV
LETTER TO HIS FATHER

NEW JERSEY

Lips form an O and smoke escapes to assume their form. The body draws itself on the air, inside-out. Death comes in. What is poetry? Words estranged from each another on a page that speaks out of nothing, to no one, from no plausible "I." A poem is like a story that picks up the reader and drops them with a short sharp shock back into their own life, none the wiser, no less lonely. It's no wonder most people, like Marianne Moore, dislike it, finding in it neither a place nor when it comes down to it value for the genuine.

In the New Jersey suburbs, ten miles and a universe away from the world she once knew how to navigate, the deserted island of Manhattan, my mother sat in yellow light tuned to the hum of an IBM Selectric and wrote a poem:

> *I am watching*
> *the sun / set*
> *among dark*
> *clouds;*
> *it is /*
> *was an extraordinary*
> *red.*
> *Thunderstorms*
> *passing over.*

When I find it in her papers it's called "Found Poem." Where did she find it? In the air, in the charge given to her senses by the atmosphere? Or someone else's words that she picks up and drops again, nearly at random? She sucked on a cigarette. She looked around the basement sewing room where she kept the typewriter next to a slithery stack of paperbacks. Upstairs her thirteen-year-old son was deep in his own paperback, by Isaac Asimov probably, or a *Star Trek* novelization. Her eleven-year-old daughter was at a friend's house. Her husband was at work, the strange galaxy of his work, following the elliptical arc that took him every morning away from the house into a secret life that each evening revealed its banality or else congealed into domestic chitchat tense with unhappiness. It was hazy outside, there was no "sun / set," not yet. Where did she find them, her words?

She called a friend on the phone, for gossip, for company, and her laughter was faintly audible to the son upstairs discovering girls and his distance from them. He crept to and fro in stocking feet with one of his dad's dirty magazines under his arm. Back then all the nude women had pubic hair, which made them seem more naked than today's model; today's naked women are stripped, invulnerable. His mother will catch him at it, more than once, and red-faced slam the door and ask him or herself or the suburbs at large, *Why?* It's a question without an answer. Looking down at her own plumping body, shaky with its polluted lungs. Hand to the door: *Those women, you understand they're not real! Are you listening to me?* But no words could fill the space between them: the unhappy woman, the unhappy boy.

Later he'd show her his first poems, climbing into the bed where she rests in the afternoon to present her with the pages typed and retyped on the same pale blue Selectric with its jittery hum, its leaping lettered globe. He won't read them aloud, he'll only huddle there, near but not too near, eyes on her eyes as they flicker across the page. Until she looks over at him and smiles.

Same bed she will die in, the years like pages. I was at the library when she died. Checked out. Searching the stacks. While my father and sister waited for her on the far side of the bed. She's gone.

In 1986 she's still alive, in remission. She quits smoking, volunteers, entertains. Sometimes she holds her husband's hand, walking down the streets of the little New Jersey town, fortunate to have streets with a little life in them, not the sidewalkless suburbs of Chicago where they go twice a year to spend a few empty hours with Bubbe, with Zeyde. They go to the movies, to Baskin Robbins (at fifteen I get my first job there, skip a shift in the second week, get fired for the first but not the last time), stroll across the village green. The hot summers are only hot summers, nobody yet understands that we've turned the world into a body as feverish as our own. The two of them are polite to each other for weeks, summoning gestures of distant affection—a brief kiss on the threshold, shy smiles in the kitchen. But always arriving sooner or later a burst of rage followed by bitter silence. When nobody's home I sneak forbidden TV (*Doctor Who, Knight Rider,* Cinemax After Dark) or put on an LP by Beethoven or The Cars and turn the volume way up, lying on the shag carpet gazing at the ceiling while the house shudders and shakes. My sister passes in and out of the house dressed for lacrosse, a spark between synapses, light. When the phone rings I don't get up to answer it: it's never for me. I go up to my room and write poems.

All ribs and hipbones, naked and preposterous in the bathroom mirror, wondering where I went wrong. Dad tries to interest me in baseball, in tennis, in golf. I flail haplessly at balls, scream at him to leave me alone. You won't teach me anything, I say. I'm no good. I go inside and read.

There are flashes, images to live for and try to capture: fragments of memory from the incomplete years, before the permanent reel-to-reel started running: age seven, age six, age five, age four. A red-haired girl named Zöe, clutching her hand, running down a grassy New England hill. The ferry to Star Island off the coast of New Hampshire watching the buoys bob, ringing their lonesome bells. My sister, a selkie, shivering in a towel in the early morning light after a polar bear swim on the island: she has always possessed the physical courage I lack. The long walk to the evening chapel in a line of children, each carrying a candle planted in a tinfoil star to catch the wax, sheltering the flame with the other hand, singing. The old hotel lobby with the lithographs of hanged pirates, the green leather settee like an inverted donut, the defunct switchboard like so many eyeless sockets. Thirteen or fourteen or fifteen years old, in my room at my desk or lying on the floor with my eyes closed straining to recapture those images, looking for the fork I took from my happy childhood into ordinary unbearable misery, finding no pattern, only a feeling of connection with something that pierced me and pieced me together, before there were words, before I fell into the inferno of my semi-autistic adolescence, before I understood that my parents were unhappy. Were they always unhappy? Had they never been in love? Fragments, fragments, flying together and apart when I screwed my eyes shut tightly enough to flash colors: Mom with long hair wearing a crown of flowers, Dad strumming a guitar by a campfire, warm and living lights in nature's darkness. Pine needles, the spooky glaze of a night in the woods, the painful push of my bladder but it's just before dawn and I'm afraid to leave the tent. I listen for my parents' breathing. No one moves.

I found the poem in a letter I didn't read until long after she was gone, part of my inheritance, a box of papers holding her birth certificate, the bill of divorcement from her first husband, some notes from a course in psychology she took later in life. Puzzling over those slashes, which academic convention dictates are used to indicate the line breaks when placing a verse quotation into prose. Here one divides "sun" from "set," a break inside the line—caesura—and another redundantly separates "is" from "was." They echo each other as they divide the present from the past. Light from obscurity. The ordinary "it is" from the "extraordinary / red." The slash *is* the poem—its turn, its clinamen, its volta—derailing ordinary sense and sending the reader along multiple forking paths of sound, of image, of possibility. It is the cut in speech that demands rereading, obsession. No wonder we think of poetry as dead, like the poets themselves, who demand like murder victims an exact and forensic attention. Uncrowned coroners, we extract proof of life from these wounded words, evidence that others felt, sorrowed, burned: *That in black ink my love may still shine bright.* Cut the word-lines and the future leaks out, Burroughs claims. But the slashes are also sutures. The past shines through them.

Fate is meaningless until you remember that it—the *it* of your life—might have been otherwise. There is a left as well as right. In the newspaper I read that Caroll Spinney, the actor who's played Big Bird on *Sesame Street* for exactly as long as I've been alive, was invited to fly on the Space Shuttle but the invitation was canceled after it was determined there wasn't enough room for the costume. That was in 1986 and the shuttle was the *Challenger* that exploded a few seconds after takeoff. Before 9/11 for my generation there was the Space Shuttle's plume of smoke ballooning on a convex screen rolled into the classroom on a metal cart, to be replayed for the next several nights on the evening news. A plume attached to nothingness, leading nowhere. We've seen that movie too many times. It's imprinted on the backs of everyone's eyelids, the disaster we were trained for. Smoke changes the light and we are afloat in a world innavigable. The pillar of fire by night.

Would a thousand fewer, a hundred fewer, a dozen fewer cigarettes have saved her life? Or is there another toxin to blame, maybe history itself? Can I blame Three Mile Island? New Jersey? The tinder of Auschwitz, the Mengele moment that came for my grandparents in their separate lines of *Selektion*. Right to live. Left to die. If either of them had been sent the wrong way, I might not exist. However well-hidden she was, ghetto-child, to have lost either parent might have twisted her out of recognition. She might never have been my mother.

It's 1986. It's always 1986 somewhere. Fifteen years old, scribbling raw in a notebook, making promises to my future self.

Downstairs she stabs out her cigarette and gets up, telling herself: *That was the last one.*

THE SAILOR

I have eye floaters; once you've seen them they're impossible to unsee. Little ghostly thready presences, insectile, like webs clinging to my corneas. Caused by decay of the vitreous humor, harmless, appearing after age fifty, a normal part of the aging process. I am not—quite—age fifty. I do wear glasses, I am myopic, these are risk factors. Hard not to feel old before my time, hard not to see—almost literally—old age marching my way. Decayed humors. I am in this body for the not-so-long haul. Wikipedia tells me they're most noticeable when looking at a light background. Looking at the desert. Looking at the sea. Staring at the cursor winking on a blank white screen.

I said my farewells this morning outside the hotel, piling the rest of the Muttering Sickness into a taxi for the airport. Hugs all around: I knew it wouldn't last but in that moment, our last as companions, I felt lovingly toward these men. We've been strangers in a strange land together, the ring of foreignness making our differences less relevant. They were only slightly puzzled by my change of plans.

"You're not coming home with us?"

"I caught a different flight. A later flight."

George and Ringo looked at one another, shrugged, smiled tightly. John tapped his phone: time to go. He clapped me on the shoulder before he got into the car, looking up into my eyes. "Please give your father my best regards."

The cab rolled out of sight. They were off to Madrid to catch the connecting flight home, a flight I was supposed to be on. Their wives and girlfriends will pick them up; I imagine them observed by my own wife, circling in our car around and around the ring of O'Hare, wondering where I am, our daughter kicking impatiently in the backseat. The ring tightened like a leash: alone, my skin thinning, the sky fell more blindingly into my eyes. On the screen a seven-second video of my wife and daughter smiling and waving, shot too many days ago to mean anything. Where's Daddy? Daddy isn't here.

I stand with my suitcase between my knees in front of the hotel, checked out, in the middle of Tangier, hesitating between north and south on the elastic leash of lies. South to Marrakech as Mr. Ahmed suggested; north to Spain and my uncertain rendezvous. Or south farther still, following the path of Bowles' hapless Americans into the desert, riding a camel, in thrall to my Orientalist fantasy, shedding at last the shell of the self. Let that part of me die like Port in a post of the French Foreign Legion, let what remains drift like an abandoned wife into abjection and madness. *Reach out, pierce the fine fabric of the sheltering sky, take repose.* The idea of it, so close, like the hot inland wind that swept through the train that carried us to Fez. I could actually do it. I could disappear.

The driver of the petit taxi turns around in his seat and grins at me. "*Où voulez-vous aller?*"

"*Le ferry, s'il vous plaît.*"

The sun shines on the Boulevard Pasteur but in the brief

time required to wind our way around the old city down to the coast road a strong wind from the north brings with it a rag of overcast sky tossing down dirty bricks of rain. The driver switches on the windshield wipers, which have absolutely no effect; I cling to the door handle with both hands as the cab lurches blindly over the stones. Gray sheets of water are sweeping across the terminal quay when we arrive, and the driver and I both just sit there quietly for a moment, listening to the rain drum on the roof like so many flat hands. He says something in French that I don't quite catch.

"Sorry? *Comment*?"

"You still want to get out here?" he says in English.

"Yes," I say. "I think so."

He glances back at me over his shoulder and shrugs an eloquent farewell.

The rain pauses long enough for me to climb out of the cab, hauling my suitcase behind me, and to hustle over to the terminal building. Once inside I discover why the cabbie was looking at me the way he did: ALL FERRIES CANCELED says a handwritten sign taped to the glass partition of the ticket counter. I stand there steaming damp until a clerk appears.

"All ferries canceled," he says without missing a beat.

Perhaps it's a sign. If I've missed my flight, if I'm not going home, instead of crossing the Mediterranean back to the comparative familiarity of Europe I must be destined to stay in Morocco or to journey to points even further south, beyond the Maghreb into Africa proper, across the Sahara into Mauritania, Senegal, the Gambia. My phone buzzing in my pocket. How far would I have to go, now, to be completely and legitimately out of touch?

Dad's going home, my sister texts. *He doesn't want to be here anymore.*

The ambiguity of the words *home* and *here* buzzes burningly in my brain.

I could be on a plane in a few hours. It might even be possible to catch up with my original flight from Madrid, if I take a taxi to the airport right now. But instead, I find myself walking out from the ferry terminal out to the highway, following a path that parallels the shore road, bumping my suitcase behind me. The squall has passed and sun glints in puddles and in the cracks in the concrete. I climb above the fragmented beach, and glancing down notice a man on horseback riding in the direction of the Casbah, head high, a figure out of dream but incontestably real. The horse is gray with a spray of black dots and dashes spattered on its haunches; the rider wears black trousers and a T-shirt and holds his magnificently mustached head high. I stand indecisively for a while, shielding my eyes from the tormenting light skimming up from the water's white blade. If I keep walking this direction I'll leave the body of the city behind, climbing higher hills until I can look out over the Mediterranean to the north and the Atlantic to the West. I could crawl into the Caves of Hercules and look out through the keyhole of light toward home. But it's starting to rain again and my back is tired from hauling the awkward suitcase on its plastic wheels. I turn around and head back toward the ferry terminal.

Standing in drizzle with a two-euro coin in my hand. Heads I go home, I say. Tails…

A taxi pulls up in front of me with the window rolled down in spite of the wet; I recognize the driver who brought me here. "Monsieur! Do you still want the ferry?

"Excuse me?"

He jerks a thumb toward the back seat. "I have two other gentlemen for the ferry. Please get in!"

He pops the trunk for me. After the slightest pause, I heave my bag inside and go around and get into the front passenger seat.

Useless windshield wipers still slashing at the flying water, we go rumbling in a U-turn out of the terminal and back into city traffic. The driver explains that the biggest boats dock at Tangier Med, the giant new port facility nearly an hour's drive east of the city proper. "They sail in every weather!" I ride in the front seat, two laconic Germans or maybe Austrians in the back, backpacker types, or maybe they're Swiss, speaking or pretending to speak no English, looking somehow hungover—well, not every non-Muslim in this country feels obliged to abstain from alcohol, and in any case hash is easy to find and profoundly strong. One is short and one is tall, I catch their bleary malignant eyes in the driver's rear-view, the shorter one stretching his neck to whisper something into the ear of the taller one, who nods grimly. Meanwhile the Ville Nouvelle unfurls and spools behind us, turning into a succession of hotel-resorts clearly designed as cheap vacation destinations for people with euros or pounds to spend. We spiral out of town onto green bluffs that remind me, inevitably, of the hills where my sister lives. I see white cars; I turn and twist in my seat, half-expecting to see one upside-down on the flats below, wheels still spinning. If our driver, who has an alarmingly casual two-fingered driving style, were to twitch a hair to the left it would be our car that took fleetingly to the air, spinning on its axis until we came crashing down onto jagged rocks, a Moroccan and an American and a Eurotrash Mutt and Jeff forever bound together in shattered glass and exploding gasoline and death. But the resemblance to Marin is limited by the litter that climbs every hill: half-finished construction sites, garbage piles, the occasional concrete minaret. The short one has taken out an electric shaver and is using his phone as a mirror while he scrapes the bristles from his neck. The tall one looks asleep or dead, his head tilted back on the seat so that I can see straight up the black holes of his nostrils. The driver clenches the wheel between his knees and lights a cigarette as we go skidding past an oncoming truck with inches to spare, nearly costing him his driver's side mirror. I look at him and he lifts his dark eyebrows waggishly, as though to say, *That's how it goes.* He takes the wheel again gingerly with two fingers of his left hand and lets the smoke chimney out of his mouth into the backseat, making the passengers cough. I stare straight ahead, trying not to look like I'm bracing my body against the dashboard against what seems an inevitable impact. But nothing happens; we drive on, trapped in the amber of transit, the purgatorial space between the city and its secret boundary. I look, reflexively, at my phone, and see with secret relief that the battery is dead.

The port is massive, industrial, newly finished and barren, braced for the reception of container ships, "Tangier" only as tangential manifestation of the city, not as a place in which people live but a theoretical point, a port of entry instead of a port of saints, where certain abstractions of the world economy are made manifest to the naked eye. Vast empty asphalt plains ready to be stacked high with shipping containers are swept by cyclones made of fog and dust. The taxi meanders endlessly around the enormous parking lot, finally dropping us off at a glassed-in building as cavernous and empty as the port itself. The two Europeans get out and stand there scratching themselves, conferring. The tall one limps up to me with a crinkled piece of paper in his hand and a hopeful look in his eye. "Speak English?"

"Nope," I say, and walk away rapidly through the automatic doors and into the endless purgatory of the port, all gleaming yet somehow grungy steel and linoleum and dead bright LED lights, walking for what feels like hours before I find the embarkation area. Standing around eating a chocolate bar, waiting for the shuttle bus that will take me and a dozen or so travelers through the thin rain to the dockside where the ferry, as big to my eyes as a cruise ship, awaits. We're ushered past a line of cars and trucks waiting to board, into the belly of the beast, coughing on fumes, climbing lurching stairways to the passenger decks above. Already I can feel things shifting, long before the engines start to churn, before the green coast of Africa is swallowed by the washed-out stainless sea. Europe takes me into its exhausted arms; I am back in the West I never really left, of which I am a disabused fragment. Relief. Loss.

The ferry plunges through arching waves: this is the real sea. Speaking pigeon Spanish at the snack bar, paying for my sandwich in euros—bereft of the melodious French and Mahgrebi I'd been swimming in. The ferry is sparsely populated by Spaniards returning home from cheap vacations, by American backpackers, by scruffy luggageless men with the hunted look of migrants, clustering together in small groups and then breaking apart again fore and aft. The water throbs like Thom Yorke's voice in my ears: black water spiraling, Sisyphus stretch, in algebra. The black umbilical of my earbuds transmits my movements like a stethoscope, like a new precarious sensory organ dangling across my chest, rasping against the buttons of my jacket or vibrating in the wind as I step out onto the open deck, slipping on spray for a view of the Rock sliding into view like a vast black table in vertical mist, distant listless sliver of England, empire in the old style before empire migrated inward to capture our imaginations in the name of consumer choice. I have my choice of music to plant in my skull but music only ever says Yes—even punk, even twelve-tone, even a raspy recording of Burroughs fulminating against the all-powerful boards and syndicates of the earth. I climb the doomy chords, wallowing in pointless assertion: *No one knows where I am.*

Table of land. Drawn into the mouth of Gibraltar. We have crossed the belt of the sea between the Pillars of Hercules. And for a moment, out on deck, the blank horizon surrounding me, I close my eyes and feel my return to another homeless home, like the Manhattan my mother dreamed of, the Europe she fled from and returned to throughout her too-short life, mostly in her mind, a restless asymptotic syncopation that I too take up and slide with. Hinge of many worlds, Atlantic and Mediterranean, European and African, Old World and older. A moment overexposed in the misty white sun. Open to it. The arrow of time throbbing in my heart.

Grim, gritty Algeciras. I find a cheap room over a cheaper bar and wander the streets. People promenade in a pedestrian mall or linger in outdoor cafes in spite of the autumn chill—the Italian habit of *passeggiata* seems general all over the Mediterranean coast. I drink a glass of beer under a heat lamp, watching handsome middle-aged couples and matrons passing by arm in arm, phone a dead weight in my pocket. Drifting in search of food I stumble across a tract of Roman ruins near a park, stunned by something as prosaic as red brick inside of ancient walls. The world's grown old. I stand in the park looking at the ruins with a bag of McDonald's French fries in my hand.

Algeciras, Westernized version of part of the Arabic name for Spain (*Al-Jazeera*, "the peninsula"), portal to *Al-Andalus,* "the West" or "the Atlantic" or "country of the Vandals" or "to become green at summer's end," depending on whom you ask. The mark of eight hundred years of Muslim rule is elusive here, or maybe it's just that it's getting dark and I'm tired and the colors, tastes, smells of Morocco have slipped entirely away. I lie in the lumpy hostel bed over the raucousness of the bar—it's so loud I might as well be lying on top of the bar itself—and leaf through Washington Irving's

Tales of the Alhambra, the book that was largely responsible for the rescue of the crumbling palace and turning it into one of the world's premier tourist spots. The strange elusive soft power of books. What Irving wanted to see—a ragged fortress haunted by a thousand years' worth of Muslim and Christian and a few Jewish ghosts—could not be represented in the form conducive to Irving's imagination, with its shadows and hollows and whiffs of danger: "give me the rude mountain scramble," Irving wrote, "the roving, haphazard, wayfaring; the half wild, yet frank and hospitable manners, which impart such a true game flavor to dear old romantic Spain!" Game: the flavor of that which has been hunted, muscles flooded with fear, or else half-rotted. Venison, civet, jugged hare: "First catch your hare," the earliest recipes say. Irving, remembered these days if he's remembered at all for kitschy stories about time-traveling graybeards and headless horsemen, caught his stories by living in the palace for about a month, chatting with local informants, admiring the architecture of the Muslim kings and deploring their ruined state, criticizing by implication the supposedly more civilized Christians who had allowed such a wonder to go to pot. Even then Americans were adventurers swamped with high regard for their own high-mindedness, and to an American the word "adventure" is scrubbed of the stink of imperial oppression that it holds for the rest of the world. We slither across the haunted grounds of the earth, not realizing that we ourselves are haunters, spirits of innocent greed, innocent malignance. *Why do they hate us?*

Jews were tolerated, even welcome in Al-Andalus; in Spain they were persecuted, hunted, until those who wouldn't convert to Christianity were driven back across the water to Morocco or points farther east and south. The Romani or Gypsies or Gitanos are deeply embedded in Andalusian culture—Lorca's *duende* and *cante jondo* are unimaginable without them—but they remain minorities with all that minority status entails: high rates of imprisonment, unemployment, and drug addiction. And all Spain remains scarred by the Civil War and the years of Franco—to mark just one of many open wounds, it has only recently been revealed that as many as 300,000 children were taken from their Republican parents by nuns, priests, and doctors and sold to "politically approved" families. Imagine the story, like something out of Dickens: you are born, you grow up in a family, you love and hate your family, like anyone. Then you discover the keystone of your fate: you are someone else's child, your life depends from a phantasmal branch. Do you rejoice? Do you weep bitter tears? Do you seek yourself a different father's face?

I wake to grainy dawn with my phone fully charged. Weirdly, there are no messages. I feel vaguely insulted at first, and then frightened. Have they forgotten me? Do I deserve to be forgotten? Do I still exist? I swipe frantically at my wife's name.

The wifi connection is spotty and the screen goes black more than once on my wife's wary expression. "Where are you?"

"Spain."

She shakes her head in wonder. "It sounds made up. All these places you've visited."

"Have you slept with him yet?"

She eyes me thoughtfully. "Why are you asking?"

"I just want to know."

"No," she says, shaking her head. "I don't think that you do."

"Dad's going home. Did you hear?"

"Of course I heard." She stares at me. "I talk to them. Every day."

Two thieves grappling in the dark for a moral authority neither can honestly claim. We wrestle into the silence.

"When are you coming home?" she says finally. "We need to talk."

"Does she ask about me?" My daughter.

My wife pushes some hair out of her face; I am undone by her expression of gentle exasperation and by her words: "Every day."

The silver cord between us has stretched to its breaking point. Her life is in the world, on the stage, with our child; mine has fallen into the tangled constellations of *soledad*. Travel leans in on me like shifting walls. Is it really so different at home? Daily we fall past from each other into our separate lives. "Life is an affair of people not of places," wrote Wallace Stevens, "but for me it is an affair of places and that is the trouble." The poet hardly went anywhere: for the most part his seventy-six years were an unbroken succession of ordinary evenings in New Haven, broken up by the occasional fishing expedition in Key West. That did not stop him from being an astronaut of the mind, impossibly distant from his insufficiently adhesive wife and world.

Lie of the dark unrevealed by sentences: *I miss you. I miss our home. I'm trying to get my right.*

And as for Edward? I find that I don't believe in Edward. Or is it possible that I simply no longer give a shit?

Woe that is in marriage.

There is a fullness, a kind of plenitude of being, that emerges only in the experience of travel. The simple yet urgent challenges of getting one's body from one place to another is wholly involving, especially when it must be negotiated in another language. Put another way, traveling one is always on the brink of disaster and its exhilarations. Dad was visiting his daughter for a few days, a brief parenthesis in a busy retirement taken up by golf, tennis, and travel. He woke in the dark; he wanted his coffee; there was no coffee in the house. My sister was still asleep. He can go out and get some and be back before she's up. He slipped on his tennis shoes in the dark, padding downstairs. There, glistening on the kitchen counter, are her keys.

There's an early train. I shower in the cramped plastic stall, dressing efficiently, zipping my suitcase shut and slipping my shoulder bag onto the handle. Out into the narrow sloping hallway of this bric-a-brac B&B, walls the color of tea with too much milk in it, and down the stairs, dodging rips in the runner. Out into the dark cool early morning, following the GPS on the phone in my left hand, pulling the rolling bag with my right, the only sound except for a few birds, a few cars. When I reach the red pin I stop and look around. There's a train station all right, but it's defunct: a granite low-slung building back of some tracks that looks like it's in the process of being converted into shops and offices. Son of a bitch. Staring at the screen, then back at the disassembled building, willing reality to conform to Google and not vice-versa. I look around but there's no one to ask, and in any case I don't speak Spanish. Fortunately I remember passing another station, the new station, not too far from the ferry terminal the previous day; I guess at the direction and strike out. It's a few minutes before six and the train leaves at 6:15 AM; I am sweating; I can't spend another hour in Algeciras, let alone another day. The buildings are blocky and charmless. I follow one deserted street to its end, then another, then catch sight of a familiar overpass. Crossing the street against the non-existent traffic and exhaling sharply at the sight of the station roundabout. Inside there's movement and life: I stand impatiently in the short queue, unwilling to risk the ticket machine. It's my turn: the pudgy uniformed clerk regards me sleepily. "*El próximo tren, por favor?*"

"Granada."

"Granada? *Si.*"

The train to Granada is a ghost train, dark and unliving in the dark, and I wonder for a moment if I'm getting on the right one. Then I wonder if there can be a right train for someone in my situation. As I'm stashing my suitcase in the darkened car the lights and air conditioning kick on, then kick off again. A few fellow passengers join me in the dimness, most of them young: a woman traveling alone, a young couple huddling into each other's bodies, a man in a suit with eyes closed, an older couple riding backwards who sit down without speaking, close their eyes, and immediately go to sleep. The sweat from my hustle has dried, I'm chilly in the superfluous AC, I pull on a fleece and sip tap water from a half-crumpled plastic bottle. Made it. The details of travel, filling every cranny of consciousness with their banality, which compels all our attention because disaster and diversion can never be far away.

Granada, city of Lorca, a poet I've loved for his goofy charisma, the camp outlines of his life, his elastic grin, until politics and tragedy deformed him into a saint. "In Granada we say 'Late, but on time,'" Lorca once remarked. At 6:15 exactly the train to Granada pulls out into the morning dark. The darkness persists longer it seems it should: the brightness of the Mediterranean light made me forget it was really November. By 7 o' clock well out of Algeciras there is still no light. At 7:25 the same. At 7:41 exactly the first fingers of dawn start picking out shapes. Half-asleep, cheek pressed to the cool window, I watch the prehistoric landscape defined by the rising sun. Dim blue light. Purple streaks. A breadth of land and then a ridgeline. Tall narrow leafless trees planted in rows, an orchard. Fields. White farmhouse with a red roof. Sudden fall of the ridge line scooping out more sky. A few lights in the distance winking out in the hazy sun. Blurred grays resolve themselves brown mountains, green fields. Eight o'clock. Orchards, palms, cypresses. A little factory. A highway. No snack seller on this train so I munch on sunflower seeds from a vending machine, trying not to eye the ham sandwiches of the couple sitting across from me. Red earth, an arched bridge or causeway, wind turbines. Metallic clamor of an olive grove.

I text photos of the things I've seen to my sister and my dad. I get back photos of him in his wheelchair, smiling dully for the camera, giving the viewer an anemic-looking thumbs-up. In one photo he's sitting in the passenger seat of a van, looking straight ahead and surprisingly normal. He gazes abstractedly at the pastoral landscape through which he once strode on long legs like mine. Where is he going? And when?

The train curves east, parallel to but distant from the Mediterranean coast, climbing into the Sierra Nevada, which seems to culminate just beyond Granada, a spectacular and unearthly white table that hovers above the Alhambra, which itself thrusts into the sky over the city like an immense eagle's skull. Noon. There is a sense of altitude, there is wind. Wheels clicking on cobblestones, I set out for my latest berth, trying to ignore the weariness that has settled deep into my chest, just above the hungry space in my stomach. When your body's your only home you're a traveler at last.

IN THE FLESH

Her last room was beautiful and overwrought: she had painted it, with the help of a friend, turning the walls of an ordinary suburban bedroom into an elaborate Arcadian mural. Mirrored sliding closet doors made the room leap larger upon entering; you saw yourself in the shade of an immense tree painted over the bedroom door, its branches and foliage climbing over the lintel, onto the molding, and across part of the ceiling before giving way to a blue sky tufted with torn cottony clouds. Long grasses lined the walls, spotted with wildflowers and the faces of small peeping animals. A television was mounted in the wall facing the bed; wittily, she had painted a Greek column on the wall there to give the impression of a pagan idol; it was a ripe shade of pink. And opposite this, over the bed's headboard, two winged putti held a curling golden banner between them with the legend AMOR VINCIT OMNIA. Underneath this banner, for weeks and years, up to the last interminable days of December, 1991, lay Mom in her last illness, just a few years older than I am now, eyes fixed on the TV. Fleshless, hairless, wearing enormous eyeglasses, she looked something like a TV herself as she stared down CNN day after day, on which a year previous in somewhat better health she had watched, incredulous and aghast, the unfolding of George H.W. Bush's Gulf War. It was cancer. It had been cancer before, in the early 80s, when she had had to have one breast removed. She quit smoking, quit cooking for us, cut her hair short, studied social work. As she was finishing, not long after I had started college, back pain sent her to the doctor. In those days there were no cell phones or even landline phones in dorm rooms; if you wanted to make or receive a call you went down to the lobby and stood in line for a chance to use the white telephone mounted to the wall in a little alcove with a door that slid shut for privacy. My father's voice hummed down the line to my ear, and then my mother's. I said nothing that I can recall. When I slid the door open again I had to walk past the line of other undergraduates girding themselves for the weekly task of calling their own families, chafing at this last long cord connecting their college selves with the children they had been. (I can't imagine what it's like for my own students nowadays who walk around with their parents in their pocket.) I went upstairs to my room and shut the door, then opened it again, hoping one of my friends might chance to call, unwilling or unable to make the call myself. Nobody came. I sat alone with my mother's voice reverberating in my ears. Concentrate on school, she'd said. Don't worry. I'll be fine.

Over the next two and a half years she tried everything that there was to try: crystals, chanting, and chemotherapy, the last of which took away the thick dark hair she had worn short since the Seventies and the extra flesh that had tormented her for so long, though she had never to my eyes been seriously overweight. "It's one hell of a diet," she said to me on the phone, voice gravelly as if she had taken up cigarettes again. It was a shock to come home from college that first year, only a month after the diagnosis, to discover how diminished she already was, how much smaller, how low, spending days and nights under the banner promising that love should conquer all. She received the news of my latest disastrous report card with disquieting equanimity. "I don't have the energy to worry about this," she said frankly. "You want to fail, fail. You're on your own."

"I love you, Mom."

Did we say anything like those words?

I was an awkward child grown tall, old enough to vote or to fight in the war, collecting Ds and B-minuses, failing astronomy and French. I stared at the crone in her bed. She was simply my mother, the paramount being in my life, telling me what she'd been telling me for years: I was on my own. The man who wavered into focus at her side, caring for her, guilty with health, was my father, and entirely beside the point. The degree zero of writing started with her: mothertongue, *Muttersprache.* In book after book I have circled the bright outline of her absence: in poetry, in fiction. It seems I am doomed to do so once again, even in this book about Dad, like an assassin called out of retirement, digging up the old weapons, going out to kill in service to a tarnished, half-forgotten ideal. Is she the target, or the ammo? I sat by her bed leafing through the yellow book that's lain in one corner or another of the house since my childhood, *Zen and the Art of Archery.* "The shot will only go smoothly when it takes the archer himself by surprise. It must be as if the bowstring suddenly cut through the thumb that held it. You mustn't open the right hand on purpose."

Mom. On a bleak afternoon in December, the same day that Wikipedia tells me is the day on which the Alma-Ata Protocol officially dissolving the Soviet Union was signed, she lay curled in the bed, no longer watching TV, no longer doing anything but breathing, closely and shallowly, fists clenched like the claws of an unborn bird beneath her chin. The adult son at the bedside of his infant mother, both of them cast adrift, embodied, shrinking. Mom's Europe, past and future, feels impossibly remote and breath-haltingly present: the death the Nazis planned, that her parents postponed by fleeing, has come to find her at last. What lay before me forever was the terrifying and impossible task: to give birth once again, in writing, to her death. On the other side of the bed, remote as Mars, father and sister huddled together in the raw red winter light. Dad was brown, young-seeming in his bewilderment and grief, the age I am now writing this. Bent, eyes moist. Where had he been sleeping? Where had he been sleeping all this time? His place in the bed, the right side (she always slept on the left), was eerily pristine, piled with colorful pillows. Did he lie beside her in the night, the emptying vessel that had been his wife, bound by ties he could never describe? Did he listen all night to her foreshortened breathing? Was he braced, at every hour, to be awakened by silence? She waited for us. My sister and I came home from their respective colleges and this was the first time all four of us had been in the same room together for several months. It was the last time, ever, but we did not let ourselves know this, in the piety of willed unknowing. *Vigil* is the root of *vigilant* and *vigilante*: it means to keep watch, to stay awake, to wait. What does one wait for? A sign.

We watched; we waited. There was little conversation. My sister was raw, a shock of untamed curly brown hair atop a pale streaked face normally tanned and strong: a jock, graceful and athletic, always happy and surrounded by friends. Now her enormous eyes swallowed the rest of her face. She buried her head in Dad's lap, and he stroked her hair. He was always emotional, with his mobile face, too emotional for a father, and yet absent of mind, as though the humors and appetites of his body were calling him constantly away from whatever was happening. He could look straight at you, nodding at what you were saying in answer to a question he had asked, but some other voice was calling him away, and this explains maybe his excesses, his need to overstep bounds, to suffer too obviously on one's behalf or to touch with too great an intimacy, kissing his children on the lips, so that I at least flinched away, ashamed of my shame. I couldn't bear to be in his presence, worse than her presence-absence in the bed, the wasted body curled like a semicolon. I wanted to flee, and did. I prolong this moment, this scene, as carefully preserved and as static in my memory as a school diorama, a churchyard crèche, a long shot in an Antonioni film in which the actors remain motionless for longer than seems artistically reasonable or humanly possible. There was a sound in the room of breathing. The body in the bed maintained, in a wholly minimal, almost notional way, its intimate contact with the air and thus with the world, familiarly referred to as the land of the living. Her voice was gone like her hair, her consciousness vanished, leaving skin and bones behind. And dreams. She was somehow still alive. She stays alive in this moment, this scene I play and replay. I looked at Dad at last.

"How long will she be like this?"

I would not hold onto her in her suffering. And you, Dad? Her body dissolved a long time ago. He is pinned like a butterfly by his accident, wings beating weakly, glistening behind glass. His body is preserved in mine, walking on his own two feet.

I was bored by dying, so I left them and went to the library. She could linger for hours, I reasoned, or for days. I wanted a book, like Ophelia's, to cover my loneliness. I drove the blank ribbon of the suburbs from our house to the county library, walked into the lobby hubbub, staring at nothing. I heard someone calling my name.

Because of reading I missed the last moment with Mom. They called me and I came home and she was gone. I couldn't believe it.

She will not breathe her last until I do not breathe at all.

DEEP NATURAL
PORT OF STARS

"Being born in Granada," Lorca wrote, "has given me a sympathetic understanding of those who are persecuted—the Gypsy, the Black, the Jew, the Moor which all Granadans have inside them." Granada, city of the *duende*, the spirit of the "black sounds" of flamenco and *cante jondo*, the "deep song" that fed the springs of Lorca's poetry. "My poetry is a game," he wrote his friend Fernández Almagro. "My life is a game. But I am not a game." Sounds of what was lost, what departed from Al-Andalus when the Catholic monarchs expelled the Arabs and the Jews, "in order," Lorca said, "to make way for a poor, cowardly, narrow-minded city, inhabited at present by the worst bourgeoise in all Spain." Gay Lorca was born out of place, which made his love for that place all the more passionate. But it's beauty—a river-forked city framed by snowswept mountains—that first presents itself to my beauty-soaked eyes. Lorca said that "the melancholic and contemplative man goes to Granada, to be all alone in the breeze of sweet basil, dark moss, and trilling nightingales exhaled by the old hills near that bonfire of saffron, deep gray, and blotting-paper pink—the walls of the Alhambra. To be alone, to ponder an atmosphere full of difficult voices, in an air so beautiful it is almost thought." "A city of grays without a skeleton," he says elsewhere. "A vertebrate melancholy."

My parents came here once; in a photograph Mom leans over a garden wall of the Generalife in a yellow dress with her hair in its characteristic bob. I picture the two of them strolling there, in sunglasses, holding hands, drifting and passing in a slow sort of dance, bewildered by beauty. Human flowers, out of place, tourists with children in their wake.

It's past noon when I set out for the *Casa de Lorca*, the Huerta de San Vicente in which Lorca's family spent their summers. I walk from the city's modern anonymous western edge, which was once *campo*, countryside, into a gridded park under the weak November sun to find a rather ordinary white house with green windows surrounded by parkland of a peculiar barrenness. It was here that Lorca lived, it was from this house that he was abducted and assassinated by the Falangists on the nineteenth of August, 1936. I look for Olga, for Viktor in his gorilla mask, for Gabriel even, but no one seems to be waiting for me. Well, it's not quite three o'clock. There's time.

In the little gift shop I buy a ticket for the tour from a dumpling-like woman with a distracted air; having managed to accomplish this without saying anything more than "*Uno, por favor*," I find myself part of a small group of tourists snapping pictures of each other with their phones. The guide, a hipsterish young man with raffish sideburns, thick-framed glasses, stovepipe pants, and high-tops, leads us through the main entrance into the cool shadowy ground floor with its tiles and whitewashed walls. The house has that curious empty underfurnished feel of all museums, with paintings and photos of Lorca and his family on the walls, as well as a few of Lorca's own whimsical drawings that look as though they were rendered in crayon and pencil. I pause before Gregorio Toledo's portrait of the poet wearing a yellow, vaguely kimono-esque robe: his position, sitting in three-quarter profile with his eyes glancing to the right, echoes that of his sister in a portrait by Antonia Martin: she is wearing white and plays a piano while her eyes engage the viewer. That piano, or at any rate *a* piano, a baby grand once played by Lorca himself, is tucked into a corner of the living room surrounded on three sides by paintings. The guide, thankfully, doesn't talk too much: after making his initial speech to us, in Spanish naturally, me trying to imitate the looks of understanding on the faces of the other guests, he lets us wander the rooms, though we are not permitted upstairs until an indeterminate number of minutes have passed. I examine the kitchen, the dining room, the living room, the parlor. The windows look out on the park, which is deserted in the middle of the day. It's easy to imagine the Andalusian sun beating down in the summer, the cool white retreat that the small-windowed house would provide. Finally the arbitrary moment arrives and the guide permits us to climb the staircase, passing more portraits of the poet's family. Suddenly we are standing in Lorca's modest bedroom. The floor is tiled, red and blue. A window overlooks the scanty trees of the park—I look for without recognizing the "corpulent poplars" Lorca mentions in his poems and letters. Opposite the single bed is the poet's desk, surprisingly large, with two raised wings on either side of the main work area, facing a poster for Lorca's traveling theatrical company, La Barraca; a photo in the room depicts Lorca posing in front of that same desk, that same poster, wearing the spotless proletarian coveralls that were the company's uniform, a form of drag for the queer little rich boy who managed to transform himself against all odds into the people's universal poet. Again that clean unnatural uncluttered feel: can a desk with no papers, no knick-knacks or books on it, be in any sense a poet's desk? The guide finishes a long speech and then walks out of the room, followed by most of the other guests. I wait to be alone in there. I have a sudden urge to climb into the poet's bed, to pull the bedclothes over my head and go to sleep for a long, long time.

How many times must Lorca have lain awake in the little twin bed, listening to chickens scratch in the yard below, the wind in the poplars, picturing in his mind the churning of the trees atop the Alhambra, the light scattering itself on the city and plain below. As a young man, dreaming of glory; as a middle-aged man with the Fascists closing in, fighting the terror of the martyrdom that would eventually be his, lost in "a vague astronomy / of abstract guns."

I look at my phone: seventeen minutes after three o'clock. Have I missed the meeting? An impulse strikes: I crouch down onto the floor and peek under the bed. There's something there. I have to lie prone, to wriggle under and seize with my hand the folded plastic bag that's been thrust a corner. It drags heavy into my hands. From a squatting position I unfold it and look inside. A round metal case a little bit larger than a paperback book, and coiled inside it, a reel of film.

One of my fellow tourists, a middle-aged woman in a saffron dress, stops in the doorway and stares at me through enormous red-framed sunglasses. I smile weakly up at her. She glances into the room, as though to confirm that no one else is there, sniffs audibly, and leaves. I scramble guiltily to my feet, stuffing the film into the leather satchel I purchased in Morocco, where it bangs against my leg as I hustle down the stairs, past the bewildered tourists, and out the door into the naked light of the city.

Under the looming prow of the Alhambra, in a thin drizzle I follow the walled-in Rio Darro past bodegas and trinket shops and theaters promising *flamenco auténtico*. Thick green ivy falls down the stone walls and trees with golden leaves crop up occasionally: there are balconies, bushes, moss. Along the trickle of the Genil, tributary of the most beautifully named river in the world, the Guadalquivir, you can find any number of bodegas and bars huddling in the immense shadow cast by the ancient palace of the Moors. I stop at random and am seated by a gesticulating waiter at one of the outdoor tables—I feel safer there, somehow, more anonymous, than I would indoors. And to return to the rented room with the film in my possession seems like the height of madness—I imagine myself stalked there by my own paranoia, wild with the excess of solitude that my travels have brought me and into which I've already so deeply sunk.

The film. I take it out of the satchel and rest it in its container on the table, sipping a beer while keeping one eye on the passersby to see if anyone will take notice—will those bicyclists or that strolling couple in matching sunhats or that gang of boys on skateboards suddenly metamorphize into Olga and Viktor, into Gabriel, into the Man Within himself? No one pays me or my contraband any mind, so I undo the container and heft the heavy reel in my hand. I pluck out the leader and hold it up to the light, squinting with my middle-aged eyes at the miniscule frames. There are the numbers. Yes, a bit further on, a series of gray smears that projected will resolve themselves into a view of the Tiergarten. If I unravel the whole thing so that it spills and reams all over my table I'll find those famous faces, miniaturized to a fantastic degree. I roll it all up again.

"What," I say to it aloud, "am I supposed to do with you?"

A sallow-faced man with a dark mustache and mutton chops passes among the tables with a stack of flyers and he lays one delicately atop my table. His bones seem to squirm underneath the thin, unhealthy skin. He stares at me and moves his lips. "*Flamenco autentico*" are the words that I hear.

"*Gracias,*" I say after a beat. His eyes are bloodshot. Is he waiting for a tip? Suppose I were to place the Burroughs film into his hand. What would he do then?

"*De nada, senor.*" The tout flashes yellow teeth and moves on.

I know where to find the real *flamenco autentico*. Once upon a time to acquire local knowledge I'd have to actually talk to a local, but nowadays if it's not online it isn't worth knowing, and several websites and message boards have assured me that the best and most authentic flamenco in the city is to be found at the Peña La Platería, a private club that claims to be the oldest establishment devoted to flamenco music in all of Spain. *Peña*, rock, is almost *pena*, which to an Andalusian signifies something far beyond pain: call it the profound suffering of identity, something close to the American blues. "Andalusian pain," Lorca wrote, was "the struggle of the loving intelligence with the incomprehensible mystery that surrounds it." It is the flip side of the objectless desire that guides Lorca's poetry, which he found in the deep song, *canto jondo*. Lorca insisted beautifully on the *impurity* of this "purely Andalusian singing"; against the racist and xenophobic tenor of his times he celebrated the music, as he celebrated Andalusia itself, for being the product of the Byzantine, Arab, Romani, and Jewish cultures that shared the Iberian Peninsula before the intolerant regime of Ferdinand and Isabel banished and suppressed them, launching their campaign of terror in the same year that they commissioned an Italian adventurer named Cristoforo Colombo to cross the Atlantic and claim the Western Hemisphere for Spain. Lorca was guided in his approach to this music by the composer Manuel de Falla, with whom he helped to organize a *cante jondo* festival in Granada in 1922, the occasion of one of Lorca's first lectures, from which he eventually evolved his most famous statement on poetics, "Theory and Play of the *Duende*." It was the composer who opened the pathway for Lorca, son of a wealthy landowner, toward his celebration of the common and popular, by transforming his distance from "the people" into a virtue. How was it possible, de Falla asked in an essay, for a French composer like Debussy to "crystallize" an "intense feeling of Spain"? His composition *Evening in Granada* "is something of a miracle if one considers that it was written by a foreigner, led only by his brilliant intuition.... Here we are actually given Andalusia, the truth without the authenticity, as it were; for although not a single measure is taken from Spanish folklore, the whole piece, down to its smallest details, brings us Spain."

Truth without authenticity. The rallying cry, probably, of all artists who bring a measure of abstraction and distance to their work, who are necessarily estranged from their most intimate materials. Think of the Statue of Liberty as envisioned by Franz Kafka, who never saw the real thing: his Liberty carries a sword instead of a lamp and is all the realer for that fact. Lorca the poet of the people is a true fiction: long before his martyrdom at the hands of Franco's forces the sheer power of his imaginative ambition had made him synonymous with Spain. Martyrdom, of course, doesn't hurt; Lorca's disappearance into a mass grave makes him emblematic of the unhealed wounds of the Civil War. But it's in the poems. He romanticized the common people, the gypsies, yes, but he also transformed them, brought them into contact with the groundwaters of myth. His "Gypsy Ballads," where his ineffable color recurs—"green flesh, green hair"—narrate a mysterious quest through rituals of violent death that have been enacted for millennia. "It's the same as always," our speaker reports to some members of the Civil Guard—a force for terror and repression as well as order—"four Romans are dead / and five Carthaginians." *Carthago delenda est*. Rituals of death and rituals of love combine in scenes of natural beauty and visions of *la pena negra*, "pain of the gypsies, / clean pain, always alone, / pain from a hidden spring / and from a distant dawn!" The Andalusian landscape and its people are as real-unreal to Lorca as Heaven and Hell were to Milton and Dante. When the real is subjugated by the imagination, what happens? Does the suppressed authentic cry out against imperial truth? What do I surrender of the real Granada, sitting by the river's edge reading these poems?

"The real Granada." As though there could be any such thing for a lone traveler, a shy traveler, on the downslope toward home and the judgement awaiting me there, carrying a roll of film on which the literary celebrities of another century cavort to no certain purpose. The waiters turn on the heat lamps as the evening chill starts to creep up from the river; I drink more beer and sample a plate or two of tapas—thin slices of bread with savory slices of ham or cheese or dollops of potato salad heaped on top. The parade of tourists is constant. I hear English, French, German, Japanese. A tall blond kid in a salmon-colored windbreaker steps in and out of the roadway as cars and buses pass, pressing leaflets into the hands of passersby. More *flamenco auténtico*. His sallow compadre, or boss, or lover, passes the cafe again and turns to stare at me with his black haunted eyes. I ignore him. The Alhambra is all lit up and its squared-off towers gleam whitely above me like a close-up of the moon.

When I'm done with my beer, I stroll a little deeper into the Albaicin or Arab Quarter, and am confronted by a statue of a flamenco dancer in a Travoltaesque pose. The small plaque names him Mario Maya. Following GPS I turn away from the river and up the hill toward Sacromonte: the narrow streets here evoke without imitating those of a Moroccan medina. A cat with black, white, and orange patches rubs against my leg and the street lamps gleam against the mortaring of the cobblestones. Suddenly there's no one around.

A figure materializes from a doorway and I tense myself for flight. It seems to me for a moment to wear the sardonic face of the gorilla mask that Viktor wore in Berlin. But no: it is Viktor himself wearing the mask of his own sneering face atop his squat, muscular frame, wearing a football jersey and cradling an unlit cigarette at his cocked hip. He glances left and right and then, wearing a conspiratorial smile, crooks his finger at me. *This way.*

To enter the Peña la Plateria you pass through a stone archway onto a broad patio where metal tables and chairs rattle in the evening gusts. A few people mill about but most are already inside the long low room that serves as an auditorium. Viktor saunters up to the doorway and produces a pair of tickets from his back pocket. He makes the crooking gesture with his finger again. *Flamenco autentico,* whether I want it or not.

The concert room, tunnel-like, feels vast yet intimate,

lined as it is with long wooden banquet tables and remarkably uncomfortable wooden chairs. The walls are covered with photos and paintings and sketches of famous flamenco singers and dancers; I recognize the face of Enrique Morente smiling benevolently down like a spirit near the stage. There are two chairs, two microphones. A white-haired man in a string tie is standing on the edge of the stage speaking conversationally to the audience of mostly middle-aged and older couples, occasionally raising his voice over the hubbub; I can't, of course, understand him at all. I wonder if Viktor can. He's found a chair and is patting the seat next to him. What the hell. I sit down.

"You have the merchandise?" he asks, his breath tickling my ear.

"I guess so."

"You *guess* so?" Viktor pulls back so that I can see the full rich amusement of his eyes. His eyebrows are light, almost invisible against the pallor of his face, giving him an expression of perpetual astonishment. "I expected an American to be more decisive. You have the film or you do not, *nicht wahr*?"

I open my satchel to show him what I've got but he puts his hand on mine and closes the bag again while shaking his head slowly and emphatically. "Yes, I see. But not here, not now. Music first."

A weathered-looking guitarist with skinny arms and skinnier legs has taken the stage, followed by a singer, Tomas, an extraordinarily, even comically young man, eighteen if he's a day, cherubic in a black suit and white shirt.

The guitarist looks at least twenty years older, with his cropped hair and boots and long laconic cowpoke's face. Baby fat jumps on the singer's cheeks as he addresses the audience in a high, nervous voice. They're both sitting. Why do they sit? Because the music has its origins in people sitting around a kitchen table or campfire? Because attention normally goes to the dancer in his or her black and red clothes? Tonight there is no dancer. Maybe it's because *canto jondo* means drawing the music up from literal depths, requiring a titanic effort, like a fisherman bracing his legs against the sides of his boat. Maybe it's just more comfortable. Now the guitarist begins to play, with an easy stroke of his right hand followed by intricate fingerpicking. His head is bent in concentration while his fingers move like a spider's legs over the strings. The tune is fierce and melancholy. The singer listens, takes a sip of water from a plastic bottle perched on a nearby stool. Then he raises his right hand into the air to about the height of his shoulder, opens his mouth, and sings.

"Ah!" Viktor throws his head back, eyes shut, mouth tense, whether in parody or sincere ecstasy I don't know.

The song is an electric current, a synapse that fires between singer and audience and the deep past of this place. Tomas is transformed, no longer a bashful boy but a man of sorrows. The baby fat on his cheeks shivers into an old man's jowls as he wrings the high, keening notes of the *siguiriya,* filling the air with pain too pure for a man so young to understand. His slicked-back hair seems to vanish in the thin light of dark music. The audience is moved, literally: they sway, they clap sporadically, there are cries and murmurs, *Olé!* Like the bullfight, but muted, in response to a particular note, a particular sequence on the guitar, or just the expression of effort and suffering on the singer's now ageless face. The room, the sound, astonishingly full: I am present at an ancient ritual, again I see it flickering, the movement transmitted from body to body, thrilling in my chest. In this low-ceilinged room, in a foreign language, seated next to a possibly insane German smuggler, I am again in the presence of Pan.

"It is a song without landscape," said delirious Lorca, "concentrated in itself and terrible in the shadows, shooting its golden arrows that pierce the heart. It is like a formidable archer of azure whose quiver is never emptied." This young-old boy-man, head bent, fists clenched on his knees, suddenly lifting his face as though struck by an arrow indeed, one hand taking flight with the song's cry. Truth without authenticity. It is the song of my father's fall, the infinite split second from the cliff's top to its bottom. Once I too survived a car accident, driving a jeep in icy conditions on the southeastern edge of Idaho. The car lost its grip on the whiteout road and hurtled into the oncoming lane before the front bumper struck a snowbank and sent me rolling end over end three times, the car landing, like my sister's, on its roof. A splintered eternal moment wresting the word *no* from my mouth, followed by a total blank blackness, like going under general anesthetic. I could have died right then. Maybe I *did* die. But when I opened my eyes I was upside-down and unhurt, crawling from the wreckage. A passing couple let me shelter in their warm car, too polite to mention the stink of the gasoline that had somehow soaked all my clothes. Later still an Idaho state trooper delivered me to my destination—a ski lodge where, yes, I was meeting my father and his new wife. He hugged me close, in spite of the terrible smell. *I'm so glad you're all right. I'm so glad you're here.* And the next day, we went skiing.

I am shivering. Out of the corner of my eye I see Viktor with his clenched fist pressed against his mouth, eyes filled by the singer.

When the song ends young Tomas smiles bashfully, a boy again, speaking softly to the audience in his high girlish voice. No trace of pain remains on his face, only the flush of effort and pleasure. But the music itself, like the blues, bears inside it the cellular knowledge of suffering, the hole in Spain, continually crushed by the boot of empire, hubris, conquest, xenophobia, civil war, terror, disappearances, real estate bubbles, economic collapse. I strain to hear the Jew in it, the Arab, the Gypsy. Of course I can't understand the lyrics; I have only Lorca's poems to pore over later that night in the bed in my rented room. Love and death in cycle, as in the songs I heard in Joujouka, the pure mesmeric repetition that maddens you until you realize that to stand outside such cycles is to stand outside of life. The singer continues, I try to be part of it, I clap at the wrong times and sway when no one else sways, and too much beer plus not enough food plus darkness and lateness and the endless ululations draw me to the edge of fitful sleep. The concert ends like it began with almost no ceremony: bright lights dazzle our eyes. I feel a hand on my shoulder. Viktor, beckoning. *Come.*

> *Llora flecha sin blanco,*
> *la tarde sin mañana,*
> *y el primer pájaro muerto*
> *sobre la rama.*
> *¡Oh guitarra!*
> *Corazón malherido*
> *por cinco espadas.*

> *Cries the arrow without a target,*
> *the evening without morning,*
> *and the first dead bird*
> *on the branch.*
> *Oh guitar!*
> *heart wounded by*
> *five blades.*

DEAR DAD

An hour before dawn, you're awake, staring up from the mattress, not sure for a moment where you are. Your daughter, breathing, there. She is a child again and you are a young or at any rate a much younger man, and in a moment she will call to you out of her sleep and you'll go to her. You feel around on the floor for your glasses before realizing that your daughter is a grown woman, and she's asleep in the little hillside house in northern California where you've come to visit her, and you're an older man now, a much older man, but not old—not old—and New Jersey and youth and childhood are far away.

Light claws its way up cold panes smoky with their breath. You sit up in the bed—it's an air mattress, actually, sagging beneath your weight. California real estate being what it is, your daughter's house is little more than a cottage, a shed or shack on the hillside property of the preposterously prosperous people who rent the space to her for however many thousands of dollars per month. You can make out her bed at the room's edge where she lies breathing in the shadows. You've always been an early riser. You swing your legs out and the soles of your feet brush against the cold floor. You sit there for a moment, a little slumped, looking down at your ugly toes—years of aggressively played tennis have torn and blackened and deformed the nails and grayed the skin around them. You flex them; they work well enough. Shake your head at the smallness of the room and the bareness of the kitchen. Your daughter doesn't drink coffee and even if she did there'd be no way to make it without waking her. So you sit at her desk chair and pull on your trousers, then shrug into a blue fleece against the chill of Mill Valley in spring. The shoes go on last. Her car keys are on the counter.

Silently, you open and then shut the door behind you and stand stretching for a moment on the hillside, feeling the little pangs and tickles of age popping in the middle of your back. Your daughter's cottage is on the property of a little compound or ranch owned by a family of four, built into the side of one of the mazy hills rising to the west of town. One of their dogs comes loping up and pushes its snout into your hand. You pet it clumsily, then push it gently away. A few years back, you were bitten badly on the wrist by a camel in a petting zoo and you've been shy of animals ever since. Can't be too careful, you tell yourself.

The sun you can feel more than see as it rises, warming the air, winding its way up through the maze of redwood trees. A few birds chatter, and you can dimly make out— again, more of a feeling in your skin than a sharp-edged perception—the murmur of Old Mill Creek as it makes its way down the hill, cutting across and under the narrow switchbacked precarious road, falling down into town past the public library and the park and on into downtown where there's a square and a bookstore café. How many mornings you've gone down there, on visits to your daughter, to sit for a while at one of the outdoor tables while the town warms up around you, checking emails or calling sales reps. But you're retired now. You sold your business last year and you're as free as you've ever been. Nothing awaits you below besides coffee and the newspaper and the pleasures of open time. Maybe you'll call your wife, for whom it's already mid-morning, and you can discuss the details of your upcoming European river cruise. A few years ago you did the Rhine; this time it's the Danube, a leisurely tour through Europa, starting in Amsterdam, winding down through Germany, pausing in Vienna for a night at the opera, carrying on to pass between Buda and Pest, down through Belgrade and terminating at Girugiu, just short of the Black Sea. From West to East, from present to past. Retirement opens its wings, lofting you gently upward into a rosy indefinite future. There's time, now, for everything.

A steep flight of wooden stairs leads down to the roadway and you grip the handrail as you go, wondering to what destination your native agility has fled. You'll be seventy-four next year, but you don't look it. Yes, what's left of your hair has turned into a seafoam halo surrounding the sunbrowned crown of your head—you like to joke about being mistaken for Larry David by the strangers you encounter in hotels and on planes. But you've never gained weight—your belly is as flat as it was when your children were young—and your arms and legs are lean with muscle, the profuse hairs on them still mostly black. Tennis and golf keep you fit and sharp. It's true that you like a nap in the afternoon now, though you pretend that's not the plan—I'm just going to sit down for a minute, you say, and take out a book or your phone. In a couple of minutes you're snoring, mouth open, dead to the world. Wake up blowing like a whale. Where did the time go? Seventy-three years on Earth. The days fly past and are over and done, but the years—the years remain.

The road winds narrowly through these hills, narrowly enough that when the well-tuned Audis and Land Rovers of the neighborhood meet each other there's always a standoff before one of them wedges itself into the hillside or pulls up against the crumbling edge so that the other vehicle can pass. Your daughter's landlords have a garage built into the hillside, but her VW is always parked on a postage-stamp sized platform of space at the road's edge, practically hanging over a sheer drop to where another loop of road winds below. It's not a legal parking space but there's always a car parked there, hers or someone else's. The sun has yet to show itself from behind the profusion of foliage, but light is falling from everywhere, radiating from the ridged edges of the redwood trunks, trickling up from the creek that rolls between the switchbacks down to town, gleaming off the polished gray of your daughter's little car. She's always driven stickshifts, says it's the only way she can feel the road. You squeeze the fob and the four locks of the doors pop themselves open with a comfortable snap. You pull open the driver's side door and fold yourself inside.

With a grunt, you bend down to press the lever that slides the seat back. Your daughter is short like her mother was and it takes a while for the motor to shift back the seat enough to accommodate the length of your legs. The mirrors, too, are all wrong. You take a moment to adjust the rearview, work the switch to adjust the angle of the side mirrors, giving yourself the clearest possible view of what lies behind. That's the hill, the house. To either side, the green cascading trees. In front of you, thin air.

Your mind has always been busy with what's to come, not what's in front of you—everyone knows this about you. You're a restless man and seldom still. You reflect rarely upon the past while your mind ticks over with thoughts of the future. Later today, you're heading out with his daughter to a home improvement store to replace some worn-out shelves. You have a tennis date for the afternoon—how many times you've faced each other down in your whites, she fast and agile, you slower than you used to be but relentless, tasking yourself, still scolding yourself when you blow a shot by shouting out your own name in disgust. After that blur the events to come: your flight home, your wife's complaints about the deer in her garden, theater tickets in the city, the riverboat trip. You will be returning to territory you first saw with Mom, waltzing down the Danube through Germany and Austria toward her city of origin: Budapest. You were there together, a few years before the Wall fell. Do you remember the Chain Bridge marching its Gothic way across the river, the baroque splendor of Fisherman's Bastion high on the Buda side, and the dark restaurant where you dined on blood sausages and plum wine? Do you remember the Gellert Baths, where an enormous, mustached man with gray hair corkscrewing from his bare belly massaged you nearly to death with his horny hands? You told her the story, laughing, in the dingy hotel room with striped green and red wallpaper, the air nauseous with the stink of Soviet cigarettes. You flung open the window and the two of you made, carefully, on a bed covered with thin dingy towels to protect you from Communist bedbugs. How you'd laughed! The next morning, however, in the hotel's windowless breakfast room, she was unaccountably strange, silent, distant. You tried to tease her out of her mood but she remained lumpish, shielded behind her glasses, crushing out cigarettes one after another. You probably don't remember the nondescript housing block she stood before in silence, the Pest building in which she'd been born. The place she'd remained with her grandparents while her parents rode the cattle-car to Poland. She never explained to you how it felt, did she? She never found the words. You walked back to the hotel, your jokes about the secret police falling flat, back to the dingy room with its carnival pinstripes and pale sun curling like pencil shavings on the gritty carpet. How could she have conveyed to you what it must have been like to wake every day to the stink of cabbage, and cheap cooking oil, and the lavender her grandmother used to cover the stink of their unwashed bodies, because it was the winter of '44 and the pipes were frozen and fresh water was almost impossible to find, though the river was just blocks away? The river riven with floes of ice, and here and there a body, another body, more and more bodies, fallen like so many stars into the path of the war, floating away to the Black Sea.

The engine purrs. You've got one hand on the wheel, one

hand on the gearshift. The metal tongue of your undone seat belt thrusts itself teasingly into the light. A German stickshift does not follow the American H pattern, with reverse in the lower right position and first gear in the upper left. In a VW you push down on the stickshift knob to maneuver it into the lower left position to reverse. If you shift as if you're driving an American car you'll pop it into fourth. Most likely the engine will stall, but if you rev the engine hard enough, you'll fly forward instead of back. Somewhere Hitler is smiling. The car will launch itself into nothingness, into the empty space of your suddenly foreshortened time on earth. It will flip itself over once, twenty-two feet per second, and land on its unprotected roof. On all four sides of you the windows will explode outwards, popping like balloons, pebbling glass all around the crushed roof in patterns like the petals of a flower. It will take the jaws of life to extract your unconscious body. EMTs and nurses and technicians and orderlies will drive themselves against the odds on your behalf. Surgeons will perform miracles. Your wife will do everything possible to summon you back to life. *Don't you fucking leave me*, she'll say. You will close your eyes. You can still do that, Dad. To the end you'll retain that last power possessed by us all, marking the territory between the incomprehensible exterior landscape of the body and the mind's interior territory. You can close your eyes.

I want to leave you like that, suspended forever in the moment before the moment, still anxious with life's possibilities, filled to the brim with plans, whistling a tune maybe, picturing yourself sauntering across the town square to the café where you can sit for a while with coffee and a croissant, reading the news or watching the faces or simply closing your eyes to the sun.

Instead you depress the clutch, grip the stick, and put the car in gear.

I loved you, Dad.

GREEN
I WANT YOU
GREEN

I climb out of the hangover and into my clothes, stumbling downstairs and out into slanted streets. In a cafe I eat slices of ham and melon and drink too much coffee and then wriggle my way to gleaming Plaza Nueva, to begin my stagger to the Alhambra. Some of the narrower alleys off the Cuesta de Gomérez are done up in imitation of an Arab souk, reminding me once again how deeply the Mahgreb has left its imprint upon Spain, in spite of all attempts to eradicate it. It's a steep climb to where an even steeper climb begins, a long green avenue repaved by fallen leaves. But there are still a lot of leaves left to fall, even in late November and with a gale blowing. The *Poniente*? Lorca writes somewhere of the gentleness of Granada's winds. Perhaps he was having us on. Or maybe here as elsewhere the weather is broken, on its way to breaking everything else. The wind lashes the trees and pushes me uphill, leaves whirlpooling at my feet. The wind is older than the Alhambra—something a poet might say. But not of this wind.

Lorca, 1928: "I am fashioning now a sort of VEIN-OPENING POETRY, a poetry that has EVADED reality with an emotion reflecting all my love of things and my mockery of things. Love of death and joking about death. Love. My heart. That's how it is."

In the labyrinth of the Alhambra, we tourists evade reality, stepping between centuries, made conscious of the division between the inner and outer life. Within the walls it's a palace, a garden of earthly delights, carved archways and statues and fountains. Without them a fortress, a medieval Death Star that fell out of orbit and crashed into the Sierra Nevada, a craggy skull looming over the city like a half-forgotten conscience. The heavy stamp of Al-Andalus, whipped by the autumn winds, the palace which as Lorca said "is not and never will be Christian." Everywhere gray stone superimposed on by colored leaves in motion. "The dark struggle continues," Lorca intones, "without being expressed... the fatal duel throbbing in the heart of every Granadan." It's the deep past that makes the deep song: Roman, Carthaginian, Arab, Judaism, Christianity, Islam. From the Alcazar, the old fortress, I have a tremendous view of the city to the west and the mountains to the east. The Alhambra itself is ringed all around by a wavelike frenzy of yellow poplars. The wind whips maps written in a dozen languages out of people's hands and sends them scurrying into the sky or along the alleys of the gardens of Generalife. In the Moorish palace itself, in the walled-off courtyards and gardens, a fragile peace prevails. Water streams gently from fountains into pools. Arabic script, like that in the Medersa Bou Inania, covers the walls like stucco. Carvings of astonishing intricacy, on an astonishing scale, range up and down pillars the color of ancient ivory. In the Palacio de Carlos V, which has a Louvre-like exterior but an interior resembling nothing so much as a vaster Roman Pantheon with the roof taken off, a number of exhibitions are taking place. A celebration of the life of Enrique Morente charms me for an hour, and there's also an exhibition of the work of the abstract Granadan painter José Guerrero: strong yellows, reds, and blacks. In yet another chamber of the Palacio there's an exhibition called "Variations on a Japanese Garden," whose individual works bear an at best abstract relation to the clichés such a title conjures: the significance of white space, the precision, the presence of absences. In an underground chamber they're screening Yoko Ono's 1965 *Cut Piece*. People, mostly men, come up to where a cross-legged Ono sits on the stage, and with a pair of scissors, cut up the clothes she's wearing. A couple of years before, I witnessed a re-enactment of this piece in Paris by the poet Laura Mullen; she wore a wedding dress, making the politics of the piece more pointed. Every time someone cuts Yoko's clothes, be it just a little incision or the severing of a bra strap, you can see a reaction in her eyes. The soundtrack captures murmurs, nervous laughter, the scrape of shoes on the floor. A stopwatch indicates, what? A young man with a smirk on his face is cutting the cloth between her breasts. High-waisted sixties pants and long hair—he looks like Alex from *A Clockwork Orange*. She asked for it, yes? She put the scissors there, she invited the audience to come up and in a controlled way express its aggression toward her. Her courage appalls me. Think of the Lennonists and how they hated her. She closes her eyes, covers her breasts with her hands, imaginary cut flower in the museum's imaginary garden. There's a limit she reaches before the film runs black. In a moment it will start again.

"The tradition of Spain is the tradition of reality," says Wallace Stevens. I call bullshit. I find nothing here except art.

What time is it in America? Edward. *Edward.* Ed. Eddie. In his foppish little costume, or as I'd seen him once before, at the opening night cast party, lanky and handsome in black turtleneck and jeans, his arm around her, both of them laughing, at me.

Where is Yoko in the eternal loop? In New York at the end of the Sixties with my parents. Hysterical with pain a decade later at her murdered husband's side. Here in the Alhambra, with me. What would I have done? Picked up the scissors and approached her, that wounded woman on the stage, to make my own incision in her shirt, as her eyes looked pityingly into mine.

Of nothing, free.

The wind is stronger than ever on the descent—alarming, really, like a small hurricane, thrashing the branches and kicking up fallen leaves into my eyes like sand. People cling to each other and laugh nervously at the racing sky. I don't know what's normal any more. The moment by its nature is fragile, febrile, unrepeatable, and yet in simulacrum endlessly reproduced, held in the mind indestructible. More than ever from below in the sunset the Alhambra seems like a massive ship sailing away from the night, with the white crest of the Sierra following it like a tsunami. It hangs dizzy in space like the angel of history, mouth an O, hurtling backward and away from the rapidly accumulating ruins of the past.

When the Spanish Civil War began, the military armed the Alhambra for the last time, firing cannon downward at the Albaicin where Republican rebels made their last forlorn stand against the Falange. The terrified Lorca took refuge first in the Huerta de San Vicente and then in the home of friends who were themselves Fascists. On August 18, 1936, Lorca's brother-in-law, the socialist mayor of Granada, Manuel Fernández-Montesinos, was shot. Later that same afternoon they came for the poet. He had pleaded his fundamentally apolitical stance; he even asked that money be donated to the Fascists in his name; he begged shamelessly for his life. It was all in vain. He was driven out of town with three others and held overnight somewhere near the Fuente Grande, or Great Fountain, near the little town of Alcafar. The four men were shot just before dawn— the first of thousands to be executed by the Falangists, in Granada alone—and buried in a mass grave that has never yet been found.

Like everything in Andalusia the fountain has two names, in Spanish and in Arabic. *Ainadamar*, the Fountain of Tears. It has been dry for a long time.

In my pocket, I finger the roll of euros given me by Viktor in exchange for acting as his mule. Wind and stars of the previous night. We stumbled wordless out of the world of the ancient young singer and stood in the alleyway outside the Pena de Plateria with lit cigarettes like lovers reluctant to part.

"What happens now?"

"Madrid," Viktor said. "I will meet the client there."

"And who is the client?"

He wagged a finger at me. "I paid you not to ask questions."

"Take it back, then."

"Put that away." Viktor shook his head. "You are a very strange American."

I sucked smoke. "He's going to destroy it. You realize that?"

"Perhaps he will cut it up," Viktor shrugged, "in the spirit of the Man Within. Can you imagine that Burroughs would have objected?"

"Why don't you just digitize it?" I said. "Put it on YouTube. Let the world see. Two old white men meeting awkwardly sixty years ago in a room in Berlin. Writers. Who's going to care?"

Viktor rubbed his thumb and finger together. "I paid you," he said, "so that I can be paid more. Do you have a better offer to make?" I didn't answer. He held up the plastic shopping bag into which he'd placed the film. "You want it back?" He held it, teasingly, just out of my reach.

This was vandalism, nihilism. A cut-up into oblivion. Viktor chuckled. The coal on the end of his cigarette glowed.

Silence, Burroughs once told an interviewer, is the most desirable state. "Beckett," he added, "wants to go inward. First he was in a bottle and now he is in the mud. I am aimed in the other direction: outward."

"When is the rendezvous?" I asked Viktor. "Where in Madrid?"

Viktor rubbed his chin, eyeing me, face puffy and rigid as if he had donned his gorilla mask. "I believe that concludes our business together. *Gute Nacht.*"

He dropped his cigarette, nodded, turned on his heel, and walked out of the alley into the scented evening.

After a frozen moment, I dropped my own smoke, and followed him. On the Calle San Juan de los Reyes there was still foot traffic: people standing in groups outside of bars and clubs, smoking, laughing, snapping selfies. A man on a motorscooter zipped by with a woman in an elegant emerald dress perched behind him, both of them wearing sunglasses against the nonexistent midnight glare. Viktor strode through the crowd, the package in its plastic bag bundled tight between his elbow and his chest. He didn't look back. I followed him under an archway into a brief tunnel, past entwined couples who paid us no mind. He swung left, climbing into the hills of Sacromonte.

These are the gypsy caves for which the city is famous, refuge of the Romany, and of those Jews and Muslims that had managed to survive the expulsions of Ferdinand and Isabella in the year of our lord 1492. An outlaw space, domesticated and touristified, authentic as an Old West town in which shootouts take place every high noon for the edification of visitors. But in the November dark I felt the shiver of the original inhabitants, barnacled against the tides of history, burrowing away. Red lights burned from windows cut into the hillside, and from housefronts, ordinary-seeming but for the way their walls ran flush into the stone. Viktor left the Camino del Sacromonte and climbed fast, almost running, up the steep slope of a street that was little more than a trail, the plastic bag flashing whitely in his hand. Panting, I climbed after him, ducking clumsily behind a bush when he paused, turned around, and looked over his shoulder for a moment at the view of the city that was unfolding behind him, with the Alhambra still throwing off its plumes of yellow light. Then he stepped inside a red door in the white plastered stone wall of what I took to be an inn or B&B and disappeared.

I climbed a little further to a gravel patch at a turn in the path, catching my breath and wondering what I was doing. The inn presented me with a dark blind wall, but it was topped by an awning that I realized after a moment covered a kind of elevated deck or patio, and there was someone on that patio, leaning on the wall's top, looking out. A moment later, I heard voices. I crept a little closer, closer still, until I could almost touch the wall of the inn, as the voices sharpened and took on edges, not yet distinct. In another moment, I was pressed against the cool stone, directly underneath, the doorway just a few inches away. I could hear the voices now, and recognize them. Olga and Viktor.

Naturally they spoke German. I strained for any word I could catch, but it was impossible. Viktor spoke rapidly in a low tone that occasionally pitched up into excitement. Olga spoke more slowly and interrogatively, her tone sleepy or bored. Once I distinctly heard her say the word *langsamer*. Slower. And then I distinctly heard another word from Viktor's mouth, a word not German at all: Goya. Goya? And two more German words that I could understand: *Morgen Nachmittag*.

Goya, tomorrow afternoon. It was his rendezvous. It had to be.

And Goya, I understood, was not a who, but a where.

The voices had stopped. A wet, sticky auscultation. A sigh.

The red door was open. It led into a courtyard with the guesthouse on one side and a set of stone stairs on the other. Silently I climbed them, craning my neck, until I arrived at a round patio like the turret of a castle, smelling strongly of soil and jasmine. Peeping, I saw the couple entwined on the wall, entirely absorbed in one another.

The bag with the film inside it was leaning against a concrete planter just a few feet from the top of the stairs. I crouched, pulse throbbing, expecting at any moment to be caught. Seized the bag, wincing at the rustling plastic—but as luck would have it a wind came sighing down from the mountain, sending a cascade of dried leaves whirling up from the patio, clicking together like insects. The wad of euros I stuffed down into the dirt, so that only the edges of the bills still showed. Maybe they'd find it, maybe not. I got the hell out of there.

Expecting at any moment Viktor's shout or a hand grabbing my shoulder I crept away from the inn until I reached the crest of the hill, then broke into a run. I glanced back at the cave inn, set into a ridge underneath a chalk-white night sky, and thought for a moment that I could still see them entwined on the patio's edge, a pair of literary terrorists deprived of their prize. In my way, I wished them well.

Stumbling, the river, the night.

THE NOVEL

In the small hours I spring awake with a hand to my chest, convinced my father is dead. I pick up the phone and check for messages. Nothing new. Scrolling back a few hours my sister reports, *They're on the ground. He's home. Dad is home.* And the unasked, unanswerable question: *What now?*

Perpetually half-written, incomplete, like life. At the foot of my bed a shadow in a three-piece suit, his profile cut out against the light on the window blind. He's smoking a cigarette. What light there is gathers in the pool of his eye.

"Mr. Ahmed!"

Mr. Ahmed takes a deep drag on his cigarette and releases the oddly fragrant smoke into the little room. "So what is your novel about?"

"It's about my mother," I say after a while. "Like every other goddamn thing I write."

"Your mother." He takes another drag. "And when it is done, will you write about your father?"

"I don't think so."

Mr. Ahmed shakes his head. "A mother is to be loved, of course, even revered. But for a father one must feel more than reverence. A father is to be feared. A father is dread."

"My father wasn't like that."

"Wasn't?"

I sit up a little higher in bed, pull my knees to my chest. "Isn't."

Mr. Ahmed nods. "You will soon be a father yourself."

"I already am."

He doesn't seem to hear. "You will understand one day it is the destiny of a man to become his father. To walk in his path."

"You don't understand," I say. "My mother is the one who wrote poetry. My father never wrote a thing in his life. He wasn't an artist. I'm not him. He's not me."

Mr. Ahmed's posture is strange: he sits at the foot of the bed with his back to me but twists his shoulders and head around to face me, contorted and unnatural. He holds up his cigarette like a tiny baton in the air, mouth twisting open like a tunnel. Sings:

> *Little Lamb who made thee*
> *Dost thou know who made thee*
> *Gave thee life & bid thee feed.*
> *By the stream & o'er the mead;*
> *Gave thee clothing of delight,*
> *Softest clothing wooly bright;*
> *Gave thee such a tender voice,*
> *Making all the vales rejoice!*
> > *Little Lamb who made thee*
> > *Dost thou know who made thee*

"Christ," I say, staring.

"No, Jew," Mr. Ahmed says in his fierce whisper. "Not Christ. *Dost thou know who made thee?*"

"I have to save them," I say, not knowing who or what I mean.

He rises like a winged shadow to the ceiling of the room

and beats there looking down at me, a plump and formal man, stinging my eyes with his smoke. A line from Burroughs: *The face of evil is the face of need.* His face floats inches from mine: the rough sweet stench of cologne wraps me. If I open my mouth I will swallow him, or vomit up something more terrible.

Does he say, *That is why?*

Or does he say, *Stop telling lies?*

The crippled father stands up in his bed, eyes glaring, all-powerful, one finger terribly outthrust: *I condemn you to death by drowning.* The son flees to make good his command.

The covers are twisted around my sweating legs when I wake. If I wake.

The glowing phone. *Your daughter says come home.*

REACHING
THE ATOCHA STATION

Every moment I expect to be accosted by a grinning gorilla-masked Viktor or a sourly triumphant Olga, but there's no sign of them on the street, or in the waiting room of the train station, or on the train itself. I only relax once we're actually crossing vasty Spain, out of Andalusia into Castile, passing mountains shaped like faces staring at the sky. An old couple slumps facing me in the compartment, snoring loudly; I stare at them until I'm sure they're not German art-terrorists in disguise. The sun leads us through topaz-colored fields and ochre mountains into the plains of Castille. The old man awakens, froglike, with a series of astounding snorts, coughs, and gurgles on the brink of speech, as though drowning, as though he has no idea where he is. *In the pass, the muttering sickness leaped into our throats, coughing and spitting in the silver morning.* He looks around him wildly, smooths down his few white hairs, I look away before he can catch me staring. His wife murmurs a few words without opening her own eyes, pats his arm, and he turns and looks at her with an expression of bewilderment, even horror on his face. Now I can't avoid meeting his eyes. He's ill-shaven, though well dressed. His wife, eyes still closed, turns her head to the window where the gray light falls into every wrinkle on her face. The man senses me looking and offers up the tiniest of shrugs, as if to say *When I boarded this train I was young, even younger than you.* I look down at my book. When I raise my eyes, they are both asleep again, arms folded together, a pair of dolls rocking comfortably with the train.

Outside Madrid I see an English graffito writ large on a concrete embankment: REMEMBER OUR NAMES.

Atocha is modern, gleaming, offering no sign to my unpracticed eye of the violence that tore it apart a decade ago on March 11. According to Wikipedia, one hundred ninety-one people died during the morning rush hour and more than eighteen hundred were wounded during "Spain's 9/11." The entry includes the following paragraph under the heading, "Reactions":

Using the Emotional Climate Scale, the dominant personal emotions in response to 11 March were sadness, disgust, anger, and contempt. The most intense reaction was sadness rather than fear. These negative emotions declined after two months. According to a study with 167 participants, some people experienced post-traumatic growth. Mostly women experienced post-traumatic growth, especially if they were indirectly exposed to the attack. It is believed that post traumatic growth [sic] may even lead to a more fulfilling and meaningful life.

Does the Emotional Climate Scale have any means of registering an uptake in sleepless nights, persistent and unnamable anxieties, migraine headaches, feelings of despair, the need to read certain poems over and over again so that fragmentary lines occur when you least expect them, like *low, dishonest decade*? Probably it does. There is nothing that can't be quantified. There is nothing in our experience so foreign that it can't be metabolized and made part of our-selves. Except perhaps the gap in experience itself. I pic-ture Proust's Combray in reverse, a provincial town folding itself up like a circus tent and disappearing beneath the surface of a steaming cup of tea gone undrunk by its author, who never rediscovers his childhood, who never becomes an author at all.

Madrid organizes itself around a series of radiant cen-ters spilling magnificent avenues lined with buildings that walk the line between the imposing and the human-scaled. But its charms are largely lost on me once I've walked my suitcase down one of those avenues and installed myself in a narrow apartment owned by a friendly couple who speak no English. When I log on, reflexively, to their wifi I see new messages from my sister and stepmother piling in the inbox, three missed calls on FaceTime. No threatening messages from Viktor. Nothing from my wife. It was an ear-ly train, I barely slept, I'm exhausted. But it's already noon, and Goya, Viktor's contact, is waiting.

Francisco Goya is one of those artists you can't remem-ber seeing for the first time: he's in the art-historical air. *The Third of May 1808* is inscribed on the lid of modernity, the hinge between art and witness, prototype for Picasso's *Guernica* and the war dead of Matthew Brady and the photo of a South Vietnamese general shooting a prisoner in the head. Only after waiting in line with my head twisting this way and that, scouting for familiar faces, concealing my own with sunglasses and a baseball cap, in the cool halls of the Prado I behold for the first time the painting's companion piece, *The Second of May 1808*, which depicts a citizens' uprising against their French occupiers. A heroic subject, but the turbulent violence that Goya has organized around the still center of a French mercenary's white horse seems every bit as appalling as the mechanized slaughter that a firing squad is permanently about to perpetrate against the uprising's participants one day later. What makes the difference is the eyes of the central figure, the man in the shirt white as a flag of truce, implicitly as red as the blood with which it's about to be stained, his hands thrown wide in a gesture less suggestive of surrender than of the desire to be seen.

Elsewhere in the museum, one can see examples from Goya's series *The Disasters of War*, black-and-white prints that depict, with mordant accuracy, war's indiscriminate cruelties. The focus is on the suffering of individuals; as in the Vietnam photo the viewer's eye is helplessly drawn to the agony on the dying man's face as he is shot. Surveying Goya's pictures, with their intense near-chiaroscuro and their intimate scale, it is difficult not to think of another black image—all the blacker for having been rendered in color—the hooded Iraqi prisoner perched precariously on a box in Abu Grahib, a strange black stain spreading on the wall behind him, arms spread in a pose more horizontal and crucifix-like than that of Goya's white-shirted victim. It's an image predicted if not replicated in countless paintings here, the hood replacing the halo that typically rings the head of the suffering saint, limbs arranged to display the artist's mastery of hands. Goya understood, because he looked. The image was in him because he saw it everywhere. His accomplishment lies in turning that single repeated image into a language—bringing it inside the tradition of the representable which turns the meaningless noise of suffering into martyrdom. Before Goya, you had to be a saint to suffer. Then, for a while, suffering could turn you into a saint. But Goya saw more deeply than that. As he aged, growing stranger and more reclusive, separated from the world by the gradual loss of his hearing, he began to understand the truth. Language lies. The words *saint* and *suffering* can never be brought into meaningful conjunction—cannot, in fact, be made to mean anything at all beyond themselves. And so he surpassed language, into the *Quinta del Sordo*, the Deaf Man's House. He retreated from the world and locked himself inside. Two hundred years later, we are all locked in there with him.

The Deaf Man's House! That's where I'll find Viktor's contact. I wind my way through the moving maze of tourists, still in my sunglasses, until I reach what feels like the bottom of the world: the U-shaped, tunnel-like room in which *las Pinturas Negras* are on display.

It's like being inside Goya's skull: an Emotional Climate. My body thuds in place, as the other tourists shuffle around me. Turning slowly to take them in, taken in, the fourteen paintings painted by Goya in oils directly onto the whitewashed walls of his house, surrounding himself with pictures from the abyss: where he ate, where he slept. He was already old when he painted them, venerable by the standards of the early nineteenth century: seventy-two, in poor health, as documented in his 1820 painting *Self-Portrait with Dr. Arrieta*, which is not in the Prado, it shows a pale and small-seeming Goya with lips parted being gripped from behind by his doctor, wearing a face compassionate or blank, offering or perhaps forcing upon his patient a glass of medicine. Whatever was in that glass worked, or at least did no harm, for Goya lived eight more years, only to fall further into deafness and black painting, bringing his art inside his house or to bring his house within the limits of art. No one commissioned them, hardly anyone saw them, apart from a few visitors and Goya's housekeeper or mistress Leocadia Weiss. A strange name, for a Spaniard. A Jewish name? She was by all accounts beautiful—one of the paintings is said to depict her in mourning dress that may have been added later—and she had a daughter, Rosario, rumored to be Goya's. Research has determined that the first murals Goya painted on his walls were full of color, registering the artist's cheerful defiance of mortality and of the tyranny into which Spain was plummeting. But something happened, something changed. The Black Paintings began to appear—talismanic, bleakly funny, terrifying. They are like an incantation in an unknown language. The world they depict is pagan and apocalyptic, the human figures distorted and close to devils—literally so in the case of the figures crowded around the figure of a black goat—and the most famous image is undoubtedly the one called *Saturn Devouring His Children*, in which the domination of black that gives these paintings their name is stained by bloody red. I stare at it for a long time, and at the other grotesqueries: old women giggling behind a masturbating man; two shriveled pointing figures, one with a bowl of soup (this apparently decorated Goya's dining room); the floating sinister figures of *Atropos* or *The Fates*; the mad pilgrims, mouths contorted by song, arranged on a vast sooty horizontal canvas like a David Lean film leached of color. Not all the paintings are grotesque: *Asmodea* could be the poster for a postapocalyptic superhero movie with its foregrounded flying figures (one of them wearing a red cape or cloak) levitating over a line of pilgrims or soldiers wending their way through a barren landscape toward— or is it from?—the mountainous fortress or citadel in the background. Are the flying figures here to save the city or to destroy it and bear witness to its destruction? Black is less dominant here than ochre, a dirty desertlike color, and this is also the shade of the painting known simply as *The Dog*, which shines out from the end of the gallery opposite the door, drawing me irresistibly and finally toward it. "There is not a single contemporary painter in the world," claims the Prado's curator, "that does not pray in front of *The Dog*." The image is simple: the small black head of a dog—perhaps a spaniel, judging from the fur of its visible ear—peeks out over an undefined brownish mass that curves up to the right. This is at the bottom quarter or so of a vertical canvas, the rest of which is taken up by that grubby ochre acreage, with shades of brown and gray mixed in, and what might be a small black cloud smeared in the top right corner, at which the dog's gaze seems to be directed. The black streaks running from it are an eerie match to the black streaks on the wall in the Abu Grahib photo. History's readymades flash in and out of focus, bearing as much or as little meaning as the expression on the face of Goya's mutely suffering dog.

Art is affliction: that's what Goya tells us. Old, ill, deaf, he walled himself off, alone with his own mind, and made it a doorway into something as universal as death. Even a sign of life, his beautiful companion Leocadia, wore death's mask under the deaf man's gaze. My right ear is ringing and has been since the Master Musicians blasted me from Pan's deep past of Pan in their village in the Rif, since I lifted my phone to it with my sister's scream leaking out. In the Prado it sings to me, death's tinnitus, its electrical piercing whine. Black sounds. These are paintings of black sounds, the language of refusal, eyes in the night. Old man Goya trapped in his doctor's ambiguous grip, peering out at us, defying us to do something about it.

I have been looking for a long time, deaf to the world and to the quixotic mission that brought me here. People surge into the room's U, look, recede. Sometimes I am nearly alone with one painting or another, except for the museum guard, a dark-skinned older woman with dyed black hair piled high upon her head, sitting on a metal stool with her arms crossed and her eyes fixed on the floor. Slowly she lifts her large, beautifully sculpted head to look straight at me—no, past me. Someone touches me on the shoulder and I flinch, pivot, raise a hand to my eyes as if to shield them from light. "Viktor! I can explain!"

"Can you?"

It's John in an impish grin.

"John," I say. "Jesus. What are you doing here?"

The first and most visionary Beatle, cool and compact in dark slacks and a gray windbreaker, squints up at me with his Mona Lisa smile. I want to tell him I just saw his wife, just cut her clothes off of her with a pair of scissors that she herself placed into my hands. But the thought passes.

"I guess you're my contact," John says after a moment. He laughs lightly. "I never would have guessed."

"Neither would I."

"You've got the film, I suppose." He nods to my Moroccan leather satchel, the one he helped me bargain for. I nod back.

"I thought it would be Gabriel."

He shrugs. "It's both of us, actually. But Gabriel has a busy schedule; he had another conference to attend, in Brussels."

"But why?"

A surge of schoolchildren scatters their way into the room, talking in high excited voices. The guard, who's been watching us suspiciously, leaps to her feet and begins gesticulating and scolding. John takes my elbow. "Come on, I'll buy you a coffee."

Outside the brilliant labyrinth of avenues and shining leaves. Coffeehouses, cinemas, luxury boutiques, people rushing everywhere just like they do back home with their noses pressed against portable screens. The air is cool without crispness. John steers us to a nearby cafe and sits us down at a table, ordering two espressos in startlingly clear and authoritative Spanish. He gestures. "Mind if I have a look?"

I fish Viktor's plastic bag out of my satchel and slide it across the table to John, who slides it out, nods, and sets it down again on top of the bag. The plastic rattles in the breeze. He's looking me barefaced, without his customary smirk.

"Have you figured it out yet?"

John and Gabriel are rivals, frenemies of long standing, each jockeying for the paper crown of top Burroughs boy. What Gabriel wants destroyed John wants to preserve. Or does he just want the pleasure of destroying it himself? And why should any of it matter? Burroughs, Beckett, Sontag, Ginsberg: a brief convergence of twentieth-century literary glamor, at maybe the last moment when it even made sense to speak of such a thing. What would become of such personalities now—three cold Apollos and an anxious Artemis, chaste and self-contained, biting the cultural hand that fed them, self-willed ecstasists, writing for fame? They'd be laptop wizards, YouTubers and musicians. Burroughs would have a podcast, Ginsberg would be a tech bro, Sontag a talking head, and Beckett would be silent. John in his way wants to destroy literature, Gabriel too. Why shouldn't they work together then, having built lives in the shadow of a junkie conspiracist who murdered his wife, whose diminishment to minor cult figure matches the diminishment of literature itself as a force to be reckoned with? John watches me, takes a sip of his espresso. I want to tilt my head back and scream at the sky.

John says, "Do you remember when my father died?"

The question is unexpected. I regard him from across the table in silence.

"It took him nearly four years," John says. "He was dying for all of that time. At first he seemed happy enough, living alone. He spent all his time going to lectures and talks at the community college, on almost any topic at all. Quantum physics, cooking classes, presidential biographies, you name it. He dressed up for every class: wore a jacket, combed his hair. His favorite part was the coffee before and after. He'd flirt with all the ladies there, and of course there were more of them than there were men, so he made himself popular. I think he even took a few of them home with him. He was only sixty-nine when he died. Younger than your dad.

"I saw him once a week, on Sundays. I'd drive about half an hour to get him and bring him to the house, or I'd bring the girls to see him. He'd tell us all about the latest lecture. He had a good memory and he was a good mimic. He could make my girls laugh talking about how this one guy had a bow tie that came undone in the middle of a talk about ancient Rome and spent the rest of the time holding it together with one hand. And he'd tell me about his conquests when the two of us were alone in the car. 'Mrs. Fleischman,' he'd say, 'remember her? The blonde with the big bazoongas?' 'Dad.' 'Do you think her curtains match her drapes?' 'DAD.' 'No, she's a very nice lady. She brought me over some schnapps. You should try it some time.' I never knew whether he meant schnapps or Mrs. Fleischman.

Probably he was pulling my leg. He liked being an old man who could say anything. He'd led what he'd call a good life. An electrical engineer married to one woman, my mother. Every year they went on a cruise somewhere. Finally they moved to Florida, but when Mom died he moved right back. We got him the townhouse, close but not too close. He was moving a little slower but he seemed all right. And he was on the young side like I said. He took my daughters to Cubs games. They had a blast.

"The stroke when it came was massive. We had a woman who came in every Tuesday to clean, Mrs. Flores, and she found him curled up on the floor in front of his bed like a cat with his tongue sticking out and his face white. The doctors said the stroke had only happened a few hours earlier, which is kind of a miracle, because he could have been lying there for hours. I had just spoken to him that morning and he sounded the same as usual. He had a date with a woman who'd never been married, he said, 'a very special girl.' I didn't find out her name so I couldn't call her to tell her he wasn't coming. That bothered me for a while. Somewhere out there is a woman who thinks my father stood her up, and it wasn't his fault. His brain had been ambushed. He'd never be the same." John looked into his empty espresso cup. "I should have known something was up. He had a headache that morning, a bad one he said. But it wasn't going to slow him down. I should have called the doctor. But what did I know?" He met my eyes and shrugged. "People get headaches."

"It wasn't that bad at first. He still had his gross motor

skills. His speech was badly slurred and he complained of numbness on his right side but he still seemed like himself. The first day after the stroke I could tell from the way he was grinning that he was saying something in poor taste, even if I couldn't understand what it was. He spent a week in the hospital and came home. We got an aide to come and fix his meals for him, help him get dressed, that sort of thing. I saw him every day, then every other day, then I'd let a few days pass, though I'd call every morning just so he could hear my voice. He didn't like talking anymore because hardly anybody understood him, but I could hear him breathing while I told him the latest about work or the kids. His appetite was good and on the weekends I'd take him to the pancake house or the deli or for a curry, the things he liked. Wasn't so bad. The kids got used to him—Cassie would sit on his lap and they'd watch *Dora the Explorer* together, and when he saw the baby his face would light up. The new normal.

"Things unraveled bit by bit. Whenever we saw him he was sweet as pie, but Dad had always had a temper and it started to come out more and more. Once we were at the pancake house and I took the girls to the bathroom and when I came back to the table there was a ring of people standing around it, a waitress and a couple of busboys, and Dad just sitting there red-faced muttering to himself. The manager took me aside and told me he'd thrown a jar of syrup on the floor because the waitress tried to take our plates away. Another time we went to the Chinese restaurant he used to like and he got so frustrated trying to tell the waiter what he wanted that he started screaming *Motherfucker* over and over again at the top of his lungs. Fortunately I was the only one who could understand what he was saying. After that I stopped taking him to restaurants. Then his home health aide quit without explanation; we hired a second one and after a week she called me up to tell me that she wanted to quit too because he was screaming abuse at her. That same day a neighbor called to tell me she'd seen him wandering around in the backyard of the house with only a T-shirt on. It got so I was afraid to bring the kids by because of what he might say or do. My wife helped when she could but she'd just started a new job downtown, so most of the time it was me on call. And I knew the calls would keep coming, more and more often.

"The second home health aide quit and we started talking about putting him in a nursing home. It felt like a betrayal to even talk about it. My whole life he'd been telling me that he'd rather we shoot him than put him in a home. But we were running out of options. Medicare and veterans benefits couldn't cover all the costs. We were paying out of pocket for the new aide, a really sweet and patient guy named Enrique. Enrique was from Guatemala and he would just walk out of the room when Dad started yelling and wait for him to be quiet before he came back. *You goddamn spic get back here,* my father would yell. I had never in my life hear him use words like that. It was like the stroke undid something in his brain. Whenever I came over he'd be sitting in his armchair and Enrique would be on the couch and they'd be watching Fox News. Dad would rant and fume and spittle would accumulate at the corner of his mouth. Enrique would wipe his chin like a baby every time a commercial came on. *Fucking immigrants,* Dad would say. *Goddamn wetbacks. They're driving this country straight into the shitter.* When Dad's dad emigrated from Poland just before the war. I don't know how much Enrique understood; his English was good, but I don't know if he spoke Stroke. He kept his face neutral like a mask when I came over. I did the same. Sometimes I could get Dad to switch to the ballgame and then he'd relax a little bit. And the three of us watched all the World Series games together. That was the last good time. Then in December Enrique quit and went back to Guatemala. Maybe he'd seen enough of Fox News by then to feel like he wasn't wanted. Probably he had other reasons. We were scrambling. And then Dad had the second stroke."

A broad golden oak leaf from one of the trees in the avenue comes skimming over our table, wheeling horizontally through the fading afternoon light. "Why are you telling me all this?"

John signals the waiter, who brings us a fresh pair of espressos. "After the second stroke, he couldn't live at home any more, not without twenty-four hour care. We found a place for him in town, which was lucky; it was only about half an hour from our house. It was clean, bright, well-maintained, about as good as nursing homes get. But Dad hated it. I could tell, even though it wasn't possible for him to speak any more. He was paralyzed on his entire right side, so that his face always had the same goofy expression on it, like he was trying to get a little kid to laugh. Cassie said that he looked like he'd just smelled a fart. The folks there would get him out of bed at least a couple of times a day and wheel him into what they called the day room, where he'd sit with the other twisted and crumpled residents, all of whom looked like victims of some sort of plague. In the day room they watched TV, in his own room he watched TV. At first when I came by I'd sit by his chair and read to him, *The New York Times*, mostly, like I was trying to deprogram him. Eventually I'd just sit with him and we'd both of us watch the TV. He watched the TV, I mean, and I watched him. His right eyelid sagged and the iris had a tendency to roll up, so that he looked blind in that eye. The left eye looked mostly all right. I'd sit on his left side and look at his profile and he'd seem almost normal, except for the drooling. This is my father, I told myself. This is the man that raised me, who taught me how to ride a bike and throw a ball and balance a checkbook and all that other dad stuff. He did everything right, everything he was supposed to do in America in the twentieth century as a father. He went to war when they told him to and he came back again alive. He went to college and to graduate school and he worked for a reputable firm and then went out on his own for a while and then back to his old company, and he made a decent living. He took care of his wife and his kids, and when his wife died and he retired he looked forward to golden years of listening to lectures and flirting with widows. And then it's like a hand reached down and squeezed his brain until it was dry and left him there, an empty Fox News-watching shell. Except he wasn't a shell. That was the worst part. He couldn't speak anymore, he barely ate, he lay there or he sat there. But the light wasn't out. I saw it in his eye, the one good eye. *He was still in there.* A prisoner, trapped. The man my father was. He wasn't gone."

John leans forward. "Your dad is still in there. You understand? Whatever happens to his body or even his brain. He's still your father and you have to deal with him."

It's a beautiful autumn evening in Madrid, with only the occasional uncanny gust of warm air rising as it were from the ground to remind us that the world is out of wack, that we are all tilting slowly and yet suddenly into an abyss. I see again the executioners in the desert, the knives, the men in jumpsuits kneeling to their doom. Which is more insane, the fanatical defense of a way of life or the daily accession to drift, to comfortable habits, to the blandishments of power? *Donald Trump is in the White House.* No novel written in these years can gainsay that fact.

"What about the film?" I ask. "Burroughs and Beckett. What are you going to do with it?"

"I don't know," he shrugs. "Burn it, probably, like Gabriel says we should."

"In God's name, why? Why is it so important that they be kept apart? Is anyone really going to believe that Beckett and Burroughs worked for the CIA? And so what if they did? Just a couple of old white guys making small talk that no one can hear. Who cares?"

"Maybe nobody," John says. He looks at me, smiles sadly. He says, "Stop. That's my message for you."

"Stop what?"

"Just. Stop."

A breeze rattles the plastic bag in his lap, the film coiled there, a little bit of literary history found and soon to be lost again, deliberately this time.

He sips his espresso. "I visited my father in the dayroom for sixteen months. Every day I arrived there, I thought to myself, 'Maybe he's dead.' I wished that it were so. Do you understand? I wanted him dead. My own father. And it wasn't because he'd been a bad father, or because he'd turned into a conservative nutjob, or anything like that. I wanted to be released. Free." His eyes are steady. "And finally, one winter day, I was." He picks up the bag with the film in it, places it on the table, pushes it toward me. "And so will you be."

He sets down his cup, stands, puts down a few euro. "I'm catching the next flight," he says. "See you home."

Night comes fast. I drift in the city, seeing everything, registering nothing, eating tapas, getting almost drunk on dry thin wines. I take out my phone, then put it away again. I don't want to call my wife, my sister, my stepmother, my father. I see nothing. I don't want to hear about my wife's affair or how my daughter is getting on without me or whether my wife still wants to be married except from her lips, her actual lips, her voice as breath from lungs, from a body before me in the same room, on the same street, standing together looking out at Lake Michigan waiting for the axe to fall. I don't want to look into my father's ruined face. My time is up. It's time to disappear. But instead of following John to the airport, I wander and wait.

Walking the plazas I find my way into an American jazz concert at another Café Central, where an elderly American Jew in a beret plays the piano and whispers Dylan to a sparely syncopated, almost bossa nova beat. *You gotta serve somebody... Might be the devil, might be the Lord! You gotta serve somebody.* I stick around for a while. I'm almost ready, I think. Ready to resume my responsibilities.

But something is in the way.

EVERYTHING WAS SLEEPING AS IF THE UNIVERSE WERE A MISTAKE

"What is it you want, then? Edward?"

"I don't *know*. No." Her voice is ragged in my ear—phone pressed to my ear, a real phone, a real call, transatlantic, from the last phone booth in Europe, back of the Café Central. We are almost touching, for the first time in I don't know how long, in the moment in which she slips away.

"I don't want Edward, no. He *is* gay. But I don't want *this*, either."

"What is *this*?"

"What is this?" she echoes.

I say nothing, breathe. The weight of the receiver in my hand, against my ear, my jaw, my cheek.

"There's a phrase that keeps running through my head, I don't know where it comes from. *Sometimes you have to be broken to be whole.*"

"Are we breaking?"

Are we broken?

Thousands of miles. She's so close. I say her name through a scrawl of static.

Come back new.

Madrid dawn, November, cold in the streets, cold in my room, where I open my computer and stare at what's there, the book unfinished and unfinishable. I tried, Dad. I tried to write your life, the beginning of mine, but Mom sucked up all the oxygen, as usual, and then it was you, or if not you your body, the body you steered across golf courses and hurtled at tennis balls and loped over beaches with little me on your shoulders feeling taller than I ever would again. We can't see you, Dad, as you fight for some kind of life. I remember your body: the large, deeply brown, slightly protuberant Bassett-hound eyes: my eyes. The hairs that cover every inch of you except your scalp, now shining ghostly as an egg, fragile as a moon, perpetually rising away and apart from your astonished face. A new shyness, a smiling in skin gone argent gray, thin as parchment. The loud colors and clashing patterns of the clothes you wore. Hair on your knuckles. The big, sloppy, sensuous mouth that I have tried and failed to discipline. "I like your smile," said the lean little cowboy I met once in a bar in Missoula, trying to pick me up. "The little reluctant twist." What should I have said back to him? *It's not mine.*

Dad asks so little of me. Certainly not for me to write about him. He doesn't ask me to write anything at all. He wants phone calls and visits with his only grandchild. I have been grudging with these things. I want to shout into his puzzled face: WHY HAVE YOU ASKED SO LITTLE OF ME? WHY HAVENT YOU EXPECTED MORE? Why, why are you and every Jewish immigrant ancestor you represent so GRATEFUL to see me become a family man, employed, useful?

Too cruel to say or even to think such things about a

man trying to decide whether to live or to die, trapped in a broken body, all remaining sensation transferred to his upper chest and back, his shoulders, his arms, his fingers, his neck and scalp and face, centaur to himself, as trapped by his own flesh as Winnie is trapped by sand in Beckett's *Happy Days.*

It's my mother, gray demon, who pushes her face through the veils of black water, veils of black lace. Demanding that I write for her.

I can't make my father love me by writing about him. My dead mother either. My wife least of all.

So how do I go on?

My father was paralyzed from the chest down, from a point that begins exactly at the vulnerable, pointless male nipples. I will never again see him standing. I can't bear to see him as I see him now, in my mind's eye, twitching his puzzlement. He never understood his own wife. Did he try? In a wheelchair he's come to rest, wearing a sadness so profound it's almost wisdom. I touch his hands, squeeze. He squeezes back.

Wind from some Spanish plain tunneling through the city, rattling the wooden shutters over my windows where dawn is creeping in. A kind of answer: the turning world.

The only answer I'm likely to get. A sign. That I invent.

The wind stirs a little water in my eye. My body makes a feeling. I follow.

I want to live, Dad says. *But not like this.*

There is a kernel in me that blooms, stirs its limbs, ho-munculus of hurt. Back to the beginning—no, that doesn't matter, it's what makes the beginning, what comes before. The gleam in Dad's eye. Interior spaceman, on a long umbilical that sometimes inexplicably crimps. He seizes up there, at the belly, losing love. He bends to cover his face, which is no face anyway, the curved silver terror in place of a face that spacemen wear. Mirroring what he sees. He sees? An astronaut living out his life alone in a white room. Eating, breathing, growing old, dying, reborn. Sitting stunned with the closing credits, whispering to his date: "What *was* that?" The star child hath ever but slenderly known himself. Yet with Emerson will he lift his hands to the screen and say *kosmos*.

Mom, I'm still in space, rocking imperceptibly, systole and diastole of persisting beyond you and your death, toward my own death, toward my daughter-your-granddaughter's overheated horizon. The day she came into language remembers you.

Amniotic universe that must be cradled and cared for by something larger and deeper and more strange.

And Dad, you have begun your journey, in a way we could never have expected, back out of all this now too much for us. Back to the womb with you in your newly crippled born body.

I put myself in play, in dreams I remember for their fixed elements: a shore, a distant woman, an overwhelming wave. Free, my legs flashing whitely, like a boy in the sand, I play awhile in the margin of loss, between she who made not only my body but the course of my life, and the oblivion into which each of us will fall. Fate, and image, drained of color, tense with life: an eye, a coil of hair, a wondering, a wave. I call out to her and hear my own name in reply. Running. Her arms—

Dad watching safely from the shore, lifting his own arms, letting them fall.

What?

Who?

NO!

SHE!

Interiors of time vibrating with each other like notes in a chord. Notes in space named by the bad outside we live in.

Save me from writing, my life.

Everything was sleeping as if the universe were a mistake— the title of an installation at the last museum I visit, with a few hours to kill before I head to the airport, in a former power station converted into gallery space, distinctive for the living wall or vertical garden of green plants and shrubbery that smooths and softens the brutal modernism of the architecture. Roni Horn's artwork tends toward abstraction but this work presents a human face, that of a woman—not the artist, but somehow not *not* her—swimming in a thermal pool in Iceland in a series of photos titled *You are the Weather.* Other pieces are literary: plastic rods lean against the wall with sentences from Emily Dickinson's letters written along their edges. "I give you a Pear that was given me— would that it were a Pair, but nature is penurious." What holds them up, these rods of near-poetry? The room is a forest in language.

The floor of another part of the gallery space is inscribed with *Rings of Lispector (Agua Viva)*, spirals of text taken from Clarice Lispector's antinovel, one of those peculiar texts whose title always goes untranslated, like Huysman's *À Rebours*. The words cannot be read unless the visitor turns in space to follow them, and even then there's overlap, and the obscure marks of other visitors' footprints, so that your movement eclipses the text: you are more and less than your reading. A triptych of rings: *The tulip is a tulip only in Holland. A single tulip simply isn't. It needs an open field to be.* Another single ring declares: *The tiniest piece of mirror is always the whole mirror.* In another the last words fall into the circle: *Today is Saturday and it's made of the purest*

air,

only

air.

Today is Saturday. Tonight I'll fly to Dublin and I'll sleep by the airport. I'll sit in one last anonymous hotel, a blank scrubbed space in which to return to my blank scrubbed self. I'll turn over the pages of my notebooks. Tomorrow I get on another plane and fly to Chicago, come down from thin air to rejoin my wife and daughter at the edge of the water. Rejoin the treachery of the present. It feels glad and right to end with the writings of women, transmuted into forms of navigating space.

On the way out of the exhibition there's a photo booth that the curators have put up, to remember the art by, if not the artist. I picture her, imagining a woman in late middle age, vigorous, in glasses, with short gray hair. I picture Mom, had she lived, what she'd have done. Dying at a different time, dying later, late enough for us to discover each other, she as other than my mother, me as other than her son. How much can a man bear before he breaks? Dad knows.

The booth. You sit in it, and a green light flashes, and it takes your photograph. There's a screen on the wall, by the exit, where these pictures are shown in rotation with the pictures of other guests, most of them smiling or making faces at the camera. Lines from Dickinson's writings are inserted at random, as captions, in Spanish, naturally enough. I translate them back:

Done with the Compass—
Done with the Chart!
And:
Day and I - in competition ran—
Who made these faces for me? Sailor, spaceman, far from home, hyphen between my daughter and my parents, evolutionary function discharged, I make a parabola, slingshot around the sun (*I send Two Sunsets -*), day for night. Dad has commenced his brief old age, his vertiginous decline, in a movable chair, picking up the pieces. He can still feel the wind on his face, touch the sun. We have time, blessed time, for goodbyes.

Amphibious light of morning, autumn in New York, winter in Chicago. The apartment door opens and the man holds it for her as the woman walks in carrying an impossibly tiny bundle in her arms, wrapped tight like a burrito, the whole room spiraling inward to reorient itself around that little face. The father steps lightly, incredulously, afraid of false moves. It's morning, bright and early, in October or January, New York or Chicago. In the sun outside the hospital for a moment the baby's breath shines in the chill like a cloud. Something new under the sun, given of itself, spark of natality, readymade. Mom and Dad look into one another's exhausted eyes, bright with terror and reflected light.

Anything, it seems, can happen.

ACKNOWLEDGMENTS

Thanks to the friends and interlocutors without whom this book would not exist: Ken Babstock, Ava Gorkin, Richard Greenfield, Ulf Peter Hallberg, Benjamin Hollander, John Hunter, Harold Kooden, Sandy McCutcheon, Don Meyer, Richard Pettengill, Jennifer Savran, Davis Schneiderman, Donna Stonecipher, and G.C. Waldrep.

Thank you to my readers, editors, and encouragers: Jay Besemer, Evan Lavender-Smith, Connor Stratman, and the ever-loving Tod Thilleman.

For their patience and forbearance, my family of origin and my families of choice.

With a special thank you to Andrew Kerr and the third floor!

And Emily, always.

Joshua Corey lives in Evanston, Illinois and teaches English at Lake Forest College. This is his second novel.

www.ingramcontent.com/pod-product-compliance
Lightning Source LLC
Chambersburg PA
CBHW011157190726
48286CB00009B/2816